DIAGNOSIS AMOR

VOLUME ONE

OFELIA MARTINEZ

Library of Congress Control Number: 2022911244

First Edition

ISBN 978-1-954906-19-8 (paperback)

ISBN 978-1-954906-20-4 (eBook)

DIAGNOSIS AMOR

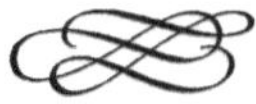

OFELIA MARTINEZ

READING CACTUS
PRESS

To Carla and Johanna from Amor en Paginas
Thank you for bringing sexy back to reading

ALSO BY OFELIA MARTINEZ

The Heartland Metro Hospital Series

Carolina & Hector's Story: Remission

Valentina & Rory's Story: Contusion

Izel & Logan's Story: Incision (Novella)

Camila & Leonardo's Story: Palpitation (Novella as part of the *Heroes with Heat and Heart Vol.2* anthology)

Sara & Ramiro's Story: Sensation

Mandy & Elio's Story: Adhesion

The Industrial November on Tour Series

Sofia & Bren's Story: Hiding in the Smoke

Lola & Karl's Story: Running from the Blaze

Erica & Friedrich's Story: Scorching to the Touch

Anthologies

Camila & Leonardo's Story: Heroes with Heat and Heart Vol 2

Collections

Diagnosis Amor Vol. 1: A Heartland Metro Hospital Collection

REMISSION

HEARTLAND METRO HOSPITAL: BOOK 1

REMISSION

CHAPTER 1

SATAN IN THE AUDIENCE

The interview was going well, and I hadn't barfed or passed out once. As we neared its conclusion, the muscles in my legs relaxed, and I uncrossed my legs, taking a taller posture in my chair. The question-and-answer bit, my favorite part, was next. Reaching young girls and women wanting to become doctors was reason enough to put myself through the stress of getting on stage to lecture at universities.

"Dr. Carolina Ramirez, everyone. Can we all please give her a round of applause?"

The packed auditorium erupted, and my cheeks would have been tomato-red had I not prepared with extra layers of makeup. I was thirty-five years old, for crying out loud. I should've been over stage fright by this point in my career.

"Please, that's enough. Thank you," I said, waving down the audience.

"We would like to thank you so much for being with us today," said the interviewer. "Before we turn it over to the audience, I would like the students here today to know that when you signed on for this guest lecture and interview, you did so only on the condition that there would be extensive time for a Q&A."

"That's right. It's a standard request on all of my speaking contracts."

"Why is that important to you?" The young journalism student interviewing me smiled as she asked. She let the note cards rest on her lap, a sure sign the interview would soon be over. During the course of the interview, she had collected a constellation of sweat droplets on her upper lip and continuously wiped her hands on her black slacks. I had done hundreds of these interviews, and on this occasion, the interviewer seemed more nervous than me. I smiled reassuringly at her as if to say, *We may both be nervous, but we are in this together.*

"If I'm honest, if I could, I would skip the lecture and interview, and instead take each of you for coffee to talk one-on-one. Sadly, unless I clone myself, time does not allow that luxury."

"If anyone could manage *that*, surely it would be you," the interviewer said.

I laughed. "No. For now, I'm still going to focus on my oncology research and my patients. I will always follow my passion. Let's leave the cloning to someone else."

"We have a few people with microphones in the audience. Please raise your hand if you have a question for Dr. Ramirez."

I placed my hand in front of my forehead to block the blinding spotlight, so I could see the person asking the first question.

The young woman couldn't look up at me as she clutched my book in her shaky hands.

"Dr. Ramirez, I loved your book—" Her voice cracked a bit.

"Thank you. What is your name?"

"Araceli."

"Hi, Araceli," I said with an encouraging smile. "It's nice to meet you."

"You too, Dr. Ramirez," she said, giggling. She tucked a strand of hair behind her ear and fidgeted with the book. "Your book is mainly about research. Honestly, a lot of it went over my head, but I couldn't stop reading. You made it seem . . . accessible . . . but you also talked about how you struggled to advance your career in this field. Why was it important to include that in a book that would have otherwise been a dry and boring publication about research?"

"Thank you, Araceli," I started. "That is a huge compliment to me. I worked really hard to make my book readable to anyone, even those not already in the medical community, hoping it might spark an interest in medicine. We need more soldiers in the trenches. But to answer your question, I was writing to my younger self, which means I was writing to any young woman intrigued by medicine but too intimidated to pursue it. The many female doctors who came before me made it so much easier, but it still is really, *really* hard to become a doctor. It's harder if, like me, you are a woman. Even harder if you are a minority. Even harder if you grew up with little money or opportunity. The list goes on and on. I want women in my same circumstances to know that it *is* possible. It won't be easy, but I swear to you that you will find mentors to help guide you in your career as a doctor."

"Thank you, Dr. Ramirez."

"Oh, before we go to the next question, Araceli, I see you have my book with you. If you'd like me to sign it, please stay after the Q&A. I'd love to chat with you some more."

Araceli smiled as though she had won the lottery, and I wondered if one day the letters M.D. would follow her name.

The next girl's name was Stephanie. She was much more self-assured, though she asked a more basic question.

"Why did you get into medicine?" she asked.

I hid my judgment because I would never embarrass someone publicly like that, but I always dreaded that question, and to my annoyance, it was the one most frequently asked. It was a simple question, but I didn't like sharing that truth, so I always gave a partial answer, which was not the same as lying. Not really. "Anyone who gets into medicine wants to save lives. If that is something you are interested in, then medicine is for you." I smiled, dismissing her more quickly than I had Araceli.

The microphone went to the next person, who was, unfortunately, sitting directly below the position of the spotlight, leaving me completely blind and unable to make out a face. I adjusted in my chair and craned my neck, trying to see the person, but it was no use.

"Hello," the voice said. This time it was a man.

"Hello." I smiled. "What is your question?"

"Your first grant," he said, and my blood went cold.

That voice. I knew that voice as well as I knew human anatomy.

"You got your first significant grant at a very young age. Most doctors are fellows or attendings before receiving that kind of research funding, but you were only a resident," he said.

My heart launched itself against my ribs, and, I swear, my poor lungs were caught in the crossfire because I couldn't breathe. The words were getting in, but I wasn't computing—not yet. I squinted, trying to make out the face that I knew in my bones belonged to the voice, but the lights were too bright. I had to give up.

I steeled my spine. *Fake it till you make it,* I reprimanded myself. *Feel confident. Be confident.* "I'm sorry," I said. "I'm not hearing a question in there."

"Please forgive me," he said. His accent had gotten softer over the years, but that voice was undeniably his. "My question is—where did you get the inspiration for your first research grant?"

The bastard. He was goading me. Here. In front of all these people. Fine. I could play his game. I could give as good as I took.

"A researcher was working in the sub-specialty of cancer research I was interested in at the time. I read all of his research, and I found a way I could improve upon his work."

"Isn't that plagiarism of someone else's research?" he asked.

"That is actually a misconception," I fired back. "All medical advances are built on the foundations laid by research before them. A mentor once told me that research was a dance. One doctor takes a step forward, and the next doctor picks up the lead, spinning the research into a twirl, pushing it further." I grinned and challenged him with a raised eyebrow before realizing he was probably too far away to make out my facial expressions.

"Sounds like a wise mentor," he said.

"He had his moments," I said, and just like that, our banter was back. "Medical research doesn't necessarily mean living in a laboratory like a mad scientist inventing new medicine, though it could certainly involve that. A lot of research, mine included, is about adjusting existing medications and protocols into new modalities. There are drugs that are used now for one thing but were originally intended for something else. I haven't invented any of the medications or radiology methods in my research. Other scientists did that long before me. But what I *have* done is change dosing and experiment with different combinations of medications. A lot of my research also involves psychological components—how much can a patient take mentally before it becomes too much?" I sat back, pleased with my answer. He wouldn't publicly ruffle my feathers—he had already taken enough.

I hadn't heard that voice in over seven years, not since he left town after nearly destroying my career. Despite my hatred of him, the familiar back and forth we had always shared returned, and I resented the excitement that simple fact brought into my body.

"Thank you, Dr. Ramirez. If I may, a second question, or rather a request—"

"Sure."

"I also have a copy of your book here with me. Would it be okay if I also stayed behind to get a signature?"

"Of course."

The last thing I wanted to do was speak with him, let alone sign his book. And what business did he have buying my book anyway? I took a deep breath; this was the worst possible time for my hatred of Hector Medina to rear its head.

I answered about twenty more questions. The entire time, I couldn't see him but knew his glare was glued to my skin. I managed, somehow, miraculously, to concentrate on the questions, but I know I wasn't one-hundred-percent on my A-game. Luckily, my B-game was also rather spectacular. When the interview wrapped up, I took a break backstage to gulp an entire water bottle in hopes of cooling off and calming down.

After the auditorium emptied, I came back on stage to meet with Araceli, as promised. The spotlight was turned off, and I was aware of the second figure in the room only by my peripheral vision, but I refused to look at him.

I sat on the stage, my legs dangling off the edge as I took Araceli's book. I chatted her up for about ten minutes to get to know her a little better so my dedication could be personalized. She left with a dazed look, as though she might swoon, and I grinned like a fool after her.

I didn't see him move so much as I sensed him approaching, drawn to him like the pull of a magnet that had always been there between us, binding us together. That hadn't changed, and alarms started blaring in my brain.

"That was very kind of you, Dr. Ramirez," he said.

Crossing my arms, I finally turned to him as he walked over to me, his steps a loud echo in the empty auditorium. I liked this position of power, sitting on top of the stage like a queen waiting for her peasants to come up to her from below. I smiled and clung to that image to give me the strength I would need to deal with the person I hated the most in this universe.

"Dr. Medina," I said. "How . . . *nice* to see you."

"Please call me Hector, Carolina," he said, his voice trying to soothe me like a child. The nerve.

"That's 'Dr. Ramirez' to you, *Dr. Medina*. Let's keep this professional."

He finally stood in front of me, and I reveled in this view from the higher vantage point. He looked up to meet my face from several feet below. Letting out a breath, he handed me the book. I arched an eyebrow.

"I wasn't kidding," he said. "I would very much like a dedication."

"You are kidding." I scoffed.

"No, Carolina. I'm serious. I'm very proud of you."

Proud? That gave me pause. Why would the man who nearly ruined my career be *proud* of me?

Disbelieving, I snatched the book from his hand. I opened the cover to the third page, which had the most blank space for a dedication. I smiled devilishly. I couldn't resist:

To the Devil himself—
>*You couldn't pull me down to hell with you.*
>*Hate always,*
>*Dr. Ramirez*

Jumping off the edge of the stage, I landed squarely in front of him and handed him the book. Standing on his level, I hated the height difference. I was tall, but he still had a good three inches on me. He encroached on my space too much with his height. I damned him for looking more handsome than ever. In the seven years since I'd seen him, his impossibly good looks had actually improved. His dark-brown, tanned skin glowed even more. What had once been salt and pepper hair was now nearly white at the temples, and his face was a bit rounder. He'd gained weight. The good kind. He was broader at the shoulders than he'd been back then, and I hated myself for noticing he'd clearly been working out. The man was like freaking wine.

He opened the book to read the inscription and laughed.

"That's funny, huh?" I said.

What in the world was happening? I didn't understand any of this. Why was he here? Why was he happy, smiling of all things, and *proud* of me? Nothing made sense, but I would be damned before I'd ask him.

"I will treasure this forever," he said, clutching the book to his chest. "I see you remain judgmental and critical of me."

"I see you remain tactless and careless," I shot back.

He laughed, and I noticed the sparkle in his eye. A sparkle I knew well, but it was so much brighter now.

I slung my purse over my shoulder, ready to get going and forget this crazy day ever happened, but Hector grabbed my wrist as I turned to leave.

"No, Carolina, wait." I looked at his hand on my wrist at the same time he did, and we both froze. We only connected for two, maybe three seconds, before he withdrew his hand, but those seconds electrified us. Nine years since the first time I'd touched him. Seven since the last time I'd spoken with him. I couldn't believe my body still reacted to him the same way after all this time.

"I'm sorry," he said.

"It's okay," I said, palming my wrist with my other hand to calm the fire on my skin.

"Can I please take you out for a drink, or coffee perhaps?"

I was speechless, so I could only shake my head.

"Please, Carolina. I have so much I have to say to you."

He said my name in nearly every sentence like he was pleading. I took too long to answer, and he pulled off his glasses to clean them. I knew that tell well. He was thinking. He wanted to find an argument that would persuade me to have drinks with him.

"Even if I wanted to," I said, "which I don't, I can't. I have a flight to catch."

"How about in Kansas City?" he asked, hopeful.

My entire body stilled. "In Kansas City?"

"Yes. Tomorrow. That little café on Westport Road you liked so much. Wait, is that still open?"

"It-it is, but you're going to be in Kansas City?"

"Yes. Does five sound okay to you? Tomorrow?" He smiled, and in that moment, he looked like a little kid.

"Why?" I asked, closing my eyes, seeking patience from within. "Why are you going to be in Kansas City? Please don't tell me you're coming back."

"Is the idea so terrible?"

"I-I, um, I have to go."

"Okay, but please. Meet me tomorrow. Five p.m."

I finally nodded. I would at least have to find out why my nightmare was back in my hometown. Then I ran out of the building as fast as I could because there was no air left in the vast auditorium.

CHAPTER 2

NINE YEARS AGO

THE RESEARCH GOD

"Ugh." Valentina, my twenty-four-year-old patient, rolled her eyes and turned away from me as I entered her room and looked at her chart on the laptop in the hospital's computer cart.

"Well, it's nice to see you too," I said.

"I fucking hate you," she said.

"No, you don't. I'm your favorite doctor." I smiled at her, looking up from her labs, which were good enough to widen my smile even further.

"You keep saying that, but you're not really my favorite doctor. You only think that because I'm your favorite patient," Valentina said.

"I have no favorite patients. I love you all the same."

She drew her finger in her mouth, pretending to gag.

"Are you really going to be sick?" I asked, only slightly concerned.

"No, but you look disgusting. It should be illegal."

"What should?"

"For doctors like you to walk around in front of patients like me."

"Doctors like me?"

"Yeah, you, strutting in here in your pencil skirt, white coat, with your—with your honey skin, amber eyes, and legs for miles. Flaunting all that in front of pale skeletons like me. It should be illegal for you to be that perfect."

I snorted. "I'm not perfect, Valentina. Far from it. And you are not a skeleton."

"I am. I'm a skeleton of my former self . . ." She trailed off, her gaze miles and miles away.

I hated seeing her so defeated. Damn it, Valentina. We knew. We knew the fight we had ahead of us. She couldn't give up on her treatment now. She wanted to be aggressive, and we'd only barely started. I was disconcerted by how low her spirits were so soon after beginning treatment.

It's only the start. She is in a bit of shock, just adjusting. I made a mental note to, if she was still in this mood in a few weeks, explore adding psych to her clinical team.

I sat on the chair next to her and brushed a long strand of hair away from her forehead. She smiled, though it was weak.

"But seriously," she said. "Why are you all dolled up? And hey! You weren't at rounds this morning," she complained.

"I wasn't at rounds because I'm off today. And I'm not dolled up."

Valentina arched an eyebrow. "So, *that's* how you dress on your days off?"

"What? This is professional!"

"No hot date? I'm disappointed. Remember, I have to live vicariously through you!"

I laughed at that. "No hot date. I'm here for a meeting. I get a new boss today, and the people upstairs are having a bit of a welcome thing for him."

"You dressed like *that*, and put on all that makeup, for a new boss? I smell something fishy. Give it up, Ramirez." She spoke with the authority of a coach.

"*Doctor* Ramirez. It cost me to get my degree, so you best show respect. I'm just trying to look professional. My new boss is kind of a big deal. I thought I should put my best foot forward."

"A big deal?" she asked, not buying it.

"Yes, and you should think he's a big deal too."

"Me?"

"Yes, you. It was *his* research that led to the clinical trials that make your treatment as effective as it is right now."

"Oh my god, is he that guy you won't shut up about? What's his name?"

"Medina. His name is Dr. Medina. And it's his research I won't shut up about. Not him."

"You clearly have a lady boner for him."

"Valentina!" I scolded her, and she pulled the bedsheets over her chin as if she weren't a grown woman.

"I'm dying," she said in a little girl's voice.

"You are not dying," I said, pulling the sheets back down. "Don't be a martyr."

"Is he hot?" she asked.

"Ew, Valentina, I've never seen him, but he is probably old. So unless you like bald and big-nosed with uncombed Einstein-like hair, which is how I've been picturing him, then yeah, he's probably hot."

She giggled back into her bed, and I felt lighter having left her in better spirits as I headed to the conference room.

Even if he did look like the troll of my imagination, I was still very nervous about meeting my godlike professional hero. Especially because I thought I'd never get to meet him in my life. His giving up a job at the FIHR, the Federal Institute of Health and Research, to come work here was like a miracle. It was such a coincidence that he would end up at my hospital, of all places. It would be like telling the average person they were going to meet Brenner Reindhart—from the best rock band of all time, *Industrial November*—and that he would be their boss.

I scanned the faces in the room eagerly. About half the staff were there early, and I smiled when I saw Sara, predictably standing by the lunch spread.

"Thanks for the heads up, Caro," said Sara, my best friend at the hospital. "This stuff is way better than what the nurses get at our meetings. *We* need the sustenance," she said, though the last word was muffled by the large piece of cantaloupe in her mouth.

"You're welcome." I gave her a side hug.

When we parted, Sara glared at me up and down. She put a hand on her hip and waited to swallow the bite she was chewing before speaking. "You look *really* nice," she said.

I pinched the bridge of my nose. Not this again. "It's not that weird," I snapped.

Sara laughed. "Yeah, honey. It is. Thanks again for the tip," she shouted as she left, a plate full of food shamelessly in her clutches.

Sara did have the right idea. My stomach rumbled at the sight of all the food. I had been so nervous all day that I hadn't eaten a bite, but now in my doctor's coat, and in the hospital—my favorite place in the world —I felt calmer, which in turn made me hungry.

As I piled fruit onto a plate, three doctors entered the conference room. I didn't have to see his face to know one of them was Dr. Braxton Keach. He was handsome, with black hair and blue eyes, but anything pleasant about him ended with his pretty-boy status. I swear Dr. Keach carried the stench of evil wherever he went, and I could sense his presence well before he made himself known. Though really, it was the excessive body spray that reminded me of so many of my high school memories. He didn't seem to understand that most of his patients were severely nauseous most of the time.

While we were both vying for the same prestigious fellowship offered by the hospital, my distaste for him didn't stem from friendly competition. No. It was the way he looked down on his patients and treated them as inferior. His disdain was subtle, so much so that it wouldn't be actionable in court, but I recognized his prejudiced behavior because he often turned it on me. For everyone else in the department, he turned on the charm. It made my teeth grind that no one else saw him for what he was.

Adding to my ongoing dislike of Dr. Keach, no one else noticed his double-face. Not only was Dr. Keach classically handsome, but he could bullshit like the best of them. The few other female residents in the room gravitated to him the minute he walked in and giggled like little girls. I rolled my eyes and wished I could sit them down and remind them they were doctors and should behave better. But Dr. Keach's presence would likely still prevail. Add to his handsomeness the fact that he was wealthy—from one of the most prominent families in Kansas City —and that meant everyone turned a blind eye to his more-than-lacking skills as a physician and his superiority complex. The result was a honey-tongued devil. But I knew.

"Dr. Ramirez," he said with his oily voice.

"Dr. Keach." I turned to the front of the room, my plate in my hand, ready to find another friendly face, any face, but he spoke before I could make my escape.

"Isn't this funny," he said with amusement in his eyes.

I didn't want to take the bait, I really didn't, but it was my day off so I could leave after the meeting. It was probably better to deal with it now than at my next shift when I would be trying to work.

"What is?" I said, indulging him.

"Last time we had a meeting like this was a year ago. You remember. The Chief of Oncology was handing you a bouquet of flowers. The youngest resident to get a ten-million-dollar grant."

"I remember," I said. "Your jealousy is showing, Dr. Keach."

He laughed. "No, not jealous. Don't you find it weird?" he asked as he grabbed a wrap from the table and placed it on his plate. "Now, the chief has brought in Dr. Medina, the very man whose research you based your own grant on."

"Is there a point to this little speech?"

He shrugged. "I don't know, Ramirez. If I were you, I'd be a little suspicious. He did just come in kind of stealing your thunder. Seems like the chief traded up. You think he'll give him a bouquet of flowers too?"

He grinned, and I clenched every muscle to restrain myself from punching him in the face. I admired Dr. Medina. I wanted to learn from him. This was the best opportunity of my career, and Dr. Keach wanted to twist it into something it was not. This was what he did. He constantly tried to make this program difficult for me. He had wanted me to quit from the moment he'd met me, and the more I pushed back, the madder I made him, and the more he tried.

"Not everyone is as twisted as you are, Dr. Keach. Some of us are here to cure cancer. We have bigger fish to fry."

"Do you hear yourself?" he asked. "You sound like a child. Cure cancer? *You?*"

"Maybe not today," I said. "But I'm one step closer than I was yesterday." I turned away from him and waved goodbye with my napkin, showing how little respect I had for him.

I walked over to join colleagues I liked better. I was ready to drum up conversation with them when the back doors to the conference room opened, and chief Stuart stepped in, followed by a tall, dark, and handsome man. My eyes immediately widened. It couldn't be Dr. Medina. Could it?

The man who followed him wore a navy-blue suit with a crisp white shirt and a grey—almost silver—tie. His black hair, thick and wavy, was meticulously combed back. He had a little bit of salt in his pepper-colored hair, which made the contrast to his deeply tanned skin much more noticeable. His strong brow shaded his eyes, so I couldn't see his eye color, but his face was chiseled except for a full bottom lip. I could sense the chiseled shape of his jaw despite the salt and pepper-speckled beard.

My lips parted, and my gaze followed him the rest of the meeting. He stood to the chief's right, scanning the faces as if he were looking for someone.

"Thank you, all," the chief started, "for being here. We'll make this quick. You know from my email last month that we have a new attending on staff. Please help me welcome Dr. Hector Medina."

Every doctor not holding a plate of food clapped. The noise snapped me out of whatever trance I had been in, and I found myself closing my mouth, which had grown dry. I needed to stop. Not only was he my boss, but I wanted him to be my mentor; *if that* weren't enough, the glistening gold band around his ring finger put me in check.

The chief continued. "We are fortunate to have him. He left a leadership position at the FIHR for an attending position here. That's a demotion if you ask me." The chief brought a hand to Dr. Medina's shoulder. Dr. Medina looked on the room with confidence and a smile that made my knees a little bit weak, though I'd never admit it to anyone. "But his decision also speaks to his character. He wants to refocus on patient care and rejoin research from the trenches, but I'll let him speak more about it himself. Dr. Medina, would you like to say a few words?"

"Thank you, Dr. Stuart. It is an honor to work with you and to be at this hospital with such great eager and young minds." His voice was deep and severe, and it carried a bit of a Spanish accent. "That's why I took this demotion, as you called it. I want to find new inspiration for my research, and the best source of inspiration I've ever had has been my patients. I know I will be a boss to most of you. To you, I say, I am a tough boss, but I am a fair boss. I look forward to working with you and, more importantly, learning from you."

He paused to look through the faces in the room as if he was searching for someone he knew. He took so long in his visual assessment that we all looked at each other, hoping to find the source he was seeking. Not settling on anyone in particular, he continued.

"I've been following research coming from this hospital for over a year now, and let me tell you, I've been impressed. That is why I chose Heartland Metro Hospital as my new professional home. There is one trial going on now that fascinates me. The grant proposal came across my desk at the FIHR a couple of years ago."

Oh no, I thought. If he was about to say what I thought he was, I was going to be sick. Two years ago was exactly when I first submitted my research proposal. Was he here to check up on my trial? Or worse still, did he intend to take back his work? I set my plate back on the conference table and straightened my jacket, hoping I was wrong but preparing to be right—the story of my life.

"If I remember correctly," Dr. Medina said, "the trial is underway now, and it deals with changes in cervical cancer treatment protocols in women under thirty."

I felt the moment when everyone turned to look at me, and I closed my eyes. *Traitors. The lot of you.*

Dr. Medina zeroed in on me. He planned it beautifully. Once he mentioned the trial and those few specifics, everyone pointed right to me. I envisioned a giant red arrow with blinking lights floating above my head. Perfect. *Well played, Dr. Medina. Well played.*

He kept his gaze on me for the remainder of his little speech. "Imagine my surprise when I read this grant proposal and found that it continued precisely where my research left off before I left for the FIHR. It was as though someone cloned me and left half of me behind to keep the research going, only much later, of course," he said and laughed at his own joke about his old age, though he could barely be pushing forty. It wasn't that funny, but everyone still joined in with a burst of nervous laughter. Suck-ups.

"I'm guessing you are Dr. Ramirez?"

Oh, how could you tell? I cleared my throat and instead said, "Yes, Doctor. Carolina Ramirez. It's a pleasure to meet you."

"Do you have a patient to see after this meeting?" he asked. His eyes narrowed.

Shit. Shit. Shit. "No, Doctor. I'm available."

Dr. Keach snickered next to me. *Shit.* Why did I have to phrase it like that? Real smart on my part.

"Perfect. Meet me in my office when we are done here. No, uh, actually, wait for me. I'll need you to first show me to my office." Everyone in the room laughed in earnest, then. I simply nodded.

Dr. Medina talked about his mission and vision for the residency program now that he was at the helm and his strong direction toward innovative research. I stopped listening. I was equal parts excited to work with him and petrified he was here to take over my trial. Why else would he leave the FIHR? It was all beginning to make sense. I worked so hard on the trial, and the results so far had been promising. For me to lose control of it now would be a devastating blow.

Dr. Medina glanced at me frequently. He would turn his attention to someone else, then return to me. I felt like I might be sick and suddenly was very thankful I hadn't eaten.

The meeting ended after Dr. Stuart said a few closing remarks, and everyone trickled out of the room and back to work.

Before departing, Dr. Keach didn't miss the opportunity to get in one more dig. He leaned in close and whispered in my ear, "What did I tell you?"

Fuck off, I thought, but only glared in response. Dr. Keach left, and then Dr. Medina and I were alone.

"Lead the way, Dr. Ramirez."

I nodded and opened the door for him.

"Thank you."

We got on the elevator, and, simply to have something to say, I informed him, "Your office is on the seventh floor." I kept my eyes glued to my hands the rest of the elevator ride. I paid no attention to who got on or off the elevator, and the three floors up seemed to take ages. My back started to break into a sweat.

We got off the elevator, and I led him to his office where I opened the door and gestured for him to go in.

"Thank you, Dr. Ramirez. Please, take a seat."

The view from his corner office was spectacular. The sea of lush, green treetops concealed the bustling metropolis below as if the hospital were the solitary structure for miles. Of course they would lay out the red carpet for him. I'd kill for this office and this view.

I heard shuffling behind me, and I turned to look at him. He closed the door to his office, hung his suit jacket on the hook by the door, and then took his tie off.

"I hate these things," he said. "They are always trying to strangle me." He looked at the tie like it was his personal enemy, and I smiled at how he took offense at the strip of fabric. I then remembered I was in danger of losing control of my trial, and the smile was wiped away.

As he walked to the chair, he rolled up his sleeves. He sat down, and looking at his desk, he filled his cheeks with air. He let the air out slowly and grunted. "Well, this is stupid," he said.

I looked at the desk, not finding anything wrong.

"Um, you don't like the desk?"

"No, the desk is fine. But such an American thing to do."

"What is?"

"This view. It's perfect, and then you place this monstrosity of a desk in here facing away from the view."

"I'm sure we can call facility services, and they can rotate things around for you."

"Yes, yes. That will be great." He looked up, smiling at me, and I found myself relaxing. He was so strange and inconsistent, not to mention manic with his shifts in attention.

"You are probably wondering why I wanted to speak with you."

"I assume to . . . take away my clinical trial?" I said with a wince.

"Take your trial? Why would I do that?"

"You don't think I ripped off your research?"

"Is that what you think?"

I thought about that. I never had in the past, until freaking Keach said it.

"No, Doctor. You made suggestions for future steps, sure, but I definitely took those and ran with them in a different direction," I said.

"Then why the doubt?"

"I had no doubts, to be honest, not until it was suggested to me—"

"By whom?" he cut in.

I looked up at him, and his face showed genuine concern. "It doesn't matter," I said dismissively. "But if that's not why you called me into your office, then I am curious."

"I didn't want to say it in front of your peers and make things tough for you, but I'm only here because of your research."

My jaw dropped. Had I heard him right? I shook my head, blinking. Keith Richards basically just told me he sought me out because of my guitar solo. I could have died right then and there and been happy about it.

"Excuse me?"

"Where you took your grant. It was brilliant. Well, don't get too cocky. It was brilliant *for a resident.*"

Was this man trying to tease me? My hero. Teasing *me*? Here for *me*? I must be dreaming. And had my boss just called me cocky?

"We can do great things together, Dr. Ramirez. You are wrapping up year one of the trial, right?"

He said *together.* I relaxed in my chair, realizing my earlier fears were unfounded. They had to be. I wrote them off as parasitic ideas deposited by one Dr. Keach.

Dr. Medina was here to mentor me.

"Yes. It's a five-year grant."

"I have a feeling it will be successful."

"We won't have statistically significant data until at least the conclusion of year three."

"Yes, yes, I know. But I'm confident. You should be too."

My heart swelled with pride. If my mother could be here now, she would be so happy. I refocused my attention before my eyes became watery at the thought. I couldn't very well cry in the presence of my boss.

"I would like to propose that we write your follow-up grant together. Dr. Ramirez, what you are doing with this trial reminds me of why I got into medicine in the first place."

"I'm honored, Doctor. I honestly don't know what to say."

"Say thank you. With my name as a co-investigator, you will get as much funding as you want. Once we get year three data, I want us to write a proposal for lifetime follow-up with the patients from this trial. We can design other trials as well if you'd like, but that's the one I'm most interested in."

"That would be amazing. Thank you."

"That is all, Dr. Ramirez." He opened his laptop, dismissing me as if he hadn't just changed my life.

As I turned the knob to the door, he called after me. "Oh, before I forget, Dr. Ramirez, if anyone asks, just say I wanted to be brought up to speed with your trial." He put his index finger to his mouth conspiratorially before saying, "Our little secret for now."

CHAPTER 3

DAY OFF

Sunday mornings off were a rarity, even more so when those mornings off aligned with Sara's, which meant I would inevitably be coerced into going on a run with her.

She ran in front of me, fast little thing that she was, and I couldn't help but stare at her cute little behind. Her short, blonde ponytail bounced with her stride. We often laughed together because we both knew people always wanted something other than what they had, especially when it came to a body. I'd kill for a tiny body like hers, and she wished for my Amazonian physique complete with muscular thighs. I wished my hair was blonde like hers, and she lusted after my thick, dark brown hair.

I was stronger and could lift way more than she could, but her low body weight made her fast. So fast. I could barely keep up with her on our runs.

When we finished, we splayed out on the grass and stretched. Sara took her earbuds off and pulled mine down as well to grab my attention. The weight of my hair pulled the hairband loose, so it was sliding down my ponytail. I took it off and regathered the ponytail, tightening the hairband more securely.

"What are the chances I could persuade your dad into making *chilaquiles* for us?" She grinned so wide it was hard to deny her, but I had to. At least this once.

"Rain check?"

"Um, okay. That's a first. I'm guessing you don't want to go elsewhere for breakfast, either?"

I shook my head and brought my water bottle to my lips, buying time from having to answer.

"Caro? What is it? Should I be concerned?"

Damn her and her closeness with my family. Dad loved her like a second daughter, and he'd never say no to her if he could help it, especially if she was asking him to cook for her.

Sara basically lived with Dad on her days off. I think the only reason he survived me getting through med school was that she kept him company when I was studying nearly twenty-four hours a day.

"Fine," I said finally. "I haven't told Dad, okay? I don't want you to be a nosy ass and spill the beans before I have the chance to talk with him."

"What on earth are you talking about?"

Sitting on the ground, I massaged my calves and tried to answer nonchalantly. "I haven't told him Dr. Medina is my new boss."

"I didn't know that was something to tell him." She crossed her arms in front of me.

"Okay, I'm going to tell you, but you have to swear to take this to your grave."

"You very well know if you ask me to, I will."

"Okay, here it goes. When I was in high school, I was a bit obsessive about Dr. Medina—or rather, his research."

"God, you were such a nerd," Sara teased.

"Anyway, Dad knew about it. I just want to tell him in person without anyone there to sway his thoughts about it."

"What? You mean, like mention that you actually combed your hair, *and* you wore something other than scrubs to meet him?"

I eyed her menacingly and pointed with one finger. "Yeah, something *exactly* like that."

"I doubt Mr. Ramirez remembers. And if he does, why would he care anyway?"

"You don't get it. I had three posters on my wall growing up. One was of *Industrial November*. One was a vintage cover of *Jane Eyre,* and the last was the abstract of Dr. Medina's published paper on his first clinical trial."

"You are such an enormous nerd that if it weren't for the *Industrial November* poster, I don't think we could be friends."

I introduced Sara to my favorite band during our freshman year in college when I met her. She hadn't listened to much music before that, so it would be a stretch to say she had any sort of musical taste, but after hearing Brenner's deep, raspy voice, she was a goner for heavy metal. "Yeah, *Industrial November* has saved me more times than I care to admit."

"Me too," Sara said with a broken voice. College was a dark time for her. Her family had been neglectful of her as a child—her parents were drug addicts—and she was just starting to break ties with them our freshman year. There was an anger in *Industrial November* lyrics that I think reflected what she was feeling, and she could finally let it out after bottling it up for so long.

"Fine, just tell Mr. Ramirez he owes me *chilaquiles* because of you."

"I will. Oh, and my shift ends at ten tomorrow. Want to grab drinks?"

"Woo, drinks on a Monday night. What a party girl."

Sara was standing now, and I threw my water bottle at her, which, of course, she caught before walking away with it.

Dad would take the news well. I had no doubt about that. He would actually be very proud Dr. Medina was so interested in my work. Most fathers wouldn't know the first thing to do about their daughter having an idol as strange as Dr. Medina, but Dad always understood and fostered my drive. I think he always realized how important Dr. Medina's work was to me. To a certain extent, his work was also important to Dad.

Still, I didn't want Sara or anyone there to suggest anything nefarious. It was strictly a professional relationship. One that I was getting very excited about. If Dr. Medina had been a woman, no one would have questioned my interest in her mentorship.

When I got home, I pulled my cell phone from my leggings pocket and texted Dad that I wanted to have breakfast with him.

Dad: *Claro, mija! I'll cook for us. Smile emoji, laugh-cry emoji, wide grin emoji.*

I shook my head with a laugh.

Me: *I'll be there in about an hour.*

Dad: *Besos.*

I drank a tall glass of water and picked out my clothes before heading into the shower.

It was unclear to me if it was the endorphin high from the run, the conversation I'd had with Sara about Dr. Medina, or the steam fogging up the glass shower door, but I couldn't tear my thoughts away from him. It would be hard for anyone with a pulse not to notice how handsome he was.

I lathered my body with soap as I thought of his gaze and those dark eyes roaming the conference room and landing on my face. He had rolled up his sleeves, revealing muscular, veiny forearms, and I bit my lip at the memory. I remembered his lips grazing his finger as he hinted at our secret—a secret we now shared.

Bringing my hands to my breasts, I circled my nipple gently. The hot water ran down my body, gliding the suds away from my skin. A flashback of his gaze with those dark eyes entered my brain, and my hand trailed away from my breast and down my soft stomach. I could nearly hear his voice in my head with that slight Spanish accent. The image of him taking off his tie and rolling up his sleeves would be etched on my brain forever—that handsome of a man starting to undress? I'd nearly reached my goal between my thighs when I snapped out of it.

What are you doing, Carolina? I slapped my own hand with a reprimand. I had just texted my *father* of all people with those very hands.

It had to be the suggestiveness of everyone around me. I had been a fangirl, and Valentina, Sara, even Keach, would all use that to insinuate something inappropriate. I didn't like him like that; I was only susceptible to those jerks placing ideas in my head.

But who was I kidding? I was lying to myself. I found Hector Medina very attractive. I needed to stop thinking of him that way.

I washed my hair much too vigorously and turned on the news to turn off my body as I got dressed in my standard jeans and white t-shirt. I didn't brush my hair. All that went on my face was sunscreen and lip balm before I grabbed my car keys.

The smell of *chilaquiles* hit my nostrils the second I entered Dad's tiny house. It was as if he could read Sara's mind. My mouth watered, and I felt only the slightest bit guilty about Sara not joining us for breakfast. This was probably the only time during our entire friendship that I had uninvited her from my family table.

Before me, Dad set a heaping plate of the reason I'll never have a body like Sara's: *chilaquiles*, fried beans with a fried egg on top, and avocado slices. I loved this man so much I could cry.

"*Gracias, Papi,*" I said.

"*Que gracias, ni que nada.* I'm not the one you need to thank." I rolled my eyes but took his hands in mine—his head already bowed. He said grace in Spanish and finished it off with a cross over his chest. "Amen."

"Amen," I echoed if only to appease him.

We ate, and we chatted about work, mostly.

My dad had owned *Tavo's Auto Repair* since before I was born, and though it was hard work, I knew he loved his job. "How's work?" I asked.

"It's doing great. I'm getting older though, and I have to tell you, I couldn't do it anymore without Ramiro's help running the business side of things. He's a great manager."

I ignored the comment about Ramiro; at this point, I was used to him mentioning Ramiro *casually* to me, always making sure not to leave out his many amazing qualities. As if I hadn't known Ramiro my entire life. I shook my head.

When we finally finished our breakfast, I refilled our coffees and sat back down to give him my news.

"*Papi,*" I said. "Do you remember that doctor I used to look up to back when I was starting to think about going to med school?"

"Hector Medina," he said right away. "How could I forget?"

Well, he wasn't going to make this easy for me. "Yeah. Him."

"I remember you wouldn't shut up about him."

"That's the one. You see—"

"Said you were going to marry him when you grew up—"

"What?" I nearly spat the coffee over the dining table.

"Yeah. You were on the phone with your *Tía* Jacinta. You didn't know I heard—"

"Dad!"

"I wasn't eavesdropping, I swear!" His hands drew up defensively. "I was walking past your room, and your door was open. It's not my fault you have a big mouth sometimes."

"Oh my god, Dad." The truth was, I had zero recollection of ever having said that about Dr. Medina but knowing how big of a fangirl I had been, it did sound like something I might have said.

"A dad doesn't forget something like that," he said. "It broke my heart to think of you one day marrying someone and leaving me. I knew you wouldn't marry him, mind you, he was too old for you, but the mere thought of it drove me crazy."

"You don't make things easy for me," I admitted.

"What are you talking about?"

"I have a new boss." Better to rip off the Band-Aid, I figured.

"Don't tell me—"

"Yep." I swung my arms back and forth nervously. "Dr. Medina is the new attending at Heartland Metro and my new boss."

"Well, that'll teach me," he said.

"What?"

"When you said you wanted to marry him when you grew up, I comforted myself with the knowledge—or what I thought at the time was knowledge—that you'd never meet him."

"Please don't worry, Dad. He is married," I said, remembering the gold ring on his finger. "You know I would never—"

"I know, sweetie." My dad patted my hand with a reassuring smile spread wide on his face.

"There's more, though," I said. "He is here because of my research."

"*¿Cómo?*"

"I didn't know he was a grant reviewer at the FIHR. He read my proposal and came to Heartland to work on the trial. He wants to mentor me."

I'm not sure what I was expecting. Perhaps teasing like what Sara had done, or if not that, congratulations on this exciting next direction in my career. *Pero no*. Dad could still surprise me.

"Of course he wants to work with you. I'm sure he is very grateful you are willing to work with him." He stood to take our coffee mugs to the sink, and I could only blink after the man I loved most in this world.

CHAPTER 4

THE LONG SHIFT

The first day of rounds with our new attending ran smoothly. Dr. Medina was mostly quiet; we all knew he was assessing us, making his mind up about our worth as doctors. The other residents were shifty and insecure with their answers, but not me.

Having a secret with him gave me armor. He felt human to me now, no longer the god he still was to my peers. My confidence must have shown through because he was receptive to all my treatment plans and encouraged me to keep speaking. In short, I was killing it. Poor choice of words for a doctor, but I didn't care. I was.

I would have been on cloud nine if it weren't for the dark cloud Dr. Keach kept sending my way. He stood next to me always, so I could clearly hear his heavy breathing and puffing. *I get it, Keach, I get it. You are pissed.*

But his fragile little ego wasn't my problem. If he wanted attention from his mentors, he'd have to work hard for it, just like anyone else. I pushed him out of my thoughts, so I could focus on what was important —caring for our patients.

Dr. Medina looked down at the list on his tablet. "Did we cover everyone for rounds who is not on Dr. Ramirez's clinical trial?" he asked.

"Yes," I said. "We have five potential trial participants left to assess and one participant already on the trial." I always called them participants. I hated the term 'subjects.' It made patients feel like lab rats, which they most definitely weren't. I had a hard enough time educating the public on what clinical trials were, persuading them that they would still get treatment even if it wasn't the experimental one, without making them feel like *things*.

"Great. I will join you. The rest of you—get to work. You have your marching orders," said Dr. Medina.

The circle broke, leaving me standing there awkwardly with him.

"Whenever you are ready," he said.

"Excuse me?" I asked.

"Lead the way, Dr. Ramirez," he said with obvious impatience in his voice. My first slip of the day.

"Yes, of course, Doctor. This way."

We saw my first three patients, and Dr. Medina introduced himself as a new member of their care team. He was confident and charismatic, so each of them instantly fell into a trust with him. I was most impressed when he lingered in Valentina's room and got her to warm up to him. She was so guarded, she hardly let anyone in.

I opened up the rounds, even though it was just the two of us in the room with Valentina.

"Valentina Almonte. Age twenty-four. Diagnosed two months ago. Accepted into the trial last month. Blinded standard treatment protocol for the last week." Valentina's arms danced like a symphony conductor's, and I paused speaking long enough to pin her hands down with my own. I arched an eyebrow as a warning.

"Okay, okay," she said. "I give." She squealed in her bed.

"Patient is responding well to chemoradiation." I let go but continued to pin her with my stare.

"You have a good team of doctors here, Miss Almonte," he said.

"Valentina, please."

Dr. Medina took his time in the room, reading her chart. He set it down on the counter in front of her bed, and Valentina took the opportunity to turn to me. She mouthed, *oh my gawd,* dropped her jaw, and fisted her hands to motion humping the air. My eyes widened with alarm, and I begged her to stop, waving her down as discreetly as I could. Dr. Medina didn't notice a thing.

"Valentina, I look forward to being on your care team."

"Thanks, Doctor," she said while batting her eyelashes. She was so obviously flirting with him, and I couldn't help but smile. I approved of anything that would bring her spirits up, and if that was Dr. Medina, then I would gladly throw him into the fire.

Dr. Medina caught me grinning like an idiot as we walked into the hallway. He rolled his eyes. "Stop," he said sternly.

"Stop what?"

"You know what."

"You must get that a lot, Doctor," I said, batting my eyelashes just as Valentina had. His eyes narrowed. I only stopped when I noticed the set of his jaw, and I wondered if he was too stiff and serious for a bit of joking banter. I checked myself and schooled my face back to its professional side.

"I apologize, Doctor. I forgot myself. If it makes you feel any better, that's the first time I've seen Valentina smile in weeks. Her spirits have been really low. With all due respect, if interacting with you will help her emotionally, I'm willing to sacrifice your dignity a bit to her whims. On the whole, she's harmless."

"I feel used, Dr. Ramirez," he said before turning to walk away from me. He shook his head all the way down the hallway, but I could swear, even by just looking at the back of his head, that he was snickering.

I didn't see him again until late that evening. I'd finished all the work I needed to with my patients, and now all that was left was to chart on my last three consults of the day. I grabbed my laptop, deciding to chart from the doctors' lounge where I could relax a bit. I hadn't gotten a chance to eat during my shift, so I grabbed a *Twix* bar from the vending machine and set it next to my laptop on the table. The details I was charting swallowed me for nearly an hour, which meant I forgot about the chocolate. That was incredibly slow charting, but I wasn't merely charting. I was analyzing every aspect of their disease: its presentation, treatment, and outcomes so far. I was scanning for clues. Anything that would help me beat this bastard called cancer.

The door swung open, and Dr. Medina walked in and settled in one of the sofa chairs. He didn't notice me at first.

"Hello," I said. "How's your first day going?"

He turned to me, startled to find me sitting in the corner. "It's technically my second day."

"Okay, how's your second day going?"

"All right. Nothing special." He walked over to the table and sat across from me.

For some reason, that comment stung a little. He smirked, and I realized he was teasing me.

"What is this?" He picked up the *Twix* bar.

"Dinner."

"*Dinner?* This isn't *food*, let alone dinner."

"Don't judge." I snatched the chocolate from his grip. I opened it and grabbed one of the two chocolate bars inside. As if to prove my point, I took a healthy bite. My eyes rolled back, and I moaned with pleasure. A thin strand of caramel fell to my lower lip, and I licked it off once I swallowed the bite. I opened my eyes to a stunned Dr. Medina. His mouth was parted, and he cleared his throat after a moment.

Then it hit me. I realized what he must have seen. He didn't know that was my standard response to chocolate. He probably thought I was still flirting with him and probably *not* in the joking way I had earlier after our visit with Valentina. I was about to apologize and further stick my foot in my mouth, but he beat me to it, breaking the awkward moment.

He reached for the other half of my chocolate. "I think I will try it after all—"

I snatched it away before he could. "You can't come in here judging my snack, insulting chocolate no less, and then ask for some."

"You *do* know I'm your boss, right?"

"And being my boss while forcing me to give up half my dinner is an abuse of power."

He opened his mouth to speak when the door burst open. Sara marched in with murder in her eyes. *Shit.* What had I done now?

"Carolina. Isabel. Ramirez. Fuentes," Sara huffed. She stood directly in front of me, both hands on her hips as she glared me down. She had long ago picked up Dad's trick of letting me know precisely how furious she was.

My full name. *Double shit.* "Chocolate?" I offered with a grin.

"Why didn't you tell me?" she whined.

Dr. Medina jumped in. "I'm sorry, this is the doctors' lounge, maybe you should—"

Sara brought her hand up to his face silencing him, and I cringed. "Do you enjoy changing your own patients' bedpans, Doctor?"

"Is she talking to me?" he asked, perplexed because Sara's glare never left me.

"Yep. I think so."

He gulped. "My apologies, Sara. Won't happen again."

It didn't escape me that he had learned her name.

"You are new here, so I'll let it slide. *This time.*"

"What's this about, Sara?" I asked.

"Your dad just texted me. You didn't invite me to the cookout."

"I'm not going to the cookout," I hissed.

"Yes, you are. I just paid off a resident to cover for you."

"Sara, you didn't!"

"I did. And you are going."

I slumped back in my chair, crossing my arms. This woman was giving me a headache. "I hate my birthday, Sara. You know that."

"It's not for you. It's for your dad and anyone else who loves you. Don't be so selfish."

"Selfish? It's *my* birthday."

"It's settled, missy. We have a bigger problem."

I groaned. By this point, I had wholly forgotten Dr. Medina was witness to this embarrassing exchange.

"It's Valentina," she said. I moved to stand, but Sara gestured me down to my chair. "She's okay. But it's time."

"Time?"

"I was brushing her hair tonight, and—"

"Oh," I said. My eyes watered. Valentina wasn't vain, but her hair was so beautiful. I was sure she would mourn the loss.

"She's having a bad night. I wouldn't go see her now. She wants to be alone. Let her cry. Tomorrow, we'll take care of it."

I nodded.

"How do you want to handle this?" Sara asked.

"Mary."

"You want to pull a Mary?"

"Yeah, I have the morning off. I'll do the shopping, and I'll meet you in her room at noon."

"I'll bring the equipment," Sara said. "And I *will* take the chocolate, thank you." She grabbed the wrapper on the table with half my dinner and walked away. She waved at us with the chocolate. "We're still having drinks at ten," were her final parting words.

"Sorry about her," I said. "She's a bit—"

"Shameless?" Hector asked.

I laughed, even as a tear escaped my eye. I wiped it away quickly as if nothing had happened. "Yeah, that's the best way to describe Sara. *Shameless.* You'll get used to it. The sooner you learn she runs this place —and we'd be lost without her—the easier your job will be," I said. "I'm sorry, I didn't mean to cry." I shifted in my chair.

"Never apologize for caring about your patients," he said softly.

"No, I know. I'm apologizing for crying. It's why so many people can't take women doctors seriously."

"No," he said, matter-of-factly. "Don't carry that weight on your shoulders. Any man who thinks that way is a piece of shit. I've cried for patients before. I'm not ashamed of it. I'm human. Some of them just get under our skin. It doesn't make us bad doctors. It makes us better ones."

He left then, understanding I needed a moment and giving me what I needed—my privacy. Even though what he said was true, the idea was so ingrained in me that I couldn't bear to cry in front of my boss.

CHAPTER 5

LA OFICINA

I was well on my way to becoming an alcoholic, and I had precisely zero shame about it. The job could be so rewarding, but it could also suck your soul straight out of your body and shred it to pieces. I downed a tequila shot, wondering how in the hell I was supposed to go into Valentina's room tomorrow. Yes, I was her doctor, and I was fighting for her life almost as hard as she was, but I just kept taking from her. I'd taken her autonomy, her pleasure, heck, her normal. Tomorrow, I would have to go in there and try to cheer her up as I took her hair.

She would not be the first one. I'd had many patients just like her, and many much worse. But Dr. Handsome's words swam in my head. *Some of them just get under our skin.* Yes, they did.

I tapped the tiny glass on the bar. "Barkeep! Another!"

Sofia walked over to me, shaking her head. "Slow it down there, Doctor," she said. "Sara isn't even here yet, and you don't want to outpace her. She'll never forgive you." Sofia grinned at me with those incredibly full lips of hers. If I swung that way, I would so dream about kissing her all day.

She wasn't just the friendly neighborhood bartender. Sofia was one of my closest friends. Sara and I drank for cheap, and sometimes free, ever since I stitched up Sofia's hand at no charge when she cut herself cleaning up a broken glass. We'd been friends ever since.

"You're probably right, but at this moment, I'm the one mad at *her*, so I don't give a rat's ass—"

"Okay, okay," said Sofia. "Who the hell am I?"

"And top shelf, darling. Something at the very least *reposado*," I said. Sofia never broke eye contact as she filled the shot glass to the rim. "Has anyone ever told you that you are like a dark angel? I envision your wings covered with raven-black feathers that match your hair."

"Are you already drunk? After your first drink?" Sofia asked only half-kidding.

"No. Bad day. I'm trying to distract myself. Just being silly."

The second shot, I savored. I'd never down good tequila without savoring it. I smiled as the silky liquid hit my stomach, sending the tiniest heat wave through my body.

"You know—"

I heard his voice, and I turned to face him.

"They say a woman who can drink tequila without making a face comes from hell."

Had he been there the entire time? And why was he everywhere? I laughed at his statement. "The person who said that never had good quality tequila. Also, they were sexist."

"Drinking all alone?"

"No. I have friends."

"The bartender doesn't count."

Sofia jumped to my defense. "Normally I'd agree with you, but this is one of those rare exceptions. Caro here is my girl."

I laughed because Sofia said it so motherly, so protective of me, and it warmed my insides almost as much as the tequila had.

"Stand down, love," I said to her. "We must be nice to him. He's my boss, don't you know?"

I brought up my glass and clinked it to his. "Cheers."

Sofia pursed her lips, then reached her hand out to him. "In that case, welcome to *La Oficina*. I'm Sofia."

He shook her hand. "Hector."

I snorted and nearly spat my drink. "Hector?"

"Yes. That's my name."

"I'm sorry. I just assumed you introduced yourself to everyone as Dr. Medina."

"Dr. Medina?" Sofia asked with interest. "Isn't he the one you—" She stopped herself when she saw the daggers I was shooting her with my eyes. "I have some inventory I have to do in the back. Help yourself if you need anything else, Caro."

Dr. Medina stared at me. "We are not at work. Why would I introduce myself by my professional title?"

I shrugged. "I guess I just assumed—"

"Has it ever occurred to you, Carolina, that you make a lot of assumptions about me?" He grabbed his drink and walked to another table, leaving me stunned. That was the first time I'd heard my given name on his lips, and I wasn't sure how I felt about it. I wanted to keep all my interactions with him professional. I wanted him to mentor me and work with me on my research, our research, but every time we were together, the universe played sick jokes on me, giving me foot-in-mouth disease.

I walked around the bar and poured two more shots of the most expensive tequila I could find. Sofia thankfully walked back out to chat with me, and in time, I completely forgot Dr. Medina was even in the room.

One hour into my drinks, I got a text from Sara.

Sara: *Please don't kill me. I can't make it tonight. I love you forever. Kiss emoji.*

"Let me guess," Sofia asked as she carried out a case of beer. "She can't make it?"

"Nope. One guess why."

"Don't go there, Caro. She's a grown woman."

"I know she is, but he is such a piece of shit. Why can't she see she deserves so much better?"

"Give her time. She needs to see for herself what a piece of shit he is. The more we tell her to dump his ass, the more she will withdraw from us. And when this blows up in her face, she will need her friends. We can't alienate her right now, no matter how much it kills us to not say anything."

I told her what I've told her a million times before. "You sure you aren't a clinical psychologist?"

Sofia laughed. "All bartenders are psychologists. Occupational hazard."

"I'm heading out. I have to get up early tomorrow."

I leaned over the bar and gave her a peck on the lips because I could never resist it. She smiled back at me. "Stay safe."

"I will."

I was grabbing my purse when I saw him again and remembered he was there. Dr. Medina was cleaning some of the drink that had spilled on his shirt, and I rolled my eyes. Poor guy couldn't handle a simple peck on the lips by two women. This, ladies and gentlemen, was the man I chose to follow blindly into my career. I shook my head in disbelief and walked out of the bar.

I searched for the car service app on my phone. I'd hit my self-imposed three-drink limit, so even though I felt mostly sober, three drinks were too many to drive. Sofia didn't even ask, because she knew me well enough, but given how quickly Hector, I mean, Dr. Medina, found himself outside with me, he clearly didn't trust that I wouldn't drive. He grabbed my arm above my elbow and started leading me away from the bar.

"I'm driving you home."

"No, you are not."

"Yes, I am. You've drunk too much."

"I know." I searched his eyes. "I'm not driving. See?" I showed him my phone and the app I was scrolling through when he found me. He sighed, and his features softened.

"Good. I'm glad you weren't going to drive. But I'd still like to drive you home."

"It's really not necessary."

"You would really rather pay for a car service than take a free ride?"

He had a point. I relented and let him lead me to his car. I was surprised to find he didn't drive a ridiculously expensive sports car like most doctors of his status. The newer model Honda sedan was discreet and unassuming.

We spent the first part of the ride to my apartment in silence, and oddly, it felt comfortable. Halfway there, he said, "I liked that bar."

"The bar or Sofia?"

"Why would you say that?"

I shrugged. "Every man who meets Sofia falls head-over-heels in love with her. I couldn't blame you if you did. It's almost inevitable. Hell, I'm completely straight, and I'm half in love with her."

He side-eyed me. "No. Not Sofia. She was nice, but I like the bar. The name is . . . interesting."

"*La Oficina*? Yeah. It was great when it first opened. We could always just say, 'hey, meet you at the office,' and anyone would think we meant we were working. The city smartened up, though, and now it has backfired."

"Backfired?" he asked.

"Yeah, now everyone knows about the bar named the office, so you have to be careful. If you say you're meeting someone at the office, people can assume—"

"Got it. So, meet you at work is the accepted vernacular."

"Correct."

"This is a strange city."

"Your first time in Kansas City?"

He nodded. Even though I told him it wasn't necessary, he insisted on walking me to the door of my apartment building.

"Thank you. You really didn't have to—"

"Good night, Carolina."

THE TEMPTATION TO search for him online had never won me over. Not even when I was a teenager and a devout disciple of his work. It had always, always been about the work, about the magic of his brain, never about the man himself. To me, he had only been a brain—a disembodied organ innovating genius advancements in medicine, improving cancer treatments for all patients. Back then, I knew, just knew it in my gut, that he would have saved *her* if he had been her doctor.

But now I had met him. The man, not just the words he typed onto a keyboard hundreds of miles from where I stood. He was also now my boss, and knowledge about him could only serve to help me in my professional relationship with him. *Tell yourself whatever you need to do the deed, Carolina.*

I got ready for bed and curled up with my tablet.

Surprisingly, there was quite a bit of information about him, probably because of his wife. Andrea Medina. According to the search engine, she was the daughter of a prominent philanthropist. They attended many of his fundraiser events in Maryland, where they lived, and in New York and Washington.

I found a picture of them at a charity event for children's cancer research. She was leaning into him, her whole body pointing to him, and wearing a wide smile that spread to her eyes. He had his arm around her waist, and his head was bent as though she was whispering something in his ear. She was gorgeous. I had to admit it. She was a tall, slim, leggy, blonde with beautiful green eyes and delicate features.

He certainly had a type, so I didn't have to continue to feel awkward around him. I'd barely admit it to myself, but there was the tiniest bit of a barely-there crush somewhere in a dusty corner of my heart. But knowing it would never be reciprocated actually made me feel better about working with him and seeing him day in and day out.

Then I saw it, and my jaw dropped—a picture of them holding hands walking in New York City. He held one of her hands, and she grabbed her enormous pregnant belly under a beautiful blue sundress with the other. They both looked incandescently happy. I smiled at the picture of them, hoping my future held that kind of love.

He had to be a good man if his wife looked that happy. I scanned the screen for a date on the picture; by my math, his child would be about eight years old now. I usually find it in horrible taste to search for celebrity children. Even if he wasn't a true celebrity, I had the same feeling about looking up their child. But I wasn't looking for a tacky tabloid. It was purer than that. I wanted to see the human manifestation of the happy couple in those pictures.

In the search bar, I entered: *Andrea Medina and Dr. Hector Medina daughter.* I smiled, thinking about a little girl with his tanned skin and her bright green eyes popping in contrast, but nothing came up. Next, I entered: *Andrea Medina and Dr. Hector Medina son.*

There it was—the first hit—a headline from two years ago. Intense grief snaked into my bloodstream and latched on to my heart. I forgot how to breathe for several seconds as I read the headline: *Six-year-old grandson of prominent Maryland philanthropist dies in freak accident.* Two years ago.

My hand came up to my mouth, and I couldn't hold back the sickening feeling gripping me. I couldn't bring myself to click on the link. When I searched for his family, I wasn't expecting to see this kind of tragedy. I couldn't bring myself to pry into his private life any further than I already had. His loss wasn't for entertainment. I shut off my tablet and tried to fall asleep.

CHAPTER 6

THE MARY

My hair was still dripping wet from my shower, clinging to my shoulders, when a knock at the door interrupted my morning routine. My brows furrowed. I wasn't expecting anyone. Once at the door, I bent to peek through the peephole. I couldn't make out his face, but I stared straight into a dress shirt over pecs I'd recognize anywhere. What the hell was Dr. Medina doing here?

Toothbrush still in my mouth, I opened the door.

"What are you doing here?" I tried to ask, but it sounded more like, "Wha a you dohee?" I gestured for him to come in then went back to the bathroom to get rid of the brush and rinse out.

"How did you get into my building? And more importantly, how did you know my apartment number?"

"I have my ways." He grinned.

I rolled my eyes and went to the kitchen to make a green smoothie. I had to offset Dad's cooking somehow.

"I'm surprised," he said as he walked over to the kitchen bar and sat on a stool.

"About what?"

"You look great."

I shot him my most insulted look, and he laughed.

"That's not what I meant. I just expected you to have a hangover."

"On three drinks? I'm not sure how you party, but three drinks won't get me there. And I also have *my* ways." I grinned back at him.

"Oh?"

"Yep. I stick to straight tequila, never switch drinks except some-times maybe a beer, and I drink tons of water. The most I ever have in the morning is a slight headache."

"I've learned my lesson, then."

Horror struck, and I panicked at what I'd said. "I don't, uh—I don't actually drink very often. I just know my limits and what my body can take."

"Relax, Ramirez. I wasn't accusing you of anything."

I changed the subject. "So, what can I do for you?" I filled my blender with spinach, pineapple, carrots, and fresh ginger root.

"What do you mean?"

"Why are you at my house at eight in the morning, boss?"

He raised an eyebrow at 'boss' and took his glasses off to clean them.

He waited until I was done blending before speaking again. "Your car is at the hospital," he said.

"I have a car service app. Maybe you don't know this about me, but I'm a pretty independent woman. I've gotten around all on my own my entire adult life."

"I don't doubt that, but I was also curious about *the Mary*, and what that meant."

My eyes misted over at that. He'd heard Sara and me making plans for Valentina today. My heart ached as I thought about what we were about to do, but the point of the Mary was to be as freaking cheerful as possible.

"Then I guess you are taking me shopping."

"Okay, but drink that. There's no way I'm letting you take that green sludge into my car."

"You want one?" I asked and wiggled my eyebrows.

"Not for all the salsa in Mexico," he said.

He drove, and I respected his wishes not to bring my smoothie into his car.

When he parked, he groaned. "The mall?"

"Yep." I got out of the car and led him into a department store.

"What are we getting?" he asked.

"Oh, this and that. Follow me."

I picked out a beautiful silk scarf that was a deep ocean blue and got a gift box for it. Dr. Medina didn't say much while I browsed the store. We made our way to the makeup counter, and I got a coral-pink nail polish and a cream blush that complemented the nail color. It was only three items, but I had spent two hundred dollars, and it was worth every penny.

"Okay," I instructed. "When we get to the hospital, you can't be in the room. We will need privacy. But if you want to, in about half an hour, find yourself at the nurses' station by Valentina's room. You'll see what the Mary is." He nodded, parked his car in the parking garage, and we parted ways.

SARA MET me in the locker room. I changed into scrubs and followed her out, Valentina's gifts in my arms.

Sara walked into her room first, pushing a cart in front of her. The top of the cart was hidden from view with a towel draped over it. Valentina smiled at us weakly.

"Good morning," she said. I shot her a wicked smile.

"What?" she asked.

I didn't answer. I placed all the items on the counter and hooked up a speaker to the wall. I brought my phone out and played *Girls Like You* by Maroon 5/Cardi B because Cardi B was life and she could make any woman feel like a boss bitch. Valentina needed to feel that power.

I turned to Sara, who was already half dancing, half jumping around the room. I couldn't turn the volume too high, this was still a hospital, but I let the lyrics seep into the hallway just the tiniest bit.

I walked up to Sara and bounce-danced with my two left feet right next to her. It's a complete stereotype that all Mexican-American women know how to dance. I didn't care if I looked silly, though. Actually, if it cheered up Valentina, that was even better.

Valentina threw her head back with laughter that we hardly heard over the music. She was hooked up to an IV and too many wires to get up and join us, plus she wasn't strong enough, but she adjusted her bed so she could sit up. She bobbed her head and shoulders as Sara and I made complete fools of ourselves.

Our patient couldn't help but grin every time a nurse walked by the room, poked their head in, and belted a single line of the chorus before walking away again. I didn't miss when one of the residents popped his head in and sang the line as he locked his eyes with hers, and she blushed in response.

He wasn't *her* doctor, so I decided to look the other way and not say a thing about it. I wouldn't be the one to take any further happiness away from her. Some other doctor would have to say something if anything more came of that exchange.

Next on my power playlist was Cardi B's *I Like It.* Sara and I stopped dancing. She removed the towel covering the contents of the cart, and Valentina winced at the sight of the hair clippers but then nodded at her.

I grabbed the nail polish and sat at the end of her bed, cross-legged. I brought her feet up to my lap, and I started painting her toenails in the bright coral shade. She smiled at me, though her eyes glistened with tears as Sara began working on her scalp.

When Sara was done with the clippers, I handed her the nail polish, and she got to work on Valentina's manicure. I brought the volume down so we could talk over the music. I wrapped the beautiful scarf around Valentina's head with a bow at the back. I smudged a little bit of the blush on her cheeks, and even as thin and pale as she'd gotten, she was still absolutely beautiful. At least to me. She smiled up at me and squeezed my hand as if to say *thank you.* I squeezed back.

The next part of the Mary was to talk about boys in general.

Sara jumped in first. "Did you guys see that *Thor* movie?" She was still finishing up her manicure as she asked. "That Hemsworth kid. Mmm." She sounded like she was enjoying a juicy hamburger. Valentina and I eyed each other and busted out laughing.

"I don't know," said Valentina. "I kinda like my men nerdy." I gave a side-glance toward the door, trying to remember the resident who had made her blush. Sure enough, Dr. Dennis was a bit on the skinny side, had huge glasses, and bright red hair. I said nothing, though.

"Oh, *really?*" Sara said.

"Absolutely. I like me a big brain on a guy," said Valentina.

"*Just* a big brain?" Sara asked, and we all giggled like crazy at her suggestiveness.

Valentina asked Sara, "Do you have a boyfriend?"

"I do," she said without looking up from the hand she was working on.

"What was that?" Valentina asked me.

Uh-oh. "What was what?" I asked.

"That." With her free hand, she pointed back and forth between my eyes. "Your crazy expressive eyebrows almost did a back flip, you looked so angry when I asked Sara about her boyfriend."

Sara finally looked up and smiled at me but answered Valentina first, saving me from having to voice my honest opinion. "Oh, she doesn't like Brian."

"Brian?" Valentina asked.

"That's my boyfriend. Dr. Ramirez here doesn't approve."

"What's wrong with him?" Valentina asked.

"Oh," Sara saved me again, "she would never say. She's too good a friend."

When she refocused on finishing the manicure, I mouthed to Valentina: *piece of shit.* She nodded with a sad smile.

"How about you, Dr. Ramirez?"

I stiffened. I knew Dr. Medina was probably listening.

"I'm too busy concentrating on my career for that. I'm focused only on you."

"Uh-huh," Sara said. Done with her work, she sat back on the chair and crossed her arms. "What about Ramiro?"

Valentina perked up at that. "Who is *Ramiro?*" she asked, rolling the r's seductively.

"Lord, help me," I said, looking at the ceiling. "Ramiro is my oldest friend. He and I grew up together, and now he is a mechanic at my dad's garage. But I absolutely do not see him like that—"

"But *he* sees *you* like that," Sara said.

They were both staring at me now, expectantly.

"Guys, stop. I get enough of that from my dad."

"Oh yeah," said Sara. "He's already planning your wedding."

I rolled my eyes.

Neither Sara nor I asked Valentina if she had a romantic partner. She never talked about it, and we both intuitively knew it might be a touchy subject for her. Since I'd been her doctor, she'd never had anyone join her at any of her appointments, and no one came to visit when she was admitted overnight. This led me to believe she was alone in the world.

"Well," said Sara, "I have to get back to it. Let me know if you need anything, Valentina."

"Guys, thanks for this." We both nodded and left her room.

It was the absolute girliest thing to do. Neither Sara nor I were girly, and I knew Valentina wasn't either. Still, somehow, bonding over something as trivial as makeup was soothing to the soul. I knew we all felt lighter than we had yesterday.

I expected to find Dr. Medina at the nurses' station, watching our little show unfold and poking fun at us, but he wasn't there, and I sighed with relief. Thank goodness he was probably too busy to listen to us make fools of ourselves. He'd question if I was actually cut out to be a doctor.

CHAPTER 7

A GRILLING

I was hesitant to leave my shift on Friday. Valentina had been nauseous all morning, and now she lay in bed, tired, panting, and weak. We couldn't force anything into her body that she didn't bring back up. I sat next to her, watching helplessly. We'd been battling her cancer for weeks—battling it aggressively—and I knew it would get worse before the tide turned. Even though I was a doctor and knew better, there was that tiny voice in the back of my mind telling me this was not a battle to be won.

"Valentina, we need to explore—"

She raised a hand to silence me. "No," she said in a breathy voice that broke me.

"It's okay, honey. You don't have to stay on the trial. We can explore other options. Less aggressive treatment."

Valentina grabbed my wrist, and I could tell from her body shaking that she was trying to squeeze my arm fiercely, but the grasp was so gentle, my eyes softened.

"Okay. You are strong. So strong. I'm going to trust that you know your limits."

"I told you at the start, Doctor. I want to live. Put me through hell if you have to, but be as aggressive as you can. I can take it."

"I don't doubt it."

"I've gone up against ruthless fighters, bigger, stronger, more experienced. Sometimes they've beaten my body to a pulp, but I've still found a way to rise and keep fighting. Trust me, this right here," she swept her hand across her body as if it were on display, "this is nothing compared to some of the fights I've won. I'm a professional athlete—a *fighter*. This all you got, doc?"

I smiled at her confidence. This is what it took. *Sometimes.* Sometimes it took better doctors, but she already had the best. I didn't mean me. She had Dr. Medina now. It was at that moment that I knew deep in my gut that Valentina Almonte would live. She had what it took, and so did her care team.

Before I clocked out, I finished noting in her chart and met Sara in the doctors' lounge. The week had kicked my ass. Valentina's case was only the tip of the iceberg. I had many other demanding patients and a group of new interns who didn't know an esophagus from a rectum. I was exhausted and wanted nothing more than to sleep through my day off tomorrow. I was frowning when Sara spoke up.

"Don't even think about it."

"I didn't say anything."

"You are not bailing tomorrow. I won't let you break your dad's heart."

I groaned. "Fine. What time do I have to be there?"

"Six is good. And please do something about your face. I want pictures."

"I'm not doing my makeup for a cookout."

"Fine. But if you don't do your own makeup, I'll be doing it for you."

Sometimes I couldn't understand why I'd become best friends with such a bossy and intrusive woman. There was no way out of this, and I knew it. A voice we weren't expecting startled us.

"Am I invited?" It was Dr. Medina. We heard him but couldn't see him. Then, he sat up from where he had been lying down on the couch. He turned to face us.

"That's the second time you've mentioned a party in my presence. It would be rude not to invite me, don't you think?"

"Uh—" I'd never seen Sara at a loss for words, and this was amusing.

"I'm not sure it would be your thing, doctor," I said.

"Why not?"

"It's very casual. My Dad is hosting it, and the guest list does not include many, um . . ."

"Doctors," Sara finished for me, saving me from having to say, *dude, you'd stick out like a sore thumb in the barrio.*

"I don't only socialize with doctors." He looked from her to me. "And I don't know any people in this city. It will be nice to have a conversation with someone other than my cat."

I couldn't help the snort that escaped me. "You have a cat?"

"Is that funny?"

Who the hell was I to judge? "No, Doctor. Of course not. We'll see you at six." I rattled off Dad's address, and he asked for my phone number.

"In case I need help finding the place," he said lamely.

After he left, Sara studied me with a massive grin on her face.

"What?"

"He asked for your phone number." She wiggled her eyebrows up and down, or tried to, anyway.

I shook my head at her.

"Your children will have the eyebrows of gods."

"Shut up," I said.

"I don't think Ramiro will be very happy with you bringing home a date."

"It's not a—" but Sara had left the lounge with my soda in her hand before I could finish speaking.

OF COURSE, I didn't arrive at Dad's at six. I knew that man, and he would be working all day to get ready for the cookout. I wasn't even a little surprised when I showed up at ten in the morning, and Ramiro was already there helping.

I turned into the driveway, and the sight of his black pickup truck forced a sigh out of me. I loved Ramiro very much, but I'd never been in love with him. He was more like a brother to me, but he didn't see me as his sister. Not yet.

Both Mom and Dad had told me that after I was born, they had somewhat jokingly agreed with Ramiro's parents that I would marry their son one day. When we were little, and girls still had cooties, even Ramiro had recoiled at the idea. But as we grew up, his view changed, while mine remained the same.

When we were in high school, he told me he would wait for me forever, that I was his soul mate, but I knew deep down that I wasn't. I told him not to wait. He'd dated women over the years, but he always swore, even before starting anything with someone else, that he was only waiting for me to get back to him.

Ramiro kept waiting even when I insisted there was nothing to wait for. First, he waited for me to finish college. Then, he waited for me to finish medical school. Now, he claimed to be waiting for me to finish my residency, so I would be less busy. I'd assured him things wouldn't slow down after that. My career was not the reason I wasn't with him.

I couldn't deny part of the fault lay in me. I'd dated some, though no one seriously. Every man I'd ever given a chance to never went past a few dates. Either he hadn't understood the demands of being a physician, or he was a fellow physician who had a schedule as busy as mine, and we never saw each other. Each relationship was doomed before it had a chance to take off. But even though I'd dated plenty, and I was no virgin, I never had the heart to tell Ramiro; I swore to myself that the minute I got serious with anyone, I would tell him. Of course, I used to be sure there was someone out there for me, but these days, I wasn't so sure.

In middle school, I once tried to make true the future that seemed predestined. I caught Ramiro off-guard, and I kissed him. It could very well have been that kiss he held on to, even if I'd explained a million times that I'd been in a bad place when I'd done that. My mother had just died, and I'd honestly believed she wished for me to grow up and marry Ramiro one day. I knew now that she would much rather have seen me happy with someone else than unhappy with the boy she knew and had once chosen for me. I had long ago let go of that dream, but my poor *papi* still clung to it.

Dad was predictably in the kitchen, pouring spices and beer over trays of thinly sliced meat for the *carne asada.*

"*Buenos días, Papi.*" I kissed his cheek.

"*Pero,* what are you doing here? I told that *güera* you weren't supposed to be here until six. She never listens."

I laughed. "I wanted to help."

His shoulders slackened in resignation. "Fine. Go help Ramiro outside."

It was a herculean effort, but I resisted the urge to roll my eyes. I loved spending time with Ramiro, but more and more, I avoided it. I needed them both to understand that Ramiro and I were never going to happen.

What Dad clung to, I believed, was his inability to let go of his roots. Every immigrant parent's dream was for their child to become a doctor or a lawyer, but then I did. And he wasn't careful with what he wished for. Now, he was having a hard time letting go of the fact that I would never be the homemaker, traditionalist, child-bearer he'd envisioned his daughter being. He couldn't have it both ways, and the sooner he realized it, the better.

Because that is what it would be like. Ramiro wasn't the type who would be okay with my sixteen-hour shifts and overnight on-call rotations. He was the kind of man who wanted a homebody who would have his favorite meal ready on the table every Friday when he got home from work, tired from a long week at the garage. That woman could not —would not—ever be me. Whomever that woman ended up being would be very lucky to have him, but she wouldn't be me.

Ramiro balanced on a chair as he wrapped a string of twinkle lights around one branch of the tree in the backyard. He had earbuds in and didn't hear when I called to him. He wore dark denim jeans and a black ribbed tank. He was tall and barrel-chested. A heartbreaker in every sense of the word. If only I could have loved him back.

He turned, and his eyes lit up at the sight of me.

"Caro!" He jogged over, picked me up in his arms, and swung me around. "Happy birthday, *Corazón.*"

"Put me down!" I smacked his giant shoulders. He was well built and hit the gym often.

"You weren't supposed to be here until six. We aren't ready."

"I came to help dad. Ramiro, you really don't need to be here helping him. That's what I'm here for."

His face fell for only one second before he shook it off. "You know better. You get treated like a queen on your birthday."

"You two spoil me almost every day, not just my birthday. How can I help?"

"You can tie the tablecloths down, so they don't blow away. That would be great."

With the three of us, everything was ready by four in the afternoon, and all that was left was to fire up the grill when guests arrived. Ramiro left to get a bit of rest and change clothes. I went to my old room and took a quick shower.

I hadn't thought to bring clothes, of course, so I had to settle for whatever old items I had in my closet. Luckily, one of my favorite deep green dresses was there. I wore this dress on very rare occasions, but I loved the square neckline that showed off my collarbones without too much cleavage. I had more than plenty in that department, so I didn't need to be highlighting it more than necessary. The deep emerald looked beautiful on my dark, caramel-honey skin. It was also the perfect outfit for the hot, Kansan summer day.

Because it was so hot outside, I knew something was up when I laid eyes on Sara dressed in an outfit more suitable for fall. She walked in wearing a thin, long-sleeved blouse and didn't remove her sunglasses even when she was indoors. Not this shit again. I was going to kill him. Oath or not, I was going to kill him. I took a deep breath before leading her upstairs to my room—I couldn't take more control away from her.

Leading her to sit on my bed, I sat on the chair in front of her.

"Honey—" That's all it took. One word, and she broke into a sob.

"I'm sorry, Caro. I don't want to ruin your party, but I also couldn't miss it. I promised your dad . . ." She trailed off into her sobs and wiped at the tears on her cheeks.

"Oh, sweetie." I brushed her hair back. "You aren't ruining anything.

You know I hate these things anyway." I smiled, and she laughed weakly. "Why don't you tell me what happened?"

Sara squared her shoulders and took her shades off. She'd done an expert job with the makeup, covering the blue and green bruises I knew were under that thin layer of pigment, but I couldn't be fooled because the swelling was clearly there. My fists clenched at my sides, and I couldn't help but bite the inside of my lip.

"Don't say it," Sara said. "I know he is slime. I know. I'm leaving him, okay?"

I'd heard this before, and there was not a shred of conviction in her voice, just like the last time. I wanted to shake her so badly, but just like the last time, I restrained myself. Even though it broke my heart, I couldn't help her out of this until she decided she was ready. So much power is taken from a domestic abuse victim, I couldn't bear to force her into anything she didn't want, even if it did everything short of killing me to hold my anger in check.

"When you're ready, I'm here for you. *We* are here for you; *Papi*, Ramiro, Sofia, and me. We got you. You got it?"

"I know."

"Why don't you stay up here and sleep it off? I'll tell Dad you're sick and resting here, and later I'll sneak you a plate of food."

Sara smiled up at me as I stood. "Did you make the salsa?" she asked.

"Yes. I made the salsa."

"The *molcajete* salsa—your mom's recipe?"

"Yes, with the secret ingredient."

"Bring extra?" she said as she curled into a ball under the blankets.

It was hard to get into the partying mood after that, but as tough as it was, we moved on. It was horrid to think it, but as often as that bastard Brian had beaten her up, Sofia and I had started getting used to it. And wasn't that just the shittiest bit of it all? We were the only two who knew because we were the only people in the world she couldn't hide her bruises from. We were too analytical.

Dad was happy, and we both knew this party was more for him. He'd invited all the neighbors—Ramiro's parents weren't present because they were vacationing in Florida—all of the mechanics from the garage, among whom were Ramiro's best friends, and Sara, but I kept her tucked away in her tower—my room.

The music came to a stop at six-thirty when we thought everyone had arrived. Dad said a few words, in Spanglish, of course.

"I want to thank you all for being here today to celebrate my *hijita*. It is a special day for me. She turns twenty-six today, and I'm the proudest dad in the world." As he spoke, out of the corner of my eye, I saw Dr. Medina enter our backyard. He carried a box wrapped in navy blue paper, finished with an orange bow. I smiled at him, and he waved back before placing the box carefully on the gift table.

Dad continued, and I returned my attention to him. "*Mija,* you are smart, strong, and beautiful. I don't know what I did in my past life to deserve a daughter like you, but I'm glad I did it."

"Don Gustavo." Ramiro jumped in, beer in his hand. "Mind if I say a few words too?"

I panicked. Oh, god, no. *Please, Papi, don't let him.*

"Of course, *mijo.*"

"Thank you," Ramiro started, and I sank into my chair. "I would like to propose a toast to Caro. *Todo el barrio* loves you. You treat patients for free at their homes when you can, and you are always helping your dad. You come from a hard worker, and I know you are a hard worker too. It's been a privilege to grow up with you, and I can't wait to start the next chapter of our lives. To Caro!" He raised his beer, and glass bottles clinked all around me.

Ramiro walked to the spot where I sat on my chair and offered me a hand. I grabbed it, smiling tightly, and stood to hug him. He went for a kiss, but I gave him my cheek instead of my lips. As I turned my head, I saw Hector still standing by the gifts, his eyes shadowed completely by his strong brow—his face unreadable.

I grabbed my drink before walking over to him.

"Dr. Medina. Hello."

"You look surprised I showed."

"To be honest, I am a little bit. I'm glad you came, though. You will be a novelty here tonight."

"I doubt that. They have you."

"I don't mean because you are a doctor." I laughed. "These people here, *my* people, are working-class people. The offspring of migrant workers, for the most part. I don't think you'll find many fancy Mexicans here tonight besides yourself."

"I'm a fancy Mexican?" he asked. At first, I thought he was joking but stifled my laugh when I sensed his earnestness.

I eyed him up and down, hand on my hip. "Yes. Definitely a fancy Mexican."

He stiffened when I laced my arm in his and led him to the opposite corner of the yard where Dad was grilling and talking to my uncle. I didn't miss when Hector used his free hand to straighten his tie.

"*Papi!*" I said. "I want you to meet someone."

Dad said a few more words I couldn't make out to my uncle and then handed him the apron and tongs. He came around the food table next to the grill. He smiled at me, but his lips thinned, seeing my arm was still linked with this strange man's.

"*Papi*, this is Dr. Hector Medina. My new boss."

Dad leaned back a bit and narrowed his eyes, studying him. Finally, after what seemed like years, he reached out his hand to shake Hector's, making him realize he had to let go of my hand.

"It's a pleasure," Dad said.

"Likewise. Thank you for inviting me to your home." I covered up my snort with a pretend cough. *Invited?* This fool invited himself.

Dad wanted to interrogate him further, but he heeded my glare. This was my boss after all, and I owed him respect. He couldn't treat him like any other man I might bring home—not that I had brought anyone home for him to meet anyway.

"Can I get you something to drink?" I asked Dr. Medina, trying to break the awkwardness.

"Water would be great."

"Let's go into the kitchen, and I'll get you some ice."

He followed me back into my childhood home, and I suddenly felt very nervous about him seeing where I grew up.

"This is a nice house," he said, and I couldn't tell whether or not he was mocking me.

"I was happy growing up here."

Once the glass of water was in his hand, I suggested going outside for a plate of dinner, but he shook his head. "How about a tour instead?"

I almost choked on my beer. "A tour?"

"Yes. I'd love to see the rest of the house that was so happy for you growing up."

I cocked my head, unsure if I should give some excuse as to why that was a bad idea. I envisioned his childhood home in Mexico—probably a mansion—and I recoiled at the thought of showing him around. I couldn't come up with anything, so I led the way.

The living room was cozy, and I was glad I'd come early to help dust and tidy up a bit. I knew Dad abhorred dusting or any other household tasks besides cooking.

A row of picture frames lined the fireplace mantel. Dr. Medina's eyes zeroed in on them, and he walked over.

He picked one of me at the pool when I was six. "This is you?"

I nodded. "I'm an only child."

"That explains a lot."

"Excuse me?" I asked with mock-offense. "It's my birthday. I will not be put down on my birthday."

"My apologies, Dr. Ramirez. I meant nothing by it."

So, we were back to *Dr. Ramirez*. Okay. That was fine. "None taken, Dr. Medina," I said pointedly.

Next, he picked up a photo from my *quinceañera*, my coming-of-age party, when I turned fifteen. I winced, and my pride couldn't take it. I nearly snatched the photo from his hands, but it was too late. There I was, standing next to Dad, in the monster of a dress engulfing me in pink tulle.

Under different circumstances, I would have died before having the classical Mexican coming-of-age party. I would have opted for hell before agreeing to wear the Pepto-Bismol pink monstrosity, but as it was, I couldn't find it in my heart to say no to Dad.

"That's, um, a pretty dress—" my boss started to say. He tried to hold back a chortle but failed, and I couldn't help but smack his arm playfully.

"I did it for my father, okay?"

"No, really, really," he said between the laughter, "you were a very pretty cotton-candy."

"Where is your mother in the photo?"

And just like that, all the laughter went out of me. He sensed the clouds behind my eyes and started to apologize.

"It's okay," I said. I brought a hand up in a friendly gesture. "She had been gone a while by the time I turned fifteen. It's been my Dad and me ever since."

"I'm sorry, Carolina. That must have been very hard."

We were back to *Carolina,* and I offered him a weak smile. "It was, though it would have been much worse if my father had been anyone other than the one I got. He really is amazing."

"He must be," he said.

"What is that supposed to mean?"

"To have a daughter like you, he must be pretty amazing."

"Well, that's it. The house, as you can see, is pretty small. Not much else to see."

"Isn't there an upstairs?"

"Yes, but—" and just like that, he was off toward the stairwell.

I'd forgotten Sara was resting in my room but exhaled when I opened the door and she was gone. The sneaky little twat—she'd get it later. Instead, I found myself in my childhood bedroom with a very tall, very handsome man who was also my boss, barely fitting in the tiny space.

I froze when I realized what he was staring at on the wall next to my bed. It could only be one of three things. He was likely not a fan of *Jane Eyre,* so it wasn't that poster. He would certainly get points for being an *Industrial November* fan, so it could be the enlarged *Metal Red Day* album cover that drew him to the wall. Even if that were the case, that's not what he was staring at now. Sandwiched between the two was the first page of the abstract to his first published paper in a journal of medicine.

I forced my legs to move next to him. His mouth was parted slightly, and he swallowed. He was trying and failing to speak, and I couldn't find what to say in my defense.

If the earth could have swallowed me whole in that moment, I would have dived in head-first.

"Okay, please don't freak out. It really is not what it looks like."

He nodded but said nothing as he stared at his name printed on the page so carefully taped to my wall.

"Dr. Medina, I'm sure this must seem really inappropriate, but I swear, I'm not some stalker or anything like that." I cleared my throat. "I've known I wanted to do cancer research since I was ten. I was in high school when I first heard of your work, and at the time, I had no idea you would one day be my boss. I never thought I'd meet you."

The silence stretched as I allowed him a moment to answer, but he seemed incapable, so I, unfortunately, continued with the verbal diarrhea.

"I'm not in this room much, or I would have taken it down now that I know you." Everything I said after that sounded weak even to my own ears.

"It's okay, not a big deal," he said, finally putting me out of my misery. "Why don't we go back out, join the party? They must be missing you."

Once back outside, Ramiro's gaze latched on to us. I ignored it and introduced Dr. Medina to the neighbors. Merengue blared from a sound system that hadn't been in the yard before. Hector grabbed my hand. "May I have this dance?"

I laughed so hard, Hector frowned. "I'm sorry," I said. "It's just, I have two left feet. I don't dance. And this song," I kept talking between fits of laughter as I listened to Esa Muchacha by Los Hermanos Rosario, "is about a girl who can dance really well."

"Everyone can dance—"

"*Mija,* can you do me a favor?" my neighbor Mrs. Garcia called out to me.

"Sure, *señora.*"

I shrugged at Hector but was glad to be called away. It warmed me to my core when he took off his jacket and tie and rolled up his sleeves, so he could pass a soccer ball around with the two Garcia boys from next door. I sat with the boys' grandmother.

"I had a little accident in the kitchen. You mind taking a look?" She brought up an arm to display a burn on her inner forearm.

"*Hay, Mamá!*" Francisca, her daughter, and the mother of the boys now playing soccer with Dr. Medina, said. "I told you, she is not that kind of doctor anymore." She turned to me. "Sorry, Caro. I wanted to take her to the doctor, but she refused."

"Don't talk for me like I'm a child," Mrs. Garcia said as she glared at her with a fire I wouldn't like to be on the receiving end of. "Why would I go to a doctor," she continued, "when I know it's so minor and that Carolina would be happy to look at it?"

"I'm so sorry, Carolina," said Francisca, completely flustered.

"Don't worry, Francisca, I'm happy to help. Let me go inside and wash my hands. I'll be right back to take a look."

The burn was barely an inch in length, and only superficial.

"The good news is, you don't have to go to the doctor," I said to her with a smile.

"And the bad news?" Mrs. Garcia said, her brows furrowed.

I laughed. "No bad news. You just need to keep it clean and covered until it heals. If it's nice and pink, it's good. Once it scabs, it's good. But if it turns any other funny color, or gets any type of smell, we'll have to take a look at it again."

Mrs. Garcia stuck her tongue out at her daughter, and I couldn't help but laugh. "See?" she said. "I told you it would be nothing."

"Ramiro!" I called for my friend. "Do you mind grabbing my first aid kit from the upstairs bathroom? I also need a notepad and a pen."

He nodded and ran inside. I followed, leading Mrs. Garcia into the kitchen, where I washed her forearm with soap and water. Ramiro came back with the supplies, and I applied antibacterial ointment to her burn and bandaged it. I wrote down the name of a cream to use to treat it on a piece of paper and took it outside.

Ramiro and I walked Mrs. Garcia back to her chair. She wasn't too old or frail yet, but we knew she'd been dipping into the beers as usual. We sat her down, and I handed Francisca the piece of paper.

"It's really no trouble," I reassured her. "I'm always happy to help your mom. She *feeds* me when Dad is busy working."

It had been true once, though not so much since I'd moved out to my own apartment. But I still had a lot of love for the woman next door who had kept an eye out for us after Mom died. Like many at the party, she was more family than neighbor.

Not much longer after fixing up her mom, Francisca caught my attention as she chatted it up with Dr. Medina. And no, I was not jealous. Not one little bit. I loved Francisca almost as much as I loved her mom. Francisca was a single mom, sure, but she was a super-hot single mom. Not that I was jealous.

And because I wasn't jealous, I walked up to them to see what they were chatting about.

"It was great to see you," Dr. Medina said, "but I have to get going. Happy birthday." He said his goodbyes to Francisca then found Dad to do the same before parting.

"He is very handsome," Francisca said with a twinkle in her eye.

"Sure. If that's your type," I said dismissively.

"What? The tall, dark, and handsome type? Or is it the hot doctor type? Or the sexy Spanish accent type?"

I said nothing.

"So, you are not into him?"

"No! He is my boss." I was getting tired of having to tell everybody that.

"So you wouldn't mind if I gave him my number?"

My head snapped to her so quickly, she threw her head back with laughter and walked back to her mom, who was seated alone and happily kept company by a nice cold one.

DAD WENT to bed shortly after the last guests left at one in the morning, with promises he would pick up tomorrow. I remained to, at the very least, throw out the leftover food.

Grabbing my last beer of the night, I laid down on the hammock under the tree, looking up at the lights Ramiro had hung. The smell of the citronella candles had diminished now but was still detected by my strong sense of smell.

It had been a good night, as much as I had fought it. I liked seeing my dad so happy; he was in his element cooking for his friends. It still hurt that Sara couldn't be a part of it, but Dr. Medina showing up when I hadn't imagined he would made up for any shortfalls of the evening.

It was in this reverie that I found myself when the sound of a chair being dragged across the grass, and landing next to me, distracted me. I turned to meet Ramiro's handsome face.

He clinked my beer with his.

"*Salud*," he said.

"*Salud.*"

"Was it a good birthday?"

"Yeah. Mostly."

"Mostly?"

I shrugged. "Just some drama with Sara. I'll talk with her about it tomorrow—err . . . today, I guess."

"I noticed she wasn't here. Was surprised."

Shrugging again, I took another swig of beer and placed my hand behind my head, looking up at the sky. I was definitely downplaying what had happened with Sara, but I wasn't sure how much she would want Ramiro to know.

"I was also surprised," Ramiro said, "that you brought someone else from work. That was a first." I glanced at him. We both knew what he was dancing around.

"You know Sara and her big mouth. She mentioned the party, and he heard. It was rude of her not to invite him, so she did. Trust me, I was just as surprised when he actually showed."

A small noise that sounded almost like an "uhuh," escaped him.

"You like him?" he asked.

"No," I said automatically. This was starting to sound rehearsed, it was asked so often.

"I saw the way you looked at him."

I sighed. "I looked at him the way you would look at David Beckham. He was my hero when I first started thinking about medicine. Now, I'm over the moon he will be my mentor." I didn't even notice when my tone turned. "And, quite frankly, I'm sick and tired of everyone assuming I'm in love with him or something. Maybe I'm in love with his work, but I want mentorship. That's all. If he were a woman, we wouldn't be having this discussion."

"Okay, okay. I give," he said with a gesture of surrender.

"I'm sorry. I shouldn't have snapped. I've just been getting a lot of that recently."

"I bet," he said.

I sat up on the hammock and dangled my legs off to the side so I could face him. I kicked off my sandals, and he tried to grab my foot and place it on his lap, but I bounced it back toward the ground.

"Ramiro—" I said before he cut me off.

"You know, if he had been a woman, and you were in love with her, I might've been into that," he said, trying to lighten the mood. This was the problem. We knew each other too well. It muddied the waters, and it had to come to an end.

I kicked him playfully, and we both laughed. "Ramiro, we need to talk—"

"Not this again, *corazón*. Please. Not tonight."

"It's never a good time. You never let me talk because you know me so well, you know exactly what I'm going to say."

His gaze dropped to the ground, and he buried the beer bottle in the grass. "On your birthday. That's when you want to do this?"

"It's one in the morning. It's not my birthday anymore."

Ramiro gulped a big breath and motioned with his hands for me to lay it on him.

"Ramiro, you need to move on. I've never seen you as anything other than my brother. What do I have to do for you to believe that will never change?"

"It's because of him—"

"No. It's not because of anyone. This might hurt for you to hear, but I may never end up with anyone. I'm not someone who needs a relationship. I'm not saying it will never happen, but even if it does, there is one thing I am sure of. It will never be with you."

Because I loved him so much, the look of pain on his face crushed me. He winced as though I had stabbed him in the gut, but he wasn't surprised. He couldn't be. He'd known how I felt all along, but he wanted to pretend. I couldn't let this go on any longer. I wouldn't let a disease spread because the treatment might cause temporary pain, but somehow, I'd let it go unchecked in Ramiro.

"I want nothing more than for you to be happy," I continued. "You need to stop distracting yourself with women who aren't worthy of your love and find someone who is. You need someone who wants to care for you the way I know you will care for the woman you end up with. I wish —I wish with all my heart that woman could be me. It would make things so much easier—for both of us. And *I do* love you. More than you know, but I love you like a brother. It will kill me if what I'm saying takes you out of my life."

He didn't say anything as he let my words sink in. Instead, he stood and offered a hand as he had done earlier in the evening. I stood, and we were about an inch apart. He looked into my eyes, finding the same truth there that had come out of my mouth. He kissed my forehead, and I brought up my hand to his cheek so I could look at him again.

He was too manly to cry, but the glistening glare hurt as much as if he had shed tears.

"You will find someone, Carolina. You are too spectacular not to have a million men fall at your feet."

"Ramiro—"

"Maybe years from now I won't feel this way, but right now, the very thought of the man you choose in the end, well, I think it will kill me to watch. Though I have a feeling I just met him tonight."

"Don't do this, Ramiro. *Please.* We are family."

He shook his head. "No. I mean, yes. I will stay away. For a little while. Please do me a favor, huh?"

"Anything," I said, and I meant it.

"Don't reach out until I do? I'll be in withdrawals from you, and you know my ego can't take you seeing me as anything other than the virile man that I am."

We both laughed, but it was forced, and I punched him playfully.

"You'll come back to us?" I asked.

"You are my family, first and foremost," he said, reassuring me.

"You promise?"

"I promise."

CHAPTER 8

ASSUMPTIONS

*W*here once there were two men in my life, now there were none. Three months had passed since the cookout, and I hadn't seen Ramiro at all, and I'd barely spoken to Dr. Medina.

Ramiro went to join his parents in Florida, Dad told me, but then stayed there when his parents came back. He asked Dad for extended leave from the garage, and considering it was his daughter who propelled him away—his words, not mine—he found himself obliged to consent to the request.

Dr. Medina, on the other hand, had pulled a one-eighty on me. He withdrew from the friendly banter we had started. I was given no attention at rounds, and it was almost as if he couldn't stand to look at me. I had no clue what was up his ass, but I refused to let it affect my work. Never meet your heroes—the best piece of advice I ever got that I stupidly ignored.

Focus on work, I told myself. It wasn't easy on this particular day. I'd drawn the short straw, though I suspected foul play from Dr. Keach, and had gotten stuck teaching a sensitivity training to our year-one residents.

"We've had four complaints this month," I said to the packed conference room, "of poor bedside manner." Some of the residents had the decency to feign some semblance of shame, and some shifted in their seats. "So," I said, "we are going to practice."

Groans skipped down the row of doctors like stones on water, so I lifted a hand to silence them. I pinched the bridge of my nose. "I don't want to be here any more than you do, but this is *your* fault, not mine, so take it up with the chief if you don't like it."

They shut it at that. Even among these baby doctors, I could tell which ones had issues with women doctors or women telling them what to do in general. It was the ones who took out their cellphones when I spoke or started hushed side conversations. I narrowed my eyes and called on that type first.

"One of the complaints was from a woman who said the doctor, and I quote, 'walked in the room, didn't so much as say hello, read my chart, and never even looked up at my face. Then, he took a thermometer and shoved it in my mouth. He didn't say what he was doing, and he didn't even ask me to open my mouth. He was very rude.'" I glanced up from the screen when a couple of the doctors cackled. They shut it immediately and straightened their postures.

One hour of hell later, I dismissed all but one of the residents.

"Dr. Dennis, why don't you join me? We have a patient who was admitted a bit late this morning, so we haven't been to round on her."

The redhead nodded. I purposefully selected Dr. Dennis because I remembered a distinct smile on Valentina's face when he was around. If she had to be back in her hellhole, at least she'd have a friendly face.

Valentina had been discharged, had been feeling a bit better, but then took a bit of a turn. Now, she was back, and I'd had to admit her for major surgery. I told her last time I discharged her that I hoped not to see her until her next round of chemo, but my wish was not granted.

We found Valentina standing at her bed, facing away from the door. She rummaged through a duffle bag, muttering something to herself. She was in her hospital gown, and the part down her spine provided just enough of a peek to see her light pink underwear. I cleared my throat to announce our presence. She whipped around and smiled at the sight of me.

"Doctor Ramirez!" Her grin broke mid-sentence when her eyes drifted over my shoulder, undoubtedly seeing Dr. Dennis. She drew her hand toward her backside to seal the mighty hospital gown gap. She turned chili-pepper red, but I couldn't bring myself to care. I was happy to see some color on her. "Rory—I mean, Dr. Dennis. Hi."

"Hello, Miss Almonte," he said.

"Valentina. Please."

"Of course. Valentina. Hello."

I let a moment pass between them before speaking again. "So, I thought I told you to stay away, young lady."

"I'm trying, Doc. I'm trying really hard."

"Are you ready for tomorrow?"

She nodded. "I remember the drill vividly."

"I know," I said. "But I still have to go over the procedure with you. Risks, all that."

Valentina rolled her eyes. "Yeah, I know that drill too."

In that second, I got paged to Dr. Medina's office. *What now?* It felt like I was being called to the principal's office. We had barely spoken since my birthday and at work, had only interacted when absolutely necessary.

"Well, missy, if you are that bored of my rambling, maybe I'll have the capable Dr. Dennis go over the paperwork with you. Do you mind, Dr. Dennis? I was paged."

"Sure," he said, taking the clipboard with the consent forms from me.

I TOOK a deep breath before knocking. Hector's mood lately had all of us in the oncology department avoiding him. I wasn't prepared to go into the lion's den.

"Come in," said Dr. Medina's gruff voice from the other side of the door.

"You paged?"

"Yes, please sit down." He smiled at me, but it wasn't the same smile as before. There was no playfulness in his eyes, and his lips were tight.

"What's this about?"

"You haven't seen your email today?"

"Not since two in the afternoon. I was in charge of a training with the residents today—"

"Yes, yes," he said, cutting me off. "Statistics got back to us. The preliminary data of the trial is in."

"It is?" My heart raced. This step of the trial wouldn't make or break it, but if it improved outcomes, it could mean . . . I couldn't go there. Not without the numbers to back it up. Dr. Medina simply nodded.

"Yes. A lot of it looks promising, but I have some questions, and I'd like to go over the data with you," he said.

"You looked at the data already?"

"Well, yes," he said, his brow furrowing.

"Why did they send it to you?"

"I asked the statistics department to cc me when the results came in—"

My pulse quickened with a rage I knew I wouldn't be able to tame. "You had no right. That is my data—"

"I thought you agreed we would work on this together?"

Dr. Medina looked aghast as if he couldn't understand where I was coming from. I counted to ten to suppress the anger building. He was overstepping on *my* trial. He wasn't used to people telling him 'no,' I could tell. But someone had to.

Taking a deep breath, I said, "Dr. Medina, from now on, I'd appreciate being the first one to see the results of *my* trial."

"A sensitivity training is not more important than this," he countered.

"No. But I won't set aside my other hospital duties. Research is one big part of the whole. I'm also expected to teach—"

"I don't see the problem here," he said.

Clearly, I thought. "You are overstepping on my trial, Dr. Medina."

He leaned back in his chair and scratched at the stubble on his jaw. "I'm not sure what to do here."

"Look, moving forward, I'd like to be in charge of the trial *I* wrote. I'm grateful for your mentorship, but that doesn't mean you can just take over—"

"I see—"

"I mean no disrespect, Dr. Medina."

"Well, what's done is done. I'd still kill to go over the preliminary data with you."

He offered no reassurances, but I was already on dicey ground with my boss, so I let the matter go. We could always re-visit the conversation if he continued to overstep.

"Fine. I have time this evening," I said.

"No, I can't this evening. I'm on call tonight."

"Oh." I slumped back in my chair, thinking about my schedule.

"How about Friday night. You're off, right?" he asked.

"I am. But I can't Friday. I have plans."

He cocked his head to the side as his eyes narrowed. I could swear a storm was brewing there.

"*Cancel* your *plans*," he said between gritted teeth.

"I'm sorry. I can't. I can work with your assistant to find a time that works for both of us if you'd like—"

"No. I can do it this Friday. I want to get it over with as soon as possible."

Over with? I hadn't asked him to do this. He wanted to work on the trial. I never asked him to, and now he was trying to make it seem like some great inconvenience while at the same time overstepping on it?

"No," I said. I took a deep breath. "I'm afraid the plans I have on Friday can't be canceled."

My shift was over, so I stood to leave. "I'll find a time with your assistant."

"Dr. Ramirez, we are not done here," he said.

"I'm afraid we are, Doctor."

Putting distance between the hospital and me was the best thing I could do for my sanity. It had been a challenging day between the sensitivity training, Dr. Keach hovering over me, and now this. I speed-walked to the conference room where I'd left my tablet earlier.

"Caro?" I heard Sara's voice as I sped by her. "What's wrong?"

"I gotta go," I said.

I'd just grabbed the tablet when I heard steps behind me.

"Not now, Sara, we'll talk later."

"It's not Sara," he said. I turned to face Dr. Medina, who I hadn't realized had followed me out of his office.

"We weren't done talking."

"Yes, we were. I have to go now."

"No. I need you to cancel your plans Friday."

"And *I told you*, I can't do that. I don't know what else there is to talk about."

He shook his head and took off his glasses to wipe them with a cloth he produced from his pants pocket.

"Your plans can't be more important than this."

"Frankly, it is none of your business."

"You can drink another time," he hissed.

"Excuse me?" I reared back. Had I heard him right?

"I've seen you outside of work exactly two times, and both times you have been drinking."

"Dr. Medina, with all due respect, sir, you are out of line." How could I tell off my boss? I couldn't. Not without risking my job.

"I don't think I am, Dr. Ramirez. If I think that it's getting in the way of your job."

"*What*? Getting in the way of my job?" He was silent for a moment—the audacity. "Dr. Medina," I hissed right back at him, "you might have seen me drinking two times, but if you can, please use your brain. Was I drunk or even tipsy? I don't drink often; you happened to be around for one special occasion, and the other was a girls' night out. I would never drink and come to work. How could you imply I would endanger my patients like that?"

More silence.

"The bottom line is, I have plans on my day off that I can't cancel. If you have a real complaint about my work, take it up with HR." It was his turn to rear back. He hadn't expected me to hold my ground. To anyone else, he may be a god, but I could see him now for what he was. His ego had everyone fooled, and he wasn't used to not getting his way when it came to work.

I couldn't escape because Sara had also followed me and now stood between the door and me. Why was she everywhere? She placed one hand on my shoulder with force to keep me in place and firmly inside the room.

Dr. Medina glared at us, his eyes darting back and forth from her face to mine. He wanted to say something, but he'd come to think twice about messing with Sara, just like every other doctor on the oncology floor. If only she could stand up for herself the way she stood up for her patients and loved ones.

"Dr. Ramirez," Sara said as she shot daggers at our boss with her eyes, "volunteers at the free clinic on two of her days off a month. You know how many days off a resident has, yet she gives most of them up. She would *never* break her commitment." Sara loosened her grip on my shoulder when she was done talking.

Dr. Medina's mouth fell open, and he hung his head but said nothing.

"Forget it, Sara. It's no use," I said as I walked past her and out the door. I could just imagine the stare down that was taking place in the conference room. I had to get out of there.

I was nearly at the locker room when Dr. Keach caught up to me. *Not this. Not now.*

"Fallen from grace so soon, Carolina?" he asked. I glared at him, and he backed off, but not before saying, "What did I tell you?"

If he tripped, fell, and broke his nose, I would not be upset.

CHAPTER 9

THE DRUNK DOCTOR

"Sofia? What is it?" I asked with my heart lodged in my throat.

I was used to getting calls at three in the morning, but they were usually from the hospital. Seeing the name of someone close was jarring. *Please don't let it be Sara,* I thought.

"He's, um—*here.*"

"Who? Where?"

"Your boss. I closed the bar a few minutes ago, but he is barely coherent. I wasn't sure if I should send him in a cab or not."

She was asking me. I pressed a hand to my heart, calming myself down. It wasn't Sara. I rubbed the sleep off my eyes. "No—uh, no. I'll drive him home."

"Mind letting yourself in?" Sofia asked. "Got someone upstairs waiting for me in bed," she said playfully, and I smiled, shaking my head. I didn't even bother asking who it was because it was usually a different person every time. It would take someone incredibly special to make it into her bed on a repeat night.

"Yeah, I got the key. And hey, Sofia? Thanks for calling me."

"No problem."

She hung up the phone, and I slipped into sweats and my white sneakers. I grabbed the first pullover I could find. At three in the morning, the air would be crisp.

Dr. Medina was twirling an empty shot glass on the bar with his index finger when I found him. All the lights were out except for one near him. He looked up when he heard the door open.

"Carolina!" he said with a huge grin that reminded me of his first week on the job. "Look! It's Carolina Doctor, I mean—Doctor Carolina."

I looked around, but there was no one else in the room but him. "Come on, hotshot. I'll take you home."

"But the drinks are here." He looked at the glass bottles of liquor on the shelf.

"I'm sure you have drinks at home."

He shook his head. "No alcohol in my home. Ever. It's a rule," he said, nodding like a child.

Oh my god. Was he an alcoholic? Is that why he was so angry when he believed I was partying on all my days off? That would explain a lot. It would certainly explain why he was murderous on the night he drove me home when he thought I'd be driving after drinking.

"I'll get you some more on the way home," I lied. He'd pass out as soon as he got there.

I stood next to him, letting him lean on me for balance.

"I have to pay," he said.

"It's okay—"

"No. The pretty bartender. Where'd she go?" He looked around the bar as if he just noticed Sofia had left.

"She knows you're good for it. Besides, she knows where you work. You can close out your tab tomorrow."

Leading him to my car proved difficult. He was more off-balance than I thought he'd be, and suddenly I regretted not asking Sofia to stay up and help me. Funny how the lives of doctors and lives of bartenders are so similar; we both get our sleep when we get our sleep. Or we don't.

Before I opened the passenger door, I grabbed his wallet from inside his jacket. I was no skilled pickpocket, but he was so far gone, he didn't notice. I pushed his head down with my free hand to protect him from banging his head on the roof of the car.

Once behind the wheel, I grabbed his driver's license and copied the address onto my navigation device. His home was less than fifteen minutes away.

We entered the security code to his front door incorrectly twice before getting it right. He kept mixing numbers at first. Once inside, I was surprised there was a security system at all. There was nothing anyone would want to steal. The house was spacious and luxurious, with its crown molding and marble kitchen island, but there was no furniture on the main floor. Not a single item decorated the walls. Maybe he had just moved in.

After asking where his room was, he led us there. Getting up the stairs was more challenging than getting him in my car, but we finally made it. I was relieved to see he had a bed, even if it was the solitary item in the room apart from a dresser.

It was beyond awkward standing in a bedroom with my drunk boss. I thanked my lucky stars Sofia was the only one aware of this debacle, and I knew she'd never tell a single soul. Not even Sara.

The thought of his wife sent a shiver through my body. Where was she? From the pictures I had seen online, I would have bet five dollars that woman would have this house filled with cozy beige and white furniture. *She* should have picked him up from the bar—certainly not me. Hector had been in Kansas City several months—long enough for furniture, and long enough for his wife to join him.

I needed to stop thinking of him in any capacity not related to work. His personal life was none of my business, even if I now found myself in the precarious situation of having to drag his drunk ass home. He groaned on the bed, looking up at the ceiling. I took his shoes off, which I reasoned with myself was not crossing a line. I wasn't taking them off to touch him. Not at all. I was being a civil servant. Serving my fellow man.

"Good night, Hector. I think the person who picks you up drunk at a bar at three in the morning gets to be on a first-name basis."

"You're leaving?"

"Yes. I have to go to work in a few hours."

"Don go," he said, his words slurred, missing consonants.

"I have to."

"I'm hungry. I can't sleep if I haven't food."

I groaned. This fool was going to slice a finger off if he tried making something.

"All right, let's see what we can find in your fridge. But then I *have* to go."

He sprang up, and it was only a little funny when he clung to the rail for balance as he descended the staircase.

There wasn't much in the fridge, but I managed to find enough to make a turkey and cheese sandwich. I started a pot of coffee to hopefully sober him up.

As I worked, Hector sat on the single stool at the kitchen island. He bent over, his arm on the counter, and his head rested on his shoulder.

"How is Ramiro?" he asked with the subtlety of a bulldozer.

I winced. I tried not to think about him but answered after handing Hector his plate. "I haven't seen him since my birthday party."

He looked up from the sandwich after the first bite.

"You haven't?" he asked.

I shook my head.

"Why?"

"He's in Florida." There was no way of knowing whether the move was permanent or not, so I refrained from voicing any assumptions.

"I'm sorry," he said.

"For what?"

"I'm sorry that you broke up."

"Broke up? Ramiro and I have never been a couple."

I tried not to get angry when he smiled.

"You haven't?"

"No."

"At the party, I could have sworn—"

"He's like a brother to me," I cut him off, wanting to be done with this conversation.

A soft 'meow' distracted me momentarily. That's right. He'd mentioned a cat. "Come here, kitty, kitty." I smacked my lips as I searched for the source of that soft sound.

"Canica," said Hector.

"What?"

"Her name is Canica."

"Marble? You named her Marble?"

He shook his head. "No. I didn't name her."

I had to assume he meant it had been his wife who named her, though why would the cat be with Hector and not her if it was *her* cat was beyond me. *None of your business, Caro.* "Canica, come here, girl."

"She's shy with strangers," Hector said.

I would be lying if I said it didn't melt my heart that he knew his cat's personality. "Right." I searched the kitchen floor until I came upon her food and water bowls tucked away in the corner. Hector didn't have much in the pantry, but he did have several cans of cat food.

I filled Canica's water bowl first and emptied a can of food into the second bowl. Lingering by the food, I hoped she'd come out to my offering, but she didn't do so until I stood a couple of feet back.

When she did reveal herself, she walked carefully to her dinner. She had a beautiful silver coat and piercing, bright yellow eyes. Once she was done, she approached me tentatively and wrapped herself around my left leg before springing away toward Hector. He picked her up to land a kiss on the top of her head before putting her down again.

"I'm sorry I had it wrong about Ramiro," Hector said, bringing back the subject to where we'd left off our conversation. He took another bite, and I handed him the coffee, which he took black. "But I guess that leaves hope for Dr. Keach."

I dropped the package of cheese I was stowing in the fridge. *What in the hell?*

"Dr. Keach? What in the world are you talking about?"

"He likes you. I never thought he had a chance—you know, thinking you were with Ramiro, but now . . ." His left eyebrow lifted as he trailed off mid-sentence.

"Dr. Keach does not like me."

"Yes, he does."

"No, he doesn't."

"Does."

"*Hector.*"

"*Carolina.*"

Oh, brother. We sounded like little kids.

"Remind me to never pick your drunk ass up again."

"Why do you think he is always in your face?"

"He *hates* me."

"Nope. He can't stand to be away from you. Always finding excuses to be around you, to get a rise out of you—provoke you."

It was that moment that I realized he'd been paying attention. He'd been watching me this entire time, not with the interest of an employer for his employee, but with interest in my personal life.

He scarfed down the sandwich and coffee in record time. Slowly, his words became more coherent, and he found his center of gravity again.

"Why do people say that?"

"What?"

"That when a guy is mean to a woman, it means he likes her. I used to hear it so much as a kid. *If a boy teases you, it means he likes you.* Mom used to say it. Dad said it. It's so wrong. It's so ingrained in us from the time we are little kids." I shook my head. "No wonder so many women grow up to confuse abuse with love." My mouth dried up at the thought of Sara.

"I'm sorry, Carolina." I found nothing but sincere repentance in his eyes. "I'm sobering up with the food and am starting to realize I've placed my foot in my mouth quite a bit tonight."

His words were indeed less slurred. I nodded in acceptance of his apology, and his muscles relaxed.

"Besides," I said dismissively, "if it happens to be true that Keach likes me—which I very much doubt—I would never accept affection from a man who chooses to show a woman he likes her by torturing her and messing with her. That wouldn't be my type at all. Too childish." I crinkled my nose.

Hector raised an eyebrow. "What *is* your type, Dr. Ramirez?"

I thought about it for a second, and he patiently waited. I had never been in a significant relationship, not that I'd tell Hector that. I'd dated, of course, but nothing had ever gotten serious. I finally settled on saying, "I'm trying to think of a throughline in the men I've dated, but they were all so different, I don't think they fit a particular type."

"Okay, but you must know what you like—traits you value."

"Yeah. Sure. Let's see. Smart. Smart is a must. Mature. I like a man who is self-assured, but still humble—not that you would know anything about humility. Balance, I guess. I'm so boring, aren't I?" I chuckled.

"No, Carolina. You are not boring. And I don't know what you are talking about. I'm the best at being humble."

"You realize that very statement proves otherwise?"

Hector threw his head back with laughter.

"I really have to get going. I won't even have a chance to sleep now, but I do have to get ready to go to the hospital."

"I'll walk you out."

I let him stand first to make sure his balance was sufficient for him to climb the stairs by himself. He was steady enough, at least for me to avoid being in his room again. That would be a mistake.

"Carolina." He stopped me before I could open the door. "Thank you for tonight. And I'm sorry for what I said. There is no excuse."

"It happens. I believe intent is important, and I know you weren't trying to be malicious."

He stepped closer to me, nearly pinning my back to the door. "No. It was not my intent to be malicious."

My breath caught in the back of my throat. He leaned in closer—the distance between us now nearly nonexistent. He bowed his head until our noses almost met. My heartbeat loudened until it was all I could hear. I looked at his eyes, but his gaze was frozen on my lips. My eyes dropped to his mouth—I couldn't help it—and his lips parted.

There was no confusing this moment. It was *want*. I wanted him, and his body made it clear he wanted me too. It was a beautiful fantasy, but it could never be more than that—*a fantasy.*

Hector's lips hovered over mine, and his gaze drifted back to my eyes, a question written in his. He was asking for my permission to seal the kiss that lingered like a ghost on our lips. I felt his movements as his arms went past me, and his hands landed on the door behind me. The muscles in his biceps tightened, and deep blue veins bulged to the surface. Restraint. He wouldn't deliver on the promise of contact—not until I accepted it.

I couldn't. My body almost gave in, but I was too practical. I knew if I let go, I would regret it. Not to mention he wasn't completely sober yet. My *good head on my shoulders* would be the ruin of me. I couldn't succumb to an affair that would undoubtedly hurt everyone involved.

Everyone.

"Andrea," I whispered her name, though the syllables tasted bitter on my tongue. His arms dropped from their iron grip on the door behind me, and he stepped back.

My hearing returned as my heart slowed. We both sobered and killed the lust we'd let escape to the surface for a moment. How could we have been so careless? I guess we were only human, after all—not the gods we played at on a daily basis at work.

"You are married," I said, more loudly now.

He nodded and looked down at the gold band around his ring finger. He twisted the band around a few times before laughing. "Right. My *wife*," he said, but there was something off about the laugh. "Good night, Carolina. Thanks again for everything."

"I think you mean *good morning*, Dr. Medina."

CHAPTER 10

WORK AS A DISTRACTION

To my surprise, things were better after our near-miss. Hector remained respectful of me and all our interactions were nothing but professional, but his good mood was back. He stopped ignoring me, and it felt almost how it had when he'd first joined Heartland Metro.

Now that Dr. Keach had planted that seed of doubt, however, I was once again the main target for his jabbing. I hadn't pieced together why Dr. Keach had backed off, but my bliss had only lasted while Hector ignored me. Now that I featured back on Hector's radar, Dr. Keach gravitated back to pestering me, taking any opportunity to put me down in the presence of Dr. Medina.

He found me at the nurses' station going over my next patient's chart. "I see all is well in paradise again," he said.

My eyes narrowed. "Excuse me?" I didn't look up from the screen.

"You and Dr. Medina. You're back in his good graces, I see."

"You should be careful what you insinuate, Dr. Keach. Your daddy's name can only protect you from so much. You sure you want to antagonize someone like Dr. Medina?" I raised an eyebrow.

That's right, Dr. Keach, I thought. *The mom and baby wing may be named after your father, but even your last name plastered on the hospital's wall is laughable.*

There was simply no way he would have gotten matched to this hospital without some serious money being involved. His father was a physician here before his retirement and was a regular—and generous—donor to the hospital. But Dr. Keach was not worth more than the research funding Hector could bring in.

Dr. Keach's lips thinned and his nostrils flared. No one had ever called him out on his bullshit. I'd been tempted many times before, and I wasn't exactly sure why I'd finally done it after all this time. Probably because before, his attention only affected me, but now he was also soiling the name of a mentor I valued. I refused to acknowledge any other feelings for Hector—even to myself.

"You really are clueless, aren't you?" asked Dr. Keach.

"Please, enlighten me," I taunted.

"Dr. Medina will be selecting the recipient of the fellowship in two years. The chief wanted fresh eyes on the graduating residents next year."

I shifted in my seat. Of course Dr. Keach would have this information. The Chief of Oncology kissed his ass constantly. It came as no surprise that he would give him the advantage. It also stung a little that Hector hadn't offered me the same upper hand by telling me his role in selecting the winner.

Hector wasn't witness to any part of this exchange. Dr. Keach was tactical in his attacks on me, and I knew that taking it to HR would only result in his word against mine. It chafed knowing that at this moment, his word would be worth a heck of a lot more than mine.

I didn't see Hector until the next day when I had to work out his schedule with his assistant. We managed to free up the latter half of the day so we could go over the statistical report we had been neglecting.

Hector hadn't changed much in his office in the few months since he'd joined Heartland Metro. From what I could tell, the only change was the appearance of a solitary picture frame on his desk. Once I sat down, I turned the photograph over to see what could be the only thing in his life important enough to look at every day. The simple black frame contained a black and white photograph of Hector and an older, shorter woman standing next to him. "Who is this?" I asked.

"That is Marisela Medina." He smiled, and I put the frame back to its original spot on his desk.

"Your mom?"

He nodded. "Ready?"

We were going over the numbers together. We made a promise to open the email at the same time—he hadn't gotten that far before we'd fought about it. He read one line, and I read the next.

An excitement very close—though also very different—to what I had felt at his house two nights ago crept up. My heart began racing.

"Are you seeing this?" Hector asked.

I couldn't look up from my screen. My mouth dried up, rendering words inaccessible. I only nodded.

"What did I tell you?"

I looked up at him then, the question clear on my face. "Is this real?"

"Carolina, you are amazing. It's going in the right direction."

I nodded, too stunned to speak.

The results were what I was expecting—*eventually.*

Hector read out loud, letting the words wrap me in an embrace. "Thirteen percent difference in remission between the control and experimental groups at six months. Carolina, the experimental group treatment is thirteen percent more effective than the standard of care. I can't wait to see data from year three and year four. I bet you it could go up as much as fifty percent when it's all done . . . Carolina? Are you okay?"

I bolted out of my seat and ran out of his office. Luckily, the bathroom wasn't too far down the hallway from his office. I made it just in time to vomit. I rinsed my mouth, and when I exited the ladies' room, Hector was leaning against the wall across from the door, his brows knitted together.

"Are you okay?" he asked.

I nodded and walked back to his office. I sat and tried to listen to whatever he was saying, but I couldn't. My eyes prickled with tears. He said he thought this could be up to fifty percent better than the standard of care. That, plus all the advancements in medicine since I'd lost her, meant she could have beaten it if she had been diagnosed today instead of so many years ago. I tried to do the math in my head. *Yes.* I was confident she would have lived.

"Carolina." Hector stared at me.

Taking a deep breath, I met his gaze. "Sorry," I said. "I think I'm in shock."

"It's okay. Take a minute."

After a long silence during which I tried to compose myself, he finally spoke.

"Who was it?"

"Who was what?"

"The loss that drove you to this mad battle against cancer."

I pressed my lips together in thought, not sure I was ready for him to know so much. I didn't like talking about it in general, not even to Dad, with whom I shared everything.

"You don't have to tell me if you don't want to, but I very much want to know, Carolina."

His eyes were so soft, so full of empathy, I couldn't help myself.

"My mother."

He nodded but didn't ask any more questions.

"I'm sorry." His glasses came off as he searched for whatever he was going to say next. "Please don't get offended by what I'm about to say. It's hard to put my feelings into words."

"Okay . . ."

"I envy you. Not because you lost your mother, obviously that's not what I'm trying to say. I only mean many people who lose someone do nothing about it. You decided to go into the toughest profession and fight for a spot in a competitive residency so that you could save another little girl's mom."

"No offense taken," I said. "I think I understand what you are trying to say."

"I also envy that you have a reason, a strong one, for doing this."

"What? You don't?"

"No. Not really."

"So then, why did you decide to be a doctor and get into oncology?"

"See, this is where I find it tricky to explain myself. When I was younger, I was very concerned about my legacy. About what contributions I would make to the world before I died. I guess I still am, in a way."

"I think that's a great reason."

"There is nuance there if you look carefully. It sounds noble to aspire to do good in the world, but no one ever admits the selfishness of the sentiment. All of us dreamers and would-be philosophers have the same thing in common: our bloated egos. You'd think we'd want to do good in the world for the world's sake, but it's more selfish than that. We do it for the personal satisfaction." He grinned, pleased with his explanation. "See? Selfish."

"I don't think it's selfish at all."

"You don't?"

"No. Had you been my mother's doctor and been successful in saving her life, do you think I'd have given a rat's ass about what led you to that success? Dr. Medina, you've done so much good in this field. I expect you will continue to do good in the latter half of your career. The patients you save—and their *families*—don't care why you do it, so long as you fucking do it."

He chuckled. "God, Carolina. Sometimes I think you know me better than I know myself." He paused. "Could you be any more perfect?"

I adjusted in my seat. I refused to turn this moment into something uncomfortable. This was my first significant trial, and all signs were pointing to success. I'd also had a beautiful moment with my mentor. We couldn't turn this into something else and mar my memory of this day.

"Well, I'm getting hungry. Would you like to get a bite?"

"Dr. Ramirez," he scolded me, looking at me from above the line of his glasses, now back on his face. "We have a lot of work to do."

It was true. Now, we needed to adjust the treatment protocol and submit it to the internal review board (IRB). In phase two of the trial, all patients would receive the experimental treatment, but not before the IRB approved the protocol change. The process would take a few weeks, so the trial would be placed on hold until then. Suddenly, I had a few more days off.

"We don't have to go anywhere," I said. "I can have my RA order us some food and bring it back."

"You have a research assistant? How come I haven't met her?"

"She works at the information desk mostly, so she's not around much. Doesn't need to be. She schedules appointments, interviews prospective trial subjects, handles data entry—that kind of thing. She was only working the front desk part-time, and when my grant got funded, I offered her a part-time position as an RA. Now, she is employed full time by the hospital and eligible for health insurance benefits."

"That was nice of you."

"I'm lucky to have her. Amanda is pretty amazing. She's more than just an assistant. She's a great visual artist. I'll introduce you sometime. Do you like sushi? I'll have her bring it right over."

"Sure. Sushi sounds great."

I needed to go to my locker and grab a credit card to give to Mandy, but before I left, I turned to him once more. "Oh, and Dr. Medina?"

"Yes?"

"I'm far from perfect. I have my own demons and insecurities, just like anyone else."

CHAPTER 11

THE BROKEN GIRL

*V*alentina's test results from last week were back, and I called her in for a follow-up appointment.

She waited patiently in exam room five. My face fell when I saw her. She looked better physically. Her hair was growing back into a sort of a pixie cut, and some of her weight was back, though her muscles weren't yet. But what threw me off was her pale complexion, her tightened lips, and, most of all, her perfectly-shaped eyebrows, almost fully grown in to their previous length, pulled-in, a crinkle forming between them.

"What's wrong?" I asked her. "Are you not feeling well?"

"You tell me," she said.

"Nothing's wrong, Vale. But you look as though you've seen a ghost."

Her expression not changing, her gaze fell to the floor.

"I read on the forums," she said, "that if it's good news, I get it over the phone. If it's bad, they call me back in for a follow-up."

"Oh, Vale, honey—"

"It's back, isn't it?" Her breath hitched as she formed the question.

"No!" I hastened to answer. "Valentina, I wanted to give you the good news in person. That's all. Please stop reading about treatment or procedures online. It's not the first time it's gotten you in trouble." I arched an eyebrow at her.

"Good news?" She looked up, hope misting her eyes.

"Yes, Valentina. Good news." I grabbed her by the shoulders and squeezed them gently. "Six months remission. It's a great milestone."

"Really?" A tear spilled over and ran down all the way to her neck. Something inside me moved. Despite the hell and pain I put her through during her treatment, this was the first time I'd seen her cry.

"Really," I said. "I thought we should celebrate. I'm actually not working right now. Let's go across the street to the bar. Champagne. My treat."

WHEN SOFIA ASKED what we were celebrating, I looked at Valentina. It was her choice who she wanted to tell—if she wanted to tell anyone at all. Many of my patients who didn't want family around for the treatment didn't tell them unless the treatment failed. I was in awe of Valentina. Not a soul helped her or took care of her, not that I knew of. She had zero support system, but she made it through. It was incredible.

"Six months in remission," Valentina said fiercely. I imagined this was what she looked like after a fight.

"Wow. Congrats!" Sofia said.

"Thanks," Valentina said.

"On the house." Sofia placed two glasses of her best champagne in front of us. "All cancer ass-whipping is rewarded at *La Oficina*." Then, she turned to attend to her other customers.

Valentina and I looked at each other, and we started giggling as we grabbed the glasses. I was about to raise my glass to make a toast when Dr. Dennis approached the table.

"Dr. Dennis," I said.

"Please, Dr. Ramirez, call me Rory outside of work."

"Okay, then, please call me Carolina." I smiled at him.

"What are we celebrating?" he asked.

I turned to Valentina who was trying to tame her pixie hair back into place. *She is self-conscious all of a sudden,* I thought.

"You want to tell him?" I asked her.

"I, um—" the fierceness with which she'd told Sofia was absent from her voice. "Remission. Six months."

"That's great!" he blurted a little too enthusiastically for my taste.

Dr. Dennis had never been part of her care team. He was present at one of her rounds, from what I remembered, and I asked him for help maybe one other time. I didn't think going over a consent form with her counted as being a part of her care team, but he was teetering on crossing a line. I was sure of it. He was still a doctor, and she was still a patient in the same department.

I couldn't say shit, though. I was in a grey-area myself. Drinking with one's patients wasn't precisely in the hospital's manual, but I couldn't imagine it being okay with the oncology department leadership.

I rarely broke rules. I was too practical. But fuck it. Valentina had no one. She'd hinted at being estranged from her family, and the fact that no one ever visited or accompanied her to any follow-ups made me think she was alone. This was an important milestone to celebrate, and if she had no one, well, damn it, I was going to celebrate with her. To hell with the rules.

"Rory," I said. "Why don't you join us?"

He turned to Valentina, ensuring it was okay with her too. I smiled approvingly at him. Valentina nodded, and he sat across from us.

"Sofia," I called out. "One more, please?" She tipped her chin, and soon after, a third glass of champagne joined the table.

I raised my glass, and they followed suit. "To kicking the shit out of cancer," I said.

"To kicking the shit out of cancer," they both sing-songed after me, and we all took a sip.

Rory had started asking Valentina about a fight she had won prior to getting sick when I heard the buzz of my phone coming from my purse.

"Excuse me," I said, and pulled out the phone.

There was one text waiting to be opened.

Sara: *Can you please come to the emergency room?*

Something wasn't right. I wasn't on call, and this wasn't an official hospital page. There was no reason Sara would be unofficially paging me to the ER. This wasn't for a patient.

I had every intention of standing up and running, but the stone in my stomach pulled my center of gravity down.

Valentina must have noticed because she nudged me. "Is everything okay?"

"I don't know," I said, with my eyes still glued to the text. "I, uh, have to go."

"Sure," Valentina said.

Rory nodded at me, and I felt perfectly comfortable leaving them together.

∼

HER NOSE WAS BUSTED—A bandage covered it from cheek to cheek. I reached for the computer to look at her chart, but the ER doctor rolled the medical computer cart away from my grasp.

"It's okay," Sara said. "She can see my chart."

He nodded and rolled the small cart back toward me.

Sara grinned at me with her eyes closed.

"She's had quite a bit of pain meds," he said. "Someone will come shortly to take her up to X-ray."

"Thank you," I said.

Sara was drifting in and out. When her eyes opened, she would look up at me and grin. I schooled my face. I was too angry, and there was no point in arguing with someone that far gone into their morphine. She would likely not remember this anyway.

I scrolled through the chart to avoid looking at her and landed on the physician's intake note.

∼

```
Patient presents to the emergency room with
blunt force trauma to the nose, left arm, and
ribs. Paramedic administered morphine on-site
due to patient complaining of severe forearm
pain. X-rays of right forearm and ribs have
been ordered. Social work consult recommended
```

<pre>
after patient is admitted. Awaiting patient
transfer to x-ray.
</pre>

I ROLLED the computer cart away from me and sat in the only chair in the small exam room. Sara woke up when the x-ray technician walked in, ready to transport her. I followed them to x-ray and waited outside while they completed her scans. This was where Hector and Chief Stuart found me.

"Is it true?" asked the chief. "We just heard—"

I nodded.

"I'm sorry, Dr. Ramirez. I know she is a close friend," said the chief.

I nodded again. Other than the *thank you* I'd offered the ER doctor, I hadn't said a word to anyone since I saw her.

When I thought of the asshole's name, Brian, a sensation like a thousand tiny snakes slithering through my veins coursed through me. He was a revolting man who did a revolting thing. My fists balled. I wanted to punch something. I'd never punched anything in my life. I am too controlled, and I suddenly understood the allure of Valentina's profession. I never so much as punched a pillow in anger. Yet, here I was, the eternal pacifist, ready to punch something, if not someone.

"Do you know who it was?" Hector asked.

I nodded.

"That's good. I'll call the police," said the chief.

"No," I protested, finding my voice.

"Excuse me?" said the chief.

"You can't take that away from her. Let her be in control of *something*. When the medication wears off, I'll let her tell me what happened. It's up to her if she wants to press charges. Believe me, chief," I added at his expression of horror, "it *kills* me not to call the cops right this second."

"She's right," Hector said. "We can't be the ones to take more power away from her."

I stared at him, surprised he would agree with me. Most men in my life would go in search of the guilty party and serve their own justice.

His cool head gave me comfort—a comfort that was a constant recurrence whenever Hector was around.

Think positively, I told myself. She's alive. She likely had some broken bones, but she would live. I hoped this was her rock bottom—the catalyst she needed to leave him once and for all.

"Can you do me a favor?" I asked the two men, and they both nodded.

"Don't be here when she comes out." Before they could protest, I provided the reason. "She will be embarrassed enough as it is. Oh, and Dr. Medina? Do you mind finding me a hospital computer? I want to see the X-rays when they are up."

Both men nodded and left me standing there. Not long after Hector brought me a laptop, Sara was rolled out in her wheelchair. An admitting nurse came to the exam room to process paperwork, and we were taken to a patient room while we awaited Sara's doctor.

It was bizarre entering the hospital via the path patients typically took. There was endless waiting. Empty moments of time in which we, the loved ones, could only worry and imagine the worst.

My work life in this hospital was always rushed. I pushed on from patient to patient and from chart to chart. There was never enough time, and the hours flew by.

Now, a single hour turned into a day. I drummed my fingers on the laptop and refreshed the page every five minutes or so. Finally, the X-rays were available. I looked at the images closely.

She had a *Monteggia* fracture. The ulnar bone was fractured, and the head of the radial bone was dislocated by the elbow joint. Her ribs were only bruised.

A different doctor walked into the room, and he introduced himself as Dr. Morgan. I'd seen him around the hospital and knew he was the chief of ortho, but I rarely interacted with the orthopedic surgeons—all except one. I shared my findings with him to get confirmation.

"You are oncology, right?"

"Yes," I said.

"And how long has it been since your radiology or ortho rotations?"

"A while."

He studied me. "You are spot-on about her fractures. If you ever want to change fields to ortho, we'd be happy to have you."

"Thanks, but I've found my calling." I smiled weakly at him. Any other day, I would have jumped with joy at being on his radar. Already, I was thinking of ways to include the ortho department on future grant proposals, but Sara groaned, and my attention drifted back to her.

"What about her nose?" I asked.

"We'll wait a few days until the swelling goes down, and I'll do another exam. It looks like a minor fracture with no major misalignment, but I'll reassess in three days."

"Thank you, Doctor," I said.

"I'll need consent for surgery to repair the forearm. I'll be back in an hour to chat about it with her when she is more awake."

"No need," I said. "I'm her emergency contact and have power of attorney. I can consent on her behalf."

"Great. I'll have someone bring the consent forms in a bit, and I can do the surgery tonight."

He smiled at me suggestively. I didn't care if he thought Sara and I were a couple. Right now, the only thing on my mind was getting her better and past this, so I didn't correct him.

The fact was that even though Dad and I had adopted Sara into our family as an adult, I still wanted to make it official. One year for my birthday, she gave me legal documents, including power of attorney. It would have seemed morbid to an outsider, but to us, it was a binding contract that made us family—officially.

Finding myself in this situation, I couldn't think of a better birthday gift that I had ever gotten.

SARA'S SURGERY WAS A SUCCESS, and I got to take her home the next day. They'd made two incisions, so she'd end up with two badass scars—the scars of a survivor.

I called Dad and told him what happened.

"*Pedaso de mierda*," said Dad—the man who never cursed. I didn't have the heart to comment about it. He was right. Brian was a piece of shit.

But Dad agreed to get my room ready for her. I wanted her safe, and I knew Brian would never show his face at Dad's.

I was helping her out of the car when I heard a *thump* from the driveway next door. I turned, and Ramiro was jogging to us, several grocery bags abandoned on the pavement behind him.

"Is she okay? Let me help you."

"Here, take this." I handed him the duffle bag I had put together with clothes from her apartment. Brian was one lucky slime ball to not have been there when I showed up to get her things. They didn't live together, but Sara's apartment was nicer, so he spent a lot of time there.

Ramiro took the bag and was doing his best trying to help but was unable to grab Sara's arm in a splint. He helped me get her upstairs, and I asked him to leave so I could help her change into pajamas. I gave her two more pain pills and went back downstairs.

"You're back," I said to Ramiro who was pacing in the living room.

"Who was it?" he asked, nostrils flaring. A vein in his forehead made its way to the surface of his skin.

"Why'd you stay away so long?"

"Stop dodging!" he growled.

Ramiro had never grown as close to Sara as I had, but they were still friends, and he treasured her as part of my family. There was no way I was going to tell Ramiro, temperamental fool that he was, anything about the person who had hurt Sara. Not until he calmed down.

"I'm not dodging. I'll tell you, but not until you calm down."

"I'm calm," he said, but he was gritting his teeth, and his jaw was set.

I snorted.

"I am," he repeated.

"First, tell me why you stayed away so long. We missed you—"

"You know why," he said, interrupting me. "Now, *please*, tell me what happened."

"It's not my place, Ramiro. I'll give you the gist, but you'll have to talk with her yourself if you want to know more. Okay?"

"That's fair."

"She's been dating this guy—"

"How come she didn't tell us . . .?" He narrowed his eyes at me as he trailed off on his question. "Wait, *you* knew she was seeing someone?"

I nodded. "Yes. It's been just over six months."

"How come she never told your dad or me?"

"I think she was a bit embarrassed by him. As you can see, he's not a great guy."

He sat down on Dad's enormous recliner. He bowed down and rubbed both hands over his short, military-style buzz-cut.

"He did this to her," he said, but it wasn't a question.

"Yeah."

"His name."

"I can't do that."

"His name, Carolina."

"I can't. Ramiro, don't do anything stupid."

"You want us to all continue to be family . . . even after everything? Families talk, don't they? I want a name."

I sighed. He'd get it out of me, or he'd get it out of Sara, and I couldn't have him go upstairs and try to intimidate her right now.

"Fine. His name is Brian."

"Brian what?"

I shrugged. "I never knew his last name."

"Where does he work?"

"Ramiro—don't. Don't go there."

"Where?" he hissed.

I sighed. "I don't know that he has a real steady job. He sounds like a bit of a deadbeat, but I remember her saying something about him doing maintenance work at an apartment building near the hospital. That's all I know."

He sprang up from the chair and left before I could protest again.

THE NEXT DAY, I went to Dad's to check in on Sara. She was still in my old room, and I knocked softly on the door in case she was sleeping.

"Come in," she said.

She smiled up at me as I walked in. She had removed the bandage from her nose, so the wreckage of her body was exemplified by her face.

My jaw clenched at the sight of the deep purple and green nebulas stretching over her nose from cheek to cheek.

"Hi. How are you doing?"

"I'm good," she said, though her words were garbled by something in her mouth. She swallowed the bite. "The splint is super itchy. It's *so* tempting to shove a pencil in there and scratch."

"You know that's a bad idea."

Sara sighed. "I know."

"What are you eating?"

She pulled a box from the other side of the bed and offered it to me like a platter. "You want one?"

I looked down at the box filled with artisan chocolates painted so beautifully it seemed a sin to eat them. "Those are gorgeous," I said.

"I know," said Sara. "I stopped myself from eating them as long as I could. But you know—*chocolate*."

"That was nice of Ramiro," I said.

Sara cocked her head to the side. "Ramiro didn't bring these."

"Oh. Dad, then?" I didn't think Dad would bring Sara something so decadent and fancy. If anything, he would bring her favorite Mexican candy: *Mazapánes.*

She shook her head. "No. Dr. Medina stopped by to check on me. You just missed him." She pointed with her chin to my dresser, where a vase contained a spectacular arrangement of yellow tulips, alien-like purple plants, and tiny little baby pineapples that could fit on the palm of my hand. Next to it sat an enormous card, flipped open to reveal signatures and well-wishes from nearly everyone on the oncology floor.

"Dr. Medina?" It made more sense to me that one of Sara's nurse friends would have dropped off a collective card and flowers. Though the signature chocolates and the extravagance of the selected flowers —*that* had 'Hector' written all over it.

"Yep," she said as she shoved another chocolate in her mouth.

"What did he say?"

"Oh, he asked how I was doing. If I was in any pain. And since your dad was at work, he offered to help if I needed to get up or go anywhere."

"Wow," was all I could say.

Sara eyed me with a glint in her eye. "Yeah," she said. "*Wow.*"

There was something so incredibly sweet about him checking in on my friend and trying to cheer her up. He remembered when she had stolen my chocolate. He was observant even about my friends and always thoughtful about what he did.

I snapped out of it. "Well, that was nice of him," I clipped, and changed the subject. "Have you moved from the bed at all, missy?"

"I got up to open the door when he showed up." She shot me a toothy grin half-smeared with chocolate.

I laughed. "That doesn't count," I said.

Sara was wallowing, but two days of it was more than enough. I told her to go for a walk. She needed to get moving and get under the sun a bit. In the meantime, I could get some work done around the house for Dad.

I was mowing Dad's front yard when the familiar black pickup truck pulled into the driveway next door.

I took my earbuds out and stopped the music on my phone so I could say hi to Ramiro. I hadn't seen him since he'd left Dad's after seeing Sara a few days ago. My lips tightened when I heard him slam the door to his truck. He sped to his front door, but not fast enough for me to miss the slight glint of red rolling down one side of his face.

"Ramiro?" I said as I started walking toward him.

"Not now, Caro."

"What did you do?"

"Not now, Caro!" He slammed the front door of his house—like that would stop me.

He groaned when the door creaked open. He was lying on the couch when I walked in. I got close enough to him to see the line of blood starting at his forehead and dripping down to his jaw. It had started to congeal, and some of it was smudged, probably from his attempts to clean it up on the drive back home.

I ran to Dad's to pick up a clean towel and my first aid kit, then went back to Ramiro's house. He didn't protest the second time I entered. I wet the towel and set the supplies on the floor next to the couch where he was still lying, looking at the ceiling.

He didn't wince when I cleaned up the blood. His eyebrow was busted, but he wouldn't need stitches.

"You found him." I wasn't asking.

"I don't know what you are talking about."

It was no coincidence that on learning Sara's boyfriend's name, he'd disappeared for a day and came back home with blood on his face.

"But you should see the other guy," he said, one side of his mouth quirking upward.

"Thank you," I said. I knew he had executed the task I had so wanted to do myself. He wanted to give me plausible deniability in case the little shit pressed charges against him, so I didn't ask him any more questions. I knew he would always protect me—us: Sara and me.

Neither of us told Sara what Ramiro did, but I knew we both had the satisfaction of knowing that justice had been served, whatever happened next.

CHAPTER 12

FREE CLINIC

"What are you doing here?"

The last person I expected to see at the free clinic was Hector.

"I thought I'd volunteer a shift," he said. "Check it out."

"Right."

"I didn't realize the med students run it in conjunction with the hospital."

Hector sat at one of the desks in the shared office. The room was packed with students getting ready for the huddle at the start of the shift. We had an hour before we opened the clinic, and already the waiting room was packed.

I was the lead resident for today, so I called the huddle.

"We have six volunteers tonight, so let's work fast. For those of you who are here for the first time, you will call patients from the waiting room and take them to the conference room—no more than three in the conference room at a time. Refer any emergent patients to the emergency room and triage the rest into the clinic. Our maximum capacity tonight is thirty. Stop triaging once that quota is met and refer them to the emergency room, if necessary."

"So, what do I do?" Hector asked once the medical students had dispersed.

"Oh, Dr. Medina. Sorry. I forgot you were here."

"Thanks," he said dryly, looking hurt, but the corner of his mouth quirked up a bit.

"Sorry. That's not what I meant. I didn't really have time to get you up to speed. There's really not much to do." I clasped my hands together. "We have an assistant updating the board with patients and their room numbers. You and I are basically here to be a prescription pad if the med students need it, and if they have any questions."

"That's it?"

"Mostly. The students will start trickling in here soon. They will each give us a run-down of patient symptoms and their proposed treatment plan. We will have to approve or adjust the treatment and write any prescriptions necessary."

"I don't see the patient?"

"You don't have to unless you want to or would like to ask the patient more questions."

"Got it."

Hector fell into a quick rhythm. It didn't escape my notice that it was the female students who gravitated most toward his counsel instead of mine. They flirted, but he didn't flirt back. He remained professional and respectful the entire time.

Halfway through the shift, Hector and I were talking when one of the newer volunteers approached us.

"Excuse me," she said shyly. I turned to her.

"Yes?"

"I have a twenty-nine-year-old female patient. No complaints, but she needs a prescription for birth control."

"What? She came to the free clinic for birth control? Who triaged her into the clinic?"

The med student flushed red. "I did," she said.

"Okay, you are new, right? Routine preventive and ongoing care needs to be referred to a primary care—"

"I know," she said, interrupting me. "But please, let me explain."

"Go on," I said.

"She doesn't have a primary care physician, and I know the protocol is to refer her to one, but I think this is a special circumstance. The patient is a mother of five and struggling. She is Catholic, and she doesn't want her husband to find out she's taking birth control. She's been saving for a long time to pay out of pocket for an appointment so that it wouldn't show up as a claim on the insurance she shares with her husband."

I nodded at her, encouraging her to go on.

"She scheduled and paid for an appointment with Dr. Tyler Smith."

"No," I gasped. I counted to ten.

She nodded.

"What is it?" Dr. Medina asked, looking between the volunteer and me as we both seethed in silence.

The med student continued. "He said he wasn't comfortable prescribing birth control and sent her on her way. She is devastated and says her family is barely scraping by with the kids they already have. She used up all her savings for that appointment."

Hector stepped in and asked the student to go to her next patient; we would take care of this one.

"What's wrong?" he asked me when she was gone.

"What do you mean?"

"You have murder in your eyes. The only other time I've seen that look was when Sara was hurt."

"Dr. Tyler Smith's philosophy on birth-control is to keep your legs crossed. He probably told her that too. I'm sure she feels guilty enough as it is without her doctor putting her down."

"Maybe I should speak with her. I don't want you to say something you will regret."

"I've been a doctor a while now, Hector," I said with irritation. "I'm perfectly capable of composing myself."

"Then, you won't mind if I join you. Just to observe."

I couldn't very well argue with my boss again, especially so soon after biting his head off about taking liberties with my trial data, so I let him shadow me during my consult with the patient.

After our introductions, I pulled out my prescription pad. I handed her the prescription and told her to take it to a pharmacy for it to be dispensed. She almost cried with gratitude, as though I was handing her a lifeline.

"Don't see Dr. Smith anymore, okay?"

"I definitely won't," she said, clutching the piece of paper to her chest.

I grabbed the prescription pad again and started writing on it.

"This is my assistant's phone number. Her name is Amanda. When you need a refill, call her. She will arrange a prescription to be sent to any pharmacy you want. No charge."

"Really?" Her eyes glistened with tears as she clutched the prescription.

"Really. I do need you to keep up with your pap smears, though. You think you can get those on schedule with your husband's insurance?"

"Yes. He would have no problem with that. It's cancer prevention, right?"

"That's right. You'll want to get a copy of your results, send them to Amanda, and I will get you prescriptions for as long as you want them. Okay?"

She left, showering Hector and me with words of gratitude, even though he'd not said a word; he was likely waiting for me to say something disparaging about one of our doctors. I didn't give him the satisfaction. Besides, I couldn't do that. There was no law against what that physician had done.

When the last patient left, most of the med students had gone. The new student stayed behind, helping me tidy up the office space. I looked at the badge hanging off her short white coat.

"Dr. Stuart," I said. "Good job today. Keep it up." She must be the chief's granddaughter. He'd mentioned she would be graduating from medical school soon.

She beamed at me and waved goodbye. "Good night."

"Good night."

"I like this place," Hector said.

"Really?" I said, and my brow arched.

"Why does that surprise you?"

"Doesn't seem like you would enjoy being around . . ." I trailed off, unsure of how to remain politically correct.

"Around *what*? Humble people? Poor people? Hardworking people?"

"Yeah . . ."

"Why do you think I'm some pretentious ass on my high horse? I get that I have a bit of an ego, but—"

"A *bit*?" I laughed, and my eyes widened to the size of dinner plates when I realized the sound had escaped against my will.

He shook his head.

"Sure, Dr. Ramirez. I was born with a silver spoon in my mouth and rubbing shoulders with peasants offends me." A tone of irritation laced his voice.

"I'm sorry. I don't know what I'm talking about. Just tired, I guess."

"Apology accepted. Want to make it up to me?" His grin reappeared.

My eyebrows raised all the way to my hairline.

"Get your mind out of the gutter, Carolina. I only meant I need help shopping."

"Shopping?"

"Yeah, shopping. I hate shopping, and my mother is coming to visit next weekend. I need—"

"Furniture?"

"Exactly."

"A table, chairs, linens, towels, pillows? Hell, a second set of dishes?"

He groaned. "I knew there was stuff I hadn't thought of. I need her to be comfortable, and I have no clue about any of that. I've never had to pick stuff out for a house before."

"All right. I'll help you if only because I've never seen a pathetic side to you, and I'm rather amused."

HECTOR WAS amazed when I told him we could order most of the things he needed online and have them delivered. I would still need to go over to his house again to take another look at the spaces and measure to make sure the furniture I selected would fit. He gave me a budget and told me to pick out everything.

"Thanks for agreeing to help," he said as soon as I stepped foot in his home.

"No problem. Consider my assistance your house-warming gift."

"I appreciate that."

I set my laptop on the kitchen island and scrolled through a few online furniture stores. Hector wasn't being much help and gave no indication as to his own personal taste.

"Look," he said. "I really don't care about any of this, but my Mom will. Just pick out what you like. I'm sure she'll love it."

"All right. Tell me a little bit about your Mom's home in Mexico. Anything you remember that might give me an idea as to what she likes?"

"I really don't know, Carolina. I don't pay attention to that kind of stuff."

I pinched the bridge of my nose. This was going to be more difficult than I'd imagined.

"What about your old house before you moved here? What was that like?"

"My wife decorated it. If it made her happy, I was fine with it. But it wasn't really my style—"

"Okay, see, you do have a style!" I said. I was not going to ask him why his wife wasn't decorating *this* house, not even with the opening he offered. *Don't get personal, Carolina. It's none of your business.*

"No. I don't have style, but I can rule out hers. It was very pristine, all white, clear crystal, that kind of thing. I was afraid to touch anything."

"Okay, so practical, durable, and easy to clean. That's a start."

I couldn't resist it any longer, and before I could stop myself, I blurted out, "Why isn't your wife helping you with this?" I clasped my hand to my mouth. "I'm so sorry, I didn't—"

"It's okay." Hector's smile was lopsided now. "I'll tell you about her, but not today. Today is a happy day. Okay?"

"Forget I asked. It's none of my business."

We turned our attention to our task and moved past a subject I could already tell was a sore one. I picked out a console cabinet for the living room, some vases to go on top, and a few framed landscape prints. When I showed them to him, he shrugged. "Do *you* like it?" he asked.

"I do," I said and smiled wide. I'd kill for that kind of furniture.

"Then it's perfect."

We repeated the process for every room in his house, from his guest room and bathrooms to dining room and dinnerware. He had no opinion on anything, though he did, at one point, say he thought his mother would approve of my taste, and that fueled the rest of the shopping experience.

When we were done, I sat back, pleased with myself. His house was going to look amazing. I hoped his mother agreed when she arrived.

Without a task occupying our collective mental spaces, being alone in his home became awkward. Too intimate in the still, echoey space.

"So, that's everything. You'll have to be here for deliveries. I sent appointments to your calendar."

When I was ready to leave, Hector took my hand in his but kept it there for one second too long. "Thank you, Carolina," he said. "You are really saving me here."

CHAPTER 13

HUMBLE BEGINNINGS

$\mathcal{H}$ector was surprised at how much we got done online without having to go to any stores. But I still promised to help him on Saturday morning, after the deliveries all came in, to arrange everything and stage any finishing touches. He didn't have to pick his mom up until six in the evening, so I showed up at ten in the morning to get started.

He was right: he had no idea what to do with any of it. He had given the delivery men completely wrong instructions, making me question if he had been sleepy or drunk while everything was set up.

"Have you no concept of *feng shui*?" I asked him.

"That's the manual on how to arrange furniture, right?"

My nose crinkled at his definition. "Sort of."

"Well, what's wrong?"

"Her bed is facing the door. We can't have that. We need the headboard side of the bed up against the wall with windows, so the feet point toward the solid wall."

Hector burst out laughing.

"Are you making fun of me, Dr. Medina?"

"I'm sorry, I don't understand why it matters, but sure. Let's move the bed. And please, outside of work, let's use our given names."

I nodded. "You didn't wash the new sheets?"

"I was supposed to?"

"Oh. My. God," I said, taking the sheets and asking for his washer and dryer, which, thankfully, he did possess.

Everything was nearly ready by two in the afternoon. We were both a mess, sweaty, disheveled, and out of breath from moving all the furniture.

"You owe me big time," I said.

"I definitely do."

Hector grabbed us two glasses of water, and we sat in the living room around the coffee table. I took the room in, pleased with what I had accomplished.

The results were cozy and understated but with a modern edge. The mahogany console now displaying art and fresh flowers was to die for. The coffee table was dressed with a candle, a tray with a stack of art books, and a sculptural design I thought Hector would like. Knowing little of his tastes, I'd done my best.

"So, what do you think?" I asked.

Hector shrugged. "Do *you* like it?"

"Not this again. It doesn't matter if I like it. I want to know if you do." I almost rolled my eyes at him.

He nodded. "If you like it, then I like it."

Stubborn man.

"By the way," Hector said, changing the subject. "I never got the chance to tell you—I thought what you did for your patient was really nice."

"What are you talking about?"

"I think you called it the Mary?"

I almost spat out the water from my mouth. This entire time, I thought he hadn't seen it. "You saw?"

Hector nodded. "Why do you call it that?"

"Um—Mary was kind of a legend. She was a patient during my first year of residency and Sara's favorite patient. She was an older woman—in her fifties—and she had been a beautician. Whenever she was admitted, and on the days she had the energy, she would go around the oncology floor and give little mini-makeovers to the other patients. It might have been as simple as putting lotion on a patient's hands and giving her a hand massage, all the way to full-blown makeovers.

"Eventually, she started adding music to her rounds. Mostly hip-hop and soul music, but usually the more upbeat variety. The staff really grew to love her."

"I bet," Hector said.

"Yeah. She could completely turn around the outlook of a patient having a rough day."

"She make it?" Hector asked.

My face turned. "No," I admitted. "Breast cancer."

"I'm sorry," Hector said.

"Me too. She was an amazing woman. It's a tribute to her that we keep the tradition going. If we have a patient who is really down, we have a girl's day. It's silly but—"

"Not silly at all. You know as well as I do that patient outlook is a big factor in resilience and is as important as chemotherapy or radiation."

"Yeah, I know. Thank you."

"I've also been meaning to ask you—"

"What?"

"Why do you volunteer at the clinic?" he asked.

"Hector, if I offended you, I'm sorry. I didn't mean to place doubts on your motives for volunteering."

"Relax. That's not why I was asking. It's just . . . you seem overwhelmed by everything you take on."

I pinched the bridge of my nose with joking exasperation. "Okay. Number one, never, and I mean *never*, tell a woman to relax. You will have the opposite outcome—"

"Noted."

"And number two, don't underestimate me. Besides, I only volunteer for a few shifts a month. I can't imagine not doing it."

"But why did you get into it in the first place?"

My gaze drifted away into space as my thoughts turned to many years back. I was starting to realize that as much as I hated talking about my mother, for some reason, Hector always got it out of me.

"My mom. She didn't have insurance before she was diagnosed, so she ignored the symptoms for too long."

"And if she'd had access to a free clinic, things might have been different," Hector finished for me.

I nodded, unsure of what else to say, but the doorbell literally saved me. "You expecting someone?" I asked.

"No. It's probably another shipment of something you ordered for the house."

"Nope. I had you pay out the wazoo for expedited shipping so everything could be here before your mom arrives."

"Thanks for that, by the way," he said wryly.

"Anytime." I grinned after him.

He shook his head as he opened the front door. "*Mami!*" he exclaimed.

I sprang up to my feet and walked over to them. Hector embraced a small woman, barely five-one in height. There was no way that tiny woman had birthed him. If she did, she could run the world one day.

She wore a pink jacket, and her hair was perfectly pinned back into a low bun. I smiled, realizing she wasn't coloring the gray out of her hair. This was a woman I could look up to.

Mother and son froze for the entirety of a minute. Eventually, they broke contact, and he let her inside.

"Hello, Mrs. Medina," I said. She looked at my outstretched hand and pushed it to the side. She caught me by surprise into a hug, and I couldn't help but hug her back. It was hard not to become emotional. I hadn't embraced a mother of any kind in a long time.

"Please," she said in broken English, "call me Marisela."

Once I could see her face, I realized she wore a little bit of makeup, and short, pearl, teardrop earrings. She gave off an air of elegance, but it was understated and subtle. I could only describe her in one word: *Grace.*

"We can switch to Spanish if you'd like," I said in Spanish. After that, all our conversations were in Spanish. It intimidated me a bit. Obviously, she and Hector would speak the proper Spain-derived Spanish of the Mexican elite, while mine would be Mexican *barrio* Spanish—'hood

Spanish. I was relieved when neither of them commented on my linguistic shortcomings in our native tongue.

"Who is this?" she asked Hector but didn't move her mother's gaze away from me.

"This is Carolina Ramirez. She is a doctor at the hospital I work at now."

"Oh?" his mom asked as she studied me from shoes to face.

"Yes, Mrs.—I mean, Marisela. Your son is my boss. I helped him get the house ready for your arrival."

She looked back and forth between us, making me shift my weight from one foot to the other.

"*Mamá*," Hector whined. "*I* was going to pick you up from the airport."

"I'm perfectly capable of taking a car," she said.

"*And* you lied to me about what time your flight was coming in."

"Well, how else was I going to manage to get a car? You are too busy. I wasn't going to bother you." She playfully palmed his cheeks twice. "I'm starving," she said. "Let's go out to lunch."

"I'll be heading home," I said. "Marisela, it was so nice to meet you. I hope you enjoy your time in Kansas City."

She turned to me and pinned me with a look of warning. "No. You must join us."

"I can't . . ." I said as I looked down and pulled on the hem of the ratty old workout t-shirt I had worn in preparation for sweating and heavy lifting.

"Oh, you both can go as you are. We aren't going anywhere fancy."

"That's right," Hector said. "Mom loves going to American chain cafés when she's in the states."

"I do," she said. "Please join us."

There was no way out of this lunch. I wasn't supposed to meet his mother. My part of the deal was to help him get ready for her arrival, not to *meet* her. Still, I couldn't stop grinning.

We drove separately so I could make my escape after lunch and give them time to catch up. When we got to the café, Hector ordered our food at the counter. Marisela and I settled in at a corner table with a view of the patio.

"So," she said, "how long have you been working with my son?"

"A few months."

"Is he a good boss?"

"He's okay," I said, surprising myself.

She laughed. "I value honesty."

I smiled at her. Hector brought us our coffee after placing our order. "You two talking about me?" he asked.

"We wouldn't dare," his mom said.

"So," I said. "Where in Mexico do you live?"

"Oaxaca," she said.

I expected Hector to have grown up in Mexico City for some reason. "And do you like it there? I've never been," I said.

"Oh, it's beautiful. Beautiful people and beautiful food. Whenever you want, you have a home there," she said.

"Thank you."

"Do you have any suggestions on things to do while I'm here?" she asked.

"Let's see . . . if you are interested in art, I suggest the Nelson-Atkins Museum. You wouldn't think it of Kansas City, but we have a rather spectacular collection, including a Caravaggio." I didn't know where I pulled that suggestion from. I'd only been to the museum once and only knew about the Caravaggio in the collection because Mandy wouldn't shut up about it. I guess I was trying to impress her.

"I was thinking something more . . . *casual?*" she suggested.

That took me aback. I had always assumed Hector came from money. I expected his mother to be cultured and want to see the more elegant aspects of the city. I certainly didn't expect her to ask for *casual* ideas.

"Um—well, not far from that museum is a beautiful rose garden," I said, hoping she would be satisfied with that answer.

"I love roses," she said with a sparkle to her eye. "Maybe Hector can take me there tomorrow." She looked at her son expectantly.

"Of course, Mom. Whatever you like."

We had a pleasant and superficial conversation the rest of our lunch until Hector had to take a call from one of his residents about a patient.

He stepped outside for privacy, leaving me alone with his mother. I didn't feel as uncomfortable as I thought I would.

"Okay, now that we have a minute alone, I'd like to talk with you about Hector," Marisela said, peering out the window to confirm that Hector wasn't yet coming back from his call.

"I'm not sure—"

"I like the way he looks at you," she said.

"What?"

"He hasn't smiled like this in years," she said. "I'd like to thank you for that."

"Oh. Please don't get the wrong impression—"

"Don't worry." She cut me off. "I know you aren't together. But when you haven't seen your son happy for many long years, believe me, you will grasp at anything that brightens his life."

Hadn't been happy for years? What was she talking about?

"You don't know anything about the state of his marriage, do you?" Her eyes narrowed.

I only shook my head. She turned once again to peek out the window, then returned her attention to me. "Hector is too stubborn to let go of the past. I'm sure he hasn't told you."

"Told me what?" I couldn't help asking.

"Oh, a great many things. For example, I don't think he has told you he has been separated from his wife for a couple of years now."

My hands got clammy, and I wiped them on my jeans, grasping at the cool fabric. I wasn't sure Hector would want me to know these profoundly personal details.

Why was Marisela telling me all this? The thought of Hector being available sent my head spinning, but separated or not, he was still married. To me, there wasn't much difference between being separated and being married. Nothing could come from Marisela's revelation.

"I can tell by your reaction that I was right. He hasn't mentioned anything."

"Marisela, I don't know if he'd want me to know—"

"*I* want you to know," she said. "Andrea is a good woman. She knows about you."

"What?" Blood pounded in my ears. How in the hell did his *wife* know about me? If I hadn't been sitting down, I would have lost my balance at Marisela's words. Suddenly, I was joining Marisela in her paranoid checks for Hector outside.

"Don't worry," she said. "She is glad Hector has found someone who makes him happy." Marisela studied me for a moment as I digested her words. "And," she added, "I think she also hopes that his finding someone else means he'll finally agree to the divorce."

I was dazed, and my head swam. Surely, this is what was meant by an out-of-body experience. Not only did his wife know about me, for some reason, but she was discussing me with his mother. This was all too weird.

"Few marriages can make it through the tragedy of losing a child. I'm sure you know what happened."

I nodded, still wordless. I didn't know the details, but I knew their son had died.

"Andrea became very depressed. The poor thing. It's understandable. She ended up drinking and having to go to a rehabilitation center. Don't worry. She's doing much better now. But even before his marriage, my son had led a tough life."

The revelations about Hector were coming in waves, and I was growing uncomfortable at knowing so many details about a life which he clearly wanted to keep private. I had never imagined he'd had a hard life prior to the tragedy of losing his son.

"We were very poor when he was growing up. I'm sure you can imagine, for a poor, brown kid from Mexico to make it as far as he has in life, it took a lot. He's always had to fight. I tell you this because I think it is important for you to understand his character. He doesn't know how to not fight, or how to stop once he's started."

I couldn't believe he had come from nothing. I had always assumed he was from an upper-class Mexican home. I'd convinced myself he'd grown up with a silver spoon in his mouth. Though his mother didn't give many details, I understood that being poor in Mexico was much more dire than being poor in the United States. My heart constricted at the thought of a little boy balancing grade school and work—selling things or stealing things. Did he go hungry? Had they even had basic utilities when he was little? I couldn't have been more wrong about him.

He was what he was because he made himself from the ground up. No one handed anything to him. He had every right to be as proud as he was.

"Why are you telling me all this? It really seems very private to Hector."

She cocked her head to the side. "I tell you because he never would."

I nodded again, this time egging her on. She nervously glanced out the window to ensure Hector was still on his call. We had precious little time now.

"Still," Marisela said, "even though her mental health has improved, Andrea could only repair things with Hector at the expense of her sobriety. She is not willing to make that sacrifice, and so Hector has stayed away. At first, he held onto the hope that time would heal their relationship, but Andrea is moving on. Hector needs to also. You understand?"

"I'm not sure," I admitted.

"She's asked him for a divorce many times over the last two years, but he always refuses."

"He still loves her," I said.

"No." Her forehead scrunched up a bit. "He doesn't love her. He will always care about her, but the romantic love they shared is gone. For both of them."

"Then, why won't he give her the divorce she wants?"

"You've met my son, right?" She laughed. "He's got some ego in him. He believes himself to be perfect, and a perfect man wouldn't get a divorce. He won't admit defeat."

"So it's pride?"

She shrugged. "I don't know. I think it's pride but also something more. He took his vows very seriously, Carolina. Even now that he has met you, he is battling himself to let go of his past. The vows he has made to his first wife are still important to him, even if he isn't in love with her anymore. She is also the mother of his only child. He's having a hard time releasing his responsibility for her."

Hector joined us back at the table, and I couldn't ask her any of my million questions.

I had been so wrong about him and what I thought he cared about. I had misjudged him, and I had no right to. Marisela was obvious with her intent. I knew a Mexican mother matchmaker when I saw one. She took one look at me, like Ramiro's mom used to look at me, and decided I was meant for her son.

If Hector was indeed engaged in an internal battle to let go of the past, I couldn't be the one to nudge him in the opposite direction. While I wasn't too concerned about getting married, I knew if I ever did, it would be for life—no matter what. I understood Hector's demons now, and I couldn't stand between him and Andrea, despite what Marisela wanted. This was Hector's life, and he had to live with his own choices.

"I'm taking some time off," he said slowly as if he were trying to get my attention.

I focused on his words. "Okay," I said. "Going anywhere fun?" I sipped on my coffee.

"Yeah. I'll show mom around here for a few days, then I'm taking her to Colorado Springs before she heads back home. I've never been, and I think she would enjoy it."

"Colorado Springs is great," I managed to say.

As we said our goodbyes, Marisela drew me down to her level to embrace me. I returned the hug, and she whispered in my ear. "Give some thought to what I said."

CHAPTER 14

WARPATH

*H*ector left town shortly after his mother arrived. They wanted to take a short trip, which left me with plenty of time to think about what his Mom had said. There was no doubt Marisela hoped for Hector and me to be something . . . more.

But I couldn't bring myself to cross that line. Separated or not, I couldn't push Hector to betray that golden band around his finger—especially if it still meant something to him.

I can't say I wasn't tempted. A door had been opened for us—Marisela made sure of it—but we couldn't very well step through and forget about the real world.

A married man was still a married man, and I couldn't be budged on that point. I decided then that I wouldn't follow Marisela's counsel. Maybe I'd see her again someday and explain why I continued to stay away.

My thoughts were more traitorous than my intent, however. I daydreamed about two signatures on divorce papers, a parting of ways, and a different sort of relationship between Hector and me. We would devise new research together, discuss patient cases before bed, offer treatment adjustment suggestions. It was a type of future I was willing to envision, unlike any I had ever considered with anyone else from my past.

When Hector finally returned, he went on a rampage. I briefly worried that his mother had told him what we had talked about, but I quickly dismissed the idea. He wasn't only being an ass to me; he was treating everyone at the hospital the same.

No one at work had seen his wrath before. He had been nothing but a cool-headed boss, and he was well-liked in general. He never belittled anyone he was teaching, and he always looked at ways to improve the skills of all the residents under him.

Which is why everyone was taken aback when, after returning from vacation, he was a changed man.

"Are you an idiot?" Hector asked Dr. Dennis.

"Excuse me?" Dr. Dennis asked, his cheeks becoming rosy.

My jaw dropped. *What the hell?*

Hector shoved the tablet into the young doctor's hands.

"Look at it very carefully."

With shaky hands, Dr. Dennis did as instructed.

"Now, read the chart carefully," Hector hissed. "What did you do wrong?"

Dr. Dennis shrugged. "I'm not sure what I should be looking for—"

"He doesn't know what he should be looking for," Hector said, this time mocking Dr. Dennis.

I glanced at the patient, who was luckily heavily medicated, and she didn't stir at the loud voices in her room.

Dr. Keach had been standing next to me, and I clearly heard him snicker, though he tried to cover it up by clearing his throat. I felt horrible for Dr. Dennis who looked like he had shrunk several inches in height. I'm sure he heard Dr. Keach's laugh as well.

"Either you're an idiot, or you're trying to kill her," Hector said.

"No—I, uh," Dr. Dennis started to say, but Hector shoved him to the side as he snatched the syringe from Dr. Dennis's hands before he could administer it into the IV line.

"The dose you ordered is twice as much as the patient needs."

Dr. Dennis reddened. "I was only following the dosing from the night physician."

"And if the night physician ate shit, would you eat shit too?"

"Dr. Medina," I snapped. "We are in a patient's room. Why don't we take this to a conference room or the lounge, perhaps?"

He turned to me with a storm brewing in his glare. The hairs at the back of my neck raised. Something was wrong. Something had happened when he went on that trip. Hector closed his eyes, nostrils flaring, and I knew he was counting to ten. He stormed out of the room.

Taking the resident's tablet, I scanned the patient's chart quickly and suggested the dosage Hector would have prescribed. I knew the way his mind worked that well. While the patient could do with half the ordered dose, what the night physician—and then Dr. Dennis—had ordered wasn't outside protocol restrictions. Neither of them had done anything wrong. "Don't worry, Dr. Dennis. I'm sure this isn't about you," I reassured him, and he nodded.

I ran out of the room, trying to catch up to Hector so I could find out what was going on before he abused any more residents and scared them away from the hospital for good. He entered the physician's lounge, and I followed.

It was lunchtime, and the room was packed. I took a deep breath before approaching him by the refrigerator.

"Who the hell took my lunch?" Hector roared and slammed the refrigerator shut. All eyes in the lounge turned to him. Shit. This wasn't good.

"Dr. Medina," I said. "Can we please talk in your office?"

"It's not the time, Carolina," he said. "I'm in no mood to talk."

He'd said my first name at work, in front of my peers. My eyes closed for a moment as if I were trying to rewind the last few seconds. I felt the stares as all eyes turned to me.

"Dr. Medina, it's urgent." I pointed out of the room in a gesture for him to lead us outside.

He groaned, but then, as if suddenly becoming aware of all the eyes, he charged out of the room. On my way out, I noticed Dr. Keach. He had followed us and was lingering by the door. As I passed him, he said, "Lover's quarrel?" loud enough for anyone near us to hear.

Fuck off, I thought. "He is having a personal problem," I tried to explain.

"Oh, I'm sure it is *personal,*" he said suggestively.

"Dr. Keach, I don't have the time or the crayons to explain to you what *personal* means." I also spoke loudly enough for people to hear. I left him standing there, stunned, his mouth open.

Shit, I thought as I dashed to Hector's office. Dr. Keach wouldn't forget that public insult so easily—but that was a problem for another day.

I busted into Hector's office, and I was fuming.

He stood facing the window, arms crossed, as he looked onto a view of an autumn Kansas City turning yellow and orange and golden below us.

"What the hell, Hector?"

"I'm sorry," he hissed, but it didn't sound sincere. He didn't turn to face me, either.

"That little stunt you pulled," I said, "was so unprofessional."

"I know," he said, this time resigned. He turned and sat at his desk. He buried his head in his hands with shame. "I know. I'm sorry."

"What is happening?" I asked as I sat in front of him. He sat up and stared me in the eye.

"Carolina, I—I'm having a bad day."

"I was able to deduce that, thank you, Doctor. But you can't call me by my first name at work when you are angry. It looked like we were fighting, and you know the rumors will pick up—"

"Oh, fuck the rumors, Carolina."

Don't lose your temper. I schooled my face. "Dr. Medina, you are a well-established and well-respected physician. *I* am just starting out. I can't just say *fuck the rumors,* as you have so eloquently put it."

"I'm sorry. I know. I really meant it when I said it wasn't a good time to talk; I knew I'd be an ass. I have a temper."

"It's good to know you have flaws."

He smiled, but it was weak on his lips.

"Now, will you please tell me what's happening?"

Hector threw a sizable yellow envelope my way. "Go ahead. Open it. I don't mind."

I pulled the stack of papers out and scanned through the first page.

I took a deep breath. *Oh, no.* "Divorce papers?"

Hector nodded.

"I'm really sorry," I said.

"Yeah, me too. I had a great trip with my mom. I was looking forward to my first day home, ready to get back to work, but instead, my morning started with getting served divorce papers." Hector laughed bitterly.

"I am so sorry," I repeated, feeling stupid. But what else do you say to someone who is utterly devastated?

"Thank you . . . she's been asking me for a divorce for a while now. I've always said no, hoping we could get back to where we were, but it never happened. I guess she got tired of waiting for me to get on board with the separation—went ahead and pulled the trigger on our marriage."

"That sucks, Hector." Part of me meant it; another smaller, meaner part of me didn't.

"Yeah, it does."

"But it doesn't excuse the way you treated that resident."

"I know." He sighed.

"Nor the scene you made. Now, everyone thinks we are—"

"I'll fix it. I promise."

I wiped my clammy hands on my scrub pants. I shouldn't ask, it was none of my business, and yet I had to know. "Are you going to sign?"

His lips pressed together, but then he shook his head. "No. Not without one last-ditch effort to save things."

He was a good man, and he was doing the right thing. Why, then, did it feel like that one year Dad forgot my birthday?

"Well, I need you to do me a favor. Take the day off. Go home. Stop making an ass of yourself."

CHAPTER 15

HOT MAN READING

"You have a minute?" I asked as I peeked into Hector's office.

"Sure, come in."

I dropped the thick stack of papers organized in manila folders onto his desk, where they landed with a heavy thud.

Hector blinked at me. "What's this?" he asked.

"The admission questionnaires for the trial. We have ten potential participants, and three are borderline. I'd like to discuss them with you."

He let out a long breath and was likely considering how to get out of this, but he knew he couldn't. This was the part of clinical trials no one liked: Deciding who got in.

"Fine," he said. "Close the door."

We went through the seven I was certain we would allow into the trial, and he agreed on each of them. Then, the hard part began.

"She is so young and has a baby—" I defended my position on one of the potential participants.

"Even if she weren't young or didn't have a baby," Hector argued, "it doesn't change the staging—"

"But it's barely outside the trial criteria—"

"Say that word again?"

I blinked at him. "What word?"

"What you used right after 'barely.'"

I rolled my eyes. "Outside. You want me to say it's outside the trial criteria. I know that Hector, but—"

"Look, I appreciate you wanting to save everyone. I do too. But if we bend the trial criteria, we are skewing the results. And you know in order to change the protocol, we'd have to go through the internal review board again anyway—"

"Yeah. Yeah. I get your point."

It was so frustrating to have someone I knew would benefit from the new treatment protocol but couldn't get it because the trial wasn't yet widely available.

"Hey, thanks for this," I said after I had a moment to process my disappointment. "The trial needs your sternness."

"You can be stern," Hector reassured me.

I scoffed.

"You can," he insisted. "I wasn't always like this. When I first started out, I was just like you. I wanted to put everyone in my trial."

"You did?"

Hector nodded. "I did. But I couldn't, and neither can you."

The second borderline participant we deemed eligible, and I stacked her file with the other seven. And the last one, like the new mom, was deemed ineligible. I shrank deeper and deeper into my doctor's coat as we made those life-altering calls.

Finally, I straightened my spine. We had to do what we had to do. Moping about it wouldn't change a damn thing.

"Can I ask you something?" Hector asked.

"Sure."

"When I first started working here, you were worried that I was mad about you ripping off my trial. Why did you think that?"

I shrugged. I didn't even want to think about Keach right now. "I guess it felt like a big coincidence you came here for this trial."

"Okay, stand up," he said as he stepped around his desk.

"What?"

"Stand up, Ramirez."

This man was acting strangely. "Okay."

We stood about three feet apart looking at each other.

"Research is a dance," Hector said.

What the hell? "A dance?" I asked with trepidation.

He nodded and stepped toward me. He took my hand in his and dropped his free hand to my waist. My shoulder blades tightened. "Hector," I said, "I wasn't kidding before. I don't know how to dance."

"Just humor me."

"Fine."

The hand on my waist pulled me toward him, and he stepped back on the same beat. "One researcher takes a step forward, and the next one takes the lead," he said, then pushed me back with the hand he had in mine. "That doctor spins the research into a twirl, pushing it further . . ." As he said this, Hector lifted our joined hands over our heads and pushed my waist forcefully until I spun around.

But I hadn't been lying when I'd told him I couldn't dance. I almost lost my balance when I landed the spin, and he expertly caught me. I peered at him through my hair—now a mess from the dancing. His eyes darkened as he took my face in, and we stood there, connected for two seconds too many. I wondered if he noticed that I shivered in his arms.

"Everyone can dance," he said, finally letting go of my hand and waist. "With the right lead," he added, then threw me the cockiest grin I had ever seen.

THE NEXT DAY I called him at his office for a consult.

"What time are you off work?" he asked.

"In an hour. Why?"

"Why don't we go for coffee somewhere and discuss there? Unless the situation is urgent—"

"No. Not urgent. Sure. I know this great place on Westport Road."

I sent him the address, wrapped up everything I had left to do on my shift, and drove to my favorite family-owned café in town.

When I arrived, Hector was already waiting for me. He wore casual attire, and it worked for him. It worked for him really well. His t-shirt clung to his pectoral muscles in the most enticing way. His brow was furrowed as he turned a page on the book in his hands. Hot men reading was my kryptonite, but I shared that dirty little secret with no one. Not even Sara or Sofia knew that I frequently searched through #hotmen-reading accounts on social media.

I needed to stop gawking at him, so I took a deep breath and settled on the seat across from his. "Hello," I said cheerily.

Hector grabbed a bookmark from the back of the book and held his place.

"What you reading?" He tilted the book to show me the cover.

"*East of Eden*," I said. "That's a great one. First time?"

"Yeah. I'm halfway through. It's fantastic."

"Since you haven't finished, I'll resist the urge to geek out about it. Don't want to spoil it."

"I appreciate that," Hector said. "Maybe when I'm done?"

"It's a deal."

The mood took a serious turn when I began to discuss a new patient I'd just seen for a second opinion. I knew deep down she was hospice-bound, but I also held out hope Hector would see something I was missing.

"I'm sorry, Carolina. You are right with your original prognosis."

"I knew you were going to say that," I said with less enthusiasm.

Hector's mouth curved into a half-smile. "Then, why'd you ask for the consult if you already knew?"

"I'm a masochist?"

He chuckled.

"Thanks for your input anyway," I said.

"Anytime."

Before leaving, I had to ask him about the fellowship. Since Dr. Keach had brought it up, I hadn't mentioned it to Hector. "Can I ask you something I'm fairly certain I shouldn't be asking?"

"I have a feeling you will no matter what I say."

"You are reviewing the fellowship applications next year, right?"

"That was supposed to be confidential. How did you . . ." Hector's eyes narrowed. "Let me guess. Keach?"

I nodded, a little surprised he guessed who had spilled the beans.

Had *he* told Keach? My stomach churned at the idea of him selecting Dr. Keach over me for the fellowship. If he had, it would make sense for them to have already talked about it. "Um—" I cleared my throat. "How did you know it was Dr. Keach who told me?"

"The chief won't shut up about him. I can only assume he told Dr. Keach, who was so kind as to inform you," he said, his voice heavy with sarcasm.

I let out the breath I'd been holding. "Oh," I said. "Well?"

"Well, what?"

"Am I in the running?"

"You know I can't tell you that," said Hector, but he smiled from ear to ear and peeked at me over his glasses. That was all the reassurance I needed.

"Thanks again. I'll get out of your hair. Let you get back to your Steinbeck."

"You in a hurry?"

"Not really, no." I bit my lip. "But I don't want to impose."

"I enjoy the company, Carolina. It's nice to have someone to talk with outside of work."

"All right, then let me grab another coffee."

Instead, he offered to place the order himself and was back at our table with a smile I was glad to see again.

"Are you doing better—I mean since getting the divorce papers?" I asked him.

"It's sinking in. I'm feeling calmer, at least," he said and sipped his coffee.

"Good." I smiled in a way I hoped came across as encouraging.

"I appreciate you listening."

"Anytime. I'm glad you're giving it one last shot."

Hector's eyes narrowed. "You are?"

"Of course!" I said in a much-too-high pitch. I laughed, but it came out nervous. Could he see right through me? "I'd like to think, though we haven't known each other that long, we are friends—"

"We are friends, Carolina. You've taken my shoes off when I was too drunk—"

I laughed in earnest, remembering his drunken experience. "Well, I want my friends to be happy. And I hope you find your happiness too."

"Oh, I will," he said with a firmness that made my thighs clench under the table.

"So how are you gonna do it?" I asked.

"Do what?"

"Get her back?"

"Don't know. I'll think of something. Why? You have any suggestions?"

I swallowed hard. No. He couldn't ask me this. While it was true that I wanted him to be happy, I wanted no part in the creation of said happiness.

"Actually," he said, "this is perfect. I could use a woman's advice—"

"Hector," I whined, "I'm not sure that's such a good idea."

"I think it's a brilliant idea. Tell me, Carolina, if your husband was trying to get you back after a long time apart, how would you like him to do it?"

No, no, no. This couldn't be happening. The thought of him with another woman, even his wife, went down like cheap tequila; it burned to the core and left a bitter taste on the tongue. I'd rather have a catheter put in than talk about this. Didn't he have buddies he could talk with about this kind of thing?

"Come on." Hector nudged me. "I'm sure what you come up with will be a million times better than any of my ideas. *Please.*"

"You're being pathetic again," I said. "It makes it hard to say no to you."

He grinned again. "I know. You said."

I couldn't find a way to say no without also giving away that my feelings for him were growing. I'd have to play this cool. *You can do this, Caro.* "Fine. What did you have in mind?"

"Expensive roses?"

I shook my head. "Really? That's the best you can do?"

"Yes. That's why I'm consulting an expert."

"Ha-ha," I said in a mocking tone. "You have to think of something big. It's hard to advise because I didn't know you two as a couple. If it's personal, that's better."

"What do you mean?"

I took a deep breath and did my best to steady my voice. "One year when I was little, Mom and Dad had been fighting. I can't remember anymore what the fight was about. Let's just say Dad was in the doghouse for a week. Dad knew who mom's favorite author was, so he got our local bookstore to track down a signed copy.

"When Mom opened the gift, she started crying. I thought she would get mad all over again, but she just kept saying over and over how that author had touched the book she was holding, and now *she* was touching it."

Hector listened intently as I shared the little memory of my parents together. "That's sweet," he said. "But I don't think Andrea is much of a reader."

"You are missing the point. It's not about the gift itself. It was so effective because he knew something so personal about her. Something only he could have managed."

Hector scratched his head, thinking.

"Look, it doesn't even have to be a thing. It can be a place or an experience. Is there a place special to the both of you? Maybe take her there? Whisk her away. Women love being whisked away."

The minute I said it, I regretted every last syllable that had left my mouth. I placed the final nail on the coffin that was my jealousy. *Way to go, Carolina. You managed to make yourself jealous.*

"Maybe I'll do that," Hector said.

I cleared my throat. "Good." I smiled, but it was stiff.

No. Please don't go anywhere with any woman. I could picture them and their perfect bodies clad in swimwear in the Maldives. A romantic getaway for two, all because I couldn't keep my mouth shut.

"Are you okay?" Hector asked. "You look like you're going to be sick."

I smiled tightly at him again. "I'm fine."

CHAPTER 16

called it. I called it and then some. It was hard not to pay any mind to the rumor mill. Sara was back at work, though only allowed to do paperwork until her arm healed. She kept me in the loop of rumors, whether I wanted her to or not.

It was bad. Really bad. I knew she wouldn't exaggerate or embellish. Luckily, Hector reverted to distancing himself from me and only approached me about work. It didn't dissuade the rumors, though. I really did my best to ignore them, but after a few months of nothing changing, I was ready to scream. Or leave.

I couldn't very well quit and leave my patients, but I could do the next best thing. I asked Mandy to clear my schedule for the next four days, and Dr. Stuart was more than happy to give me a few days off since I almost never used any of my vacation time.

The East Coast Oncology Research Annual Conference was in two days. I hadn't initially planned on attending, but it was the perfect reason to get away. I needed distance from the hospital, from the rumors, and most importantly, from *him*.

I called my assistant.

She picked up on the second ring.

"Mandy?"

"What's up, Dr. Ramirez?"

"Please don't kill me," I said as I winced, even though she couldn't see me through the phone.

"What did you do now?"

"I want to go to the ECOR conference."

"I asked you about that months ago," Mandy whined. "And you said you didn't have the time."

"But you just cleared my schedule."

"I thought you were taking vacation time."

"Well, I need to get away. Can you *try*? I know it's a lot to ask."

I could hear her breath as she slowly let it out on the other end of the line. "Fine. I'll see what I can do, but I'm not making any promises."

"You are the most amazing assistant," I said.

"If you want to compliment me, say I'm the most amazing artist."

"That goes without saying," I said. "Thank you, Mandy."

Everything was booked last minute, but my amazing assistant managed to wrangle me late registration and did some sort of voodoo magic, I was sure, to get me a hotel room in the conference hotel that had been booked up for weeks.

I managed to get a window seat when I boarded the flight. I put my earbuds in, turned on soothing music, and leaned back. I wasn't nervous flying, and the flight would ordinarily put me to sleep. I closed my eyes and tried to relax.

The plane hadn't finished boarding when I felt a tap on my shoulder. "Not taken. Go ahead," I said, assuming they were asking about the seat next to me, but I didn't open my eyes. When the light tap repeated itself, I opened one eye.

"Mother f—," I started to say. I pulled my earbuds out. "What are you doing here?"

Hector blinked at me from the seat next to mine. "I'm going to the conference. What are *you* doing here?"

"I was trying to get away from you," I joked.

"Great minds?" he offered.

"More like fools seldom differ."

"Oh, I don't know. This could be fun."

"You realize I've been trying to get rid of the rumors. When everyone realizes we took the same days off, and if it gets back to anyone we were at the conference together—"

"I know, Carolina. I've been keeping my distance—"

"Yeah, I've noticed."

He looked at me, and his brows drew into a frown. "I thought it's what you wanted."

"It was—is, but now—"

"It wasn't intentional. I didn't know you were coming."

"I can't blame you for that. *I* didn't know I was coming until a few days ago."

"Let's make the best of it then, no?"

I nodded.

I could kill Mandy for putting us on the same flight to Boston, though I knew she hadn't done it on purpose. Or had she? If she had talked to Hector's assistant to coordinate flights, I was going to have to get a different research assistant.

And yet, as bad an idea as a trip together was, I found myself having to push down a small excitement that was building in my chest.

THE FIRST PRESENTATION started at seven in the morning, so most attendees arrived the night before the conference officially kicked off. Hector and I took a taxi together and were at the hotel by six in the evening.

Once in the elevator, after checking in, Hector asked me to dinner.

"I'm not sure that's such a good idea."

"Just as colleagues. You once wanted me to be your mentor. You are supposed to mingle at these things. It's kind of the point."

"I don't know."

"There will be no better time. Away from the hospital—in another city."

He had a point. To a great extent, I had let the rumors rob me of the one thing I did want from Hector Medina: his brain. Everything went sideways, and the opportunity of a lifetime dangled in front of me like a carrot I knew I would never be able to reach. "All right," I agreed with reluctance.

We agreed to freshen up after our flight, and I met him at the hotel's restaurant an hour later.

I looked the menu over and was happy the prices weren't too outrageous.

"Would you like to hear the specials tonight?" our waiter asked as he approached our table.

"No, thank you," Hector said. He ordered a glass of red wine, and I didn't miss his glare over the rim of his glasses when I ordered only water.

After ordering—he steak and greens, and I shrimp pasta—we settled into the evening, more relaxed than I would have imagined.

He smiled at me, encouraging me to lead the conversation. "Why didn't you correct me whenever I assumed you grew up rich?" I asked.

"Ah. I was wondering when this would come up."

"Your mother—"

"She didn't say anything to me, by the way, about what you two spoke about. She wouldn't do that. That said, I know my mother. I can guess what she had to say to you."

"Hector, I wasn't trying to pry into your personal life. I—"

"I know. No need to apologize." He smiled, and there was nothing but truth in his eyes, so I relaxed a bit. "But to answer your question, I didn't think it was important."

"It's not, but I've said things, insensitive things—"

"Don't worry. I think intent is important." He grinned, throwing my words back at me.

"I'm afraid my intent wasn't very virtuous. I was trying to take a jab, and I'm sorry for that. The truth is, even if you *had* come from money, I shouldn't have acted that way, regardless."

"All is forgiven."

"Would you like to have lunch tomorrow?" I asked. I was enjoying our conversation tonight.

Hector cleared his throat. "I, um—can't . . . I, uh, have lunch plans."

I took a sip of my water, wishing it was wine. "Oh?"

"Andrea is in town for work. We agreed to meet over lunch."

"I see," I said, but my stomach twisted into knots. "That's good. Baby steps." I did my best to smile. Was this him whisking her away like I suggested? If it was, it was a sorry excuse for a romantic trip.

"Yeah. If I'm honest, I'm a little nervous," he said.

"Has it been that long?"

"I haven't seen her in over a year."

I blinked. Over a year? I thought it had been months, not an entire year. "I'm sure it'll be fine," I said and was desperate for the conversation to go anywhere else. I didn't need to hear any details about him and Andrea together. My poor heart couldn't take it.

Once our dinner arrived, the conversation relaxed into a more leisurely pace, allowing me to take a breath after Hector's revelation.

"So tell me about home."

"What about it?"

"Growing up in Oaxaca. What was it like?"

He put his fork down and leaned back in his chair. He grabbed for his glass of wine, buying time.

"It's not something I like thinking about much. My only connection to the city is my mother, and she refuses to leave. It's a beautiful city, and she loves it. I understand her; her family and friends are all there. But for me—I have only bad memories."

"Forget I asked."

"No—it's okay. Let's see. My father left us when I was six. Wish he had done it sooner so I wouldn't have the vague memories I have of him. My mother struggled to support us. She had little help from my grandparents because they weren't much better off."

"What did she do?"

"What she knew how to do. She's a great cook, so she put a few pesos together and started a little food stand. She sold *memelas* because they were cheap to make. With that, she was able to provide for us. It was a humble start, but I'm glad for it."

"Why are you glad you grew up like that?"

"I don't think I'd be the person I am today if I hadn't. I know I can take myself too seriously at times, and Mom reminds me all the time that I fancy myself perfect."

"Yeah, she might have mentioned it," I said with a grin.

"I don't doubt it. That attitude of mine was probably what you were picking up on when you made those assumptions about me. But if you can imagine, think about what an arrogant bastard I am now. Then imagine how much worse that would be if I had started off in life as you assumed."

"The monstrosity," I gasped.

He threw his head back with laughter. "Indeed."

He was true to his word. The remainder of the meal was very polite, and no lines were crossed. I was pleased to see him not fighting me when I wanted to split the check with him. I wanted no room to interpret this dinner as anything other than a meal between colleagues.

I was taken aback when he exited the elevator on my floor.

"What are you doing? This isn't your floor."

"I'm walking you to your room."

"That's really not necessary."

"I don't mind," he said. Either he was oblivious to my discomfort or intentionally ignoring it.

I opened the door to my room and turned to stretch my hand out to shake his. He looked at my hand for one beat, then two. He grabbed it, finally, but didn't let go.

"Carolina—"

"Hector, don't."

"I'm trying not to." He stepped closer to me, my hand still in his.

"You're not doing a great job at it," I said, my voice breathy.

"Then you know how much I'm hating this. I hate not being in control." His voice deepened, and there was a hoarseness to it now.

I tried pulling my hand away from his grasp, but he was too strong. "Just one minute," he pleaded. "I lose all control with you. Why do you do this to me?"

"I'm not doing anything."

"You are doing it by existing."

"We really shouldn't—" I started to say, but I leaned into his personal space as much as he was invading mine.

"No, we shouldn't," he said. He closed the remaining distance between us. His hand came up to the side of my face. He pushed back a strand of my hair and carefully tucked it behind my ear. His hand then lingered on my cheek, his thumb hovering near the corner of my mouth. My chest heaved when he looked at my lips; a hunger burned in his dilated pupils.

This was a moment that could change my life if I let it. It felt very much like the night that I picked him up from the bar, but it couldn't be more different. He was sober, so there was no questioning what I found in his eyes, or what story his body told me, those muscles taut as he held himself back, his brows knitted together in pain—the pain of restraint.

We stood in the threshold of my hotel room, and he awaited the answer to the question his body was asking. He was charged like a wire, but ever the gentleman, wouldn't step a foot in my room if I didn't ask him to.

My body reacted to him too. How could it not? He let go of my hand and brought his second hand to the other side of my face. He was pleading now, and the skin on my arms broke into goosebumps at his touch.

I grabbed his hands and pulled them off my face. "I can't," I said, panting.

Rejecting him wasn't what my heart wanted, but like always, my head won over. "I want to. I really want to," I reassured him as if the reaction in my body hadn't already told him that. "But I can't. There's work to think about. I can be fired if we start anything, but I wouldn't do that anyway. Not while you're married, even if you are separated. And then there's . . ."

"What?" he asked.

"Your wife, Hector. You're going to see her tomorrow."

"I know," he hissed then took a step back.

"You wanted to try with her again, remember?"

His jaw was set now, and a muscle clicked over one side of his jaw. "Damn it, Carolina, I hate myself. I feel like I'm failing."

"You aren't failing."

"I am. I'm failing myself, and I'm failing you. I promise I'll try harder."

I wanted to reach out to him, to touch him and reassure him he wasn't failing. I wanted to ease the look of pain evident on his face, but I could only nod.

"I won't try to touch you again. I promise." It was the last thing he said before walking away from me. It was a vow that hurt more deeply than I could have imagined because now I knew.

Hector Medina was a man who kept his vows.

CHAPTER 17

UNDER FIRE

After the closing remarks of the conference, Hector and I left for the airport. Not surprisingly, he was returning on the same flight. It would be hard not to suspect this was intentional, but really, how many afternoon flights from Boston to Kansas City could there be? I let it go. There was no point in bringing it up now, not after our conversation that first night.

Hector never offered any information on the lunch with his wife or if anything came of it, and I'd be damned if I asked him, so I tried to concentrate on work. In the waiting area for our flight, I decided to check my email. I was excited to open the messages waiting in my inbox, ready to dive into work, and grateful for the distraction, but it all changed as I read them one by one.

"What's wrong?" Hector asked, no doubt seeing the concern plain on my face.

"This can't be right." I scrolled to the next email and the next, but they all said the same thing.

"What is it? You're starting to scare me."

I placed my phone in my pocket and looked up at him. "They all said no."

"Who? No to what?"

"My follow-up grant. The doctors at Heartland Metro, who I invited to sign on to the follow-up grant for the trial, all said no. I shared the preliminary data report to hook them in, and I pitched some ideas for what might be included in the proposal."

"Okay . . ."

"They all said no. Every doctor I invited to participate in the next trial." I let out a breath that shrank me like a deflated mylar balloon.

"What? All of them?"

I nodded. "Well, the physicians at the hospitals administering the current trial in California, Texas, and New York all said yes. But every doctor I contacted at Heartland Metro said no."

"How many?"

"Six. I re-invited the four on the trial now, plus two more. I wanted to add a psychological support component to the next trial, so I invited two of our top-rated psychologists as well."

Hector's jaw clenched. "Those sons of bitches."

"What could this be about, Hector? Doctors usually jump at a chance to be included in a project like this. I figured with you involved, it was an easy sell. I'd understand if one, or even two said no—especially if they were over-burdened with other projects. But *all six?* Something is off here."

"Don't worry. We'll figure it out when we get back."

We didn't have the opportunity to investigate, however, because, on our first day back, I was called into Chief Stuart's office. When I arrived, Hector was already in one of two chairs in front of the chief's desk.

"Dr. Ramirez, please take a seat."

"What is this about?" I asked.

"We'll get to that," Chief Stuart said.

"How was the conference?" he asked. "I wanted to go but couldn't make it work with my schedule."

He looked between Hector and me, and it wasn't clear to whom he had directed the question. *Shit,* I thought. He knew we had been there together. When we didn't respond, he smiled.

"Hector asked for the time off for the conference several months ago. When you asked, Carolina, I didn't put two and two together."

I nodded, and he continued. "We have a problem. I've been ignoring the rumors, but it's getting harder to—"

"Chief," Hector said, jumping in. "You have my word that the rumors are unfounded. We have done nothing that we would be ashamed of. Our relationship is purely professional."

Well, it was mostly true.

The chief turned to me, and I winced.

"Dr. Ramirez, do you have anything to add?"

"Yes, um—" Damn it, I felt like a kid in the principal's office, and all my confidence ran out the window. I cleared my throat. "I think the rumors stem from some professional jealousies. It hasn't always been easy since I got the trial funded. But I view Dr. Medina as nothing other than a mentor. I respect him, and I wouldn't dishonor his *wife* or their marriage by entering into any type of relationship that wasn't professional." And that was nothing but pure truth. I could see Hector from my peripheral vision as he turned to face me.

"Well," said the chief, "if it were all still rumors, eventually they would die down when everyone realized they were unfounded. But now, we have a bigger problem. We've received an official complaint through Human Resources."

"About me?" I asked.

"About Dr. Medina's preferential treatment of you due to an inappropriate relationship. This is why we have a hospital policy against superiors and subordinates dating."

"We are not dating. Who made the complaint?" I clipped.

"That is confidential," Chief Stuart said.

"It was Keach, wasn't it?"

"Complaints are anonymous." The chief leaned back in his chair. "But if it *was* Dr. Keach, I wouldn't be happy about it if I were you, Dr. Ramirez." He raised an eyebrow in warning. "This competition you two have going has got to stop. I realize the fellowship is prestigious and highly competitive, but that is no reason to act out. It will only ruin your chances."

"I am not competing with him. With all due respect, sir, all I'm trying to do is the best work I can, which I can do here or as an attending elsewhere."

Chief Stuart looked flustered, and he straightened up in his chair. "No one is going anywhere," he said.

Now that I was bringing in the big research dollars, Dr. Stuart couldn't afford to lose me. He would also be hesitant to let go of the Keachs' generous donations to the hospital. The chief had a choice to make, and I needed to make that clear.

"Things aren't getting easier for me, Chief. This will get back to you, so you better hear it from me. Physicians are taking sides. Every doctor I invited to participate in my follow-up trial said no. That has Dr. Keach's name written all over it. What do you have to say about that?"

"I'll talk with them," he said.

And I knew he would. He wouldn't lose out on the potential of millions of dollars in research funding for a petty little man who didn't have the chops to let his skills speak for him.

"You do that, Chief," I spat and stormed out of his office. I couldn't believe I had just spoken to the chief like that.

I ran to the stairwell; I needed a minute. I was great at keeping my shit together in front of the chief, but I was at a crossroads. How I handled this situation could make or break my career. It was such a delicate problem. One wrong word. One false accusation—and I could lose everything I'd worked for.

I sat in the stairwell, letting out the first tears I would ever shed on the clock during my professional career. They tasted bitter, and I resented them immediately. I wasn't that *girl*—one shaken up by a boy's club. This wasn't *me*—crying in a stairwell because of some rumors.

The rumors. The rumors that were this close to ending my career. My dreams. No. I wiped the tears away and straightened my light-blue scrub top. Even if it ended here, I would succeed elsewhere.

The door to the stairwell burst open, and Hector descended the stairs toward me. I was hoping there was no redness in my eyes or nose, but when his eyes softened, I knew the traitorous signs of tears were there.

"Carolina."

"No!" I hissed, and he stopped in his tracks. I looked up at him from several steps below. "From now on, it's *Dr. Ramirez* and *only* Dr. Ramirez. You will not address me directly. If you need to work out schedules, have your secretary talk with my RA. If you need to discuss a patient, reach out via email. The next grant proposal we can work on via email as well—"

"Carolina—" He closed his mouth when my glare snapped up to him at the sound of my name.

"No. You will not talk with me. You will pick a seat on the opposite side of the table in conference rooms, and as far away as possible at any presentations we may be attending at the same time."

My eyes stung when I saw him swallow hard, and his Adam's apple bobbed. But I had to continue. "If you get drunk, you will get a taxi; you will not call me. And if you see me in the hallway, do not say hello."

He looked like I had stabbed him in the gut.

"I'm sorry," I said. "I'm trying to fix this. I can't lose my career over something that isn't even happening."

He nodded.

And he followed my every order faithfully.

For two years.

The longest two years of my life.

CHAPTER 18

TWO YEARS LATER

RESULTS ARE IN

"You know they're calling you 'Flash,' right?" Mandy said as she tried to catch up to me.

"What?"

"You need to slow down—"

"Can't. I've had a long shift, and I have to finish charting before I can catch a little shuteye—"

"Carolina!" Mandy snapped, and I halted at her tone.

"*What?*"

"Here." She pushed a tablet toward me. "You haven't checked your email today."

"I'll do it later—"

"No. Trust me. You'll do it now."

I took the tablet again, this time willingly. I let out a breath. I was so tired, and all I wanted to do was go home. But then I saw the email she had already opened for me. It was the statistical report to phase two of my trial that concluded year three. I read and reread the summary in the body of the email. I looked up at her.

"This can't be right."

"It is!" Mandy clasped her hands and bounced in front of me.

I shook my head. I must have read wrong. I read the email a third, then a fourth time. No. I hadn't read wrong. My breath was coming in shorter, more rapid bursts. My pulse quickened in excitement as I realized what these results could mean. When I met Mandy's gaze once more, she was smiling ear-to-ear, and her eyes were a little misty.

"Thanks, Mandy," I said in a near whisper, and I broke into a soft jog.

I had to tell him. He had to know.

Over the last two years, we never saw each other again outside the hospital. No more lunches together or meetings in his office. But now I didn't care. I had to share this excitement with him. Even if the rumors had mostly died down. Even if I had regained the trust of my colleagues and mentors. It didn't matter. This was a mutual success. He deserved his due credit.

I bumped into Sara on the way to Hector's office. Her brows furrowed at seeing me jog.

"Everything okay?" asked Sara.

I made sure she had regained her balance before I kept going. "Yeah! Great! I'll tell you later."

"Okay, Flash!" she called after me.

Huh. I guess they were calling me that.

I didn't care if he was with someone; I barged into his office anyway. He stood behind his chair, hunched over his desk, reading the laptop screen. Luckily, he was alone. At my entrance, he looked up, startled. Then he grinned when he realized it was me.

"Is this right?" he asked, hopeful.

I nodded. "I think so."

"I don't believe it." He looked back to his screen, aghast. "Sixty-percent increased remission at year three over the standard of care national average. This is unreal." He looked up again and ran his hands through his hair. "Dr. Ramirez." His voice cracked a bit. "This is big. Really big. This will change how the world treats cervical cancer in this age group."

I nodded again. I was still stunned and breathy from my jog to his office.

"Congratulations, Dr. Ramirez!" He stood and spread his arms wide as he approached me. I didn't hesitate to embrace him back. Not even a little bit.

This was the first time we had touched since that time outside my hotel room, but it was entirely different. There was no electricity, no sensuality lacing our words, no hunger between us. It was a sweet hug of congratulations, and, dare I thought it, pride. It was a relief to be with him like this—and have it mean nothing more. He still wore that gold band on his left hand, so it couldn't be anything more.

"I couldn't have done it without you," I said once we parted.

"Sure you could have."

I shook my head. "No. You've helped so much since joining the trial team, but I actually mean your past work. If you hadn't made the strides you did, I wouldn't have thought of this. We wouldn't be here today."

I wasn't imagining that his eyes misted over, not unlike Mandy's only a few moments ago.

"This is all you, Carolina. And I'm sorry, I know I'm not supposed to call you that. Please forgive me this once. I am bursting with pride."

"Thank you."

"So what's next for you?" he asked.

"Well, cure cancer, of course," I said. Everyone always looked at me like I was crazy when I said that. I wasn't delusional; I knew I probably wouldn't be the one person who cured cancer. It would take a cooperative international effort to one day eradicate this disease from our planet, but I said those words like a promise: *I will do my part.*

Hector threw his head back with a laugh. "I don't doubt it. I feel bad for cancer. I think it has met its match."

"I have to go. I have to wrap up a few things and go tell Dad."

"Congratulations, Carolina."

DAD WASN'T at home when I got there. I turned on the television, but I couldn't concentrate on anything. I shut it off and paced the small living room. It was so quiet in the house that I easily heard the sound of tires coming up the driveway, signaling his arrival.

"*Mija,*" he said as he entered the front door. "What's wrong?"

"Nothing's wrong."

"Then, why are you here?"

I knew he didn't mean it the way it sounded, but a pang of guilt radiated through my ribcage all the same. I had overworked the last two years, completely neglecting my family and friends. The clinical trial and my patients had consumed me. I had thought of little else. I worked to fill up the hours in such a way that I could not spend a single second of any day thinking about Hector and what we had almost been.

"I'm sorry, Dad," I said. "I know I've been busy, but I have good news."

When I told him the trial results and explained what that meant in non-medical terms, he wept.

My father was a proud man. He was a strong, hardworking, old-school, Mexican man. A man like that didn't cry, and still, he'd let me see him cry exactly twice. There was never any shame in it. The first time was at my mom's funeral, and the second time was at this very moment.

"Really?" He looked up at me with those glistening black eyes. Wrinkles etched the outside corners of each eye—the echoes of constant smiling.

"Yes, Dad. Really."

He was sitting now, and I knelt before him. I placed my head on his lap like I had when I was a little girl, and he patted my head. I didn't care that his clothes were full of black stains from the garage, or that the smell of grease would end up in my hair.

"*Papi*," I croaked out. "I could have saved her."

It was a hard admission to make. I couldn't look at him. It was irrational—to feel shame at not being able to save her when I had only been a child. The scientific, rational part of my brain assured me it couldn't have been my fault. But my irrational side, the side that sometimes won out in internal battles, the side of my heart, *that side* didn't free me of the shame of failure.

He stroked my hair gently. We wept now, our sobs the only sound in the quiet house.

"I know, *mija*. I know."

"You think she would forgive me?" I asked, even fully understanding how irrational that line of thinking was.

"There is nothing to forgive," he said. "Look at me." He grabbed my chin and pulled my face up to force me into looking at him. I sat back on my heels. "Carolina Isabel Ramirez Fuentes, there is nothing you could have done. You hear me?"

"I know. But if it had been *now*, I could have—" I insisted.

"Yes. But time is stupid that way," he deadpanned. I let out a laugh, but it chortled and caught in all the snot from my ugly-crying. Us Ramirezes—there's a good reason we don't cry often. It's a fucking mess.

"This is what I *do* know," he said. "Your mother would be so incredibly proud of you. Almost as much as I am."

THE ICE over my eyes helped. I pressed the frozen spoons to the skin that had turned into bags overnight. I'd gone home after speaking with Dad and cried myself to sleep. In the morning, I was paying the puffy-eye price. Nothing about crying is attractive.

The phone buzzed on the kitchen counter, and I had to set down one of the spoons to make out the name on the screen.

When Mandy called me, it was usually either really good or really bad.

"Hello?"

"Hey, can you come in?"

"No can do. It's my day off, and I haven't actually taken one in a long time."

"Let me rephrase. You *have to* come in."

I set the other spoon down. "What is it now, Mandy?"

"Dr. Stuart came to find me at the information desk and asked me to call you. He said he needs you in his office ASAP."

Had someone seen Hector hugging me? Were they trying to dig up those long-buried skeletons? It had been two years. This was unbelievable. I was beyond annoyed. I was pissed. I wouldn't let them do this again. I had more leverage, and I didn't have a single thing to lose anymore. Not more than I already lost: the best mentor I'd ever have in my career.

I actually saw the smoke coming out of my nose. "I swear to god,

Mandy, if they are trying to bring up this old bullshit again, I'm taking my next trial to another hospital."

"Take me with you?" she asked.

"You got it. Please tell Chief Stuart's secretary I'll need an hour to get there."

Let him wait. I wasn't going to go in there, making demands and taking names, in my pajamas. I would look my best. I put on a pair of dark blue slacks and a crisp white shirt. My hair went up into a slick ponytail, and I put on the brightest red lipstick I could find. I wasn't one for makeup, but if I was quitting my job today, I was going to do it in style.

Three men waited for me—the chief, Hector, and a third I didn't recognize. They all stood when I entered the office.

"Dr. Ramirez, this is Dr. Drake."

"Hello, Dr. Drake." I shook his hand. "Have we met before?"

"No, we haven't, but you may recognize the name. I'm Chief of Oncology at Peak View Metro in California. We have two physicians administering your trial there."

"Is something wrong with the trial?" I asked, my heart lodged in my throat. Why would someone make the trip otherwise?

"Quite the contrary," said the chief. "Dr. Drake got on a flight as soon as his team got the report on phase two of the trial."

"Oh." I pressed my palm to my chest. This was good.

"I'm sorry if we scared you," Hector said, making his presence known once again.

"What can I do for you?" I asked.

"Dr. Drake would like to speak with you," said the chief. "He afforded me the respect of coming to me first before giving you an official offer."

I looked among the three men. They had been discussing me. Hector had a guilty expression on his face, and Dr. Stuart shifted his weight from one leg to the other.

"What's going on?" I asked.

"I wanted to talk with you about your plans when your contract is over here at Heartland Metro," said Dr. Drake.

"I was hoping to continue," I said. "I have something similar in mind for a breast cancer treatment trial. I was also thinking about adding a psychological component—"

"That's great!" Dr. Drake interrupted me. "I'm hoping we can compete with Heartland Metro. I trust you will find our offer more than generous."

The way Dr. Drake's long neck moved slightly when he talked made me think of a snake. He was tall and slender, and his movements were precise but unnatural. My instincts were to step away from him, but I forced a smile. I'd never willingly work for a man who interrupted a woman mid-sentence simply because he could, but he was giving me leverage with Chief Stuart. The more the chief thought I was interested in going to a top-tier hospital in California, the better.

"Why don't you give Dr. Drake a tour of the hospital?" said the chief. "I'm sure you two have a lot to talk about. I'll submit Heartland's competing offer by the end of the week. Hector, mind staying behind for a bit?"

Dr. Drake and I were dismissed. By the time the tour was over, I had him convinced that I was sincerely interested in the offer. I imagined him slithering his way all the way back to California, thinking he had tempted me.

CHAPTER 19

BACK TO NORMAL

"You are not seriously thinking about going to Peak View, are you?" Hector caught me between patients at the nurses' station. I blinked at him.

"I'm going to consider *all* offers."

Hector's eyes narrowed. "I'm sure the offers will start pouring in once we publish the first paper on the trial." His tone was frigid, but I could tell the smallest of smiles pulled at one corner of his mouth. It was almost as if he didn't care what hospital I ended up at, so long as it was my choice.

"That would be nice," I said. "But I'm not going to count my chickens. I'm just focused on my work right now."

"Very diplomatic of you," he said.

"That's me: diplomatic Dr. Ramirez."

Hector laughed, and I wondered how we could return to our old comfortable banter so quickly.

The rumors that had circulated about us a few years ago were all but snuffed out. Now, I had leverage with the chief for an attending position. And Hector was clearly still happily married, or he wouldn't be wearing that wedding ring.

So fuck it. I missed my mentor. I missed bouncing ideas off him and brainstorming for future trials. I wasn't going to keep pushing him away—not while he didn't want to remain at arm's length.

Much more quickly than I would have anticipated, everything returned to normal—the normal before we parted ways for the first time.

"This is nice," Hector said.

"What is?"

"Being able to talk with you. I've missed it."

I nodded. "I've missed you too."

His gaze fixed on mine like he couldn't believe I had said that.

"Does this mean we can go back to being friends? Work on the paper together?" he asked.

"I'd like that."

Hector smiled. "I'd also like to catch up. You free for lunch today?"

"Sure. I have a patient at one though, so it'll have to be the cafeteria."

"That's not really what I had in mind, but I'll take it."

We walked through the cafeteria line together, and I did my best to ignore the many eyes that followed us.

When Hector found his way to the hot food line, I pulled him away. "What are you doing?"

"Grabbing my lunch. The sign said it was turkey and mashed potatoes."

"Dr. Medina," I said, fighting back laughter, "have you *ever* eaten the cafeteria food here?"

He shook his head.

"Trust me; you don't ever want to go through the hot food line."

"What do you recommend then?" he asked.

"The cold sandwich station isn't bad, but if you ask me, there is only one thing here worth having."

"Please enlighten me, Dr. Ramirez." He chuckled, and I enjoyed the playfulness that was back.

"Pizza," I said.

We found a table in the cafeteria, and when Hector took a bite of his slice, I waited for his reaction.

"Not bad," he said.

"I told you."

"Yes. You did. So, how have you been, Carolina?"

"Busy," I said, taking a bite of my pizza.

"Yes. I know. I was worried you would burn out. I wanted to check in—"

"But I told you to stay away from me?"

He nodded grimly.

"I'm sorry about that. I'm not sure I handled it the best way I could have, but look on the bright side. It worked. I got my professional respect back, and I've had no issues with doctors joining my grant proposals since."

"I'm glad something good came of it. You aren't worried about being seen with me now?"

I shook my head and swallowed my bite of pizza. "No. I have options now, and it's time for Dr. Stuart to decide who is more valuable to the department."

"Good for you. I'm glad you are realizing your worth."

A flush swept over my face, so I decided to change the subject. "How about you? How have you been?"

Hector sighed. "Not quite as good as you. I was often tempted to ignore your commands and talk with you, so I took a lot of vacation time."

I blinked at him. "You did?"

"It hurts that you didn't notice."

"I was working too much," I admitted.

"I know."

"What did you do with all the time off?"

"I went to the FIHR to check on some projects I handed over before coming here. I also spent some time with my mom in Mexico."

"How is Marisela?" I asked.

"Good, though she can't forgive me for letting you go." He likely saw the shift in mood plain on my face. "I'm sorry. I shouldn't have said that. Won't happen again."

"Will you say hi to her for me?"

"Of course," he said. "I also wanted to ask you about Sara. I've seen her at work, and she seemed well, so I haven't checked in on her again."

"She's doing great. She will be finishing her graduate degree soon."

"And that mess back then. It's done?"

"That *mess* was a man who is not in her life anymore."

"Good," said Hector. It was still the sweetest thing that he worried about my friend. Sara was lucky to have so many people in her corner, even if she didn't realize quite the scope of it.

When we parted ways outside the cafeteria doors, I felt lighter. There was newfound excitement in the renewed possibility of picking the great Hector Medina's brain; with that assurance, nothing could possibly have the power to wipe the grin off my face.

I was wrong.

ALMOST AS IF evil could sense happiness, Dr. Keach got a whiff of our returned working relationship. Two days later, he sat next to me in the hospital auditorium during a grand rounds presentation.

I initially found a seat next to Dr. Bel, whom I liked and respected. Dr. Bel was an orthopedic surgeon, and though we didn't work together much, he had started residency the same year I had. Being a surgeon, though, he usually interacted with the cool kids—the jocks actually known as surgeons—of the hospital. Anyone who says cliques ended with high school is lying through their teeth. They were *everywhere.*

As we waited for the grand rounds presentation to start, I chatted easily with Dr. Bel until Dr. Keach's hot breath graced the side of my neck.

"Dr. Ramirez," Dr. Keach said.

"Dr. Keach." I nodded curtly.

"I hear paradise is back."

"If you mean Peak View was here just two days ago to offer me an attending position in their oncology department, then yes. I'm very happy about it."

Clearly taken aback, Dr. Keach stammered for only a second. His lips thinned, and he suddenly looked uncomfortable in his seat. "That's not what I meant," he clipped.

I shrugged. "No?"

"No. I meant all is well in paradise with you and Dr. Medina."

"If you mean, the results of our trial are more than we could ever have imagined, and the oncology department is still celebrating, then yes. All is well, Dr. Keach. Thanks for your concern."

His nostrils flared, and I thoroughly enjoyed the reaction I got out of him when he failed to get one out of me.

He turned to the doctor sitting on the other side of him and spoke loud enough for everyone in the vicinity to hear. "Not all of us can get into med school and get jobs because of affirmative action."

He went *there*. Dr. Keach freaking went there. When he failed at drumming up false rumors about Hector and me, he reverted to his previous favorite torture device. What he used long before Hector came to Heartland Metro. The line I thought he'd long ago forgotten, like a child with his old toys.

I froze. I didn't want to snap at him and give him the satisfaction he sought. The auditorium was nearly full, and even though everyone around us was engaged in conversation, a scene in the crowd would not go unnoticed.

Dr. Bel's hand drifted to my wrist, resting on the armrest between us, and he squeezed once. I blinked at him, but the motion was only a cause for me to be distracted.

"No, Dr. Keach," Dr. Bel nearly shouted. "Some of us get here on the coattails of our daddies." When Dr. Bel said *daddies* in such an infantilizing way, I almost lost it and couldn't suppress my snort. "And some of us keep our jobs because of the millions our families donate, not because of our talent. It's lucky, don't you think, Dr. Keach, that nepotism is still alive and well?"

Dr. Bel finished his little speech with a grin at me that said *I got you.* If I hadn't known he was happily married, I would have pounced him right then and there. Okay, maybe not right then and there, but soon. Why were all the wonderful men in the world taken?

Thank you, I mouthed to him, and he tipped his chin at me. Luckily, the presentation started soon after that, much too quickly for Dr. Keach to come up with a retort.

This was turning out to be the best week I'd had in a long time.

CHAPTER 20

FOREVER CHILD

"I once had a friend who looked like you," said Sofia. "Her name was Sara."

"Ha-ha." Sara rolled her eyes.

I had forced Sara to go out with me to *La Oficina* for a drink. In the two years since that piece of shit had beaten her to a pulp, and she dumped him to the curb, Sara had become a recluse. Her way of putting herself back together was to start her master's program in the evenings while continuing to work full time. I understood that her need to work to a point of exhaustion meant there was no energy left to think and dwell—I'd done the same thing.

It also meant we'd hardly seen each other except for fleeting moments at work. I wasn't serious about leaving Heartland, but if I got the right offer, I might consider it. Now was the time to reconnect with my friends, just in case.

BUT THE UNIVERSE wasn't on my side. Almost as soon as I sat down, my phone dinged with a text from Hector.

Hector: *Do you have a minute? Can you call?*

Me: *I'm actually out with friends.*

Hector: *It's important.*

Me: *One sec. Let me step outside.*

He sounded off when he answered the call.

"Hi," I said.

"Can you come over?"

"Yeah, I'm just across the street at—"

"No. Not the office. My house," he corrected.

"I'm not sure that's the best idea."

"I promise no one will know."

"Is everything okay?"

"No. I need stitches."

His voice was calm. Too calm. "Hector, why do you need stitches?"

"I cut myself picking up some broken glass."

"Go to the emergency room, you big oaf."

He chuckled. "Don't want them to see me like this. I, um, had a few drinks earlier. And it's really not that bad. I'd do it myself if I didn't have to stitch left-handed."

I let out a sigh. "Fine. Put pressure on it until I get there."

"Yes, Doctor," he teased.

WHEN HECTOR OPENED THE DOOR, I couldn't stop the gasp that escaped me. His grey shirt was stained with—something. He wore grey sweat-pants, which I'd never, not once, seen him wearing, and he had dark circles under his eyes.

"Thanks for coming," he said and led me to his kitchen. He held a towel firmly around his right hand.

He had been right. The cut was minor and only needed three stitches on the outer hand under his pinky finger line. He was a fool to refuse topical anesthetic, and while I could smell the alcohol on him from earlier in the night, he seemed sober now and would feel every stitch. Not to mention the hand is very sensitive to pain.

We didn't speak as I worked, and I was done quickly. He barely winced. His gaze was far off, miles away and in another time.

When I stood to clean up the supplies and throw out the used cotton balls, I took in the room. Two of the dining room chairs I had helped him pick out were on their backs. The coffee table, too, was upturned, and on the other side of the kitchen island, by the sink, shards of glass glittered on the floor.

"Why don't I clean this up?" I offered.

"Thanks."

Hector went to the living room and laid on the couch while I worked. I tidied up the place and went over to sit on the chair next to him.

He looked at his bandaged hand. "Glad I'm not a surgeon," he said.

"You still need it for other important doctorly things," I teased.

"Yeah . . ."

"What's going on, Hector?"

He looked at me with glassy eyes. "This is a bad day for me. I'm sorry. I'm not at my best."

"Nothing to be sorry about. We all have our bad days."

He nodded. We sat in silence for a while, and it suddenly dawned on me that this was about the same time of year when I had to pick him up drunk from the bar a few years back.

I couldn't remember the exact date, but it was definitely the same week. I'd bet my medical license it was the exact same day.

"What's today, Hector?"

He sat up, pressing his elbows to his thighs. He buried his head in his hands for a few breaths before looking up at me. "It's the worst goddamn day of the year, Carolina. I'm sorry you have to see me like this."

I nodded. Something inside me moved. I wanted to leach this pain from his body and absorb it into my own so he wouldn't feel it—whatever it was.

I moved next to him on the couch now that he was sitting. I placed a reassuring hand on his shoulder.

It was probably the worst thing I could have done to ask him for details, but I had to know. I repeated my question. "What's today, Hector?"

His eyes met mine, and he could no longer contain the sob. "It's my son's birthday," he said. I nodded, swallowing hard as I tried to push down the lump that had formed in my throat.

"He's gone," I said, but it wasn't a question.

"He'd be ten today," he said. "Jake. He was the best thing I have ever done, and he is gone."

My chin quivered at the sight of his pain. "I'm so sorry, Hector," I said, but they felt like the weakest words in the English language.

He patted my hand still on his shoulder. "Me too. Oh, Carolina, you would have loved him."

"I'm sure I would have. Do you want to tell me about him?"

"He was perfect," Hector said. "He didn't care about science or what I did. He said he was going to be a soccer player and play for *Real Madrid* someday. He was a good player too, for a six-year-old."

"I bet he was. What did he look like?"

"Like me. And like Andrea. He had my black, wavy hair and my deep, tanned skin, but he had her body type. All legs and arms—tall and gangly. If you can imagine, the brightest green eyes on that dark skin . . . he was beautiful."

"Perfect," I repeated.

"Perfect."

A long moment of silence followed before he pulled out his phone and handed it to me. On the screen was a school picture of a little boy precisely as he had described him. He was smiling wide—a gap in the center of his mouth from the missing two front teeth.

I smiled. "He was beautiful," I said. He took the phone back and put it in his pocket.

"When he died, Andrea and I . . . well, we couldn't cope. She blamed me, and part of me wants to blame myself too . . ."

"What do you mean?" My brows drew together with concern.

"He wanted to climb a tree. It was so stupid. Kids climb trees all the time."

"They do," I said.

"He wanted to go higher. His mom said no, but I'd always thought she was too over-protective."

My eyes widened with the horror and anticipation of what I knew followed next.

"I grew up with cousins. We were rough. We did dangerous things all the time. We climbed trees. We were boys. So I told him to go ahead. I didn't want him to grow up scared of things."

"Oh, Hector . . ."

"He kept climbing . . . a branch snapped, and when he fell, his neck broke on impact. By the time I got to him, it was too late. In an instant, he was gone."

"I'm so sorry." My tears were down to my chin by the time his story was over.

"I'm a doctor, Carolina. Do you know what that feels like? To be a *doctor* and not be able to help the person you love most in the world? How helpless that is?"

I did know. But this was *his* story. I only nodded.

"I don't blame her for blaming me. Part of me knows it wasn't my fault, but there is a warring part that blames me as much as she does."

"Hector, it wasn't your fault," I said. "Kids play. There are hundreds of things that could happen to anyone at any time. You can't stop them all."

He smiled weakly at me. "That's why this day is so damn hard on me."

"You are allowed to not be perfect," I whispered. "This may sound weird, but can we try something?"

His eyebrow arched, but he nodded. I moved to the edge of the sofa and patted my lap. "Lay down," I said.

"What?"

"Lay down. Put your head on my lap."

He hesitated.

"We've crossed enough professional lines tonight. What's one more?"

He did as I said, and I stroked his hair. This was the most comforting feeling in the world, what Dad did for me when I was upset.

"That feels nice," he said with a moan.

"Good. Now, why don't you try to get a little shut-eye?"

I startled when Canica jumped on the couch and curled up next to Hector. I remembered Hector saying he hadn't named her. I smiled, thinking of a six-year-old Jake naming his new pet. Hector's eyes drifted closed, and I kept petting his head, sliding my fingers through his salt-and-pepper hair. He was a beautiful specimen sleeping. His features softened the deeper into sleep he went.

When the slightest of snores escaped him, I waited a few minutes then wiggled my way out from under him. Neither he nor Canica stirred. I went upstairs to his room and grabbed a blanket. Bringing it back downstairs, I covered him with it.

A sharp pain lanced through the center of my ribcage, and I knew it was because he was hurting. I stared for longer than I should have. His pain was breaking me.

I loved him.

I couldn't lie to myself any longer. I was *in* love with him. If I wasn't, his pain wouldn't hurt me this much.

CHAPTER 21

THE BREAKING POINT

Hector took the week off both to give his hand time to heal and to get mentally back in the game. Officially, he called the laceration on his hand a 'cooking accident' and I was the only one who knew the truth.

I thought it would feel dirty, to have a secret with him again, but it didn't. It felt natural, as if that were the order of the universe.

We didn't see each other outside of work, either. We worked on writing and revising the paper we were submitting to the medical journal via email, and we texted constantly. At first, it was so I could check up on him, but it turned into a playful and welcome distraction.

Hector: *Just sent you the first revision. Please check.*

Me: *I'm about to see a patient.*

Hector: *This is more important.*

Me: *Nothing is more important than my patients.*

Hector: *Please clear your schedule. We have to publish this before it gets out.*

Me: *I'll get to it.*

Hector: *I'm not above going to the hospital and carrying you over my shoulder to my office.*

Me: *Please don't. Keach will have a field day. I promise before you wake up tomorrow, you will have a second draft.*

Even if I knew it would bring the rumors back, I would be lying if I said I wasn't tempted. The vision of Hector storming into the hospital and picking me up in those strong arms was a welcome one.

A fantasy followed, of me in his office, taken there by force, and thrown on top of his desk—*concentrate, Carolina.* I shook it off and reread my next patient's chart before going into the exam room.

I WAS NEARLY KEELING over with exhaustion, but I managed to address all of Hector's comments on the first draft. I almost cried when I saw all of his edits and comments. I swear, there were more red corrections than my original text. But I got it done.

He didn't receive the email until three in the morning, so I wasn't expecting the texts I got starting an hour later.

Hector: *This is good, Carolina.*

Hector: *Wait, am I allowed to call you Carolina outside of work again? You never said.*

Hector: *Just sent you the second draft.*

Hector: *I'm sorry. I just realized you are probably sleeping.*

Hector: *What are you dreaming about? Tell me when you wake up.*

Hector: *I hated not seeing you this week. Even when we weren't speaking, I at least got to see you from afar.*

I woke up at eight in the morning, ready to meet Sara for the run I promised her. A smile drew on the corner of my lips at the sight of the flurry of messages from Hector.

This was going down a dangerous road. I felt deceptive, somehow, not having told him how I felt about him.

Me: *I dreamt about medicine.*

Hector: *Really?*

Me: *No. You are not privy to my dreams.*

Hector: *Noted.*

Hector: *What am I privy to?*

Me: *Whatever I decide.*

Hector: *I can live with that.*

Hector: *When this is published in a few months, may I take you to dinner to celebrate?*

Blinking, I wiped the sleep from my eyes, not certain I was reading right. This was why I hated texting. There was no additional information provided by his facial expressions or his body language.

Was he being a boss? A mentor? Or was he hinting at a date?

More importantly, did it matter?

No. I decided it didn't. He needed to know how I felt as much as I needed to know why he still wore the wedding ring. Clearly, his wife hadn't returned to his life. Nothing had changed in his house, and there was no way he would have called me over to give him stitches if Andrea was back in his life.

He was in limbo. I wouldn't enter into any sort of romantic relationship with him while he was married, but he deserved to know that I would wait for him until it was indeed over. If he ever did get divorced, something could come of our relationship. I had to find out if he felt the same way.

Us—I was already thinking of *us*. At that moment, I decided the truth had to come out. The paper wouldn't publish for a couple of months. We could use that time to reestablish the friendship I ruined when the rumors started.

Me: *I'd love to go to dinner with you when the paper gets published.*

Hector: *Really?*

Me: *Yes.*

Hector: *What about the rumors?*

Me: *Fuck the rumors.*

IT WAS LIKE CHRISTMAS MORNING. I decided to stay at Dad's house so we could look at the website together. Sara, too, came over to spend the night with me. She startled awake when I sprang up from the bed.

"It's too early." Sara moaned next to me.

"Consider it payback for all the runs you make me do."

"Are we running after?" she asked as she rubbed the sleep from her eyes.

"No. It's my day. Now, get up."

I hurried to get my slippers on and tumbled down the stairs. Dad was already in the kitchen, making coffee. He had placed my laptop on the table, and it was hard-wired to the internet. No Wi-Fi mishaps this morning. He was nothing if not practical, and today practical was precisely what I needed.

"Good morning, *Papi.*"

"*Buenos días.*" He kissed me on the cheek, and I sat in front of the laptop.

"It's not up yet," I said.

"What?" Sara asked. Her eyes half-closed, she extended her arm until Dad placed a coffee mug in her hand.

"The article isn't loaded yet."

I ordered about twenty hard copies of the journal, which would arrive in a few days. Dad requested copies so he could give them out to our extended family. He didn't care if most of them wouldn't know what any of it meant, or the significance of it. He didn't care about any of it. All he wanted to do was brag.

Refreshing the button every ten seconds only increased my anxiety. As if sensing it, Sara stilled my hand.

"Why don't you give it a few minutes?" she said. "Maybe Ramiro would like to be here too."

At her suggestion, I ran to the door, but when I opened it, there he was, groggy and in pajama bottoms and a ribbed tank, but with a smile etched on his lips.

"Morning," Ramiro said.

"Good morning." I kissed him on the cheek. "Dad's got coffee going."

"Great," he grunted.

All three of us sat in front of the monitor. My leg shook under the table.

"Why don't you refresh it again?" Ramiro asked.

"She's done that already," Sara clipped, and Ramiro shot her a stink-eye.

I tried again anyway. The loading icon spun for a few beats longer than last time, and there it was—the article.

"Yes!" Dad yelled with a level of excitement I'd only seen from him during soccer games.

No. Something was wrong. I'd let Hector submit the final draft after his final approval, and surely he had made a mistake.

"What is this?" Sara asked.

There, on the screen before us, the article read: *Changes in Chemoradiation Treatment Protocols for Cervical Cancer in Women Under Thirty.* And listed as Primary Investigator: *Hector Medina, M.D.*

I scanned the list of contributors next. Listed were the physicians from the other hospitals, including Pike View and Heartland Metro. Listed in alphabetical order toward the end of the list: *Carolina Ramirez, M.D.*

It was a mistake. It had to be. Hector wouldn't do this intentionally.

"That piece of shit," Sara said through gritted teeth.

"What's going on?" Dad asked.

"He took credit for the trial," Sara said.

"What?" Dad asked.

"He listed himself as the primary investigator, and Carolina only as a contributor. He is saying it was all his idea," Sara explained to Dad.

"I'm going to kill that piece of shit," Ramiro hissed.

"No. No one is doing anything. I'm sure it was a mistake, and it can be fixed. We should be able to send a correction request to the journal."

"You are defending him?" Ramiro asked. He looked like I had slapped him.

"I don't believe he would do this," I said, pointing at the laptop.

"I hope you're right," said Ramiro. "But I don't think you are." He left after that, likely too angry to look at me again.

Take deep breaths, Carolina. "Okay. Here's what we are going to do. We are not going to panic. Dad, stay put. Please don't say anything about this to *anyone* until I find out what's going on. Sara, drive me to the hospital?"

My friend nodded. She didn't ask why she needed to drive. I was starting to panic despite having only seconds ago advised my family against doing exactly that. If this was on purpose, then I would be furious. My head swam, and there was no way I was going to be able to keep my attention on the road.

We both ran upstairs to change. I grabbed my dirty clothes from the day before, not caring one bit about the state of my appearance.

I found Hector's office empty—as in, he wasn't there, and neither were any of his few personal belongings. The solitary framed photograph of him and his mother was gone, and there wasn't another trace of him. Panic began to swell in my chest.

Next, I tried Chief Stuart's office. His secretary didn't let me inside his office. He was in a meeting, or so she led me to believe.

"That's fine. I'll wait." I sat in a chair in front of her desk, but after twenty minutes, I had to stand. I paced the small hallway in front of his office.

"What time is the meeting supposed to be over?"

She shrugged. "Could run long."

Meeting my ass. I would give him ten more minutes, and then I was going in there. If there was indeed a meeting going on, I would apologize for the interruption. If there wasn't, well, that would only throw more embers into the fire.

When the ten minutes were up, I ran in before the secretary could object.

"Chief," I said, looking around. No one was in the room with him, and he didn't seem to be on a video conference call either.

"Dr. Ramirez?" He looked up from his computer, but he didn't look surprised.

My stomach churned. "I'm sorry for interrupting, Chief, but it's urgent."

He motioned for me to sit in front of him, and I grabbed the chair across from his. "I don't have much time right now, but I can give you a few minutes."

"There has been a mistake with the article I submitted to the journal of medicine."

"Oh?"

I nodded. "Yes. It was uploaded to the website this morning, listing Dr. Medina as the primary investigator."

"I see." Chief Stuart clasped his hands over his belly.

"I was only listed as a contributor, but I was the PI, *not* Dr. Medina."

"Dr. Ramirez, I'm failing to see a problem here."

Was this man kidding me? This was *my* trial. Why would I let another person claim credit for it? I wouldn't. I would never.

"Chief," I said, disbelief etched in my tone, "the way the article published the paper gives Dr. Medina *my* credit. I'm sure it's a mistake. I couldn't find Dr. Medina in his office. I wanted to ask him about it before coming to you." I took a deep breath calming myself down. There had to be a rational explanation for this. "I'm sorry, Chief. I shouldn't have bothered you with this. I guess I just panicked. I'll write to the journal and request a correction—"

"Dr. Ramirez, I'm not sure how to tell you this, but Dr. Medina is gone."

"What?" My glare slashed through the chief.

"His contract was only for the duration of the trial. Now that phase two is done, he's gone back to the FIHR."

I blinked and shook my head. I couldn't have heard right. "Gone?"

He nodded.

As I stood to walk away in a daze, the chief stopped me. "And about that correction," he said. "You won't be submitting that."

I sat back down firmly on the chair. "Excuse me?"

"The more I think about it, the more realize it's better this way."

"With all due respect, Chief, I've spent the last three years of my life on this. It's the trial of a lifetime—"

"We have to think about what's best for the hospital."

"I've conducted research that will save so many lives. How is that not what's best for the hospital?" I hissed, hysterics starting to set in.

"It is great for the hospital. I agree. But you are still unknown in the medical community. Dr. Medina is a household name. The news of a follow-up trial at *our* hospital by *Hector Medina*, well, that would be great publicity for us."

If I could have taken a step back and looked at the bigger picture, I would have seen that it didn't really matter in the grand scheme of things. What mattered was that after publication, treatment protocols across the world would start to change, and lives would be saved.

What didn't square well with me was that something was being stolen from me, and it was something that would've had the potential to open many doors for my career.

It wasn't ambition for money. My ambition was one for knowledge and growth. After this trial, I was thinking of world-renowned oncology centers, hoping to do research there. Those thoughts would now be down the toilet if I were to follow the chief's orders.

"This isn't right. It's *my* trial." I felt like a child whining.

"Being chief isn't easy. I have to think beyond what's best for *one* doctor and think about the department and the hospital. I need to put them first."

"I won't let this happen—" I was going to say I was quitting and making the correction before he cut me off.

"Think carefully about what you are about to say. It will be your word against Dr. Medina's. The hospital will back up Dr. Medina's authorship of the paper. It's no secret he was your mentor and heavily involved in the trial. No one will question his authorship."

It felt like I was walking in slow motion getting back to Sara's car. She was waiting for me at the entrance, where she'd dropped me off earlier.

"Carolina?" she said when I got in the car. "Are you okay?"

I shook my head.

"What's wrong?"

"Hector's gone."

"Gone?"

I nodded. "Yeah. His contract is over. He left. And the chief won't let me correct the paper. Hector gets to keep authorship."

"That can't be right." Sara's nose scrunched up. "Did you talk with Hector?"

"No."

Pulling out my phone from my jeans pocket, I dialed his number. He had to explain himself.

"The number you have dialed is no longer in service. If you feel you have reached—" I hung up and threw my phone into the back seat, not caring if it cracked.

The sounds around me were far off and muffled like I was underwater. "He took my trial, Sara," I said.

When we got back to Dad's house, Sara opened the car door for me and helped me out—a complete reversal from when she had come home from the hospital two years ago. I leaned on her both for balance and for emotional support. Bile started to rise from my empty stomach, but I forced it down.

"What happened?" Dad asked, greeting us eagerly at the door.

"He took it," I said, still in disbelief.

"What did he take?" asked Dad.

"Everything."

CHAPTER 22

PRESENT DAY: SEVEN YEARS AFTER
HECTOR'S DEPARTURE

HOME

On the flight back home from the lecture in California, I didn't sleep as I usually did whenever I was in the air. I couldn't find a comfortable position, and I was left with all that time to think about the encounter with Hector—to think about our past.

I thought about that last week before he left seven years ago. Over the years, I had replayed over and over in my head every last thing he'd said. I pieced together conversations from memory, parsing them for clues as to why he had betrayed me. I did that for years, always coming up empty.

It didn't make sense. The self he presented to me seemed so genuine, it had been inconceivable to believe it was all an act. But as the weeks passed, then the months, and finally the years, without a word from him —I had to admit he had been simply *that* good. A master snake in the grass, and a fucking fantastic actor who had me believing that he actually gave a shit.

What followed in the wake of my destruction was devastating, and he didn't have to deal with it—I did. The humiliation had been somewhat internal. The majority of the hospital wasn't that involved, but those in the oncology department, as well as any of the physicians who knew me personally, all knew what happened.

It wasn't long before the vipers got to work with the gossip. As far as the oncology department was concerned, I was a slut trying to sleep myself to the top. Dr. Medina came out great in that version of the story. He wasn't having any of it and decided to leave after publishing *his* trial in order to get as far away from me as possible.

The worst part of it all was that I was credited with the reason for Heartland Metro losing a rockstar physician. It was a long time, many years, before I regained the trust of my colleagues.

I was lucky that I had enough people in my corner, people who knew my character well. If it weren't for them, I'm not sure I could have stayed at Heartland.

Then, there was Keach and his small group of friends who rarely let me forget what had happened.

It was a pleasure when, four years after the trial was published, Dr. Keach lost a hefty malpractice suit that resulted in the loss of his medical license. The only thing that could have made that moment better was if the demise of his career hadn't come at the cost of his patients' care.

The hospital was forced to take a side publicly. Not wanting negative publicity, Heartland Metro distanced itself from the Keach name and declined ongoing lucrative support from the family. The day the maternity ward took down the Keach name from its front door sign was one of the best days of my life. Dr. Keach was gone, and he wasn't leaving his last name behind to haunt me in the hospital hallways.

I HAD BEEN GONE a week on a small book tour prior to my lecture, so I wasn't surprised that Sara was over for dinner to welcome my return. On any other day, I would have been happy to see her, but now that I had grim news to share, I wasn't so sure I wanted her to be there to witness Dad blow a gasket.

How could I go into my father's home and tell him the ghost of one of the darkest periods in my life was back? He would find out sooner or later. I kept nothing from him.

The house smelled like heaven, but I didn't recognize the aroma as one from Dad's repertoire of recipes.

"Mmm," I moaned. "What did you make, *Papi?*"

"*Mija!*" He turned to me, apron still wrapped around his waist, and hugged me. "*Mole,*" he said. "Are you hungry? I tried to make Sara wait for you, but I couldn't stop the *comelona* of your friend from digging in." Dad pointed at her with the tongs in his hand.

"Hi, Caro," Sara said between bites of what I was sure was her second helping.

"You know how to make *mole?*" I asked Dad.

"I wish," Dad said. "*Mole* is a full-day affair unless you buy the pre-made stuff, which is really just sad. I got this from one of Sofia's friends."

"Who?" I asked. I thought I knew all of her friends, but I didn't think she knew anyone who knew how to make this.

"Ileana. She works at the bar a few days a month."

I thought back and remembered seeing her a few times over the years. Ileana was warm and friendly, and her smile radiated like the sun. It was hard not to feel lighter when you were around her—and this coming from someone who hardly knew her.

"How'd you get *mole* from her?" I asked.

"She doesn't work full time, and mainly works odd jobs. I went to *La Oficina* last Tuesday, and I got to talking to her." Leave it to Dad to make friends with a bartender. "When she mentioned she likes to cook, and I realized she lives pretty close by, I offered to pay her to share a few of her meals with me every week. She agreed to make extra for tonight, for your welcome home dinner. I didn't think she'd make *mole* when I told her it was a special occasion."

It warmed me to think of this woman I hardly knew spending two days making *mole* for my homecoming. I had only been gone a week, so I felt more than special to this stranger. I'd have to thank her when I saw her next.

It wouldn't have been polite to ruin such a perfect dinner with bad news. It could wait until we had finished our meal. My mouth watered when Dad lifted the lid to the pot of chicken smothered in brown sauce. I hadn't had a good *mole* in years. I served myself rice and a healthy helping of the chicken. Dad followed suit, and we both joined

Sara at the table, though she was nearly done with her current helping.

"What even is *mole*?" Sara asked as she licked her fingers.

"It's a special dish. I think Puebla is the place to go for *mole*."

"But what's in it? This sauce is delicious."

"Dad, you wanna take this one?"

"Let's see," Dad said and started checking off fingers. "It has four different kinds of dried chilies that are lightly fried, and tomatoes." Sara nodded, and he continued listing ingredients. "Fried peanuts. Fried raisins. Toasted bread crumbs, Toasted sesame seeds—"

"Raisins? *Bread?* In a sauce?" Sara asked as she placed a hand on her stomach. Her face twisted a little, and I urged Dad to go on.

"Yes. It also has lard, cinnamon, sugar, a bunch of spices," when he said *lard* and *cinnamon,* Sara's hand went to cover her mouth. "What else am I missing? Oh, if the cook is really good and it's traditional *mole,* they always burn a tortilla and put the blackened tortilla in the sauce. It's what gives it its color. They also use chicken broth."

"Dad," I said with my eyes on Sara, "you are missing the most important ingredient."

"What?" He looked up at me and scratched his head, thinking. "Oh. Yes! How did I forget the main ingredient? Chocolate!"

Dad's smile was triumphant, and Sara's cheeks filled with air like a blowfish. She ran to the bathroom, and we clearly heard her yell through the door. *"Chocolate?"*

I burst into laughter, and Dad glared at me. "You did that on purpose," he said.

"I couldn't help it. Most people who don't know what *mole* is love it when they try it but can't handle knowing it's chicken in chocolate sauce."

"That wasn't very nice."

"Consider it payback for when I wasn't warned baked beans were sweet, and I spat them out in the school cafeteria."

Sara glared at me when she joined us back at the table. "You didn't have to ruin it for me," she hissed.

"I'm sorry. It was too tempting."

We all burst out laughing then, and I hated to bring down the levity of our dinner. We were all so busy, it was hard to get together like this, but I knew they wouldn't forgive me if I met Hector the next day and didn't tell them about it.

"What's wrong?" asked my perceptive father.

"I have something to tell you."

Both Sara and Dad grew quiet and focused on me. I swallowed. "I saw Hector in California."

Sara's jaw dropped.

"How could you do this?" Dad asked. "After everything he did to you—"

"Dad, I didn't do anything. He showed up at my lecture. I had no idea he was there until the end when he asked a question."

He seemed to relax a little when I said that. I winced as I went on. "He wants to see me tomorrow."

"No, Carolina," he said. "I forbid it."

"I think I'm going to go home now," Sara said. She never liked upsetting my dad. "I'll talk with you later, Caro."

"Yeah. Talk later."

Chicken, I thought.

I started loading the dishwasher as I listened to Dad go on.

"You can't seriously be considering seeing him."

"I am, Dad. I need some answers—"

"After everything—how could you? You broke my heart. It was so bad, Carolina, it's like you weren't there, but *I* was. You were devastated."

I swallowed hard. I knew I'd put Dad through a lot when Hector first departed. The chief had granted me a week off work until things settled down a bit at the hospital. I hadn't cried. It was like I had no feelings, a complete void of any emotion, a perpetual state of being in darkness.

After that, it didn't get much better. I finally snapped out of it enough to get back to work, but then I threw myself into work in an unhealthy way. I became a robot. I'd been hellbent on recuperating my reputation and outdoing my first trial.

In all that, I left Dad to worry. He must have felt so helpless, seeing me go through a depression like that, and then been completely shut out from my life so quickly after.

"I know it was hard, Dad. But it's different now."

"How is it different?"

"*I'm* different now. More experienced. And I have the advantage of knowing what he really is now. I'm not starstruck. I'm the star now."

He smiled weakly. "You are, *pero mija,* I don't understand why you would even entertain the idea of talking to him."

"To be honest, I don't really understand it myself. He said he had a lot to say to me. I guess part of me still wants an explanation, or at the very least an apology, for what he did."

The dishes loaded and the kitchen clean, I turned to look at him. He cocked his head to the side, and his eyes narrowed. "Are you sure that's all it is?" he asked. "Curiosity and a desire for vindication?"

"Yes, Dad. I promise I'll be really careful."

"Tell *him* to be careful. I better not lay eyes on him."

I chuckled. "I'll warn him, Dad."

~

IN THE MORNING, I was awakened by a call from Sara.

"Does your husband know you are calling me at all hours of the morning?" I groaned into the phone.

"*My husband* is sound asleep upstairs. Don't worry about it."

"Okay," I said.

"So I know your dad already laid it on thick, which is why I decided to leave, but, Caro, you can't be serious."

"You too?"

"Yes, me too."

The truth was, I wasn't sure what I was feeling. Something about Hector made me want to trust him all over again. I couldn't quite put a finger on it. I knew I couldn't be so stupid as to fall for the same trick twice, but there had been something in his eyes. It didn't seem like threat.

"Look," Sara said when I didn't answer again. "I think, when you saw him, you probably stopped thinking straight. I wanted to talk with you before you saw him."

"Okay," I said, sitting up in my bed to fully wake up for this conversation. "Shoot."

"Think clearly, Carolina. Do you remember everything he did?"

"Of course I remember. It was seven years ago, but it is definitely fresh in my mind. I didn't get over it quickly."

"Good. But just in case, let me remind you. First, he tried to seduce you when he was *married*. Next, he let the entire hospital speak about you without defending you *once*. And for his grand *pièce de résistance*, he stole your trial. A trial you had been working on for years. As if *that* weren't enough, he took the credit for *your* trial. He left town, leaving you to deal with the fallout, and Carolina, *the rumors*, they almost destroyed your career."

While she finished her rant, I rubbed my temple. She was giving me a headache. "Trust me," I said. "I haven't forgotten any of it. Dad already covered this last night but thank you for worrying about me."

"You are still seeing him, aren't you?"

"I have to. I can't explain it, but I have to. I need answers."

Sara let out a sigh of resignation. "Fine, but *please* be careful."

"I will. Promise."

"Love you."

"Love you too."

I had to give it to my family. They had really reminded me of my hatred for Hector Medina. My blood was nearly scorching by the time I started to get ready to go see him. He was going to have to hear me out too.

CHAPTER 23

THE TRUTH

Deciding what to wear to a meeting with my nemesis was no easy task. I didn't want to give him the wrong impression by trying too hard, but I also needed to feel confident. In the end, I selected dark denim jeans, a burnt-orange chunky sweater, and topped the outfit off with knee-high brown boots. I left my long waves loose around my shoulders and took a deep breath in front of the mirror. *You got this, Carolina.*

Fall had barely begun to turn the city umber, but the chill was already prominent. Hector had coffee waiting on the table by the time I arrived at the café. He wore a thin, grey sweater that clung to every muscle of his torso—not that I noticed—with jeans and white sneakers.

"Carolina," he said. "Thank you for coming."

"Dr. Medina," I said curtly.

"I can get you a different coffee if you'd like. This one is probably cold."

I'd intentionally shown up twenty minutes late for our meeting. He needed to know who had the upper hand here. I held the cards, and that had to be clear.

"This is fine," I said, without tasting the coffee.

"You are never late," he noted.

"I'm never late when it's something *important*." I took a sip and tried to ignore the smile playing at the corner of his lips. "Dr. Medina, I'm a busy woman. You said you have a lot to say to me, so I suggest you get started." I glared at him.

"Can we start by using first names?"

"No."

He drew his hands up in defense. "Okay. This will do for now."

"What do you want? Why are you here?" I shot each question at him rapid-fire.

"I'm here for you."

I scoffed. Was he trying to pull this same old shit again? He couldn't be *that* stupid.

"I am," he repeated. "I stayed away as long as I could, but I figured it had been long enough."

"Speak clearly. I don't have time for games."

"I'm not trying to play any games. I swear."

"Then, *please,* tell me why you are here."

"I think it's time you heard my side of the story."

"Are you talking about what happened when you were last at Heartland Metro?"

He nodded.

"The right to tell your side of the story passed you by nearly seven years ago, Doctor."

He closed his eyes at my cool tone. "Just as well," he said. "I'd very much like to tell you what happened from my point of view. I owe you that much."

"You have no idea exactly how much you owe me."

Hector leaned back in his chair. He cleaned his glasses once before putting them back on his face and started speaking again.

"I'll get to it then. I submitted the paper *we* worked on after the last edits you sent me. At the time, I didn't realize Chief Stuart had a *personal* relationship with someone from the editorial staff at the medical journal."

"That son of a bitch," I hissed.

Hector nodded again.

"He knew we were submitting the paper soon. He alerted his contact at the journal, and the request to change authorship to me was made without my knowledge."

"Is that supposed to make me feel better, Hector? That you didn't want your name listed as PI? Because it doesn't. You should have requested a correction."

"I couldn't. My hands were tied."

"That's convenient—"

"Please, Carolina. Hear me out. I think you'll be glad you did."

I tried to relax my muscles a bit, but the tense situation made it difficult. "Go on."

"The night before the article would be uploaded to the journal website, I was paged to the hospital. When I got there, they told me to report to the chief's office, and he told me what he had done.

"I told him I would request the correction, but he ordered me not to. He had leverage over me at the time, and my hands were tied. Believe me, Carolina. If I could have fought it, I would have. We had a heated conversation, and I gave him an ultimatum. Either the authorship would be corrected, or I would end my contract at Heartland Metro."

"He told me your contract was over at the conclusion of my trial," I said.

"It wasn't. I had an ongoing contract, but I had the prerogative to end it whenever I wanted. It was one of the perks of being in that position." His ego reared its head.

"Don't get so cocky, Doctor. Don't forget that he chose to keep the authorship in your name instead of keeping you."

"Touché," he said.

"What I don't understand is why did he do it?"

"I have my theories, but it's probably better that you talk with him directly."

"Chief Stuart is no longer at Heartland. He retired a couple of years back."

"Yes, I know. Once he retired, I requested the correction in the journal of medicine."

"That was you?" I asked, my heart quickening in pace. He had fixed it.

All this time, I had no idea why, years later, the journal had reached out to me with the correction. Did Hector think I was going to thank him for doing the very least he could have done?

I shrugged. "But I'd still like to hear your theories about why Dr. Stuart did it."

"All right. Do you remember when the results first came in? A doctor from Peak View in California was interested in you?"

"Yes. I remember. I turned their offer down."

"They didn't pull it?"

"No, why?"

"The chief wasn't too happy about the attention you were getting. When Peak View expressed interest, the chief perked up. He couldn't afford to lose you, but he couldn't afford a hefty competing offer while at the same time offering Dr. Keach the fellowship and an attending position."

"He was always going to have to make that choice."

"Yes. But was Heartland's offer even close to Peak View's?"

"Initially, it was, but it was conditional on the retirement of an attending who would leave the spot open."

"Did it change after the article was published?"

"Yes. It went quite a bit down."

"And I bet you had already turned down all other offers, thinking you had the luxury of staying in your hometown."

"He was running out the clock," I said.

"It's all speculation on my part, but I have a feeling that version of events is pretty close to the truth. The only other thing I could come up with was that his relationship with the Keaches was deeper and more twisted than we knew. He clearly wanted to sabotage your chances."

"He sabotaged more than just my chances," I said dryly.

"I'm sure it must have been tough. Carolina, what happened after I left?"

I cupped the mug between my hands, seeking warmth, and narrowed my eyes at him. Here went nothing. "You took my reputation with you," I said. "It took me a long time to gain back the trust of my colleagues, and it was two years before I could get a doctor to sign on to a grant proposal of mine again."

"I'm so sorry. I can't begin to tell you how sorry I am."

"I'm not sure I believe you," I said.

"You are smart. You shouldn't believe me. I wouldn't take my word for it if the situation were reversed."

He let a long silence pass before he spoke again. "Despite all the damage I did, your second trial was another success. I have to admit, I was surprised by the numbers. It's rare to see two back-to-back trials both so highly successful."

"Yeah, well, I had something to prove at that point. You know what the shittiest part of it all is?" I asked him.

"What's that?"

"You remember that supplemental grant proposal we submitted, to keep following up on the patients from the first trial?"

"Yeah, vaguely."

"The grant got funded."

"It did? That's great! Why is that the shittiest part?"

"Because to the world, it was *your* trial, but in reality, I had to deal with all the work involved."

Hector chuckled. "I'm sorry about that. Maybe you'll let me make it up to you one day."

I found myself smiling despite myself. That supplemental grant had actually been a lifesaver—a flotation device in a vast and empty ocean. It had kept me occupied, and I got to stay in touch with my patients. The money awarded with the grant kept my foot inside the door at Heartland when all signs pointed to my termination.

"Can you give me time, Carolina?" he asked.

"Time for what?"

"To show you that I'm telling you the truth. That I've never lied to you, and I never would."

I nodded, without permission from my brain.

"You look the same," he said, changing the subject.

It was a lot to digest, so I didn't halt the change in the conversation's direction.

"Wish I could say the same. You look older," I clipped.

Hector chuckled. "Yeah. I'm an old man. You must forgive me. We old men are stuck in our ways."

I knew he was eleven years my senior. It was a gap that hadn't both-ered me back when I was hoping for more from him. Dad had been nine years older than my mother when they met, and they were the happiest couple I'd ever known.

"I'm not sure what you are expecting from me, exactly."

"I expect nothing," he said. "I only hope for time."

I was still suspicious, but my walls began to crumble the more he spoke. Everything he said made sense. I'd come into the café ready to tell him off, and yet here I was, doubting everything I believed I knew about him, and what had happened all those years ago.

"Listen, I have some things to get ready and some errands to run."

"Sure. I don't know how I feel about everything you've said, but I promise to think on it. There are still holes in this story."

"There are," he said. "Would you please have dinner with me on Friday? I'd like to fill in those gaps—start earning your trust back."

"I don't know, Hector. Don't you think it's better to let bygones be bygones?"

"No," he said. "Not when you don't have all the information. Just think about it. Here's my card."

I looked at the simple white card with his name, email, and phone number. The anger flooded back at the memory of that day when I had called him for an explanation, and his phone had been disconnected.

"I wouldn't hold my breath," I said.

"I'll keep trying."

CHAPTER 24

MENTORSHIP

I was picking up my mail when my phone dinged with a message.

Unkown: *Have you given any thought to dinner?*

Hector. Of course he still had my number. I'd never changed it.

Me: *I haven't decided yet.*

Hector: *Tell me nothing of what I said brought up more questions. Please let me complete the story.*

Me: *We'll see.*

He stopped messaging after that. When I got back to my apartment, I scanned through my mail and was surprised to find a hand-written personal letter. My pulse quickened when I saw the name on the upper left corner of the envelope: Andrea Carter.

With trembling hands, I tore open the letter and read, and then read it a second time:

~

DEAR CAROLINA,

I'm sure you can guess the Andrea writing this letter is also the Andrea who was once married to Hector. I've taken my second husband's last name. I wanted to explain the change.

I know it's strange to receive a letter from me—I can hardly believe I'm writing it at this very moment, but I'm forcing myself to put this in the mailbox because while I may no longer be in love with Hector Medina, I will always cherish him as the father of our child. I still want his happiness.

Marisela has informed me that he is headed back to Kansas City and we can only assume he is trying to get you back. Please don't be mad at Marisela. We only want Hector's happiness, and she has convinced me you are the key.

Can you believe I am trying to wing-man my own ex-husband? I'll have my head examined about it soon.

Hector and I check in on each other on tough dates. Jake's birthday, holidays —that kind of thing. We remember our son together and keep the memory of him alive in our hearts. It's also a time to make sure the other is doing well. The last few times I've spoken with Hector on the phone have left me worried about him. He isn't happy, and now I know that unhappiness has everything to do with the distance and years he's placed between the two of you.

I know seven years is a long time, and I so hope you haven't moved on, because Hector hasn't. If you love him even a fraction of the way he loves you, then please, give him a chance.

If you do end up together like I'm hoping, I promise to never meddle again. And I sincerely hope you'll be okay with our check-ins with each other. Please trust they are all about Jake.

From a new friend,
Andrea Carter.

WHEN ONE DOOR CLOSES, a window opens—somewhere. It may sound contrived and even useless in dire circumstances, but it is also true. I wasn't lying to that university student at my lecture when I told her that there are great female mentors in the field of medicine, even if they are rare. *Extremely* rare.

In my case, I had found a unicorn during Hector's time away.

Dr. Monica Lopez joined Heartland Metro Hospital as the Chief of

Cardiothoracic Surgery a year after Hector's departure. She was a female chief, which was rare, and Latina, which was even rarer. I had thanked the gods for sending me another mentor even if she was in another department.

Dr. Lopez understood many of the difficulties all women, and women of color especially, face when trying to enter any male-dominated field. She had been instrumental in helping me get back on track when everything had seemed lost.

She was also a no-bullshit kind of gal, so I knew she would have an unbiased opinion. I had always been grateful to her for also advising me on personal matters.

She agreed to chat between surgeries, but only if I brought food to her office, so I stole some of Dad's leftover chicken mole and rice for lunch.

"Carolina." Dr. Lopez greeted me from behind her desk as I entered her office. She wore light blue hospital scrubs and still had her scrub cap on. In her mid-fifties, Dr. Lopez was a stunning woman. She was short and curvy in all the right places. Her long, rectangular face was perfectly framed by thick, black curls when they weren't pinned back under a scrub cap. I only hoped that I aged half as well as she had. "How was your book tour?" she asked.

"It was good—mostly."

"Uh-oh. I know that look. What happened?"

"No, really, the book tour was great. All the talks went smoothly; I was able to manage my stage fright."

"No, missy, I know you. Something's off."

I handed her the lunch, and her eyes closed when she smelled the opened container. "You didn't cook this."

"No," I admitted.

"I wasn't asking. I *know* you didn't cook this."

I smirked. "No. Dad's friend did. You are safe, Dr. Lopez."

She took a bite and moaned. "You are a lifesaver, Carolina. My last surgery was ten hours long, and I have to go back in with my next patient in two hours."

"I'll keep this short then. I'm sure you'll want to sleep."

"Out with it, then."

"I would like some personal advice."

"Sure," she said between bites.

"Dr. Medina is back in Kansas City," I said.

The fork in her hand stopped mid-air on the way to her mouth. "What?"

I nodded, and she put the fork down so she could study me.

Dr. Lopez knew everything Hector had done—from my perspective. She'd caught some of the rumors when she first came to Heartland and advised me on how to handle them. She was so experienced, and she often made my head spin. I relayed all the information Hector had given me at the café.

"It's plausible," she said and reclaimed the fork to keep eating. "From what I hear, Dr. Stuart's *priorities* left the oncology department in a bit of a disarray. But your new Chief of Oncology should have more insight. Why are you talking to me and not her?"

"I respect her and value her opinion," I said. "But she is my boss; I don't really talk with her about personal stuff."

"I see you still keep up unnecessary walls."

"I'm working on it."

"Fine, so what's the problem now?"

"Hector wants to have dinner tonight. Says he has more to say. I was so angry at him then, I don't know what to do."

"And you don't want to have dinner with him?"

"I didn't, at first, but I still have questions. "

Dr. Lopez chewed as she mulled over everything I had said, so I continued. "Then, there's the fact that his wife sent me a letter."

"What?" She almost spat out the bite she was working on.

"Yeah. It was so strange, Monica. I swear I don't know what to make of it."

"What did it say?"

"She wants me to give Hector a chance."

"That is super weird," she said, but there was a twinkle in her eye, and the corners of her mouth turned upward into a smirk. "But I *like* this woman. She has *cojones*."

I threw my head back with laughter. "Yeah. I guess she does."

"Honestly, Carolina, I don't know why you are here. If you could stop listening to your head for even a second, you'd know what your heart wants."

I sighed and rubbed my temple but said nothing to that, because what could I say? She was right.

"Or are you too proud?" she asked.

"Too proud?"

"Yes. *Too proud.* Don't let an opportunity pass you by due to pride. I'll say it plainly: that would be stupid. Are you too proud to forgive him now that you know he didn't really intend to steal your trial?"

"It's not just that. I didn't have answers for seven years; that's a lot of time to forgive."

"Yes. I see it now. The pride—"

"Oh my god, it's not that—"

"It is, and we both know it. You've always had a chip on your shoulder, trying to prove yourself. I recognize it because it's the very same chip I carried on my shoulder for the first two decades of my career— only I didn't have an amazing mentor to point it out to me and help me shake it off."

"What on earth are you talking about?" I asked. "I don't have a chip."

"Yes, you do. Or are you going to tell me that proving to every man in this hospital that you belong here hasn't been the driving force of your career? Are you going to tell me that anytime someone made a comment about affirmative action being the only possible way you could have become a physician, it didn't bother you because you knew better?"

"I don't see what that has to do with Hector," I said.

"Everything, *amiga.* I saw how hard you worked to regain the respect your name once carried. You had to prove to the world, and more importantly, to yourself, that you could thrive without him. You did such a good job, now you are convincing yourself you don't need him— and before you say anything, no, you don't *need* him for your career to continue to flourish. But what if you *do* need him in your life, even when you don't need him in your career?"

"What are you dancing around, Dr. Lopez?" I asked.

"What if you love him?"

"I did once," I admitted.

"And are you so sure it's gone? Because just you, sitting here, in that chair, agonizing about whether you can believe him again or not, tells me there are still feelings there. If you are so done with him, as you seem to be convincing yourself you are, then it would be easy to dismiss him and move on without a glance backward."

Sometimes I hated this woman and all the sense she made. I narrowed my eyes at her.

"I know you, darling," she said. "And you wouldn't be here if you didn't already know what to do."

"You talk about me like I'm a petulant child throwing a tantrum."

Dr. Lopez placed the lid on the now empty container and handed it to me. "Aren't you?" she asked as she stood and pushed her chair to the side. "Feel free to stay here and think for a while if you'd like. I'm going to an on-call room to get a couple of hours of sleep before my next surgery." Before she closed the door behind her, she spoke once more. "Oh, and Carolina, when you come to your senses, I'd love to meet him."

She shut the door, and I sat there looking out the window. She was right, damn it, and it was so annoying. I knew I wanted to give him another chance to complete the story, but it would be the absolute last chance.

CHAPTER 25

RECOUNTING OF THE DAMAGE

"Fine. I'll go to dinner," I said, holding the phone to my ear. It was Friday afternoon, and I had waited until the last possible moment to agree to see him. We were on my timeline now.

"You won't regret it. I promise," Hector said.

"Where should I meet you?"

"I'll pick you up."

"Okay. Fine."

"Will you be at your apartment, or your dad's?"

"My place, but I live in a different apartment now."

I sent him the new address, and all that was left was to wait for him. It might have been safer to wait for him at Dad's, but I hadn't exactly told Dad about my dinner with Hector yet.

Mainly, he would have to tell me what leverage the chief had had on him then. It didn't escape me that he'd left that part of the conversation out. I hadn't asked him about it, thinking it might be personal, but I had to know—and he'd have to tell me.

"You look great," Hector said as he got out of his car to open the door for me. I hadn't wanted to give him my apartment number—there was still some distrust there—so I told him I'd wait outside.

I may have overdressed in a body-hugging little black dress because he wouldn't tell me where we were going. I decided to err on the side of caution in case we went someplace nice.

"Thank you," I said, purposefully not commenting on his appearance, though he looked handsome as ever in slacks and a button-down burgundy shirt.

My jaw clenched when he parked in front of his house. I was surprised he still lived at the same place he had when he worked at Heartland. Had he kept the house the entire time, or was he merely lucky to rent or re-purchase the same home?

I'd have to ask him later because I was doing everything in my power not to shout at him. I didn't wait for him to open my door; I got out of the car and started walking away from the house as I pulled out my cell to find my car service app. He was insane if he thought I was going to have dinner in *there.*

"Carolina!" he shouted. I heard the rapid footfalls of his jogging behind me. He grabbed my arm. "Where are you going?"

"I'm going home, Hector."

"Why? What's wrong?"

"You can't be *that* stupid," I said. "What made you think I'd have dinner with you at *your house?*"

"Please, just listen. This isn't something nefarious. I brought you here because some of what I have to say, it may make you a bit mad."

My eyes narrowed, but I didn't press the key to call the car yet. "Mad?" I asked.

Hector nodded. "I figured you might enjoy shouting at me or perhaps throwing something. I wanted you to feel comfortable doing that if you wanted to."

"You are not making me feel better about this dinner," I said.

"I'm sorry. I knew you wouldn't like a public scene. Listen, I've cooked, and I have nothing but dinner and your wrath planned for tonight. I promise."

"What did you cook?" I asked, only mildly curious.

"Shrimp *paella,*" he said.

"I like *paella*."

"I know." He smiled, and it melted me.

I reluctantly followed him to his place because I was weak, but I kept the car app open should I change my mind.

"I made it earlier today. I'm just going to pop it in the oven for a few minutes to warm up."

I nodded and took a glass of white wine from him. I guessed the no alcohol rule had been abolished—not that he had heavily enforced it before.

When he handed me the glass, I realized for the first time since he'd come back into my life that his wedding ring was gone. I took a sip of the wine, and it was heavenly. It was a *vino verde* with a mineral tone that made me think of the sea.

I took the room in. Nothing had changed in the house since I'd helped him decorate it. So he *had* kept the house. For a brief moment, I wondered if he had somehow remained in Kansas City under the radar but then shook it off. There was no way. He had returned to the FIHR.

"You haven't changed anything," I said.

"No," he called from the kitchen. "I wouldn't. Not unless you wanted to change something."

I cocked my head to the side and studied him as he walked back into the living room. That was a strange thing for him to say. We both sat on the couch and set our wine glasses on the coffee table.

"Okay, Hector. I'm not getting any younger."

"Why don't we have dinner first? It would be a waste if you were too angry to eat, and I worked all day to make this dinner." There was a playfulness in his eyes as he spoke, and I was finding it more and more difficult to school my face into sternness.

Hector set the dinner at the table and played Carla Morrison in the background. The soothing sound of her voice was relaxing, and the mood lifted as we ate and killed the bottle of wine. He plated the *paella* expertly, so it was almost a sin to devour it, but devour it, I did.

"No!" Hector said in disbelief when I briefed him on Dr. Keach's fate.

"Yes. It was one of the best days of my life. Okay, I won't give him that much importance, but easily one of the top twenty."

"I wish I could have been there."

"Me too. I tried to stay away from him, so I didn't actually know what was happening until it was over."

"Still, that must have been a relief."

"It was, though, by the end of his tenure at the hospital, things were already a lot better for me. The new chief is a woman, and I think she recognized his misogyny for what it was."

"I wouldn't be surprised if Dr. Stuart also knew about his misbehavior but looked the other way. Your new chief must not have been willing to put up with it for money."

"You know, I'm a little surprised at all these accusations you're making against Dr. Stuart."

"How so?"

"He wasn't the best boss, sure, but back then, before he screwed me over, I really thought he was a good man. A good doctor. I respected him for many years."

"And even after he did what he did to you, you feel this way?"

I shifted in my seat. "No. I guess it's easier to believe after that."

"Some people are really good at acting, Carolina."

"Like you?" My eyes narrowed.

"No, baby. I'd never put up a false front with you."

My guard came down, and I blinked at him. Had I heard him right? Had he just called me *baby*? I must have heard him wrong. I shook my head, but his eyes held mine. "All right, Hector. We've had dinner. Will you please stop wasting my time? Tell me whatever it is you have to say."

"Would you at least tell me if you liked dinner?" he asked.

"It was okay." I crossed my arms over my chest and smirked.

Hector chuckled. "Oh, I think it was more than okay."

"No. That's your ego talking."

He chuckled again. "Okay." He stood and started picking up the dishes. I recognized he was trying to keep his hands busy to have this difficult conversation. I did the same thing when I was nervous. I stood and started clearing the table with him, but not before kicking off my heels.

"I know my mother might have mentioned Andrea when she was here."

I tried not to show any anger on my face. Did he not know Andrea had written to me? "Your wife? What does she have to do with anything?"

"Everything," Hector said. "When I joined Heartland Metro, we had been separated for several years already. That entire time, I had refused to give her a divorce. I knew it was over, and that we'd never get what we had back, but I was stubborn."

"I believe it," I said, fully recognizing his stubbornness. So far, everything Andrea had written was matching up with Hector's account of events.

"What you need to understand is that I came to Heartland only for you. At first, it was for your work. I was excited about medicine for the first in a long time when I heard about this young doctor who was inspired by my work, pushing the envelope of what was possible."

I smiled at the sight of his excitement, but I wasn't connecting the dots yet. He continued.

"Then I met you, and Carolina, *everything* changed. You have to believe that. I was suddenly less concerned about the perfect life and the perfect marriage I had drawn up for myself. Suddenly, giving Andrea a divorce didn't seem like the worst defeat of my life."

"But you didn't go through with it," I said.

"Actually, I did," he said, wincing a little at the words.

"*What?*" I asked through gritted teeth.

"I signed that first year I was at Heartland Metro. Within a year, it was finalized."

"What?" I hissed again. I couldn't form full sentences at that moment.

"I was divorced soon after I met you, Carolina. I was hoping we could have—"

"But you never said anything," I interrupted him. "You always wore the wedding ring."

"The divorce was finalized in that two-year period when you wouldn't talk with me."

"And after that, when things were better between us?"

"I couldn't bear to do it. The rumors had taken their toll and had just started to dissipate. I would have been damned before I let them affect your career any further than they already had. So I kept it to myself and kept wearing the ring, letting everyone believe I was still married."

"Hector, you should have told me," I said forlornly. "Back then, I wanted . . . *more*," I said.

"I know, baby. You weren't very good at hiding your feelings. Neither was I. Why do you think the rumors caught fire like that?"

"I always blamed Keach."

"Sure. He ignited the rumors, but the blaze was all us. Even when it was clear we weren't on speaking terms, some still wondered if we'd actually had an affair that had ended badly."

"Don't remind me," I said.

"I wouldn't have believed us either."

"You give yourself a lot of credit."

"Come on. We've wanted each other for almost a decade. Since that first day in the conference room, I needed to know who you were. I couldn't imagine you were the doctor I had come here for. I can't tell you what it felt like, knowing it was you."

"Speak for yourself. I haven't said I've wanted you for years."

Hector chuckled. "Tell yourself what you want, baby. I know what I see in your eyes—what I've seen since the first day we met."

"What's that?"

Hector moved toward me, his chest puffed like a predator. I took a step back until I couldn't move any further against the kitchen island behind me. He caged me in with both his hands on either side of me, pressed firmly to the countertop.

"Desire, Carolina." Letting his grip off the countertop, he cupped my face in his hands, lifting my face to meet his. "I see it right there, in your eyes right now."

I dropped my gaze from him and let out a breath. He wasn't wrong, but damn him for knowing. The slight buzz from the wine electrified the sensation of his hands on my skin, and I had zero willpower to break free.

Hector grabbed me by the waist and lifted me to sit on the countertop. My eyes widened with the surprise of the movement, but then my legs parted, making room for him to press his body against mine. The air crackled around us.

He ran his fingers through my hair and cupped the back of my head, holding me in place. "Hector," I moaned his name. My breath was coming in choppy, and I didn't have the power in my limbs to push him away. I wasn't even sure I wanted to anymore.

"Tell me. Tell me you didn't want me then, and tell me you don't want me now. Set me straight, Carolina. This is your chance. Tell me I imagined it all."

My eyes met his because I was no chicken-shit. I could see from behind the light stubble that his jaw was clenched as he waited for my answer. "I can't," I said with a challenging gaze. "It wouldn't be true." His eyes roamed my face looking for sincerity in it, finding an invitation instead.

His other arm was now around my waist, pulling me flush against him. He let go of my body and brought his hand back up, this time finding my lips. With his thumb, he rubbed my bottom lip, swiping from one side to the other, while my hands pressed against his hard chest.

"I've wanted to touch you like this for so long." His voice was deeper and now suddenly raspy. When he spoke, my skin broke into goose-bumps, and my legs wrapped around his waist without my command, pulling him closer.

When his lips finally made contact with mine, the last nine years fell away. Every reason we had for not being together was gone. My hatred, even, had mellowed to a low flicker in the distance.

It was a gentle kiss—at first. He explored my mouth with restraint and grazed my teeth tentatively with the tip of his tongue. The smell of his musk mingled with the crisp taste of the wine still on our lips, and a moan escaped me. The hand he had cupping the back of my head bunched into a fist in response to the sound, sending a prickling sensation through my scalp. But the pain mixed with pleasure, and I could not voice a protest. I didn't want to.

My eyes flew open when I felt the length of him hardening through the layers of clothing. His slacks, my pantyhose, and underwear separated me from what my body *needed*.

I tightened the muscles of my legs to grip him even closer to me if that were possible. I needed to feel *all* of him. He pulled me away by the hair still in his fist, and he chuckled. The void I felt at his mouth no longer on mine was unbearable. The need for him was unmatched by anything I had felt for anyone, ever—by a longshot.

"My eager little Carolina," he said in a breathy voice. "We have plenty of time. Let me enjoy this."

Hector's grip pulled my hair, forcing my head back and exposing my neck to him. I grabbed on to his broad shoulders for balance. He kissed my jaw, then trailed kisses down my neck.

"I love you," he whispered, and my every muscle turned to stone. My hands dropped away from him and found the counter. My legs unraveled from him, retreating from his body and finding their way back to mine.

"What did you say?"

"I love you. I've loved for a long time."

My face twisted at his words, and I pushed him away. He let go of my hair so he could look at my face, which was now serious. He groaned with frustration, but he stepped back and away from me.

"You were talking about *desire*, Hector. Desire and love are two very different things."

"You must have known," he countered, now looking angry.

"No. You didn't love me. Someone who loves someone doesn't put them through what you have put me through."

"Someone who loves someone," he said, his teeth gritted, "will do anything, even if it means staying away for nearly a decade, before hurting them."

"What are you talking about?" I jumped off the counter and straightened my dress.

"Carolina, do you think I could have kept you, knowing that either way things played out, I would be hurting you?"

"Hurting me?" I shook my head. None of his words were making sense. "What are you talking about?"

"I was in a classic no-win situation. If we had been weak at the conference hotel that night, the rumors would have been true, and they would have ruined your career."

"But we weren't. We didn't do anything wrong."

"Like that mattered? Look at what happened anyway."

"Hector, that wasn't your fault."

"Yes, it was!" His voice raised a little. "And what if we had done things right? What if after my divorce came through, we had gotten together? What then? The hospital would have had a problem with it because I was your boss. But maybe I tried to solve the problem for you and left Heartland. Maybe I found another hospital so we could stay together—"

That was a beautiful possibility lost. "What would have been wrong with *that*?"

"Let's play this out. Do you think you would have the career you have now if everyone believed you slept your way to the top?"

I wanted to slap him. I wanted to slap him so much my palm tickled with the anticipation of contact, but I forced it to remain at my side. "I wouldn't have done that," I hissed.

"No. But that's what they would have all believed. But if we had gone further?"

"What do you mean?"

"What if I had proposed, because I wanted to Carolina, I wanted to propose to you back then. I was going to at our celebration dinner, but it never happened."

"You were going to *propose*?" I spoke gently, eerily gently, because the anger was swelling up in waves, and my breath kept getting caught in them.

"Yes. I was. But then I talked to the chief, and he opened my eyes. And he wasn't wrong, Carolina. What do you think would have happened if I had gotten my stupid happily-ever-after?"

"Well, I guess we will never know, will we?" I started to look for my shoes. I had to get out of there but couldn't remember where I'd kicked them off. Hector followed me around as I looked for them.

"Don't be obtuse. Dr. Stuart didn't point out anything I didn't already know, but I wanted to pretend I didn't. And you knew it too."

"I don't know what you are talking about, but this conversation is over."

"No, it isn't. Listen to me. If you had done me that honor and said yes, the honeymoon period would have ended so soon."

"Great to know you had so little confidence in the possibility of us—"

"That's not what I mean, and you know it. Carolina, would you be happy right now, if all your career you wondered if you achieved what you have achieved because you earned it, or because your husband was Hector Medina?"

I turned to face him again. "That's what stopped you?"

"Mostly." He cupped the back of his neck. He seemed calmer now, but sadder too. "The other part of it was Stuart's leverage."

"Yes, Hector, please tell me, what did he have over your head that was so important?"

"You."

"Me?"

"Yes. He was ready to sink your career if I didn't keep my name on the paper—and he could have done it too. That's why I had to wait to correct the authorship on our paper. I had to wait for him to be gone. I couldn't do that to you. And I couldn't stay and continue to have him use you like a pawn. I just couldn't, Carolina. I had to remove myself from the picture. I needed you to know that anything you achieved was because of you—and in spite of me. I didn't want anyone to ever think it was *because* of me."

"So, *you* decided."

"Don't you see? Everything I have done has been for you. I went to Heartland Metro for you, and I had to leave to protect you. I've stayed away for the same reason. Everything is always for you. You are my life, baby." He moved closer to me, his eyes softer, trying to appease me.

"No." I shook my head. "You chose. We lost nine years we could've had—"

"Let's not lose any more—"

"No. Not when *you* decide. You will never call the shots for me again, do you hear me?" I was shouting at him now, and I did my best to keep the tears pricking my eyes from escaping down my cheeks.

He looked at me like I had slapped him, even though I had the grace to resist. "You stole nine years from me and didn't have the decency to tell me. How could you do it?"

"I did it *for* you."

I found my shoes and put them on then made my way toward the door. Hector hadn't noticed when I had called the car, and I got the notification that it was waiting outside.

"Don't walk out on me, Carolina. We aren't over—not like this."

"Everything has been up to you, Hector. It's time to realize you are not my keeper," I said and walked out of his house.

CHAPTER 26

FIGHT OF FIGHTS

My driver witnessed my breakdown on the car ride home. The tears I was so hell-bent on keeping from Hector spilled over with gusto. The driver looked in his rear-view mirror several times and asked if I was okay. I could only nod.

When I arrived at my apartment, I didn't even try to get to bed. I knew I wouldn't sleep. My entire body was the nucleus of a bomb amassing energy before it detonated.

I'd loved him, and he had loved me back, but he took our chance away. I had no say in the outcome. I'd never felt so powerless.

It was like mourning, but I went straight to the second stage of grief: Anger. I left his house because I wanted to hit him and didn't like the violence that was building in me. A violence fueled by the passion of the moments leading up to the argument.

I rummaged through the storage bin under my bed and pulled out a gift box almost nine years old. It was wrapped in navy blue paper and tied off with an orange ribbon.

Opening the gift in front of everyone hadn't seemed appropriate, but then I'd forgotten about it after the party. It was placed in a box when I moved into a larger apartment. By the time I came across it again, the fallout had already taken place, and I couldn't bring myself to open it.

I'd come close a few times but never committed. Over the years, I would think about him and wonder what was in the box, but then the anger would wash over me, and I'd always put it away again.

I undid the frayed ribbon. Hopefully, it wasn't chocolate or something edible that had long ago turned rancid. I felt the heavy weight of it in my hands as I had so many times before. Breaking through the paper, I realized it was a book. I ran my fingers over the soft leather-bound tome. I turned it over to read the front cover and found the title of *Jane Eyre.*

When he went to my house on my birthday that day so long ago, I had found him in my room, frozen in place as he stared at the wall. I'd always assumed it was the copy of his paper that had glued him to his spot. I had thought he believed me to be a stalker but realizing now what he had brought as a gift, I had to believe he was in awe that he'd unknowingly selected my favorite book.

My eyes stung with tears. Anger and empathy battled within my body for a place in my heart. I wanted to forgive him, and I wanted to scratch his eyes out, all in the same breath.

It was reckless to drive back to his place with the rage still blinding me, but I was drawn to him even in my anger. We'd almost slept together, and I was too restless to go to sleep.

I gave myself several hours to calm down and returned to his house at four in the morning.

"Carolina?" Hector asked sleepily as he opened his front door. His bedhead waves fell over his forehead, and he wore a white t-shirt with light-blue pajama bottoms.

Not waiting for an invitation, I let myself in. As I closed the door, I leaned on it, needing the balance for strength.

"How could you do it?" I asked, and a tear rolled down my cheek.

"How could I not? Tell me you wouldn't have done the same thing had the situation been reversed and it had been *you* threatening *my* career. You wouldn't have stayed away too?"

"I don't know. But I would have talked to you about it."

"I couldn't." He swallowed hard, and his Adam's apple bobbed. "I knew you would convince me that we could work it out, and I would have been weak. I couldn't chance it. I'm so, *so*, sorry."

He stepped forward and wiped away my tear with his thumb. "Please believe it was one of the hardest things I've ever had to do."

I nodded but took his hand away from my cheek. He kept his hand in mine and led me to the couch to sit next to him. The entire house was dark; he hadn't turned on a single light when he opened the door.

"I'm glad you came back."

"I'm not sure why I did. I mean, I had to cool off. Your instincts were right. I did want to hit you earlier."

He chuckled. "My instincts are always right." His white teeth almost glowed in the dark through his grin.

"I can think of at least one time when they weren't," I said, and I knew it was like a dagger to him.

"What's it going to take for you to forgive me?"

"Forgiving has never come hard to me, Hector. It's not about forgiveness. I'm not sure I can *trust* you." And that was the truth of it. I wasn't one to hold a grudge, with scarce exception. It was incredibly easy to forgive the people I loved, but this was so different. A grudge I didn't know I'd been holding, for perhaps the first time in my life, had been brewing for years.

"That hurts," he admitted.

"I'm sorry. I'm not trying to be hurtful—just honest."

"I know." A strand of hair fell over my eyes, and Hector swept it back, tucking it behind my ear. "But I'm still glad you are back. Even if it's to wound me," he said.

"I um—" I cleared my throat. "I opened your gift," I said.

Hector's brows drew together. "My gift?"

"My birthday gift—"

He thought for a moment. "Do you mean from when I first came to Heartland Metro Hospital? The cookout for your birthday?"

I nodded.

"You hadn't opened it before now?"

I shook my head.

"That's a bit odd."

"Why did you pick that book?"

"What, *Jane Eyre?* I do have to say I was very surprised to find a poster of it in your room. But, um, I guess you reminded me of Jane."

"*I* reminded you of Jane? And more importantly, you've read it?"

"Don't get too excited. It was a college assignment, but it wasn't bad."

"Please don't give me more reasons to want to stab you," I said, and he threw his head back with laughter.

"Okay, it was good. Happy?"

"No. Not even a little. You still haven't told me why I reminded you of Jane. I'm nothing like her. She is small, and I am super tall. She's plain and simple, and I'm more of a fiery, in-your-face kind of a presence, or so I've been told."

Hector chuckled. "Well, you are right on all accounts. But you are also otherworldly, like Jane. You can't be from this planet. You are so . . . rare. Mainly though, if I remember correctly, Jane was Rochester's equal, as you were—are—mine. No one else could understand either of them on a deeper level, but they didn't have to even speak to know what was in the other's heart."

"For someone who only read it for a college assignment, you have a pretty good understanding of the novel. I read it once a year—at *least.*"

Hector gave me a side-glance but didn't comment further.

"What about the last seven years?" I asked him.

"What about them?"

"There hasn't been anyone in your life in that time? A St. John—if you will?"

"No." Hector shook his head. "I dated, especially those first few years. I was trying to forget you, but nothing ever got serious. It's hard to try to grow feelings for someone when you know your soul mate is elsewhere."

I scoffed. "We are scientists. How can you believe in soul mates?"

"I didn't use to." Hector cupped my hand in both of his and pressed it to his chest. He kept a grip on it, not letting me have my hand back. "But I'm not exaggerating when I say *everything* changed with you."

A long stretch of silence followed as I thought of what to say next. I wasn't sure why I was back here. I only knew I had no freewill to stay away.

"What about you?" Hector asked after a moment.

"What about me?"

"It killed me to think of you with Ramiro or with someone else all these years. It was excruciating not getting on a flight and claiming you as mine."

"Really?" My anger was rising again. "It always comes back to this. What is it with you and Ramiro? He is family. Always has been, always will be."

"So, you never got together with him after I left?"

"No!"

Hector let out a breath he had been holding.

"If you must know," I said. "In the last seven years, Ramiro has had two great loves. Neither of whom was me. Now, he is very happily married, and very much still someone I consider family."

"And there hasn't been anyone else?" he asked.

"Like you, I dated some, but nothing ever came of it. I was too focused on work, and most men can't handle a schedule as busy as mine."

Now that my sight had adjusted to the dark, I could make out Hector's face as his nostrils flared.

"I want to kill, just thinking about you with anyone else," he admitted.

"Don't be a hypocrite. You just told me you dated as well."

"And how did you like hearing that, baby?"

I shifted in my seat. I hadn't liked it one bit, and immediately wanted to know names, how long they had lasted, and all the sordid details. But I wasn't about to admit that to him.

"Are you back to stay the night with me, Carolina?"

My body answered before I could, and I found myself nodding. He stood and helped me up from the sofa. He then took me by surprise and lifted me off the ground. My legs wrapped around his waist, and my arms clutched around the back of his neck. It was amazing that he could carry me—I wasn't a light little feather like Sara, but this man was *strong*.

He kissed the tip of my nose before speaking again. "I won't be able to take you leaving again. It will drive me to insanity. Please tell me you are here to stay."

"I think I am," I said.

"At least promise you won't get mad at me again for the remainder of the night."

"You know I can't promise that."

Hector squeezed my ass, and I squealed. "Could you at least *try?*" he asked.

I nodded, and my jaw dropped when he carried me all the way upstairs and into his room without so much as a grunt.

Once in his room, he pressed me up against a wall, and my legs unfurled away from him, my feet finding the ground once again. I took his shirt off over his head, and my hands explored his upper body.

His shoulders and arms were massive, and his chest was firm, but his abdominal muscles weren't too obvious. I'd never really understood the fascination most women have with a six-pack. Hector was slim at the waist. An understated shadow hinted at the muscles beneath his tanned skin, but there were no overly pronounced striations.

But what really made my mouth water was the v-cut line of muscles that peeked out from above his pajama bottoms and pointed downward like a beacon leading me to my prize.

He flipped me over, and I gasped with the surprise of his sudden movements. I held onto the wall for balance as he slowly drew down the zipper of my dress. The soft caress of his fingers followed the trail of the zipper sliding down my back.

Damn it. Hector was taking too much time. I needed him *now.* I pulled off the rest of my dress from my upper body with urgency and turned around, not caring that I hadn't worn a bra. He raised his hands in surrender as I untied the string of his pajama bottoms. He chuckled at my desperate movements, the bastard.

"Here," he said, and carried me to his bed. He threw me on the mattress unceremoniously and peeled off the rest of my dress and pantyhose. He stepped back to look at me, and I suddenly became aware that I was splayed out in front of him in only a black thong. "Carolina," he said with a hoarse voice. "You are so fucking beautiful."

I shot up with his words, sitting on the edge of the mattress. I hooked my fingers to the waistband of both his bottoms and boxer briefs, helping him out of both.

He sprang free, and I gulped at the sight of his erection, facing me and pointing upward. He didn't say anything as I explored him. I placed a hand around his shaft and squeezed gently, feeling his girth. Hector drew in a breath at the touch, and a small drop of pre-cum escaped him. I rubbed it with my thumb around the head and brought my thumb to my mouth, licking it. The flavor of him in my mouth quickened my breathing.

My intention was to draw him into my mouth, I wanted to taste him, but he pulled out of my grip before my tongue reached its desire.

"Tsk, tsk," he said. "Not yet. I won't be able to last if you do that, and I want to devour you, baby."

I swallowed, even as I was denied what I wanted most. Still, his words stirred inside me, and I felt my pussy contract in response.

He pushed me gently by the shoulders until I lay back onto the bed. He was on top of me in no time.

When he kissed me the second time, it was different. This was not the exploration of tentative lovemaking, full of sweetness like his kiss earlier in the night. This kiss—it was all desire and hunger. He made good on his promise and devoured my mouth. His lips crushed mine, and his tongue played roughly with mine like he couldn't get enough, making me squirm under him.

His cock rested on me, his shaft nestled gently between the seam at my center, and my hips raised forward, searching for the head, wanting him inside me. He let out a deep chuckle at my desperation, and I could have killed him right then and there.

"My eager little Carolina," he said, admonishing me. "We have all night. What is the rush?"

"The rush," I said in a breathy voice, "is that we have been waiting a decade." I circled my hips, rubbing my clit against the shaft of his cock, seeking my pleasure.

His eyes darkened, and I was almost afraid of what I saw in them—almost. He looked wild, like a starving savage.

His mouth trailed down my body as he pinned me to the bed by my shoulders. He let go of his grip when his mouth reached my pubic bone, and his hands found themselves on my thighs, spreading my legs even wider.

With his index finger, he pulled my thong to the side. There was a gentle caress, teasing at my entrance, and my body writhed at the touch.

"What do you want, Carolina?"

"I want you." Damn it, I wanted him *now.*

"Say it, baby. What do you want from me?" His stubble scratched my inner thigh as his finger continued to toy at my entrance, not giving me what I wanted. I was about to cry.

"I want your mouth," I said.

"Like this?" He slid his finger deeper in me and gave me a gentle kiss on the outside of my pussy. I groaned.

"No. I want your tongue on me."

"Oh, you mean like this?" He licked at the outer lip of my pussy, as his finger twirled inside me.

"Hector, damn it! I want you to lick my clit!" I surprised myself at how loud I had said it, but my bluntness was rewarded. He chuckled as the tip of his tongue circled my clitoris gently.

He made a soft *mmmm* sound, and the sound vibrations were unlike anything I'd ever felt. He was unreal.

"Oh, Hector." My eyes rolled back with pleasure. He flicked his tongue a little faster and slid a second finger inside me, sending me reeling. I grabbed a fistful of fabric from the bedsheets and held on for life. My thighs clenched, and he pulled his fingers out of me to stabilize my legs wide and open like he wanted them.

"No!" I protested, the emptiness leaving me nearly in tears.

"Then, don't close your legs for me, got it?"

I nodded rapidly, wanting to be rewarded. What the hell? Where was the polite and respectable Hector Medina? This Hector was all teasing and power and hunger. I fucking loved it. While I didn't want him calling the shots in my career, I definitely didn't mind him calling the shots when he had his way with me.

He returned his attention to my pussy, and this time he plunged three fingers inside me, stretching me further. I was so wet by that point, there was no pain at the extra width of the fingers inside.

His tongue rolled once again over my clit, this time picking up speed, and his fingers went in and out of me more rapidly each time. When he curled his fingers slightly upward, finding that spot, I couldn't take it anymore.

"Hector, No! Please stop, I'm going to come." I didn't want to. Not yet. I wanted his cock inside me when I came.

"Yes, baby. Come for me. I want you dripping down all the way to my wrist," he said and pushed his fingers deeper inside me.

A familiar tension coiled in my core, and bursts of white lights set off behind my eyes as my body answered him, giving him what he commanded.

My orgasm came in waves, and my abdominal muscles spasmed with the pleasure. My pussy clenched around his fingers. And his mouth left me.

"Oh, Carolina," he said hoarsely at the sensation around his fingers.

He stood, and I momentarily panicked. "Where are you going?"

"I'm just going to the dresser. Need to grab a condom."

"Wait," I said. I couldn't look at him, but I needed to ask. I wanted to feel him, and not between a layer of latex. "I'm on birth control. I have an IUD," I said. "And I'm clean. I'm sure of it. Would you want to . . ." I trailed off, not able to finish my thought.

Shit. What the hell was happening? Where was the confident and assertive Carolina Ramirez? Being naked with each other had seemed to reduce both of us to repressed personality traits we avoided in our everyday lives and careers.

"Carolina, you are my every dream come true," Hector said and finished peeling off my thong. I welcomed him with open thighs as he found his way back on top of me.

One of his hands went to the back of my head, holding me in place for a kiss, just as he had earlier in the night. The tip of his cock played at my entrance, and I writhed beneath him, trying to get him deeper inside me. I groaned in his mouth, and my reward was another inch of him.

He pushed in slowly, stretching me inch by inch in the most gentle way. I was so wet that there was nothing but pleasure, and just when I didn't think he could possibly go inside me any deeper, he thrust in another inch, and then another.

I hunkered down, taking in his cock and adjusting to the size. I'd never been with a man this big, and I thought it might be painful when I first saw him, but it wasn't. It was the most delicious stretch of my life.

"Are you okay?" he asked between kisses.

"Yes," I said, and my legs wrapped around him, my ankles pushing on his ass so I could have him deeper.

"Yes, ma'am," he said teasingly, and pulled out of me almost entirely, then drove in again with force.

I screamed his name and cursed in the same breath, and he was amused by all of it. He was paying close attention, finding my eyes even when I tried to look away. He was studying me. He wanted to know what my body reacted to—what I liked. Hector Medina was conducting research on my body.

He pulled out again, this time staying away, with only his tip inside me. "Please, Hector, *please* come back," I begged.

His mouth found me first, and he drove his tongue in my mouth before he drove his cock deep inside again. I moaned into his mouth, my eyes shut tight, and that coil started building again.

My legs tightened around him, and I dug my fingertips in his back—luckily, like all doctors, I had short nails and didn't scratch him. Or at least I didn't think I had.

I took my mouth away from him, gasping for air, and my head rolled back as the second orgasm hit. My pussy tightened around him as I came, and it only made him thrust harder, sending me over the edge again.

He was wild now, his eyes darkened like a sinister, other-worldly being as he pounded into me. My pussy was still contracting from the orgasm when he plunged deep inside me and remained there. A groan that escaped from deep within him followed as he came shortly after I did. I realized he'd been trying to hold out until I came again—like a gentleman.

He pressed his forehead to my collar bone and tried to catch his breath. My arms embraced him around the neck, and I couldn't help running my fingers through his hair.

"I'm never letting you get away again," he said between breaths and while he was still inside me. He kissed my left breast and looked up at me. "But more importantly, I'll never again give you a reason to want to go."

CHAPTER 27

MORNING AFTER

The house was quiet, but the sun rays flooding through the window warmed my skin. I felt a tickle at my nose, and my eyes fluttered open. I had fallen asleep on his chest, and his thick chest hair tickled my face awake. I smiled when I realized his chest hair matched the salt and pepper hues of his thick mane.

I slept like the dead, though I didn't imagine he could have been very comfortable. I had his arm pinned under me, and nearly half of me was on top of him, my legs wrapped around his right leg.

As I rubbed the sleep from my eyes, he shifted under me. "You awake?" His voice didn't sound hoarse or groggy.

"Yeah. How long have you been awake?"

He caressed my shoulder. "An hour," he admitted.

I pushed myself away from him, horrified. "I'm so sorry, Hector. You should have woken me so I could move. You must have been so uncomfortable."

Hector only tightened his grip, pressing me to his naked body. "Come here. I wasn't uncomfortable. Actually, it was heavenly. You looked so at peace, I didn't want to wake you."

"Well, thank you," I said with doubt.

"Not that I could wake you up if I wanted to."

"What's that supposed to mean?"

"It means, my love, that you sleep like a log. I don't think a freight train could wake you up. And don't let me get started on that cute little snore of yours—"

"I do not snore!" I tried wiggling out of his grip, but who was I kidding? It was only a threat. I wasn't going to willingly separate my skin from his. I settled back into the warm nook of his body, and I couldn't remember the last time I'd felt that safe—or if I ever had.

I covered my mouth for a yawn, preoccupied with my morning breath. "That was a yummy sleep," I admitted and brought my hand back to his chest. I gathered some of his chest hair between my fingers and started twirling the locks around. This man was *mine,* and I couldn't believe it. As I played with the curls, something caught a ray of sunlight from within the chest hair and glimmered. I pulled my hand to my face and realized it was on my finger.

I shot up into a sitting position and grabbed the bed sheet to cover my breasts. Hector remained calmly lying down and drew circles on my naked back with the pad of his finger.

"Hector, wha-wha-what is this?" I held my left hand to my face and pushed aside the strands of hair obscuring my view. I was sure my locks were suffering from a severe case of sex hair, but I couldn't worry about that right now. On my hand, staring back at me, was a classically cut round diamond on a sleek and simple platinum band.

"That's your engagement ring, love. Guess I'm lucky you sleep like you do, or I would have never managed to get it on you without waking you."

Love? He had gone from *baby* to *love* in one night. "How did you get—"

"I've had it for a while now," Hector said.

"How long is *a while?*" I asked, looking at him now.

"That ring has been here, in this house, for eight years."

"What?" My eyes bulged to saucers. It was possible I was dreaming or still so groggy I hadn't heard him right.

"I was only renting at first, but when you came over, you mentioned you liked the house, so I bought it."

"You bought a house because I mentioned I liked it?"

"Yes." Hector sat up in the bed and scooted me back toward him so we could both rest our backs on the headboard. He took my left hand in his and kissed it. "I bought it for you—for us. I told you, love. I fell in love with you back then, and I was ready to propose, but you were so damned mad at me, and well, you know what happened after that."

"And it has been here this entire time?" I stared at the ring again. It was sizable and looked expensive, but it wasn't too much. It felt elegant and classic on my hand, even to my untrained eye.

"Waiting for you. That ring was going to be on your finger one day, or it would never get to feel the skin of another human. The poor thing," he teased.

"Would have been such a waste," I teased back.

"The worst," Hector said.

"And you kept the house empty? All this time?"

Hector nodded. "I couldn't bear to sell it. Doing so would have been like admitting I was giving up on us, and I never did. Not even when I tried to convince myself it was over. In the back of my mind, I always knew that I'd come back once your career was established, once I could be in your life without simultaneously destroying it."

He had been right last night when he'd asked whether I wouldn't have done the same thing he had. I was starting to understand the sacrifice of his restraint. He waited seven years for me to make a name for myself and risked me moving on with someone else. It would have killed me, but I couldn't lie to myself; I would have done the same thing if I'd thought I was ruining everything he had ever worked for.

It wasn't like he stayed away so I could keep a job. He loved medicine as much as I did and understood that losing a love like that would have all but killed me. Because he was right. I would have chosen him at the risk of my career, and if I had lost the ability to conduct research, it would have slowly killed me and taken its own particular toll on our relationship.

I dropped the sheets from my body and pulled them away from both of us. The contrast of his tanned skin on the white linens was astounding in the morning light, and I couldn't stop myself from fucking him with my eyes as I raked my gaze up and down his body.

So much had been missing last night in the dark. He had fucked me hard, with hunger and desire and longing, but it was all touch and sounds. The glory of his body was missing from the limited senses lacking vision in the night.

I smirked when his erection made its presence known, but then my pussy contracted. I was sore and swollen from what we had done not too many hours ago. He looked bigger in the clarity of daylight, and I winced.

"As much as I love you devouring me with your eyes," Hector said, "I was hoping you'd actually touch me."

"We have the rest of our lives. What's the rush?" I threw his words at him and bent over his body.

I gripped the shaft of his cock and moved to make him think I was going to have him in my mouth. But this was payback for all the teasing from earlier. He would pay.

I leaned to kiss his inner thigh and dragged my tongue from his knee to his thigh on one leg, then the other, stopping each time before reaching the spot where he wanted me.

"I shouldn't have teased you last night, should I?" Hector asked.

"No, darling. You *really* shouldn't have." I was mainly teasing him as he had done, but I was also exploring his body again, this time with my eyes. I scooted up, and my tongue trailed the thin strip of hair that led to his bellybutton, and I nipped at the skin of his stomach.

"Damn it, Carolina," Hector said, his voice hoarse. "I swear I'll never tease you again if you stop."

I withdrew from him and studied his expression as I licked my lips. "You want me to stop?"

"No! Agh! That's not what I meant. *Please* stop teasing me."

I understood now why he had done it. Him begging, saying my name, pleading drawn-out *pleases,* was like a prayer for me. It was so goddamned empowering and so fucking hot.

Rewarding the prayer offering, I bent again and gripped his shaft, pumping once, then twice. Still, I wanted to savor him, so I only licked, first along his shaft from root to head. I let my tongue linger there and circle the head, finding the saltiness of us from the night before.

Hector was still half-sitting up against the headboard, and he gathered my hair in his hand so he could watch me—I wanted him to see what I was doing to him. I drew the tip of his cock into my mouth and sucked only there, at the very edge, and he bucked his hips, trying to go deeper, but I was in control now.

"Tsk, tsk," I said as I let him out of my mouth. "This is my show now."

"I'm sorry," he said. "*Please* get back here."

"Are you going to be good?" I sat up, giving him a full view of my body, and circled my nipple with my finger. I drew my hand down, tracing a zig-zag pattern from my breast down to my clit.

"Yes, I'll stay still, just *please*—" He tried reaching for me, but I was just out of grasp. I moaned as I toyed with my clit, high on the look in his eyes as he watched.

"*Please*, Carolina. You've made your point. This is cruel."

I bent over him again and kept my balance on one hand so I could keep playing with myself with the other while I sucked him. I took him deeper into my mouth the second time, and he growled—he actually *growled*—and I etched the sound in my mind so I could take it with me for the rest of my days.

"Stop, Carolina," he ordered, and I couldn't stop myself from obeying, his power over me from last night lingering somewhere in the recesses of my brain.

I crawled up toward him and found his mouth, letting him taste what had been on my tongue, morning breath be damned, because this was so hot. I used his shoulders for support as I came up over him and slid down over his cock slowly—so slowly.

The girth of him sent a stretch of pain to my core as I slid down around his length. My mouth parted from his. I gulped some air to ebb the pain away, but he noticed my wince.

"Are you in pain, baby? We don't have to, we can stop if you are too sore." His body stilled like he wouldn't dare move a muscle lest he hurt me.

I shook my head.

The thing was, there was a pain where we joined, but also so much pleasure, and there was no way I was stopping now. I circled my hips gently as I took the rest of him in, and he groaned.

"I'm okay," I promised. "A little sore, but nothing I can't handle." I slid down further until there was nothing more to take in and rode him for all that I was worth.

Hector grabbed onto my hip bones, encouraging my rhythm. He helped me up his shaft and brought me down forcefully. His fingers dug into my skin, but the pain was masked under the pleasure of his fullness inside me. The way it felt to be with him had never been close to this with anyone, not even remotely.

He sat up fully and took my mouth in his. I moaned into his tongue, and he rewarded me by pushing me until I fell on my back. He rolled up over me in an instant, never once disconnecting from my body. Grabbing my right leg, he placed it over his shoulder, and the stretch felt divine.

"Oh," I moaned with the surprise of this new position. I tried bucking my hips, but too much of his weight was on me, and I was powerless. "Hector," I moaned.

"I'm here, baby," he said, claiming my lips once again.

He picked up speed as he drove into me over and over, and when I couldn't take it any longer, I clenched around him as I found my release. My center convulsed around him, and his body stilled. The morning light splayed across his forehead, and I could see a vein making itself known over his taut skin as he came inside me.

After we both came undone, he rolled off me. We lay next to each other for a long moment, panting. The sweat from the heat of us started to cool over my body, and I curled to his side, seeking his warmth.

We both lay there for a moment as we brought down our heart rates and our breaths. After a long moment of coming back to, Hector broke the silence.

"So I take it that was a *yes*?"

EPILOGUE

SIX YEARS LATER

THANSGIVING DAY

Hector stood in front of the fireplace mantel with all the family pictures, our five-year-old daughter in his arms. Marisela's long legs dangled nearly to his knees, and already we could tell she would grow up to be tall—just like her parents.

She wore a deep blue dress with grey wool leggings and looked positively adorable in her daddy's arms. Though physically she looked most like me, her attitude, brain, and mannerisms were all Hector Medina.

When our daughter was born, Hector had wanted to name her after my mom, but Marisela came into this world with my face—my mother's face. I couldn't handle looking at her *and* calling her by my mother's name day after day. Instead, I suggested we name her after *his* mom. Hector had grinned as he let out a tear. Marisela, who had been in her dad's arms swaddled in the tiniest bundle I had ever seen, caught the tear with her forehead.

Grammy Marisela, as we all now called her to differentiate between grandmother and granddaughter, wasn't joining us this holiday season. In her seventies, she didn't like leaving her home in Mexico to travel any longer, but we had promised to visit in the spring.

"Daddy, this is my brother," Marisela said, pointing to the picture of Jake my dad had added to the mantel.

"Yes," Hector said. "That's your older brother Jake."

"He's in heaven," she told him matter-of-factly, and the words sounded like my father's counsel.

"Is he now?" Hector asked like she had all the answers.

"Yeah!" Marisela said with a confidence not unlike her father's. "Grammy Consuelo takes care of him there." And *that* explanation definitely had Dad written all over it. Hector chuckled, and Marisela didn't notice her dad's eyes misting over, but I caught sight of it when he turned his face slightly away from her to take a deep breath.

Dad placed a hand on my shoulder. I was standing, leaning against the door frame that led to the living room, watching my family. "You know, *Mami* would be so in love with her granddaughter," I said as I clasped Dad's hand on my shoulder.

"She *is* in love with her," said Dad. I wasn't sure I believed that, but it was still comforting that *he* believed it, and he believed it enough for the both of us. "You have a package," he said. "It's on the table."

I went into the kitchen where Sofia and her daughter Audrey were smearing *masa* onto dry corn husks and helping Dad roll *tamales*. I grabbed the small box from the table so it wouldn't be in the way of their work.

I watched Audrey work diligently, her tongue poking out to the side as she concentrated on getting the perfect *tamal*, and I laughed. She was twelve now and growing into a beautiful young woman. Her dad and Sofia were going to have a heck of a time with boys real soon.

"*Tía*," Audrey said, looking up at me. "Is *Tía* Sara coming to dinner with the boys?"

"Yeah, why aren't they already here *helping*?" Sofia asked with mock-disdain.

"No, Mom!" Audrey said. "My *tía* Sara doesn't come until the food is ready."

Audrey made the accusation so seriously, Dad, Sofia, and I all roared with laughter. Hector and Marisela joined us in the kitchen, asking us what was so funny. Hector joined in with laughter when I repeated Audrey's matter-of-fact statement.

"Yes, sweetie," I told her. "Sara is coming, but it's better if she comes when dinner is ready, or do you want her tornado boys here while we try to work?"

"No!" she said with horror, and we all laughed again. Audrey returned her attention to the *tamal* she was rolling. She feigned disinterest when she spoke again, but I didn't miss her cute little rosy cheeks reddening crimson. "What about *Tía* Mandy? Is she bringing Lulu?"

Why was my niece asking about Mandy's son Lucas? I knew they were almost the same age and went to the same school, but the redness in her face amused me. I tried not to show it as I answered her. "No, sweetie. Lulu is in Spain with his other grandparents for the holidays. He'll be back after the new year."

Audrey shrugged, and I changed the subject to prevent her any embarrassment if anyone else caught on. I still had her back. I just hoped there wasn't payback from Sofia when Marisela became a pre-teen and started thinking about boys.

Hector lowered Marisela to the ground, and she ran to her grandpa who had a ball of *masa* waiting for her to play with. She rolled the dough in her hands and sank her fingers into it, giggling at the sensation. She ran to the living room with it still in her hands.

"What's the package?" Hector asked.

I had forgotten about it and looked down at the small box still resting on my lap. "I don't know. Hand me the kitchen scissors?"

"Is your dad coming to dinner, Audrey?" Hector asked as he handed me the scissors.

Audrey's little face fell, and she bit her lip just like her momma.

"No," Sofia said when Audrey didn't answer. "He's in Germany working, but he'll be back by Christmas, right, honey?" Sofia ran her fingers over Audrey's bangs, pushing them away from her eyes.

"Right," said Audrey, more cheerful now.

Opening the package, I found an assortment of Mexican candy, and I smiled. I knew exactly who these were from. The box was filled with tamarind-covered candy, my favorite watermelon lollipops, banana bubble gum, and several *cajeta* and *dulce de leche* candies. I opened the card, recognizing the familiar handwriting that found me every holiday season.

For the doctor who gave me a fighting chance,
Thank you for saving my life.
Much Love,
Valentina Dennis

"It's from a patient," I said. Hector hovered over me, looking inside the box. His hand reached toward my lap for a piece of candy, but I smacked it away. "That's *my* candy, Dr. Medina," I said.

"Is that right, Dr. Ramirez?" Hector put his hands on his hips in warning just like he did when he was attempting—and failing—to be stern with our daughter.

I sprang to my feet, opened the door to the backyard, and ran as I clutched the box in my hands. I only barely heard Hector's footfalls on the grass as he followed me, but I knew he wasn't far behind.

He caught me and gripped my waist with one hand as he tickled me with the other.

"No, daddy!" shouted Marisela, now next to us. "She is going to drop the candy!"

I wiggled in his grip. "Stop! Stop!" I pleaded through the laughter.

Hector stopped long enough for me to hand my daughter the box. Marisela's eyes widened at the sight of all the candy, and she ran with it back inside the house to show her grandpa.

"Dr. Ramirez," Hector said. "Half of what is yours is mine."

"Everything except for candy." I grinned at him, and he tackled me to the ground.

Dad hadn't raked the yard yet, and I laid on a bed of yellow and orange leaves. Hector's weight pinned me to the ground, and he dipped his head to kiss me gently—just one chaste little peck would do for now, until we got home and put Marisela to bed.

As he looked at me with that smile of his, I thought of everything we had created together and how beautiful it all was. Nothing we had ever done together was ever short of remarkable.

I had come from a tiny family, just Dad and me, but I'd slowly but surely grown it. First, with Ramiro, then Sara, then all my girlfriends, and finally, all my nieces and nephews. We had filled this house with a huge family and a lot of laughter.

I lay there, looking up at my husband, feeling the crisp autumn air nip at my skin, incredibly grateful for the family we had made.

BONUS CHAPTER

If you have already read *Remission,*
enjoy Hector and Carolina's meet-cute from his perspective in the
bonus chapter up next. This additional scene has never before been in
print.

BONUS SCENE

FIRST DAY ON THE JOB

I'm ready for my first day at my new job by five in the morning. I didn't sleep a wink my first night in Kansas City. The new house is empty and too quiet. Even though I spend my life in hospitals, the sterile feeling of the white walls in this new place makes me uncomfortable to the point of restlessness.

After a spartan breakfast of a hard-boiled egg and a coffee, I open up my laptop to get a head start on the day. I don't eat much else for the rest of the morning. At thirty-seven, keeping off the pounds is starting to get harder. Even harder is gaining muscle mass, but I do my best. Though I confess I skipped the gym this morning, not feeling up to it after my night of sleeplessness.

My email is a long list of pending requests from my old job at the FIHR—the Federal Institute of Health and Research—and at least three from the director begging me to come back.

But I can't go back to Maryland. Nothing waits for me there but the bitter memories of the perfect life I once had—and then lost my grip on. My wife moved to New York, and with her parents the only family I have left in Maryland, I have zero desire to stay so close.

The excuses are all bullshit. Because the real reason I left Maryland—the real reason I ended up in Kansas City, of all places—is that two years ago, as part of a review panel for funding grant applications, I came across a clinical trial proposal that knocked the wind out of me.

When I first read it, I was angry. At myself, mostly. This fucking baby doctor barely out of med school was doing *my* work. But I abandoned it. I let the FIHR lure me to its clutches with promises of making a bigger difference for more cancer patients. Instead, I became an extremely well-paid paper pusher.

Then I met Andrea, and my life in Maryland seemed the only path forward. Until this Dr. Carolina Ramirez, whoever the hell she was—a nobody from the sticks of Kansas City—wrote the grant I was meant to write. The project that had been in my head for years, but that I never got to . . . because I abandoned it.

I rub my temples. There is so much regret in my life—regret I never imagined I'd have at this stage of my career.

I can help Dr. Ramirez—in fact, it is my duty as a physician to do so. I would need to pass the baton at some point in my career. No time like the present, I suppose. I want to be mad at her, but I can't. If it hadn't been her, someone else would have eventually followed the data to the next logical steps—my next steps.

The two different cancer treatments I used in my unique formulation had only been utilized individually up until my clinical trial increased cervical cancer survival rates so much that I became a household name within the medical community almost overnight. It had landed me the gig at the FIHR, and fuck if fame isn't everything they say it is. I never treated a patient face-to-face again.

Now, Dr. Ramirez is pushing the envelope further with her protocol changes to those very treatments. She is pushing the boundaries of what a cancer-ridden body can take, and damn her because I know she will be successful. But she has holes in her process. Holes I can fill.

Fuck if that didn't sound dirty as all hell.

The reality is, I haven't fucked anyone or anything but my hand for the last two years. Not since Andrea and I separated. She may be dating and screwing around. In fact, I know she is—she's made it clear to me on more than one occasion. She just wants me to sign the divorce papers. But despite all that, I take my wedding vows seriously. I haven't cheated on her even during our separation—*como un pendejo.*

I guess I'm still holding out hope she'll come back to me, though somewhere deep in my old, broken heart, I know she will never forgive me for what I did. I'm sure of this simple fact because I haven't forgiven myself.

I close the laptop and get ready for the day.

I head to my new job at Heartland Metro Hospital. I'm early for my eight a.m. meeting with the Chief of Oncology, so I give myself a tour of the hospital. I get lost twice and eventually find myself at Chief Stuart's office.

A young administrative assistant greets me.

"Hello. Could you please inform Chief Stuart that Hector Medina is here?"

The administrative assistant smiles and bites her lip. She fidgets with her hair and doesn't even try to hide the fact that she is checking me out. I'm used to this kind of female attention, so I have no patience for flirts. "Sure thing. Please take a seat," she says.

"Thank you." I clear my throat and straighten my tie, blatantly displaying my wedding ring. The gesture has the desired effect because her face falls a little until she forces a smile again.

She picks up her phone and sits back at the desk. "Chief? Are you ready for Dr. Medina?" She hangs up and looks at me once again. "Go on in. It is the second door to the right."

I tip my chin at her and go into the chief's office.

"Dr. Medina," he greets me. "It's so nice to finally meet in person. I'm a big fan of your work."

"Chief. The pleasure is all mine. Please call me Hector." We shake hands, and the chief gestures for me to sit.

"I have to say I'm surprised you are reentering the world of direct patient care."

"You shouldn't be. A lot of FIHR physicians miss working in the hospital."

"But not a lot of them would give up their big paychecks."

"It's never been about that for me."

"I see," he says but narrows his eyes, clearly not buying it.

"I miss seeing patients, but more importantly, I miss conducting clinical trials."

"Yes. That's why you are here. To work on Dr. Ramirez's trial."

"Thank you for making this happen," I say. "When can I meet her?"

"We are heading over to meet everyone in the Oncology Department as soon as we are done here, but Hector—"

"*Yes?*"

"I hope you understand as an attending at Heartland Metro, you are expected to teach all residents. I can't have you playing favorites."

"With all due respect, Dr. Stuart. *I* hope *you* understand the only reason I'm here is for Dr. Ramirez's trial. I intend to take her under my wing and help make her trial as successful as my first trial was. Sure, I will teach all residents I work with. I always have. But I won't pretend I'm not here with a distinct purpose."

"So long as you can keep that to yourself and the other residents don't feel overlooked—"

"Is there anyone in particular you are worried about, Dr. Stuart?" I narrow my eyes because I'm sensing he is dancing around something, and I would much prefer that he spit it out.

He clears his throat and straightens his doctor's coat. "As a matter of fact, yes. We have a resident on staff whose family is important to the hospital."

"Oh?"

"Yes. Braxton Keach, son of Dr. Edward Keach, a retired prominent obstetrician. I'm sure you've heard of him."

"The name sounds vaguely familiar," I say.

"Well, the Keach family has donated generously to the hospital. We recently named the obstetrics wing after them. I wouldn't want Dr. Keach to think he is being set aside."

"Are you proposing I favor *him*, then?" I challenge.

"No. Just don't push him aside."

"I will treat him as I would any resident. He gets to learn from me, and if he seems like he is worth something, then yes, I will consider deeper mentorship. However, I haven't seen any grant proposals in his name. I have no reason yet to be impressed by him."

I'm not saying what we both understand. He doesn't write research grants because he is not responsible for bringing in the research dollars. His family takes care of that for him.

"I appreciate you keeping in mind the delicate situation," Chief Stuart says finally with resignation. "Now, let's head over to meet your new team."

We walk under an awning to an adjoining building and enter a large conference room. Several doctors are milling about in conversation as they help themselves to a breakfast spread. There are only four women in the room full of doctors, and one of them has to be Dr. Ramirez. If only I could skip this inane introduction and talk to her instead. I'm ready to jump into the research.

Chief Stuart opens up the meeting, and I can hardly pay any attention because in the center of the room, looking at me with interest, is a woman so beautiful, I have a hard time tearing my eyes away. I've never hated the white doctor's coat so much as in this moment—hers covers the full view of her body.

She is wearing a pencil skirt, one of my few weaknesses, and her long, thick, dark-brown hair hits well below her waist. I bet it grazes her ass as she moves. Her skin is a dark caramel-honey that I want to lick from head to toe, and her amber eyes never leave me. Her presence lights up the room like the sun, and like the sun, her beauty blinds. Fuck. I need to look away from her because I can't very well have a hard-on in a room full of doctors. But I can't look away. My eyes are frozen to her figure.

I'm a tall man, and the honey-skinned goddess is almost my height. I scan her body once again, not able to help myself. My eyes roll down her legs, and I'm surprised to see her wearing high heels. I smile inwardly because most tall women I know live in flat shoes.

The feminine shoes accentuate her calves, and I find myself wondering what her thighs look like under that skirt. Those details are left hidden by her white coat, but what I *can* make out is that her shoulders are square-set, and her posture is impeccable. This is a woman self-assured and confident. *Don't be Dr. Ramirez. Don't be Dr. Ramirez,* I plead to any gods who will listen. I can't work with this woman every day.

The chief finishes introducing me, and damn him for asking if I want to say a few words. I thank him and take over the speech. "It is an honor to work with you and to be at this hospital with such great young and eager minds," I say. I keep talking, all bullshit I'm pulling out of my ass because I can't concentrate. I need to know which of the four women she is. So I bring up the trial.

I really didn't want anyone to know I was here only for *one* particular trial. It could hardly make things easier for the primary investigator, or PI, but I *have* to know who she is. More importantly—I need to know she is not the woman with the amber eyes.

"I have been following research coming from this hospital for over a year now, and let me tell you, I've been impressed," I say. "That is why I chose Heartland Metro Hospital as my new professional home." I look between the four female doctors in the room, and everyone has realized I'm looking for someone because they are all leveling each other now. "There is one trial going on now that fascinates me." I rattle off a few details of the trial, and on cue, every head in the room turns to face the honey-skinned goddess. I clench my fists at my sides.

Fuck. Fuck. *Fuck.* This is inconvenient as fuck.

If Dr. Ramirez is rattled by my singling her out, she doesn't show it. She smiles politely as she introduces herself, and I tip my chin at her. I ask her to stay after the meeting to bring me up to speed on the trial, and, thankfully, no one seems suspicious. She shows me to my new office, and I ask her to sit when we get there.

I take off my jacket and loosen my tie. I'm buying time, not wanting to look at her. This is the doctor I chose to be my protégé. I can't blur lines like this. Why do I have to be so attracted to her? *Because she is smart as hell and hot as sin to boot, Hector.* That's right. Two extremely inconvenient reasons. Maybe she will have a shitty personality. A man can hope.

I sit in front of my desk, and my eyes linger on the flat top a beat too long. I don't know what to say, so I blurt out the first thing that comes to mind. "Well, this is stupid."

"Um, you don't like the desk?" Her voice is silken and warm, like top-shelf tequila, and my arms break out in goosebumps.

"No, the desk is fine. But such an American thing to do," I say. "This view. It is perfect, and then you place this monstrosity of a desk in here facing away from the view."

She politely suggests we call facilities services, get the furniture moved around. I've lost all sense of Hector Medina because I'm at a loss for words, discussing *furniture arrangements,* of all things.

I look up at her, and I am surprised to see her brows drawn together in concern. The look is so sultry, my body reacts without permission from my brain, and I start to harden. Thank the stars I'm sitting behind this desk—which I'm suddenly very fond of.

I clear my throat. "You are probably wondering why I want to speak with you."

"I assume to . . . take away my clinical trial?" she says like a question.

I cock my head to the side. What the hell? Why would I want to take her trial? When I stay silent too long, I voice my questions out loud. "Take your trial? Why would I do that?"

"You don't think I ripped off your research?" she asks.

What the fuck? Why would she think *that?* "Is that what you think?"

She considers this for a short moment. "You made suggestions for future steps, sure, but I definitely took those and ran with them in a different direction."

I'm baffled by her train of thought, but she explains that someone suggested she has ripped me off, and I want to strangle whoever that idiot was.

There was no plan to let Dr. Ramirez know I was here to take her under my wing, but that is precisely what I find myself doing next. "I didn't want to say it in front of your peers and make things tough for you, but I'm only here because of your research."

Her mouth makes a small 'o' before she shuts it, and her lips draw up into a smile—and my dick twitches in response.

She looks stunned, as if she doesn't believe I have actually said those words. "Excuse me?" she asks.

"Where you took your grant. It was brilliant. Well, don't get too cocky. It was brilliant *for a resident.*"

She says nothing more, and I have to get her out of my office before my dick turns to stone. I hurry up the conversation with reassurances that her trial will be a success. I offer support in future grant proposals for funding, and she showers me with gratitude I bask in.

I want her to stay, but I need her to go. I clench my jaw and snap open my laptop. "That is all, Dr. Ramirez," I say dismissively.

She is already at the door when I remember to warn her. "Oh, before I forget, Dr. Ramirez. If anyone asks, just say I wanted to be brought up to speed with your trial. Our little secret for now."

I stare after her as she leaves my office. I was right. Even through the baggy doctor's coat, I can tell her long hair *does* graze her ass as she walks.

I am so fucked.

CONTUSION

HEARTLAND METRO HOSPITAL: BOOK 2

CONTUSION

AUTHOR'S NOTE

This is a love story between Valentina and Rory. This is not a story about cancer. Specific treatment and symptom details have been omitted because I want the reader to focus on the love story.

Every cancer patient's journey is different. I am not an expert, and Valentina's specific case and the clinical trial depicted in this novel are entirely fictional.

In the United States, the National Breast and Cervical Cancer Early Detection Program assists uninsured women with free cancer screening services. You can learn more about eligibility at www.cdc.gov/cancer/nbccedp/.

*I*t's either the machine or me. *You are going down,* I telepathically warn the vending contraption holding my Pop-Tart hostage. I've never had a Pop-Tart in my life, but I haven't eaten all day, and *hangry* Valentina Almonte . . . well, let's just say even inanimate objects wouldn't want to meet her. "I train with two-hundred-and-fifty-pound men, so you better give it soon," I mutter under my breath as I think about my coach, Chema. Chema, who didn't know where I was and was probably worried. Two-hundred-and-fifty-pound Chema, who I have only been able to wrestle to the ground once. I should call him today, but not until I eat. Chema isn't fond of hangry Valentina either. I shake the vending machine as discreetly as possible.

I'm getting ready to start kicking the thing when someone clears their throat nearby to grab my attention. I turn and am faced with a red-headed, freckled man who has about four inches on my five-foot-five frame. I stare with surprise at the handsome stranger with piercing green eyes. His nose and cheekbones are chiseled like a Roman marble statue. I've never seen a red-headed person this close before, and I've always been a sucker for bearded smart guys. He wears glasses, so he has to be smart. That's the rule, right? Yet there is something manly about him, starting with his short beard and solidifying with a surprisingly deep voice considering his slender frame.

"Here," he says, extending two dollar bills my way.

"Um, it's okay," I say, self-conscious about the last remnants of my Spanish accent that I was never quite able to shake off.

"Please," he insists. "I'm afraid for its life." He points to the vending machine and smirks as he extends the bills my way again.

I cock my head to the side, unsure I should accept—my brain misfiring at what to say to this handsome stranger—when he sweeps past me to insert the bills into the machine. His arm brushes mine, and I jump back like I am dodging a strike from my opponent.

"What was it?" he asks and smiles broadly.

I point to the lopsided pastry package dangling from a corner caught on the claw of the feeding coil. "The Pop-Tart," I say. This is so embarrassing. I finally meet someone in the U.S., someone handsome, and he is buying out my hostage snack.

When the snack drops, he bends down to grab my prize, and I don't check out his ass. Not one little bit. But if I had, which I didn't, I'd have to admit it is quite a fine ass in that light-colored denim.

"Are you waiting for family?" he asks, handing me the Pop-Tart.

I look around nervously at the nearly empty waiting area. I'm not ready to tell anyone, even a stranger, so I shrug and change the subject instead. "Thanks, um—what's your name?"

"You betcha. I'm Rory," he says, and his smile extends to his eyes. He offers his hand, and I take it in mine.

"Valentina. Nice to meet you."

He adjusts the backpack strap over his shoulder, and I wonder if he is a college student because he has to be in his early twenties. "Valentina," he tries out the name in his mouth. "That's pretty. I don't think I know any Valentinas."

Except for the salsa, I think. "It's Mexican," I say abruptly.

"Is that where you're from? Mexico?"

I nod. "Well, thanks again for the snack. I appreciate it."

I'm walking toward my spot in the waiting room when he calls out after me. "Anytime. And take it easy on the equipment, tiger."

Sitting in my chair, I track the fiery-haired Rory as he leaves the waiting area. I slump back in my seat and open the silvery package—my stomach groans at the sound, and my mouth waters. I had seen Pop-

Tarts on American television many times, but by the time I was old enough to travel north, I was already in training.

My rigorous training included a strict food plan that was gluten-free, sugar-free, dairy-free, and all the other trendy '-frees' that coach Chema could throw my way. I had fought it at the time, but he'd refused to train me if I wouldn't agree to follow his rules to a T.

Chema is a coveted mixed martial arts coach, and I wasn't about to pass up the opportunity to train with him, so I promised I would stay on the food plan if he would train me. He has coached me since I was sixteen, and after eight years of training, he's more like an older brother than a coach.

If he could see me now, about to eat a gluten-full, sugar-full, dairy-full atomic snack, I'd be doing push-ups for days in punishment. I smile and take a healthy bite. My face contorts, and my nose scrunches up. Maybe I should have taken baby steps with the sugar after eight years without.

Yes. Eight years with no sugar. It wasn't a sacrifice. Well, it had been at first, but it was one I was more than willing to make if it meant I could one day get to the UFC.

I only manage to eat half of one Pop-Tart before I have to throw it out, completely *empalagada*, and I wonder what the English word is for that sickening over-sugared nauseous sensation. The search engine on my phone has no answers, and I let it go.

"Valentina Almonte," a young woman calls out, and I follow her through two sets of doors until we settle in a small office.

"Please take a seat," she says with a warm smile.

This woman has to be close to my age, and I find myself relaxing a little at the familiarity.

"I'm Amanda. You can call me Mandy. We spoke on the phone."

"Yes. I remember. You did the eligibility questionnaire when I first signed up for the clinical trial."

"Exactly. I'm Dr. Ramirez's research assistant." She smiles again and splits her attention between my face and her computer screen as she reads my medical chart.

"I have to confirm information you have already given."

"Okay," I say. I squeeze my hands into fists and relax them, repeating the motion several times. I follow my calming technique with deep breaths as I prepare for what's next.

"Please state your full name."

"Valentina Almonte."

"Age?"

"Twenty-four."

"City of Residence."

"Well, it was Mexico City, but it will be Kansas City for the duration of the treatment as well as six months of follow-up care."

"Any changes in symptoms?"

"No symptoms other than the slight back pain I already reported."

"Has the frequency or intensity of the back pain changed in any way?"

"No. It's the same."

"I know when we spoke on the phone, you hadn't received any treatment, but have you received any treatment since?"

"No cancer treatment. No. I only take over-the-counter pain medication sometimes for my back, but not every day."

"Thank you," Mandy says. "I know it's weird because you gave all the information already, but I want to prepare you. Many doctors, nurses, and even hospital staff will have you confirm a lot of the same information over and over. Please be patient with us. It's hospital policy."

I smile reassuringly at her. "Sure," I say. "No worries."

"I do have a few concerns about your eligibility," Mandy says, and my stomach drops.

No. She can't turn me away now. This is my best shot. The only one I want to take. I can't be kicked off the clinical trial before I've even started. My mouth dries up as I try to focus on her words. I picked this trial—and Dr. Ramirez—because it is the most aggressive cervical cancer treatment anywhere, and I want to be as aggressive as possible.

"You're a very special case, and Dr. Ramirez agreed to make some exceptions for you, but I want to reiterate that this process will be very difficult. Are you sure there isn't any support system you can count on? A friend, perhaps? You'll need someone to care for you after hospitalizations and drive you when you are too sedated after appointments."

"I'll be able to hire help as needed. That sounded really stuck-up.

That's the American expression, yes? Stuck-up?" Mandy nods. "I just mean I have family in Mexico who is paying for my treatment and resources while I'm here. I'll be able to hire nurses and drivers as needed, and besides, my apartment is only two blocks from here. I wouldn't compromise my eligibility into the trial. If it's money you are worried about, I understand none of my treatment is covered under the trial. Since I don't have medical insurance, I've given deposits already, but if you want, I'm happy to pay in full in advance."

Mandy's eyes soften, but I don't mind it as much as I would anyone else's sympathy. I couldn't stand Mom or Dad looking at me like that. I definitely couldn't stand Chema or my sister Pilar looking at me like that, so I keep it all to myself.

"It's more than that," Mandy says. "You'll want some emotional support."

"I don't want anyone to know. Not unless they absolutely have to—if the treatment fails."

"Okay. I'm following protocol, making sure you are going to have all the support you will need. But I'll take your word for it that you have it figured out."

"Thank you. I appreciate that. And I do. Really," I reassure her.

"Okay, then. Are you ready to meet Dr. Ramirez?"

I nod, and Mandy walks me to an exam room. I wait, shivering in the hospital gown Mandy provided before she left, until Dr. Ramirez announces her presence with a knock at the door.

"Come in," I say.

In walks a stunningly beautiful Amazon of a woman. I press my lips together to avoid gawking at her. She is tall and has muscular legs I would kill for—I can tell even through her scrub bottoms. I'm only a flyweight at one-hundred-and-twenty-five pounds, but I bet she is a bantamweight, or maybe even a featherweight, if she were a fighter. She wears a white coat over her blue scrubs. Her hair is up in a ponytail of straight dark-brown tresses that almost hit her waist, and she has the most expressive eyebrows I have ever seen on a woman.

"*Hola Valentina. Soy la doctora Ramirez. ¿Prefieres español?*"

"English is fine."

Dr. Ramirez smiles with what seems like relief. "Good. I'm Dr.

Carolina Ramirez. It's a pleasure to meet you," she says. Her amber eyes hold my gaze, and I can't help but smile back. I'm already at ease.

Dr. Ramirez grabs the chair in the corner and rolls it over to sit in front of me. "I've gone over your chart, and it sounds like your case is an excellent fit for the trial," she says.

I let out a breath, feeling more reassured that I have done the right thing by coming here and seeking her out.

She finishes my physical exam and pelvic exam, and I sit up to close the gown once again. I wrap myself in the flimsy cloth that does nothing to warm my skin.

"We're retaking some images. So long as there is no change, we will be able to start treatment this week as part of the trial."

What she means by 'change' is if the cancer has progressed further. There's still a chance this could go the other way, but I nod because Dr. Ramirez's presence is somehow reassuring, and I'm feeling calmer than I thought I would.

"It's part of the trial protocol, but I have to ask again," she says. "Are you sure you understand the trial treatment is more aggressive than the standard of care, which is still an option for you at this point? This trial will take a toll on you."

"I know, doctor. I want to be as aggressive as humanly possible."

"There's one last concern I have," she says. "I'm sorry, I must insist, you are so young and with no children. You understand the radiation will more than likely render you unable to conceive naturally?"

"Yes. Mandy went over all my pre-trial plan options."

"I'm willing to wait a few weeks if you want to freeze your eggs."

"Won't we risk the cancer spreading further?"

"That is a risk. Yes. But if having children at some point is important to you, I want to make sure I'm also advocating for what you'll need to have a happy life."

I smile. She wants to make sure that if she saves my life, she's not leaving me with a miserable one. "Look," I say. "I've never given any thought to children. I may one day want children, but I don't need that child to be biological. There are many children in the world in need of good parents." I don't say that I have chosen family I love more than bloodline family. "I'll be very happy with adoption if children ever become important."

"Okay, then. Let's do this."

Four hours of waiting and several scans later, I finally get to leave the hospital. It was all cold metal, shivering, and waiting in exam rooms, but it's not my first rodeo. I already went through all of this in Mexico when I first received my diagnosis.

I stand in front of the hospital, unsure of my next steps. Less than twenty-four hours in Kansas City, and for what is probably the first time in my adult life, I don't have a schedule to keep.

Pulling out my phone, I call a car with my car service app. I ask the driver to take me to any street with multiple car dealerships, and he drops me off in front of a Ford dealership. I look down the busy boulevard, flanked by dealerships, feeling daunted at all the options. I shrug. *When in Rome . . . or in this case, America.* I walk into the Ford dealership, and a nice old man hooks me up with a used but reliable Ford sedan. I could probably afford new, but I don't want to take advantage.

I had ordered furniture to be delivered to my apartment, but it won't show up until tomorrow. Realizing I need essentials, I pull up the navigation app on my phone and roll away in my new pre-owned car. The salesman was adamant it isn't 'used.'

After shopping, it takes three trips to get all of my supplies into my new barren apartment. I was shocked at how expensive rent is in the U.S., but being close to the hospital was a priority. I opted for a two-bedroom, thinking if it came to it, I could rent out one of the rooms to offset some of my expenses. I could only ask my sister for so much money before she got suspicious. Not that she wouldn't give it in a heartbeat if I told her what was going on, but I'm not ready to tell her.

I plop on the cream duvet over the white carpet, not sure I will be able to sleep on the floor—first time for everything, I guess. Once chemo and radiation start, wine will be off-limits, so I went to town at the grocery store's liquor section.

Uncorking the bottle of merlot, I sip straight from the bottle as I sit in my dark apartment. On the second floor, the apartment faces the busier side of the street. Two restaurants and a small used bookshop sit directly below, and I wonder if they call the books 'pre-owned' too.

The coolness of the glass in the floor-to-ceiling windows soothes my skin as I press my arm against it to look down the street. There are a few bars, and it's late enough that people are starting to go inside with broad smiles and flirty looks.

It's a beautiful city, and I wish I had come here under different circumstances. Now all I will have as souvenirs will be the bitter memories of cancer treatment.

I take a long pull from the bottle of wine, not caring when some of it spills from the corners of my mouth and down my chin, splattering over the white duvet. I'll get a new one tomorrow. I press my forehead to the glass and hug the bottle to my body while I look at the lights of the city night.

My phone is on silent mode, so I don't hear it when it rings, but the bright glow in the dark apartment signals the incoming call. I block the light with one hand as I grab the phone with the other. *Pili* is displayed on the screen—my nickname for my older sister Pilar. I've called her Pili since I was four-years-old, and she's hated it ever since.

"Tini?" I hear on the other end when I pick up. I hate her nickname for me as much as she hates mine for her. We would both benefit from a truce, but we are both too stubborn.

I roll my eyes. "Hi, Pili. How are you?"

"You promised you would call me when you landed yesterday, and I never heard from you," Pilar whines.

"I'm sorry. Been busy with training and all. I was actually about to call you—"

"Sure you were," she huffs. "Well?"

"Well, what?"

"How's it going? Are you settled in? How's the new coach? Give me an update!"

I suppose as my benefactor, she deserves information. "I just got here, but yes, everything's fine," I lie. "I got my apartment keys yesterday, furniture comes tomorrow, and I've been training all day."

"Furniture tomorrow?" She yells, appalled, and I pull the phone away from my ear for a second after her shriek. "You should have stayed in a hotel until then. Do you need more money?" she asks.

"No. You've given me more than enough. Don't worry." A million dollars should cover treatment and living expenses in the U.S., shouldn't it? I couldn't ask her for more. I just couldn't, not even knowing she could spare five times that amount without batting an eye.

"You sound tired."

"Yeah, training right after a long day of flying can really take it out of you, you know?" I never lied to my sister before my diagnosis, and I am surprised at how easily it all rolls off my tongue.

"And when are you going to tell Chema?"

I wince. "Soon. I need to find the right time to—"

"The right time was when you were here. *In person.* I hate to tell you this, Tini, but you are a little shit for not being upfront with him. He deserves to know you got an agent and a new coach. You basically just ghosted him."

She isn't saying anything that isn't true about me being a shit, though nothing about the agent or coach is true—that's my cover. I rub my temples. "I know. Trust me. I know. I'll tell him soon."

"I miss you," she says.

"Me too." Guilt washes over me for leaving her alone. My brother-in-law doesn't allow her to go out with her friends, and I'm one of the few people he does let visit her. I've left her more isolated than ever. He wouldn't have allowed her to come with me for treatment. Of that much, I was sure. Not unless he could come too, and if there is a last person in the world I wouldn't want to see, it is Felipe Conde, followed closely by Dad. "I'll call more often," I promise.

"Good night."

"Night, Pili."

Half of the bottle of wine is gone, and I pour the rest down the sink before bedtime. I lay down on my makeshift sleeping bag next to the window and stare at the smooth ceiling. Taking deep breaths, I repeat my intentions over and over into the echoes of the empty apartment, exactly as I would do before any fight.

"Get back to fighting."

"Beat the shit out of cancer."

"Get back to fighting."

"Live."

CHAPTER 2

$\mathcal{N}$othing appetizing takes up space in my fridge. After extensive research, I bought groceries to pack on the pounds. My one-hundred-and-twenty-five pounds are all muscle, and I know I'll lose weight once chemo and radiation start. I need to gain some weight before I start treatment. I'll have a hell of a time fattening up after an entire adulthood of balancing food to keep muscle up and fat down. I bought all the things the internet suggested, all high in calories, proteins, and fat, but low in volume. I look at the eggs, olives, butter, peanut butter—why are there so many butters?—avocados, and whole milk. None of it seems to go together, so I close the fridge and hit the shower to go out to breakfast instead.

The furniture delivery service won't arrive until after ten, so I have time to explore the neighborhood and grab a bite. I hardly slept a wink as I thought about my web of lies, but I didn't want to waste any more of my precious time sleeping.

~

KANSAS CITY IS FLAT. At least compared to the tall buildings of my home city. None of the structures in this neighborhood are taller than a few stories, except for the hospital that reaches a whopping seven floors and sticks out above everything else on this street. Also, unlike my home city, greenery flanks almost every road.

I'm surprised when I find a gym not too far from my apartment. I look through the window, itching to go in, but what's the point? I can't get a membership. It's not a fighting gym of any kind, but it would be better than nothing. I watch men and women go in, and I get a few friendly hellos. Maybe I could get a week's membership and just come to lift weights until the treatment starts? I'm getting ready to open the door when I hear a voice behind me.

"Don't even think about it." I turn like the kid caught with my hands in the *masa* to find Dr. Ramirez and Mandy staring at me. Dr. Ramirez's arms are crossed over her chest, and one of her brows is arched in warning. Mandy is pressing her lips together, suppressing laughter at this exchange.

"I-um, I wasn't going to go—"

"Yes, you were," says Dr. Ramirez.

I hang my head with shame. "Yeah, you're right."

"You're supposed to be softening up and trying to gain as much weight as possible this week."

"I know. I know. I just don't know how to not do what I was born to do." I smile lamely at the women, and we all ignore my eyes misting over.

"We're just going for breakfast," Mandy steps in just in time to avoid my tears spilling over. "You're coming with us." She isn't asking. She grabs my arm and laces hers through mine, tugging me away from the first place that has looked like home since I got here.

"Are you going to work today?" I ask as I sit in front of the two women looking at their menus.

"Yes," Mandy says. "We grab breakfast together Monday mornings. You're welcome to join us."

"Thank you, I might do that," I say, relieved to have someone to talk to besides a bottle of wine.

"So, are you really a UFC fighter?" Mandy asks with interest and much too loudly.

"Mandy," Dr. Ramirez scolds. "I don't think Valentina wants to talk about that."

I look between the two women who couldn't be more different. Mandy is short and has unruly wavy hair in a chocolaty dark brown shade. It's almost witchy as the tresses stir with her movements. Her skin is a smooth, cool-toned light brown. Her rectangular face meets in a square jaw, and she has one of the widest smiles I have ever seen. She is almost my height and definitely much shorter than Dr. Ramirez.

It's not just their physicality that is polar-opposite either. Dr. Ramirez moves with grace and sits with impeccable posture, while Mandy looks a bit frumpy and slouches in her seat, making her seem that much shorter. But what she lacks in physical height, Mandy makes up for in volume. Mandy is *loud*. So loud it's almost embarrassing, and I can't help but look at the other diners when she speaks.

I take a deep breath and answer Mandy. "No. I wasn't a UFC fighter *yet*. I was starting to get close—before—well, before everything happened."

"I'm sorry, *amiga*," she says and reaches across the table to grab my hand.

I smile at her choice of words and hope she is sincere because, lord help me, I'm going to need a friend.

When the waiter comes to our table, Dr. Ramirez snatches the menu from my hands, and my brows knit together.

"I'll be ordering for her," says Dr. Ramirez. "She'll have two fried eggs over-medium. Hash-browns, Texas toast with butter, two slices of bacon, and one biscuit on the side with gravy, if you have it."

"And for you, ma'am?" the waiter asks Dr. Ramirez.

"I'll have the spinach-egg white omelet with avocado slices and half a grapefruit," says Dr. Ramirez.

I blink at her, and Mandy throws her head back with a roar of laughter so magnified, several rows of tables turn to stare at us. I sink in my chair.

The heaping plate of food set before me doesn't look even a little appealing. I tug the plate, and the mountain of food jiggles. "Do I really have to eat this?" I ask.

"As much as you can, within reason," says Dr. Ramirez.

I turn my attention to a glob of something white that seems to have bits of sausage in it. "What is *that*?" I ask. It looks revolting, and despite my hunger, my stomach churns at the sight of it.

Mandy laughs again. "That's biscuits and gravy," she says with a bright, toothy smile. "Welcome to America."

"There's no way I'm eating that," I say.

"Fine," says Dr. Ramirez. "But eat as much as you can of the rest. Have a milkshake later, if you can, for a snack. When you find it hard to eat in volume, you'll be glad you can drink some calories."

"It's true," Mandy adds. "A few weeks from now, you'll be sending me on an errand to get you this very breakfast, and you won't be able to keep it down."

I take the fork and knife, one in each hand. *You can do this, Vale.* I pep myself, and Mandy roars with laughter again. My glare rises to her, and she presses her lips together.

"It's not so bad," says Mandy. "You'll see."

And it really isn't. It's greasy, and I'm not used to it, but I stop when I'm comfortable, and Dr. Ramirez nods with approval at the amount I manage to devour.

"Well, ladies," she says. "I have to get to work. Mandy, why don't you take the morning off? You haven't used any vacation time in a while."

"Thanks, boss," Mandy says, between mouthfuls of the pancakes she ordered, before Dr. Ramirez leaves us alone.

When we ask for our checks, the waiter informs us that both our tabs have been taken care of.

"Dr. Ramirez is generous like that," says Mandy. "Sometimes too generous. People tend to want to walk over her."

"Don't take advantage. Noted."

As we make our way outside, I ask Mandy something that crossed my mind during breakfast. "Hey, is it okay for us to socialize outside the hospital?"

"Not with Dr. R. Today was fine, but she won't be hanging out with us on the regular. She needs to keep a line drawn between her personal life and her patients. But I'm cool."

"You won't get in trouble?"

"No. I don't handle patient care or anything like that. The hospital won't have a problem if we're friends, if that's what you're worried about."

We are on the sidewalk, and Mandy stands in front of me. "So, what would you like to do? Seems I'm free this morning."

I shrug. "I was just planning on exploring the neighborhood a bit."

"That's great." Mandy starts to rattle off suggestions on which direction we should take when I see the glint of red hair walking in our direction. The man in front of him walks into a shop, and I can clearly make out Rory—the guy who saved my Pop-Tart. He is looking at his phone and hasn't seen us yet, and for some reason, I don't want him to.

"Let's go there," I quip and grab her arm as I haul her across the street and into the used-book store. I look out the window as Rory passes by, swallowed in a crowd of people.

When we are safely inside the bookshop, Mandy flashes me a funny look. "Okay, weirdo. What was that?"

"Just this guy I met the other day—"

"Oooh, a guy? Which one is it?" She cranes her neck after the group of people crossing the street. "Is he cute?"

"Doesn't matter. I can't really date now, can I?"

"No, but enjoy your sex-drive while you can. Trust me. It's going to take a bit of a vacation once you start treatment. Everyone handles it differently, but your body will change a lot. Sex will be the last thing on your mind."

I'm so stunned at her directness, I change the subject. "Well, I have to get back. I have furniture deliveries today."

"Oh, I'll come with. I can help move things around."

"You really don't have to."

"I want to." And just like that, Mandy invites herself over.

As we walk to my apartment, it dawns on me I don't know her full name. "What's your last name?"

"In case you have to give the cops a description?"

"What? No!" I laugh. "I just—I like to know my friend's names."

"Gomez. Amanda Gomez."

~

WHEN SHE WALKS into my apartment, Mandy whistles. "This is nice," she bellows but stretches the word 'nice' into two syllables. "I knew you were rich, but this is . . . I think only surgeons live in this building."

I stiffen. She already knows the trial requires patient insurance or upfront out-of-pocket deposits for treatment and hospital stays. This shouldn't be a surprise to her.

"I'm sorry," she hastens to apologize. "I'm working on my filter. It's not very good yet."

"How old are you?" I ask.

"Twenty-eight."

"Twenty-eight? You don't look it." It's hard to believe she is older than me. I laugh nervously. "And no worries about the filter, but no, I'm not rich. My sister is. She's bankrolling my treatment." *Without her knowledge*, I think, but don't offer Mandy that information.

"Oh yeah? What does she do?" Mandy walks around the apartment on a self-led tour as we talk. She grins when she sees the kitchen with its marble island and brand new appliances. The white subway tile back-splash particularly catches her eye. Then she walks from room to room, making sounds of appreciation at each one.

"Nothing. That sounds bad. I don't mean 'nothing.' She's a homemaker."

"Nothing wrong with that," Mandy says with a wide, toothy smile that is growing on me. She pops a piece of gum in her mouth and talks through the chewing. "My mom is too. She's amazing. So your sister, she married money or something?"

"Sort of. I mean, she did. Her husband owns a company in Mexico, but she has her own money."

"From what?" Mandy asks.

Geesh. She wasn't kidding about the filter. Is it common for Americans to talk about money like this? "From her dowry," I say like it's the most natural thing in the world, but I know it isn't.

"Her *dowry?*" Mandy's jaw drops, flashing me the pink bubblegum in her mouth. "Like Jane Austen and shit?"

I laugh. "Yeah, Mexico had colonizers too. They brought their dowry ideas with them."

"No shit?" she says and plops herself on the floor as she leans on the wall for a back-rest.

"No shit," I say.

"Will you get one too?" she asks.

"What?"

"A dowry."

My nose crinkles, and I shake my head. "Nope. Don't think so. There's a clause Dad has to approve of my husband-to-be, and to Dad, it means he gets to pick him out."

"So your Dad has money?"

I side-eye her. "Yeah. He does," I say with resignation.

"So I was right before. You're a rich girl."

"I'm really not. I was starting to get sponsors and handle my own money that *I earned* before I got sick."

"Hey, I didn't mean anything by it. I'm honestly just curious. I don't give a shit one way or the other."

"You say 'shit' a lot."

"Yeah. I like to cuss when I'm not at work or at home because it's the only time I can."

"Why can't you cuss at home?" I ask.

"I have a thirteen-year-old baby brother."

She lives at home? At twenty-eight? That can't be right, but I'm not comfortable asking such personal questions. "You know he's probably cussing already."

"Oh yeah, he says shit way worse than me. But my parents still think he's a sweet little innocent angel."

"Got it."

"Where'd you go?" Mandy snaps her fingers in front of my face when I stay quiet too long.

I'm now sitting next to her on the floor, and I know I checked out of the conversation. "Sorry. Just thinking about what's ahead."

"Hey, don't worry. Dr. Ramirez is amazing. You are going to be fine."

"How do you know so much? I mean, you mentioned about the food and drinking calories and then the sex drive thing. Do research assistants usually know so much about the trials?"

"Yeah. I also keep the database of adverse events. If any trial participants experience side effects, they call me, and I add them to the database. Expected side effects are par for the course, but if they are unexpected, we have to monitor those closely."

"I see."

"Can I ask you something?"

I side-eye her. "I have a feeling you will even if I don't say yes."

Her toothy grin spreads, but then her face turns serious. "How come you didn't tell any of your family or friends?"

I think about that for a moment, trying to find the right words. "I don't want this to define me. I was a rising star in my field, as *fresa* as that sounds. Everyone in my life has a perception of me as the strong one. I can't now be the sick one."

The doorbell rings, ending our conversation, and I'm glad I don't have to keep explaining something I'm in the process of trying to understand myself. I make my way to the intercom, and a man's voice fills the living room. "I have a delivery for Valentina Almonte."

"That's me." I buzz them up.

Three muscular men trickle in and out of the apartment as they bring in all the furniture I could possibly need. I even ordered a second bed for the guest bedroom. When I'd shopped online, I'd opted to buy entire showcase rooms from the website because I've never been good at putting together home decor. Pilar would have loved to help, but the less she knew, the better. I didn't want to slip up and have her get suspicious.

Feeling more in the way than helpful, Mandy and I press our backs against the living room window. A few of the pieces of furniture require assembly. One man goes into the bedroom to start on that while a second crouches in front of us, putting together the sectional.

"I'm so glad I came," Mandy says. I look at her to find a twinkle in her eye. It's amusing until her intentions become clear. "Go talk to him," she says in a hushed tone.

"What? No!"

"Remember what I said about the sex drive? He is so hot. Do it."

I panic because even though we are whispering and the living room is large, he is right there, and I'm sure he can probably hear us.

"Fine. You're too slow. I'm calling dibs."

"What? Mandy!" I warn, but she only puts her hand on her hip and tussles her hair over one shoulder.

"Hey," she calls toward the man. "What's your name?"

The tall, dark, and handsome man looks up at us with a bright smile. He had introduced himself to me when I opened the door for them, but Mandy was at the other end of the room. "Chris, ma'am," he says.

Mandy walks toward him. "None of that 'ma'am' business. I'm Mandy." Chris stands to stretch out his hand, and their hand-shake connection lingers for a beat too long.

Chris is much taller than Mandy, allowing me a view of the amusement in his eyes from her flirting. She finally lets go of his hand and starts rummaging through her purse. I see the corner of a piece of paper that she pulls out and hands to him. "I have a solo art show soon. You should check it out." She gives him what I assume is a flyer. "Hold that," she says and keeps rummaging through her purse.

Chris smooths out the flyer in front of him and looks at it. His mouth forms up into a smile. "An artist, huh?"

"Yeah, I'm a painter. Landscapes and portraits mostly. Here." She stretches her hand out so he'll give the flyer back, and she starts writing something on it. "My number," she hands back the flyer to Chris. "You know, if you want a sneak peek before the show." Mandy turns and starts walking back to me. She continues to ogle Chris as he works and brings more furniture in, both of them smiling like fools the entire time it takes the three men to get my apartment furnished.

"Ma'am," the man who seems to be in charge calls after me, a clipboard in his hands. "Could you please sign here that you received everything you ordered?"

"Sure." I sign, and the men leave. Mandy looks out onto the street as she watches them go.

"You are shameless," I say to her jokingly.

She turns and winks at me. "I'm so tapping that ass," she says, and I laugh.

There's not much moving around I want to do, so Mandy and I try out the sectional.

"So, you're an artist?" I ask.

"Yeah. I'm an RA, and I work the information desk at the hospital so I can have health insurance, but one day I'll make a living just from my painting," she says as she stares dreamily into space.

"I'd love to go to your show too."

"Well, duh, you are going," she says and rolls her eyes. "I have to go. Still have half a shift I have to cover."

"Thanks for everything, Mandy. It's nice to know someone here."

Mandy smiles at me. "I'll see you soon, okay? And hey, think about what I said," she says while turning the doorknob.

"About what?"

"Have a sexathon tonight, then let your body rest the last two days before treatment starts."

I throw one of the sofa cushions at her, but it only hits the door after she is on the other side.

After she leaves, I try to remember when was the last time I got some. I've been so numb and in shock since my diagnosis. Sex has been the last thing on my mind. I'm lucky not to have some of the more embarrassing symptoms many women in my situation have. Maybe a night of reckless abandon will help me feel alive again. *I'm not dead yet*, I remind myself. And the furthest thing from the act of dying is the act of lovemaking.

I've never had a serious long-term relationship. I mostly lived at the gym. Luckily, Chema's gym is full of hot men to pick from, and I have a deep bench of booty-call friends I call on when I need to scratch the itch or just relax after hefty training.

I sigh because I have to admit it has been too long, and that bench is oh so very far away in Mexico City. Maybe I could offer to pay for one of them to come here?

No. Not only was that too desperate, but I would lose a day or two before they could get here, and treatment starts in three days. Not to mention a disrespectful use of my sister's money when she thinks she is sponsoring a future UFC titleholder. Looks like the bar it is.

IN THE EVENING, I shower and throw on a pair of faux-leather leggings with a navy-blue silk camisole. My breasts are on the small side, so I feel comfortable skipping a bra and showing a bit of cleavage. I hate wearing high-heels and instead opt for black moto boots that I leave untied and slouchy.

The one girly thing I do enjoy is makeup. I don't get to wear it often because I'm always training, but now seems like the perfect opportunity to wear it.

I opt for a smokey eye with charcoal-black eyeliner. For the lips, I wear a kissable nude shade just a few shades darker than my tanned natural color to give my face some life.

Standing in front of the mirror, I look at my full figure. Taking in those slim, toned muscles I worked so hard to perfect sends me into an emotional state I wasn't expecting. I look great, and I know I won't look this way again for a long time, or maybe even ever. I can't even begin to imagine the many ways in which my body will change and am so grateful Mandy suggested this so I could enjoy my body—this version of it—one last time. I blink away the tears before they get the chance to ruin my makeup.

Not wanting to take a purse with me, I place my ID and credit card in my back pocket. I secure my apartment key into my boot laces, and I head outside.

I have several options to choose from as I walk down my street. For some inexplicable reason, I walk toward the hospital instead of away from it. I hadn't noticed the bar precisely across from the emergency room entrance. *Smart location*, I think.

The door's sign is in a simple font with white LED lights that reads *La Oficina*. Looks like I found my bar.

CHAPTER 3

$\mathcal{I}$t's early, and the bar isn't even at quarter capacity. It's easy to find a space at the bar, and I pull out my credit card to open up my tab.

A bartender so beautiful I find it hard to formulate words comes over to take my order. She has the body of a model, and I can't tell what race she is. She has an other-worldly face, fair skin, and a perfect black bob hairstyle. Her beautiful full lips move again, and I replay what she just said in my head. *What can I get you?*

"Um—sorry. Whiskey sour, please."

She takes my credit card and comes back with my drink a few minutes later.

"Here," she says. "I like your accent."

"Thanks." My face grows hot, and it's not the whiskey.

"*¿Hablas español?*"

My head snaps up to her in surprise. Her Spanish is impeccable. "*Sí,*" I say. We switch back to English after that. "Where are you from?" I ask.

"I'm Chicana. Mom's Mexican, and dad's Chinese. It throws people off. I know." She laughs easily as she says this. "I haven't seen you around here. You work at the hospital?"

"No. New in town," I say.

"I'm Sofia," the bartender says and stretches her hand out to me. "I own the place."

I shake her hand and smile. "Valentina. Nice to meet you."

"Welcome to KC. Let me know when you want another one, okay?"

"Thanks."

Sofia walks away to flirt with two customers a few seats down the bar. Poor suckers don't know she is playing them so that they buy more drinks. I smile. I like this woman.

Sipping on my cocktail, I scan the room for a potential one-night-stand. Someone muscular and handsome who won't need to ask for my phone number after. Someone alone, and more importantly, someone single. Nothing on the menu is appetizing yet, so I order a second drink and nurse it as I wait for the place to fill up.

A few guys come up to hit on me, but they aren't my type. I don't feel any attraction physically, and if Mandy is right and this is my last hurrah for a while, then I want something yummy. I mean, someone yummy. Fuck it. Men objectify women all the time, so I have exactly zero qualms about objectifying them just this once. They would be doing a humanitarian service, I decide. Would they go for it if I sold it as some sort of make-a-wish-for-adults service? No. That would probably kill the mood.

A third man walks over to hit on me, clearly inebriated. I resist the urge to roll my eyes. Could he even get it up, as drunk as he seems to be? Probably not. I smile and do my best to be nice to him—though I hate that's my impulse.

He sways a bit, but it's enough for me to notice. His black hair is slicked back with gel, like this is the nineties or something. "Can I buy you a drink?" he asks.

I point to my glass, showing it's half full. "Got one. Thanks, though." I smile curtly and divert my eyes from him, hoping he takes the hint.

"Oh, I like your accent. Where are you from, *señorita?*" he asks.

I do roll my eyes this time and take a sip of my drink. "I'm from Mexico. Where are you from?" I ask pointedly, though I probably shouldn't engage him any further.

Sofia looks at me with a question in her eyes. I roll my eyes and shake my head as if to say *I got it, thanks.* She tips her chin, and I know she'll throw his ass out if he gets rowdy. Hopefully, I can get him to back away without having to make a scene. I am here to catch a big fish, after all. I won't have a bite if I come across as drama before the night even starts.

"I'm from this here, the U.S. of A." He grins, and it feels eerily like he is about to pound his chest with his fists like a Neanderthal. He is somewhat handsome, tall, black hair, blue eyes. If he wasn't that far drunk, and he hadn't opened his mouth, I may have considered him as my boytoy for the night. "I'm Doctor Keach," he adds. When he says *doctor*, I take it I'm supposed to be impressed.

"I'm actually waiting for someone, so if you don't mind . . ." I trail off, hoping he gets the hint this time.

"Oh, come on. You look so exotic, like a spicy Latina." He says Latina with a mocking accent that I can only assume is meant to mimic my own. My nostrils flare, and I count to ten.

This idiot doesn't realize I could have him on the ground and begging for his mommy in less than ten seconds flat. *Don't use your power on civilians, Valentina.* I remind myself of Chema's anger management lessons. Leave it for the cage. *Never out in everyday life.*

"We can have a good time, honey," he slurs.

"Sorry, buddy, she's with me." A voice much too deep for the body it came out of turns both our attention. I do a double-take when I see Rory, who is in the process of placing his hand on the small of my back. He doesn't make contact with me, though, and instead lets his hand hover over my backside. He wants drunky here to believe it, and he is selling it good.

"Like I said," I tell Dr. Keach, "I was waiting for someone."

"All right, all right. No harm done." He raises his hands in surrender as he walks backward, stumbling on a few people before he turns to face the opposite direction.

"Thanks," I say to Rory.

"No problem. It didn't look like you were having fun."

"I wasn't, but I had it under control."

"I don't doubt it," says Rory. "But I thought maybe I could save you some time."

My gaze sweeps his body from face to shoes. He is wearing jeans and a grey t-shirt, but the outfit is polished. His short, reddish beard is expertly kept, and he looks fresh like he just got out of a shower. This will do nicely. Very nicely indeed.

"That's the second time you saved me this week," I say.

"I thought you looked familiar."

"The vending machine?" I remind him. "You bought me a Pop-Tart."

"That's right. That was you." His eyes squint like he is trying to place my face in that scenario.

"In your defense," I offer, "I look much better tonight."

He smirks, accepting my awkward flirting. God, I'm so bad at this. My booty-call bench is so much easier. All I have to do is text one of them, at random, so no one's feelings get hurt, and ask: Free to fuck tonight? Somehow I don't think that methodology will go over well with Rory. "Can I buy you a drink?" I ask.

"Um—" he looks toward a group of men sitting at a table in the corner of the bar.

"Hey, don't worry about it." My heart sinks a little, but I keep smiling. "I just wanted to thank you for the Pop-Tart and for coming to my rescue tonight. Let me buy you the drink—no strings. You can take it over and enjoy it with your friends."

"No, that's not what I—um, just, let me go say bye to them, and I'll be right back."

My heart flutters, and I don't understand this new sensation. It must be the whiskey. "Sure. I can order in the meantime. What's your poison?"

"A beer?"

"You got it."

I order his beer, and Sofia has it ready for him before he gets back. I swivel in my barstool to look at him standing near the table with his buddies. They roar with laughter, and one of them pats him in the back. His fair complexion makes the reddening of his neck glaringly obvious, and I smile. He palms the back of his neck as if he can feel the heat there. It's cute, really.

Rory is nerdy and slim and oh so very handsome. I hope he'll let me take him home tonight. If this fails, I have to make a mental note to hit the nearest adult toy store first thing in the morning.

He grins as he takes the barstool next to mine. "Thanks," he says as he grabs his beer and takes a long pull. He is nervous and buying time. It's adorable.

"It's the least I could do," I say, opening up the conversation for him. He seems lost for what to say next, so I speak again. "Are you from Kansas City?" I ask, starting with a safe topic I hope will engage him.

"No," he says. "I'm from Minnesota." His entire face brightens when he thinks of home, and I know I've chosen the right topic. "Here for work. I've been here a few years now."

"I'd love some advice on what to check out. It's only my second night in Kansas City. Sofia?" I call her attention, and she looks over right away. She smiles knowingly as she looks between Rory and me, and I point to my empty drink.

"Oh, KC is great. You'll really love it," says Rory.

I start on my third drink, and Rory falls silent. His brows crease like he is thinking of something and he is unsure if he should say it. "Well?" he asks finally. "What are we waiting for? Let's go."

"Go where?" I ask.

"I'm going to show you Kansas City."

"*Tonight?*" I set my drink down and wipe my mouth with a napkin.

"No time like the present."

I cock my head to the side. Is this man serious? *No time like the present?*

"Come on. You are wearing walking shoes. Let's do this."

"Can I at least finish my drink?" I ask.

"Yeah. Sure. The night is young."

I almost spit my drink. Does he only speak in clichés? "Did you just say that?"

"What?"

"*The night is young?* That's such a cliché," I inform him.

"It's going to take a lot to impress you, isn't it, Miss Valentina, um—what's your last name?"

"Almonte. And are you trying to impress me, Rory . . . ?"

"Dennis," he says. "And, yes. Maybe I am trying to impress you."

I bite my lip as I lock eyes with him, and his jade-green eyes darken. The third drink is plunging me into tipsy territory, and I push it away. As I stare deep into his eyes, I realize even his eyes have freckles.

"What are you looking at?" he asks.

"Your eyes have freckles. These little flecks of brown swimming in the green."

"Ah, that." He takes another swig of his beer. "Yeah, my mom used to tell me it was poop."

"What?" I almost yell as I ask, my eyes wide with surprise.

"Yeah, when I was a kid, she had me convinced the little pieces of brown were tiny flecks of poop floating around my irises. Said it was because I was so full of shit." He smirks and drinks from his beer bottle again.

I throw my head back with laughter. This man is funny. "Your mom sounds like a badass," I say.

"She really is."

We are both laughing and relaxed. I don't remember feeling this way with anyone on a first date. "I don't think I'll be finishing my drink after all," I say. We both stand, and I press my hand to his chest. It's firm, and my body heats at the feel of it. "Rory," I say with a breathy voice.

"Yeah?"

"If we go out tonight, I hope you understand I intend to take you to bed before the date is over. Don't leave with me if you are not interested in that."

His eyebrow arches, and he pushes his glasses further up his nose so he can better look at me. His jaw slackens, and I know his brain is misfiring. I walk out of the bar without looking back but hope he is right behind me.

I step into the warm night and take a deep breath of air. Not even three seconds pass before Rory is at my side.

"Sorry," he says. "You kind of caught me off guard there."

"You're here, so I take it you are interested?"

He nods. "You're very forward, aren't you?"

"Not really, but I don't have any time to waste," I say plainly because it is the absolute truth.

CHAPTER 4

Rory orders a car, and I frown when we arrive at our first stop. "A gas station?" I ask.

Rory nods.

Not only is it a gas station but a somewhat shabby one at that. We get out of the car, and as we round the corner, we have to walk past a long line of people waiting to go inside.

"Pro-tip," Rory says, "whenever you travel anywhere new, find long lines. Nine times out of ten, that's where the good food is."

"What could there be that's so good at a gas station?" I scoff.

"Barbecue. The best in the states, dontchaknow."

"Barbecue?"

He nods as we take our place in line. I frown. This line will take an hour before we can go inside, then another hour to wait for the food and the eat it. Maybe I should have gone with Dr. Keach instead of Rory. He was ready to go right then and there.

As if sensing my turning mood, Rory nudges me. "Don't worry. The line will move fast, and you'll see, the wait will be more than worth it."

He is right. We get through the line and have our food in front of us in less than thirty minutes. The dining area is small and crowded. People don't linger and talk, so other diners can have a table.

"This is huge," I say, looking at the brisket sandwich Rory recommended as the only thing worth having. Piles of brisket on a bun with melted cheese and onion rings tower on my plate. Adjusting to the portions in Kansas City will take time but serve my weight-gain goals well. I close the sandwich with the top bun and take a bite. My eyes draw closed. The meat is tender and smoky and so delicious.

"You didn't put any barbecue sauce on it," he says, and hands me a bottle.

I try the sauce first and wrinkle my nose. "Too sweet," I say.

He then hands me a second sauce that is spicier and less sweet. I add only a little of that to appease him.

"So?" He asks.

"It's delicious," I say and mean it. "Except for the fries."

"What's wrong with the fries?" Rory looks down at the tray with the fry mountain.

"They have sugar. Who the hell puts sugar on fries? It's like everything here has sugar. It's really annoying. Sugar is for desserts—that's it. Maybe sweet and sour at Chinese. But that's really it."

Rory blinks at me, then shakes his head. "The fries don't have sugar."

"Are you serious?"

"What?"

"They are like candied fries; they have so much sugar! You really can't taste it?"

He shakes his head. "You're crazy," he says.

I only eat half of my sandwich, even though it's so good I could probably stuff it in. I want to avoid what saucy Chema christened 'TFF' or 'Too Full to Fuck.' I heed all of Chema's warnings.

Our second stop on my tour of the city lands us at a plaza that I have to admit is stunning. The architecture reminds me of the Spanish-style haciendas typical in Mexico. We walk for an hour past restaurants, bars, and shops, never once going inside. Rory talks about his love of traveling and how he wishes he could do it more and asks me questions about Mexico, but we don't go too deep. I won't let it, even with the ample invitations he opens up.

"How's your English so good? I mean, you know a lot of colloquialisms . . . I wouldn't expect you to. I'm sorry, maybe that's a rude question," says Rory as he cups the back of his neck like he did at the bar.

I laugh. "Not at all. A lot of middle—and upper—class kids in Mexico love American culture. English is so cool when you're a teenager in Mexico. We pay attention to all the music, movies, everything that's popular here. And I did a year in a Swiss boarding school when I was fifteen."

Rory stops in his tracks to look at me. "Fancy," he says and resumes his walk.

I scoff. "Yeah. That's one word for it. I think Dad was hoping I'd come back a lady," I say wryly.

"Did you?"

I shake my head. "No. It backfired. I've always wanted to be the furthest thing from a lady that I could. But anyway, the school was mostly for Americans—though I was never quite able to completely shake off the accent—"

"You shouldn't be ashamed of it," says Rory. "You speak multiple languages, and it's easy to understand you. Not to mention, it's very sexy."

"It is?" I ask, my cheek heating up. He nods. "Rory? Are you trying to avoid going to my place? If you didn't want to—"

"No," he says and grabs my hand in his. "I just want to make sure that when we are together, we are both completely sober."

"Oh," I say, unsure how to respond to that. "I'm sober." I'll admit the food helped, and I'm starting to realize nothing Rory does is by accident.

He smiles. "Good. But I also do want you to see a little of this city before you leave—one last stop. I promise, then we'll head back to your place. No way in hell I'm backing out."

We get to the last stop of my tour at nearly one in the morning. Our driver warns us we are probably not allowed at the park this late, but I let Rory lead the way. I smile when he insists on opening my door. Men like this just don't exist anymore. Or so I thought.

"This is Liberty Memorial. The building is a World War I museum, and that is the Liberty Memorial Tower." He points to an obnoxious structure.

We walk through the park toward the tower, and I compress my lips together.

"What?" asks Rory.

My shoulders shake with my suppressed laugh. I can't hold the laughter any longer, so I let it out. "Sorry, it's just . . ."

"Spit it out, Almonte."

"The tower. Isn't it a bit . . ." I trail off and point to the tower because he has to see it. How could he not see it?

Rory cocks his head to the side as he studies the tower. His face scrunches up, and he scratches his head. "What? What are you saying?"

"It's rather *phallic*. Don't you think?"

He tosses his head back with laughter and then nudges my arm. "You are a one-track-mind kind of gal, aren't you?"

"Sure you don't want to just go straight to my apartment?" I ask and wiggle my eyebrows.

Rory shakes his head and takes my hand in his. Our fingers lace together, and I stare at our hands where we join as we walk. I blink. I've never held hands with a man before, and the intimacy of it has me regretting that I've selected Rory for this job. He needed some sort of 'date' before he could go to bed with me. He is boyfriend material, and I am not girlfriend material. This is such a bad idea. But his hand is warm and inviting, and the gesture brings us closer together so I can take his scent in again like I had at the bar. It's a mix of sandalwood and suede and so refreshing mixed with the park's cut grass.

We walk to the edge of the building until we come to a short wall where I rest my elbows on the ledge and look down at a Kansas City starting to come alive with nightlife. The lazy pulse of light traffic in the veins of the city streets flows below us. It's dark, and the lights are bright. Straight ahead, a beautiful building that reminds me of the Met in New York displays fountains on its front lawn.

"What's that?" I ask, pointing at the building.

"That's Union Station," he says.

"Like an actual train station?"

"Yeah."

"It's beautiful," I say dreamily. Would I ever get the chance to ride a train? I was so dedicated to my sport, I barely experienced life at all. You always think there is more time, *later*—to do all the things you ever dreamed of. But time is not a guarantee, and it is not owed to anyone. Too bad I learned this lesson at the expense of my life.

You are not dead yet, Valentina, I remind myself. There's still a chance.

"The inside is great too," Rory says, oblivious in the dark to the prickling tears in my eyes.

"Yeah?"

"Yeah. There's a coffee shop and a restaurant. They have all sorts of science exhibits. Maybe you'll let me take you on a date? We can go there. This weekend? Are you free?"

This weekend I'll be puking my guts out. "Rory, I don't want to give you the wrong idea. I—"

"I know what this is," he says. "I'm not asking you to be my girlfriend or my wife. You were at that bar looking for something, and I'm just the lucky bastard who caught your eye. But I'm not going to stand here and lie to you. I can't tell you I don't want to see you again after tonight."

"The thing is, I'm not sure I'll be here much longer." I mean *life*, but Rory, I know, hears *Kansas City*.

"Can we just enjoy the time we do have, then?" He ducks his head to hold my gaze, and I suddenly am not sick Valentina. I'm not cancer-patient Valentina. In his eyes, I'm hot and sexy Valentina. The girl with the Spanish accent who bought him a drink. "Please?" he nudges.

"Okay," I say, unsure how the hell I'm going to get out of this. The thing is, spending what little time I have before treatment with him sounds lovely. I can always make an excuse later if I'm not feeling up to going out on the weekend.

He leads me by the hand as we make our way back through the trees and lays down on the grass. He pats the spot next to him. "You gonna join me?"

"This is the weirdest hookup of my life," I tell him, attempting to joke, but he doesn't laugh. His beard shifts lightly with the movement of his clenching jaw.

We are nestled between two trees, looking up at the black sky through the leaves. There are no stars out tonight. I'm completely sober now, and a gust of wind makes me shiver. I press my naked arms to his body as I curl up to his side.

"Hold on." Rory shifts. "Lift your head a bit." I do as I'm told, and he slides his arm under my head so that I nestle next to him and lay my head on his shoulder. He wraps his other arm around me and rubs my arm a few times to warm me up. "Better?"

"Yeah," I say. "I get cold easily."

"That's great because I'm always running way too hot." And it's true. His warm skin soothes me, and I bet my cool skin refreshes him. I fit next to his body perfectly and can only imagine what it will be like to have him fully.

A short gust of wind rattles the leaves into the most soothing sound.

"Valentina?"

"Mmm?" I moan, too relaxed to form words.

"Why did you pick me?"

I shrug. "You're handsome. And . . ." I bite the inside of my lip.

"And what?"

What the hell. *Pa' luego es tarde*, as Chema would say. "When you were getting the Pop-Tart from the vending machine, I *may* have checked out your ass."

"You checked out my ass?"

I lift my head so I can read his expression, and he chuckles. "Yeah. I checked out your ass. Sue me. It's a cute little bubble butt."

"Oh, Valentina—"

"What?"

"I was checking out your ass the entire time you were threatening the machine."

"You were?"

"Yeah."

I laugh, and a moment of silence follows. I'm thinking about the train station and all the places I want to go one day. "Rory?"

"Mmm?"

"If you could go anywhere in the world, where would you go?"

"Easy. India."

"That's unexpected."

"I'd eat my way through India until I got sick of it."

I laugh. "Really? You chose your dream destination based on the food?"

"What else is there?"

"I don't know. People? Places?"

"Well, yeah, India has both those too."

"Smartass," I say, and he chuckles. "So, you like Indian food?"

"Don't you?"

"Don't know. I kind of live on protein shakes, broccoli, and chicken breasts. Slight exaggeration, but it's not far off from the truth."

"A picky eater, huh?"

"No. It's for work."

"Work?"

"Yeah. I'm an athlete." Or was an athlete, I think. "So my eating habits are controlled, to put it mildly."

"Well, if you can ever have a cheat day, I'd love to take you out for Indian food."

I blink slowly, then smile when he doesn't judge my eating regimen like most people do. Everyone not in the sport always assumes I'm exaggerating and should be able to cheat my diet more than I do. But Rory accepts it without question, and it's so strange to me. He also doesn't ask what kind of athlete. He wants me to open up to him because I want to.

"Maybe one day," I tell him finally.

He nods, and we both fall silent for a long stretch of time. So much so that when I wake up, I have no idea how long we've been out because next to me, Rory is letting out the cutest little snore. I poke his ribs gently, and he stirs. "Rory," I whisper.

"Mmmh," he groans but doesn't open his eyes.

"Rory." I shiver. The night got significantly cooler. What the hell time is it? I pull out my phone from my back pocket, and my eyes widen with horror. Five in the morning. We slept *all night*. What the hell are cops doing that they didn't notice us? Not only did we miss our booty call, but I slept like I had never slept in my life. "Rory," I hiss, louder this time. "Wake up. We have to go."

He stirs and wipes a bit of drool from the corner of his mouth. His eyes dart around his surroundings, trying to place where he is. "What . . ." He sits up and looks around. He starts grasping around for his glasses that must have fallen from his face in the middle of the night and puts them on once he finds them. He looks around, and what he does next, I would have never in a million years have guessed would be his reaction.

He rolls onto his back with laughter so intense, he wraps his arms around his middle to clutch his stomach. "We fell asleep!" He cries between guffaws.

"It's not funny, Rory," I say, gritting my teeth.

"It's pretty funny."

"Rory, it's five a.m."

He laughs harder. "Really?"

I stand to shake any dirt from my outfit and try to straighten my hair. I use my phone as my mirror, and I turn away from him at record speed. My mascara is running, and I look like a raccoon. My hair is knotted and has blades of grass stuck in it.

Rory stands to look at me, and I pull my face away, horrified.

"Come here," he says. He grabs my chin, so I face him. "You look adorable," he says.

"No, I don't," I whine, and I slap his torso playfully. My hands can't help but linger over his hard oblique muscles. I'm only holding on to him for balance, of course, while he pulls out blade after blade of grass from my hair.

"Here, let me get that." His finger is reaching for my eye next, and I rear back.

"What are you doing?"

He laughs as he tries to approach me again. "You have an eye booger."

"Oh my god!" I turn away from him and start walking in the opposite direction while I clear out the corners of my eyes.

"Hold on," he calls after me. "It's no big deal," he says. He continues to laugh, and I'm trying to be annoyed like I should be, but it's getting harder to suppress my own laughter.

"This was supposed to be a sexy night. I'm not going to let you clean my eye-boogers."

"I'm sorry if you're upset," he says. "But I'm not."

"You're not?"

"No. That's the best night's sleep I've had in a long time."

"Me too," I admit.

"See? It wasn't a total waste. But I am sorry we missed our night together. I'm sorry for falling asleep. Not that it's an excuse, but I had a long shift at work yesterday."

"It's on me too. I can't just blame you. Even if I wanted to," I say.

"I don't have work today," he says. "Do you?"

I shake my head. "Do you still want to . . . ?"

His expression changes from that playful-young-boy demeanor of his into a dark one full of hunger. It's like he has two personalities, my very own personal Jekyll and Hyde. He draws me to him and kisses me with greed I have never known before. He crushes his lips to mine and nibbles at my lower lip when he comes up for air. Then he plunges in again to play, his tongue on mine. His beard grazes my skin, and I whimper into his mouth. A groan comes from deep within his throat in response, and I bunch up the fabric of his shirt in my hands.

I push him away, and we are both panting. I touch my lips that now feel bruised. I can't believe I slept with him in the literal sense of the word and hadn't so much as kissed him. "We need to get a car," I say. He nods and pulls out his phone.

"Your place or mine?" he asks. "I have roommates. They'll be up soon."

"My place is fine. I live alone."

We ride in the back seat together and can't help giggling as we look at each other conspiratorially. He tries grabbing my hand, but I pull it away. He chuckles, and I can't help smiling around him. I should be mad. So mad. And with any other guy, I would be fuming if this had happened, but sleeping with him didn't seem like a waste of time—not even with the precious few days I might have left.

"Valentina?"

"What?" I try to snap but fail.

"How do you say eye booger in Spanish?"

"Oh my god. Why do you want to know?" I look over at our driver, who doesn't seem to care about our odd conversation.

Rory shrugs. "I think I'd like to learn Spanish."

"And you think the best place to start is with 'eye booger?'"

He presses his hand to his heart. "The word has sentimental value to me." He chuckles as he says this, and soon I follow with my own laugh. Have I ever laughed this much? Rory radiates a warmth that makes it hard to be mad at him and instead has me smiling and laughing like I wasn't already walking on death row.

"*Lagaña*," I say.

"*Lagaña*," he repeats.

"Excellent pronunciation," I say, a bit proud. "But next time, let's teach you something more useful."

"I don't know. It would have been useful today," he jokes, and I smack his arm as we turn onto my street.

Dawn breaks as we enter my apartment, and Rory stares into my living room with an expression not unlike Mandy's when she first saw it. *Here we go again*, I think, but unlike Mandy, he doesn't comment on how nice it is.

I'm locking the door when he comes up behind me. He wraps his arms around me, tucking his thumb under the hem of my blouse. It lingers there as he kisses my neck, his beard tickling a trail after his lips.

"Mmm, Valentina." He groans into my ear, and my skin breaks into goosebumps, forcing my hand to move of its own accord. I take his hand currently over my lower midriff and help him into my legging's waistband. I turn to face him, and his lips crush mine once again like they had at the park. He's about to tuck my pants off when I stop him. "Wait," I say.

His hands break free of me, and he looks into my eyes. His brows knit together, and I see concern there. "No, that's not what I—I still want to. We *are* going to. I just need a minute in the restroom. Freshen up and all that."

"Oh, okay," he says with a breathy voice.

"Make yourself at home. There's a guest bathroom if you need it. First door on the left." I smile and hasten to my bedroom.

I had to pee, but I wasn't about to tell him that. Then I wince when I look in the mirror. Rory had picked out most of the grass but missed many still lingering in the depths of my thick hair. I finish the job, take off my ghastly makeup, and run a brush through my hair. I can't waste time and shower, and I also don't want him to feel bad that he hasn't showered himself, so I run some water under my armpits and between my legs and hope that will do. I brush my teeth and use some hand lotion with a gentle flowery scent that will hopefully mask any odors from the night outdoors. I smirk, remembering our mishap last night.

I kick off my boots and find him in the living room.

"You took forever," he says.

"I'm sorry. I'm all yours now."

CHAPTER 5

I take my camisole off as I walk to him, and his eyes widen at my brazen exposure of my breasts. I'm about to start taking his shirt off when he grasps my wrists holding me in place. Crap. Did I miss my window? I'm suddenly vulnerable in my topless state. "What's wrong?" I ask.

He cups the back of his neck in a gesture exactly like what he did at the bar when his buddies were giving him a hard time about leaving with a woman.

"Rory?" I ask in as soothing a tone as I'm capable of. My arms wrap in front of my chest so I can cover my nipples. "Do you want to keep your shirt on? It's okay if you do." *I might cry*, I think, but don't share that last bit. I also can't imagine what he would be self-conscious about. I had felt the hard muscles of his abdomen through his shirt several times already.

Rory shifts his weight from one leg to the other, and his eyes can't meet mine. "No. It's okay. I just need to prepare you . . ." He trails off. Whatever he needs to prepare me for is difficult for him to say.

"What for?"

"I'll tell you about it later. Don't ask the story behind what you're about to see right now. Okay?"

"You're scaring me a little, Rory."

He chuckles, but it's nervous. "It's nothing bad. I promise."

"Okay?"

"I have a scar."

I laugh. "I don't have any problems with scars." I drop my arms, exposing my naked breasts again.

"It's pretty big."

I purse my lips because now I'm concerned about *why* he has this scar, but he asked me not to ask questions, and I intend to make him comfortable too. My eyes freeze over his chest for a second before I look at him again. His beautiful green eyes are frozen to the carpet.

"You never asked me what kind of athlete I am," I say.

His head snaps up, and he is looking into my eyes again, a question in his.

"Ask me what I do."

"Um, okay . . . what do you do, Valentina?"

"I'm a mixed martial arts fighter."

"Oh." He looks confused, and I know he doesn't understand where I'm going with this.

"Fighters tend to find scars sexy as fuck," I explain, and I know he can see the hunger in my gaze. I lick my lips in a blatant display of desire. He charges for me and picks me up in his arms like newlyweds in all the romantic comedies my sister likes to watch. I squeal as he lifts me. "Rory!"

He takes me to my bedroom and tosses me onto the bed somewhat forcefully. "You're fucking perfect," he declares. I sit up and then kneel on the bed so I can help him out of his clothes, *finally*.

I race to take his shirt off and lean back to admire his body. A shirtless Rory still in his jeans is a sight to behold. His fair torso is slim but well-defined. You wouldn't think it to look at him with clothes on, but this man has a six-pack with a trail of reddish hair leading to his waistband over the ripples of his muscles.

His chest hair in matching red covers a lengthy scar that starts at the top of his chest and spans down the length of his sternum. I know his chest has been cracked open, but no questions right now. I raise my hands to his chest, hovering over the scar, and search his eyes. He nods, giving me permission to touch, so I trace the scar from top to bottom.

And in a move I have no idea where it came from, I dip my head to lick the length of it. His grip tightens a bit around my shoulders, but he doesn't push me away.

I reach to touch the muscles of his six-pack, and he stills but lets me explore where I want. I follow the trail of my hands with my mouth as I kiss and lick the granite muscles leading up to his scar. When I get to it, I lick it all the way to its start. I find his neck and nibble at it while my hands work his jeans open.

Underneath, I find boxer briefs with that mushroom tip poking out of the waistband. I lift the glistening droplet of his precum with my index finger and bring it to my mouth. I look him in the eye as I lick my finger and revel in the taste of him. The saltiness of it sends a shiver down my spine my eyes close with pleasure. I open them again to find a stunned Rory gaping at me. He shakes his head to snap out of it and hurries out of his underwear.

His cock springs forward, and my eyes widen. I gulp. I'm not sure I'll be able to fit him in. His length is intimidating, but my mouth waters all the same. "It's so . . ." I trail off.

"So what?" he asks.

"So pink."

He smiles sexily and peels off my leggings and underwear next, then steps back to ogle me as I had him. Fair is fair. His jaw tightens, and his Adam's apple bobs as he swallows hard. With that look of hunger on his face, I'm not the slightest bit self-conscious. Being naked in front of Rory is nothing but freedom and delight.

He leans over me and finds my mouth. This is our first kiss without the morning breath, and it is glorious. I purr into his mouth, and he matches it with a deep groan that has my legs locking around him.

His hand draws down so he can play with the folds of my entrance. I shamelessly grind against the feel of his hand, finding his rhythm. His thumb presses my clit while he dips a finger in me. He doesn't stop kissing me, though, and it's hard to stay put and not roll my head back at all the sensations he evokes.

When he sinks a second and then a third finger inside to stretch me, I can't contain it any longer. I pull away from his mouth and scream his name.

"Does that feel good?" he asks in that husky voice of his.

"Yes!" I scream and clench around his fingers. His fingers respond by curling upward. "So good. Oh, Rory! Don't stop!"

He brings his mouth to my nipple and circles his tongue gently around it, sending me over the edge. I'm moaning and writhing under his touch as my orgasm hits, and he isn't even inside me yet. Rory is a selfless lover. I'm so smart for picking him out of everyone in the bar.

His fingers withdraw from me, and he gives my nipple a peck with his lips. "Condoms?" he asks.

"Nightstand. I'll get them."

He pulls away from me, and I rummage through the drawer and sit up so I can put it on him. His abdominal muscles clench as I roll the condom down his length.

He grabs a handful of my ass as he groans. "I love this ass," he says.

I raise an eyebrow. "Is that right, Rory Dennis?" I ask. He nods, and I reward him by facing away from him and scooting back to offer him a better view of it. After years of working my body into a machine, I am very proud of all my muscles—ass included. If one more person gets to admire it, who am I to argue?

The bed moves as Rory stands, and I scoot further back until my entrance feels the tip of his cock. I grind against him, begging for him to enter me. I am so wet from my first orgasm and so glad he took that care given his size. Both his hands wrap around my waist to hold me in place as he starts to slowly slide in. His fingers were blissful, but this, nothing could compare to the stretch of me with him inside.

"Valentina, fuck," he gurgles out, and I reward the sounds by rocking back and forth to match his gentle stroke. He stops moving for a long moment, giving me time to adjust to his size. I grab a pillow so I can rest my chest to the bed, and my ass raises higher. I want him to enjoy this view almost as much as I want to chase my next orgasm with him inside me.

He plunges into me and freezes deep inside. I clench experimentally around him, and he growls before he starts pounding into me. The grip he has on my waist tightens, his fingers digging into my skin, but the pain mixes with the pleasure, and I can't tell him to stop. I can only ask him to keep going. "Yes, Rory! Yes! Right there!"

Rory is listening because next follow a series of pumps so forceful, he is slowly scooting me further up the bed. I bite into the pillow under me as I let out a scream that gets muffled. My orgasm comes in waves this time, and he keeps driving into me, rolling me into a second climax and then a third. My legs start to shake when he sinks into me as his body clenches with his own release. I'm now regretting this position because I can't see him as he climaxes. I pant into the pillow and come up for air.

Rory kisses my back gently and withdraws from me. He steps into the restroom, probably to toss the condom before he comes back to bed and lies next to me. I curl to his side like I had done last night. "No falling asleep this time," I joke.

He laughs. "No falling asleep. Though, I don't think I could even if I wanted to. I feel well-rested."

"Oh really?" I wiggle my eyebrows at him.

"Are you trying to kill me, woman?" He chuckles. "I at least need sustenance, then maybe after that, and a bit of a rest, I will make you come five more times."

My thighs tighten at his words. His lips lock with mine again, but this time it's sweeter and with less urgency. "I'm going to hold you to that," I joke.

"First, I must get food."

"I have food, but you'll be sorry if I cook. Would you like to go out?"

"No. I prefer to spend the morning with you naked. I'll cook."

"You can cook?" I ask with surprise.

"I know my way a bit around the kitchen."

"Would you cook naked?" I ask.

He chuckles. "Can I at least wear my boxer-briefs? A naked cooking incident wouldn't be pretty."

"Fine," I say with resignation.

"You, on the other hand, I insist you remain naked while you watch me cook."

"I can manage that."

We get up and make our way to the kitchen. Rory leans toward the fridge and scratches his jaw through his beard. "You don't have much," he says. "But I think I can whip up some egg sandwiches. How does that sound?"

"Great," I say. And it does. I'm starting to love real bread with actual gluten. I don't know how I'll ever go back to my pre-cancer diet. I purse my lips because this is the first time I've caught myself making plans for the future, and I have the sickening sensation in my stomach that this new outlook has everything to do with the redhead with the broken sternum.

Which reminds me of his scar. Is it okay to ask now? I understood he didn't want to say before. I thought maybe he didn't want to ruin the moment, but *when* would it be okay to ask?

He's a one-night-stand, so maybe it's better to not ask at all. *Don't get personal, Valentina. This is just for today.*

Rory places several items from the fridge on the counter, and I watch him from my spot at the bar. I'm sitting with my arms propped on the bar top so he can have a view of my breasts as he works. My breasts swell over my forearms, and I smile at him.

He looks up at me, and the corner of his mouth quirks up into a sexy smile. "Fuck breakfast. I'm eating you instead," he says and walks around the bar to me. He takes me by surprise and lifts me to reposition me on the barstool, so I face away from the counter. Kneeling, his face is at the level of my sex. My entire body blushes, and I almost want to close my legs. What the hell? I'm not shy.

"No." He grabs my knees and pushes them wide to expose me fully to his face. "Don't close your legs." He slides his fingers down the length of my folds. "You're beautiful," he says in a husky voice. I found Rory's deep voice sexy to begin with, but when it deepens further with his arousal, that sexiness reaches an entirely different level.

My chest expands with each labored breath, and I nod. He plays with the black curls of my pubic hair and presses a finger to my clit, sending my head back with pleasure. I'm so sensitive from our time together in bed, and the sensation is so extreme, my face twists into a grimace he can't see. I feel his tongue on me next, and my head snaps down to look at him. His tongue is circling my clit, but not touching it in a teasing motion. His head moves between my legs as he teases at my entrance with his tongue, and the view of his red mane between my legs is the most erotic thing I have ever seen in my life.

My fingers find their way to his hair and tug on it lightly. I keep his head in place where I want him, and a moan escapes him. "Rory," I purr his name. "That feels amazing." He rewards my praise by pressing his tongue to my swollen clit, and my legs start to quiver. His hands are keeping my legs apart, his grip tightening over my inner thighs. I'm so sensitive, that familiar coil starts building in my core almost instantly. His lips enclose around my clit so he can suck on it gently, and I can't take it anymore. My hands fist his hair, and my abdomen convulses as I climax onto his tongue. He doesn't stop, and the orgasm keeps going. I had no idea an orgasm could stretch out that long. Rory Dennis has a magic tongue.

I can't take the maddening ongoing release anymore, and I start to beg. "Rory, please, Rory, stop!"

He encircles his tongue around my clit one last time and finally comes up for air. My legs shake as he trails kisses up my lower abdomen, licks a circle around my belly button, and trails his tongue to my neck. He stops to nibble at my jaw and finishes with a sensual kiss that lets me taste myself on his lips. He parts from my mouth to study my face, and his smirk is cocky, like he is so damn proud of himself.

"That was yummy," I say, coming down from my fuck-drunk state.

"Indeed." Rory chuckles.

I look down, and he is starting to harden again, though he isn't at his full size yet. I reach for the waistband of his boxer-briefs, but he grabs my wrist with a shake of his head. "No. That was just for you."

"Rory—" I protest because I want my turn, but he kisses me into silence.

"One down," he says when his mouth leaves mine.

"What?"

"I told you I was going to make you come five more times before I leave today. Four more to go."

I blink slowly at him. This man can't be serious. I don't know if I can handle four more.

"I'm a man of my word, Valentina. You'll see." He pulls away from me and goes back to his work in the kitchen.

I blink after him, too stunned for words. It was odd how this day started, with him shy about his chest, but the moment I licked his scar,

Rory came out of his shell. I smile at him, glad he could open up to me, even if only sexually.

I go to the restroom to clean up a bit, and when I get back, he winks at me, starts chopping onions, and tosses them into butter on a hot pan. He moves quickly, like he knows this kitchen. Before I know it, the smell of butter and eggs has my stomach grumbling.

"Here." He places the egg sandwich in front of me before coming around the counter to sit next to me.

"Thanks," I say, and we both dig in. "This is great," I offer after the first bite. He smiles and keeps chewing but squeezes my thigh.

"Valentina, how do you say 'sandwich' in Spanish?" he asks between bites.

I laugh. "How do you say 'taco' in English?"

Rory turns to me slowly, a large bite bulging his right cheek, and he blinks. He starts laughing and trying to swallow at the same time, which makes him cough. He takes a sip of water, and when he successfully swallows, he faces me again. "I don't think our Spanish lessons are going very well so far. Maybe I should give up?"

I laugh. "No, don't give up. Spanish is a beautiful language. And in your defense, there is a word for sandwich, but it's not really used. A lot of people wouldn't even know what it is. At least in Mexico."

"So you just call it sandwich, then?"

I nod. "But you have to pronounce it in Spanish."

Rory scratches his head. "What do you mean?"

"You say it like, *'sanguish'* with a soft 'g.'"

"That's weird."

"Or brilliant," I counter.

When we finish eating, I wrinkle my nose. "Don't take this the wrong way, but I can smell myself. I need a shower bad. You want to join me?"

"It would be an honor to shower with you." He stands and offers me his hand as he bows. His wavy bed-head is adorable, and even his beard is a bit messed up from our intense fucking. I smile and take his hand.

I lead him to the shower and let him adjust the water temperature to his liking. "This okay?" he asks. It's a little on the hot side for me, but I don't mind it much.

His skin reddens a bit with the heat as the water glides down his body. I bite my lip.

"Again?" he rolls his eyes. "Fine. But you're really taking advantage of my body, miss Almonte." He grabs a handful of my ass and squeezes.

I laugh. "No. Let's clean up a bit. I really need the shower."

"Okay." He grabs my loofah and the washcloth I brought for him, and I pour body wash liberally on both. We soap up and giggle as we get clean. I feel naughty, like a little kid who ate too many sweets before dinner. I wash my hair and am surprised when he shampoos his beard.

He chuckles at my expression. "It takes a lot of work to keep this beard."

"I like it," I say.

"Oh?"

"It's a great feeling when it tickles my inner thighs."

"Only for you, Valentina, I promise never to shave it off."

We are both rinsed off, and he grabs me by the waist, so my body is flush with his. His lips crush mine as he plays with his tongue on mine. He cups the back of my head as the water falls down both our faces, keeping my eyes shut tight. As we devour the others' mouths, his erection hardens against my abdomen. The water rolling down my body, his tight grip on me, and the erection twitching between us are all too much. When the hell did I become so damn insatiable that I want him again?

I break away from him and kneel on the shower floor much too quickly to give him a chance to protest. Wrapping my hand around his shaft, I pump once, then twice, while I squeeze gently. Rory groans, and his hands fist at his sides. He leans his head back on the tile, and the water now hits his chest and six-pack. I look up at his body and lick my lips. His gaze is glued to my face with hooded eyes.

Bringing my grip to the base of his shaft, I lick the head of his cock.

"Fuck, Valentina," he groans. His breathing quickens, and I take the head into my mouth, sucking on it gently before letting him out of my mouth again.

I look up. The water bounces off those six-pack muscles, making me squint. "Is this okay?" I ask as I pump with my hand once again.

"Fuck, yes," he all but screams, and I take him into my mouth again.

This time I take him deeper into my throat as I continue to stroke his base with my hand. He grips my hair in his fist and starts guiding me to the rhythm he wants, and I let him. Rory tastes divine, and seeing his body wet like this has my own wetness gliding down my thighs all over again. My pussy clenches at the sight of him with his eyes shut tight and the veins in his neck straining with the pleasure of my mouth.

"Stop," he growls and pulls me away by my hair.

"No," I whine. "More. Please."

"Fuck. It's hard to deny you, but I don't want to come in your mouth."

"I want you to come in my mouth." I reach for him with my tongue, but his grip on my hair is too tight.

"No," he shakes his head, though I know his resolve wavers. "I'm not wasting this on your mouth. Not today." He bends and places his hands under my armpits so he can lift me to my feet. He lands a wet kiss on my lips and pants when he breaks away.

"I'm about to impress the hell out of you," I tell him, and his eyebrow arches. I'm leaning against the cool tile of the shower wall, and I bring my right leg all the way up to rest against his shoulder, effectively doing the splits while standing.

"You are going to be the end of me," he groans. He presses his erection to my entrance, and I grind my clit up and down the shaft. I could come from just this friction alone.

I hear a wrapper, and my eyes fling open. "When did you get a condom?"

Rory chuckles. "I have many talents, Valentina."

He withdraws his hips away from me so he can roll on the condom, but I keep my leg over his shoulder as he does this. Taking his cock in hand, he positions it at my entrance, parting me slowly. I wince a bit, and he stills. "Are you okay?" he says. I nod. "We can stop if it's painful."

"No!" I all but scream out. "It hurts so good," I say.

With a sexy smile, he gives me another inch of him slowly, so slowly, my head leans back. In this stretched position, my tightening around him is extreme.

"Fuuuck," Rory draws out. "You feel so tight like this."

I can tell he is holding himself back with the slow, lazy strokes by the strained muscles of his arms encasing me. He keeps one hand on the wall behind me and takes the other away from the wall to cup my chin, and brings his lips to mine. I plunge my tongue into his mouth, and his pace quickens a bit.

He releases my mouth and leans back to bring his free hand between us and presses his thumb to my overly-sensitive and swollen clit.

I scream, and my leg muscles tighten over his shoulder as I come yet again for the who-the-fuck-knows-how-many times today. He drives into me so forcefully now, he is almost lifting me off the ground by his cock until he stills, effectively impaling me. His eyes tighten, and he groans out his release. I'm so glad we are facing each other now so I can see his face when he climaxes.

We both pant, and he presses his forehead to mine. "Thank you," he says.

"Are you thanking me for making you come?"

He chuckles. "Yeah. Guess I am." He leaves me, and I unwrap my leg from him, bringing it down to the ground. We rinse again, then dry off.

Rory is drying out his hair with a towel when he looks at me with a devilish grin. "Only three more to go."

Oh, for fuck's sake. "You really don't have to deliver on that. You've more than proved your sex-god status."

"Oh, but I want to deliver," he says with a teasing smile.

"Can I at least have a break?"

"Of course. So long as you remain naked the rest of the morning."

"Fine, but I'm wearing underwear at least. It's more comfortable."

"Agreed."

We both put on underwear before going to lounge on the sofa. Rory sits, and I lay my head on his lap. "What a fucking glorious morning," I say.

Rory pinches my nipple playfully. "You got that right."

I giggle.

Rory's head rests back as he looks at the ceiling and I look at him. We are both basking in the luxury of this lazy morning where all we've done is fuck and eat. A lump lodges in my throat because I want more of this. Preferably with Rory if he is up to it, but the bottom line is, I want more of life. I've hardly lived, and now I have found someone who has given me so many firsts that I'm thinking there are a hell of a lot more firsts I haven't even begun to imagine. My eyes prickle with tears. I need to live. I need to survive.

I want more time.

Suddenly I'm reminded that I'm Valentina Fucking Almonte. A new fan-favorite MMA fighter in Mexico and shortlisted for the UFC. I have never backed down from a fight; why the hell was I about to start now? I sought Dr. Carolina Ramirez like I sought Chema—I wanted the best on my team, and I got her. Like there was never an option to lose a fight, there isn't an option to die. Not yet. Not for a long time.

"Are you okay?" Rory asks, his brows creased together.

Fuck. He's looking at me with puppy eyes. "Yeah. Just a little home-sick. Wish I could show you around Mexico City."

"You mean like I showed you around Kansas City?"

I laugh. "Yeah. Exactly like that. Except for the falling asleep at the park bit."

"Let me make up for that. Saturday. I'll really show you around a few more places."

I shake my head. "Rory," I choke on my words. "I haven't changed my mind. This is a one-night-stand, or rather, a one-day-stand, but we aren't seeing each other again."

"I thought we agreed we would spend together whatever time we do have?"

Dammit. "Yeah. Okay, but let's not put pressure on this, okay? I can't really handle serious right now."

"Okay. We can take it slow."

"Thank you. I can't promise we can hang out Saturday, but if you like, you can stay over tonight." It's my last night to have him, I think.

"I can't," he says. "I have a shift at the hospital tonight. I start at four."

My eyes widen with horror, and I spring up to a sitting position like a Jack-In-The-Box toy. "What did you say?"

"I work tonight." His head cocks to the side as he tries to figure out what's wrong.

"Yeah, but you said 'at the hospital.'"

"That's right. Where we met." He smiles. "I'm a doctor."

No. No. No. This can't be happening. Then all the pieces fall into place. How could I have been so stupid? It was so obvious. I met him in the waiting area at Heartland Metro Hospital, never thinking he could be a doctor. I just assumed he was a student. He knew that Doctor Keach from the bar, which is why he backed off so easily. He was at the bar across the street from the hospital. I clear my throat. "So you work at Heartland Metro?"

"Now you want to get to know me?" He is teasing me, and I try to smile. I don't want him to know, so I have to play this off even though I already acted like a freak.

I shrug. "Just curious."

Crap.

"Why do you look like that?" he asks.

"Like what?"

"All green, like you are going to vomit."

"Just a little hot in here, don't you think?"

"I'm fine, but if you want to kick up your AC, go for it."

I walk to the hallway with the thermostat pretending to adjust it and use the time to take a deep breath and calm my racing heart. Let's think about this logically. Heartland Metro is almost a small city with lots of buildings. It would be improbable for us to bump into each other again. The likelihood of him being in the oncology department is slim. I mean, what would be the chances? And what's the worst that could happen if he finds out I am a patient there? It's not like we are a couple; it shouldn't be a big deal. He couldn't get mad because why would I tell a one-night-stand my medical history? It's not like he told me about his scar. Calmer, I walk back to the couch and lie down again.

"Better?" He asks.

"Yeah. Thanks."

I want to change the subject, so I think. I look down his slim but muscular legs. "Are you a runner?" I ask.

"Yeah. Don't usually skip a morning run, but I figure you have provided me with quite a bit of cardio for today." He smirks, and I laugh. "Why do you ask?"

"Your legs. Well, really, your build. You have a deceivingly muscular body."

"Hey, what's that supposed to mean?"

"Nothing. I like your athletic build, but you don't really show it off much with your loose clothes."

"Some things are best left to the imagination."

I DOZE off after a short while and awaken at a sensation between my legs. I have no clue how long Rory has been fingering me, but his gaze is locked on my face like he is studying.

"Mmmm," I moan. "That feels good."

My head is on his lap, but he is leaning slightly so he can reach my center. He works me until I come again, and within the next twenty minutes, he delivers on his promise with the remaining two orgasms.

We lay in my bed for a few hours, Rory asking me how to say different words in Spanish. We keep the conversation light, and I'm grateful he can read my mood so well.

"I have to go," Rory says, and I look at the clock on my nightstand. It's noon, and our morning is officially over.

He smiles. "Sex and eggs," he says.

"What?"

"Sex and eggs. I could get used to this." I smack him playfully on the arm, and he gets up to start dressing. "I hope we can do this again soon," he says.

"We'll see."

"Can I get your number?" When he sees my hesitation, he adds, "I know where you live. Would you rather I stop by?"

"Fine." I enter my number in his phone. He calls it like he is not sure I gave him the right number, but it rings in my room, and he gives me one last kiss before he leaves.

Chema used to tell me I should promise myself rewards to keep up with my training and stay motivated, so I follow his advice now. I'm going to beat this thing, so I can have Rory once more before I go home, I promise myself.

Because I haven't had nearly enough of him yet.

CHAPTER 6

With Rory gone, there is nothing else to do in the apartment except eat. I didn't want to go explore because somehow, that is something I now want to do with him. I heavily smother my fourth piece of toast with butter as I think of what to do with my time.

In another first in my week of 'firsts,' as I now fondly think of it, I have free time. I would have to thank Mandy for prescribing the sex-athon because it had been a while, and it will be longer after treatment.

Going back to the bar to pick out another hookup doesn't appeal. Plus, I doubt anyone would measure up to Rory and his enthusiastic fucking. And if that wasn't enough of a deterrent, I couldn't go to the same bar without risking bringing home another doctor from the hospital where my treatment will take place.

Mandy calls at three in the afternoon, and I am glad for the distraction from my boredom.

"I'm having drinks at a friend's tonight, and you are coming with," she says before so much as a 'hello.'

"Hi Mandy, I'm fine, thanks for asking. Sure, thanks for inviting me."

"Sarcasm doesn't look as good on you as it does on me," she says dryly.

"What time? And where do I meet you?"

Mandy sighs into the phone. "Do you even have a car?"

"I didn't really have to drive in the City, so . . ."

"Oh, my, god. Don't tell me you don't know how to drive!"

I laugh. "I'm joking. I have a car."

"Forget it. I'll pick you up at seven," she says and hangs up.

I'm ready by seven, but Mandy doesn't show up until seven forty-five. I'm sitting on the stoop in front of my building when she shows up in an old, beat-up clunker of a car. When she rolls down her window, a litany of apologies trail out.

"It's really okay," I tell her once I'm in the passenger side. "Honestly, I wanted to enjoy the nice night out."

"Okay," she bites her lip, looking guilty as she drives. "I have a hard time getting to places on time."

"No worries. So? We're going to a friend's house?"

"Yeah. They work at the hospital with me, but don't worry, they're discreet, and you don't have to tell them anything you don't want to. I know I could use a girls' night, and I figured you might as well."

"I don't know," I say. "I don't really have any girlfriends," I admit, and I'm not sure why that makes me feel embarrassed.

"Not even one?"

"Does my sister count?"

Mandy shakes her head, and her laughter fills the car. "No. Your sister definitely doesn't count."

I shrug, unsure what else to say to that.

"Don't tell me you are one of those girls who is too cool for other girls? You only hang out with men because you 'identify' better with them?"

I laugh. "No. When you're trying to be a pro athlete, it's hard to have time for friends at all. I didn't really go anywhere, so it was hard to meet people, and yeah, fighting gyms are filled ninety-nine percent with men. I mostly have male friends because of convenience, not because I think I'm superior to other women or anything."

"Okay, girl. I get you. I get you."

"Also, my resting bitch face doesn't help."

Mandy laughs again. "Yeah, you do have one of those, though I would never have pointed it out."

"It's helpful in the fighting cage, but I think people find it hard to approach me in everyday life. Except for you. You are kind of fearless, aren't you?"

Mandy shrugs. "I don't know. I think I pick people. I find someone who I think, 'this person is worth my time,' and it's not always the obvious choice, but I always have my reasons."

My cheeks raise a few degrees when she mentions picking me to be in her life. It seems like an intimate statement I'm not used to having in friendships. "What was your reason for picking me?" I ask.

Mandy thinks for a moment, then says softly, "You're like the calm in the eye of the storm. You'll learn this about me, but I'm a fucking mess. It's all chaos when it comes to Amanda Gomez. I'm guessing opposites attracted when it came to you. I was impressed at how you have kept your shit together through the clinical trial process. Usually, it's a lot of crying and emotion. I'm not saying you are emotionless; I know inside shit is going on in your head, but you keep your cool. I'm guessing it's the fighter in you."

"Huh," I take in her assessment and examine it in my mind. "I think, for the most part, people think I'm hard to get to know, that I don't let anyone in, and maybe that's partially true, but I'd like to change that."

Mandy smiles at me with encouragement, and I get the feeling this woman is going to be an important part of my life—because she has already declared me a part of hers.

A young woman who has to be much younger than Mandy or me opens the door. Mandy introduces her as Izel. She takes me by surprise with a hug and steps aside to let us in. Izel's face is round, and she has short, light-brown hair with curtain bangs. She is wearing yoga pants and a slouchy sweater that falls off one shoulder. Her body is on the plumper side, but those curves could kill.

"Wine?" Izel offers.

"Sure," Mandy and I both say.

"Take a seat, *estás en tu casa*," she yells from the kitchen as she gets our drinks. When she comes back, Izel is clumsily clutching three wine glasses much too full with red wine. "How was that?" she asks, looking at Mandy.

"Perfect pronunciation," Mandy says, and we both take a glass each.

"You don't speak Spanish?" I ask Izel.

"No. My mom is super Chicana, and so is her sister, so they gave their daughters the most Mexican names they could think of. I kind of rebelled when I was younger and rejected everything about our language and culture. I regret it now, but at the time, my own personal revolt against my parents was the most important thing."

"When you were young?" I say pointedly. "Are you even old enough to drink?"

Mandy is so close to me on the couch, her laughter startles me. "Izel is older than you," she says. "She just has a baby face," Mandy says with a baby voice and pinches Izel's cheek. Izel swats her hand away, annoyed. "Where's Tlali?" Mandy asks her.

"She was just taking a shower. She had to stay overtime today and got home not that long ago."

"Tlali?" I ask, thinking. "Izel and Tlali, those are Nahuatl names, right?"

Izel blinks at me. "Man, my mom, and Tlali's mom would love you. I bet you speak like proper Spanish, huh?"

I don't have a chance to answer before Mandy does. "Yeah. The real shit. This girl here comes from old Spanish money," Mandy says and grins at me.

Geesh. I'm annoyed she continues to find it a novelty that my family has money. "To be clear," I say. "My family has money, not me."

We hear someone clamoring down the stairs excitedly. "Did I hear the door?"

A woman joins us in the living room and pulls Mandy into a hug. She is tall and slender, with beautiful tanned skin much darker than Izel's, so it's hard to believe they are related. Her hair is wet, but I can see the thick mass of curls that hit just below her shoulders. "Nice to meet you," she says and kisses my cheek. "I'm Tlali."

"Hi. Nice to meet you too."

The four of us claim our wine glasses and relax into the evening. I'm surprised at how quickly I become comfortable with this small group of women, but it's natural, like so many things have been in Kansas City.

"I can't believe you two are related," I say, looking between Tlali and Izel. "You don't look anything alike."

"Well," Tlali explains, "our moms are half-sisters, and my dad is Afro-Mexican."

"And my mom," Mandy interjects, "is not related to their moms by blood, but they consider her a sister as well, so we are basically cousins."

"So you have all been in Kansas City for several generations?"

They all nod.

"Wow," I say. "I didn't know there were so many Latinx here."

"Oh yeah," Tlali says. "There's even a small town several hours away that is a meat-packing town, and it is a minority-majority town."

"What does that mean?" I ask.

"More than half of the population is Mexican or Mexican-American. Sometimes Izel and I take long weekend vacations just to go there. It's like being in Mexico. Amazing food and all that."

"I'd like to go there sometime," I say, feeling homesick for real now.

"You planning on moving here or something?" Mandy asks.

I shrug. "I don't know what my plan is now. It kind of took a detour."

Mandy smiles with understanding, and I love her intuitiveness more than ever because she changes the subject.

"So, I met this guy," Mandy says as she tosses her hair over one shoulder as she did when she was flirting with my furniture delivery guy.

Tlali and Izel both lean in with interest. "Do tell," says Izel.

"And thank the stars, I hope this means you're over that other *pendejo*," adds Tlali.

Mandy rolls her eyes and ignores those comments about whoever her ex was. "His name is Chris. I actually met him at Valentina's."

The two cousins glance over at me. "He was my furniture delivery guy," I explain.

"Oh, my god, there were three of them, and they were all so hot. I almost want to have furniture delivered and send it back so they can come back again to pick it up," Mandy says.

Tlali raises her glass to Mandy in cheers of approval, and they clink glasses. "How'd you pick?" Tlali asks.

"It was so hard, guys. Seriously. It was like I was a kid at a candy store."

"She was drooling like one too," I say, and Izel snorts with her laughter.

Mandy rolls her eyes again. "In the end, Chris had the thickest arms."

"And you do love you some thick arms," Izel says.

"That I do. Anyway, there he is in the living room, and Valentina and I are watching him put together her sofa. And he is sweating and looking hot as hell; I couldn't help it. I ask him for his name, and I invite him to my art show. Then I give him my number."

"And he calls?" I ask.

"No," Mandy says. "Well, not fast enough. So I call the furniture company, I got the name from the truck when they left, and I give them your address. I tell them I was impressed with the delivery service—which isn't a lie—and that I'd like to thank them personally. They give me their numbers, and I call Chris."

"Stalker much?" Tlali asks.

"Shut up. I call him up, and he sounds glad I called."

"What do you say to him?" I ask, thoroughly impressed by her *cojones*.

"I tell him he took too long to call, and his window was closing. He claims he lost the flyer and was glad I called—not sure I buy it, but I give him the benefit of the doubt. He asks me out for drinks, and I take him to the studio for a nightcap."

"So, how was it?" Izel asks.

"Amazing," Mandy says. "I'm surprised I'm walking today."

I almost spit my wine out but manage to keep it in. It goes down the wrong pipe, and I start coughing. Is this what women talk about? What girlfriends talk about? I mean, it's no worse than the locker room talk at the gym, but I've never heard bluntness like this from women before.

Izel sighs and stares off into space. "I need to get some. It's been too long," she says.

"Amen, sister," Tlali joins in, and they clink glasses.

"How long?" Mandy asks them.

"Three months," Tlali says.

"Two weeks," says Izel.

"Two weeks is too long for you?" I ask.

Izel nods and sips her wine. "Yeah. Isn't it for you?"

I shake my head. "No. I'd say months would be long, but not just a few weeks."

"Speak for yourself," Mandy says. "I'm with Izel on this one. Can't go that long. Why? How long has it been for you?"

I feel the heat creeping up my neck, and I stare into my glass like it's the most exciting thing in the world, so it's hard to look back at Mandy's face, but I do.

Mandy narrows her eyes. "You little slut," she says in a playful tone. "You did it, didn't you? You listened to me?"

I look up at the cousins, hoping they'll help, but they blink at each other.

"We're lost," Tlali says.

"I told Valentina to have a sex-athon, and I think she did."

"Fine," I say. If this is what it's like to have girlfriends, then I should go all in. "Yes. I picked up a guy at a bar yesterday, and we spent all morning together until he had to go at noon today. That's all the details you're getting."

"No," Mandy whines. "We need details. Who's the guy? Is he hot? You can't leave us hanging like this."

Izel jumps into my rescue. "Come on, Mandy. Leave her alone. She's clearly not a *cochina* like you. Not everyone shares as much as we do."

I try to communicate a telepathic 'thank you' to Izel, and she tips her chin at me. If there is a chance Mandy knows Rory, I can't give out any further details.

"You said there were *three* hot delivery guys?" Tlali asks.

"Yeah," Mandy says.

"And you have all three cell numbers?" Izel asks with interest.

I can almost see the moment when the matching floating light bulbs over the cousin's heads light up.

"I do!" Mandy rummages through her purse, producing a yellow Post-It note. She crosses off something, presumably Chris's name and number, and hands the piece of paper to Tlali.

"I'm going to go put this on the fridge door before we spill wine on it," Tlali says.

"So," Izel turns to me. "Let's get to know you. What do you do? What brings you to Kansas City?"

Mandy smiles at me, and I remember her words from the car. I only have to tell them as much as I want to.

"Well, I was training as an MMA fighter—"

"Whoa, like an actual fighter? Like a UFC fighter?" Tlali asks, now back in the living room with us.

"Yeah. Well, I wasn't in the UFC yet," I say.

"You will be one day," Mandy reassures me.

I smile at her. I don't know if it's the wine that has relaxed me or how welcome Izel and Tlali have made me feel, but I find myself confiding in them openly. "I'm here for treatment. I met Mandy at the hospital."

Tlali and Izel eye each other in a gesture I am starting to understand is some sort of telepathy or *brujeria* between them.

"I have cervical cancer, and I'm on Dr. Ramirez's clinical trial. I'll be in K.C. until treatment is over."

Izel changes seats so she can be next to me on the sofa. She wraps her arm around my shoulder into a half hug. "Dr. Ramirez is amazing," she says. "You'll be fine."

"And we got you. Whatever you need," Tlali adds with a smile of her own.

My eyes sting with tears; I am so moved by this small tribe of women who don't know me from Eve but offer a safety net for when I fall. If this is what having girlfriends is like, I never want to go back. "Can we talk about something else? Treatment starts tomorrow, and today I just want to feel normal," I say as I wipe my eyes.

I don't share all my fears with them. The prospect of going under the knife for the first surgical procedure of my life is terrifying, and I'll have to follow that up with radiation. I need my mind off it all and am so thankful these girls are here to help with that.

"Of course, *amiga*," Tlali says. "What you wanna talk about?"

"Um, what do you guys do at the hospital?"

"We all have double lives," Izel says with a grin.

"What?" I ask, confused.

Izel points her chin toward Mandy. "You know how she's a research assistant-slash front desk clerk at the hospital by day and a painter by night?"

"Yeah . . ."

"Well, I'm a surgical technologist by day, and I write by night," Izel says.

"And I'm a medical interpreter by day, and I translate novels by night," Tlali says.

Mandy jumps in. "We have a master plan that we will all one day make a living from our arts and leave our day jobs. We cheer each other on to stay motivated."

"That's amazing," I say. "What kind of books do you write and translate?"

"I write horror," says Izel. "Pretty gruesome stuff," she says with a delighted grin on her face.

Tlali rolls her eyes. "And I translate proper literature. Or want to, anyway."

"So you do speak Spanish? Or are you translating another language?"

"Yeah, Spanish."

"Your double lives—it's like Superman and Clark Kent—"

"Exactly," Mandy says. "Did you know Superman is from Kansas?"

I shake my head. "No, I didn't."

We laugh and get to know each other better the rest of the night. The cousins don't ask me more about myself unless I offer tidbits, and I realize they are trying to respect my privacy.

If I make it out of this, I hope we can all stay friends. I surprise myself because, more and more, my plans post-treatment seem to shift to Kansas City and away from home.

CHAPTER 7

"I have to ask you one last time, Valentina. Are you sure? We can still stop." Dr. Ramirez looks at me with creased brows. I understand she's just doing her due diligence, asking about fertility again. We have the same conversation we did on our first appointment, and I don't budge.

"There are more ways than one to become a mom," I say to settle the matter once and for all. "I'm not saying I won't ever change my mind about being a mom, but if I do, I'm pretty damn sure I don't want to cook my own, if you know what I mean."

The corner of her mouth slants into a weak smile, and she sighs. "You've thought this out."

"I have. I'm young, I know that, but I also have always known what I want."

"Okay. You've convinced me." Dr. Ramirez presses the nurse call button next to my bed.

A short, slim blonde walks in. She smiles broadly and moves with jerky movements like she's had too much caffeine. "Hi, Miss Almonte. I'm Sara," she says and gives me her hand to shake.

"Just Valentina, please, or Vale if you'd like."

She smiles at me and goes over to a laptop resting on a cart in the corner of my room. "I see we have surgery and radiation scheduled today."

"First round of treatment," Dr. Ramirez says. "I have to go to my next patient. Can you take care of transport, Sara?"

"Sure," the nurse says.

"For future procedures, we'll have an orderly transport you, but for this first one, I'd like to go with you. Dr. Ramirez briefed me about you, and I'd like you to have a friendly face around."

"Thank you," I say. She brings a wheelchair into the room, I sit, and she wheels me out of the room.

"So, I hear you are a fighter?"

"Yeah. I was." I say it in the past tense for the first time.

"You box or something?"

"Mixed martial arts, but yeah, boxing is one of my strengths."

"Wow. Must be amazing to be a professional athlete."

I smile, remembering everything I left behind. She keeps talking.

"Are you nervous?"

"A little. Mostly I'm eager to put this behind me," I say. *One way or the other*, I add mentally.

"I'm not going to lie, it's going to be rough, but Dr. Ramirez and I, we got your back." She squeezes my shoulder, and the solitude I carry starts to chip away at the edges.

We get out of the elevator, and she tells me we are almost there. "When you're going under anesthesia, in that freaky alien setting, and they are asking you to count down from ten, it helps to think of your happy place or a person who means a lot to you. Think about that to help with the nerves."

"Okay. Thanks for the tip."

Nurse Sara hands me over to a technician, and I'm transferred to a bed and then wheeled into the operating room. She was right; this place is freaky and alien. I smile, thinking how this is such a perfect workplace for Izel, the horror writer. She must get excellent creative fodder from everything she sees here.

When I begin the countdown, nurse Sara's words run through my head, and I think of my happy place. I'm in the locker room, getting ready for a fight. My hair is pinned back in braids. I encase my hands with the knuckle wraps and position my mouthguard between my teeth. I stretch my neck from side to side and bounce in place like I'm jumping rope.

I'm walking out of the locker room through a sea of people calling my name—only one is distinguishable, with those unruly red waves bright in the audience. The cage calls to me like a siren's song; my opponent is waiting for me. I step into the cage, and my world goes black.

The next thing I know, I'm striking the current flyweight titleholder. She stumbles back, recovers, and kicks me in the jaw with a force that sends me flying and landing on my ass. She wastes no time in clamoring over to me, and her fists rain down on my face. I go into a defense position, with my fists covering my face for only a second. I bring my legs around her torso and my arms around her neck, placing her in a triangle choke. My grip is so tight around her, her punches weaken.

When her exhaustion weakens her struggle, I swing my body with full momentum, rolling us both over. I land on top, taking the dominant position. The crowd cheers, but somehow, one voice calling to me rises above the deafening cheers.

"Valentina? Valentina? Honey, wake up," says the voice.

I open my eyes, and my brain is in a haze. It takes me a while to remember where I am and why. My face is wet and cold, and I bring up a hand to wipe it dry. I was crying.

"Sorry," Sara says. "I normally wouldn't try to wake you, but I think you were having a nightmare."

"No," I say. "It was a good dream." My voice is husky, and my throat hurts as I say this.

"Oh. I'm sorry, then. Is your mouth dry?"

Rolling my tongue across the roof of my mouth, it gets stuck with the dryness. I clasp my throat and nod. She places a cup full of ice chips on a tray over my bed, and I suck on those.

Sara looks at the monitors I'm hooked up to and makes some notes on my chart on the laptop. "Dinner should be here in about an hour." She points to a bin sitting next to me on the bed. "In case you need it. Nausea hits at different times for different people, but be prepared for it tonight to be on the safe side."

"Thanks," I say.

When I'm alone, I pull the blankets to one side and lift my hospital gown. I can't see the incisions because they are covered in bandages. I flex my abdomen gently, testing for pain, but whatever they gave me is strong enough it never comes.

It's a strange thing, going from the perfect body to one that is cut up and radiated. I don't feel any different, and I start to hope I can get back to the cage when this is all said and done.

When dinner comes, I lift the lid to find the most disgusting-looking bowl of soup. The stereotype of hospital food being gross is no joke. Despite not enjoying the dinner one bit, nausea from radiation doesn't kick in tonight. I sleep through the night, and I wonder if I could be so lucky as to avoid the horrors of side effects.

I am so wrong.

In the morning, I devour pancakes that aren't quite as bad as the chicken noodle soup, but they almost instantly come back up.

The rest of the day is a constant race between Sara and the other nurses to rush fresh basins for my vomit. If that weren't bad enough, by the evening, I'm spewing out the other end too. How the hell can you get diarrhea when you are vomiting everything you eat?

By morning, my body feels like it's been through five fights in a row, with no breaks, and lost all of them. I finally am able to keep down some mashed potatoes. It is a triumph because it means I don't have to live in the hospital until chemo starts the following week.

"I hear you finally ate and kept it down?" Dr. Ramirez walks in, pumps hand sanitizer on her hands, and sits next to me.

"Yeah. It was pretty gnarly there for a second."

"Valentina, this is only going to get much worse before it gets better."

"I know. I'm in this. I swear."

"The standard of care is also a great option. We can go for less aggressive treatment over a longer period of time. You don't have to be in this trial if it's too much."

"It's been one day, doc. You giving up on me already?"

She laughs. "No. Of course not. It's protocol that the patient understands we can stop at any time."

"I'm not stopping. Your chances are my best chances. Do your worst. I can take it."

"Okay, then. Since you can keep your food down, you can go home this afternoon. On Monday, you have your first chemo-radiation combo. Be here at eleven."

"I know. I know," I say. "We go like that for five weeks."

"With weekends off," she adds.

"I never thanked you for breakfast the other day."

Dr. Ramirez smiles. "My pleasure. Amanda is a wonderful human. I was hoping you two would become friendly."

"We did. She's great and a total riot."

Dr. Ramirez laughs at my assessment. "That's one word to describe her. I personally use 'firecracker.'"

My phone buzzes on the table, and I grab it. It's an unknown number.

"Go ahead and take it. We are done here. I'll have discharge papers here in a bit."

"Thanks, doctor. Really."

Turning my attention back to the phone, I answer. "Hello?"

"Valentina, I'm so glad you picked up." Rory's voice sends my blood pressure through the roof. Crap. Why did I pick up? I should have known it was him.

"Um, hey." I press my hand to the phone, hoping the line doesn't pick up any of the hospital sounds.

"I'm calling about that date," he says.

"I'm not sure I'm free."

"I'll check in with you Saturday morning. We can play it by ear. If you're free, you're free. If not, we can hang out another time."

"Uh, okay," I say reluctantly. The thing is, his voice is the most comforting thing in this hospital room.

"Valentina, can I say something without you freaking out?"

"I suspect you will no matter what I say."

Rory laughs. "True." Then his voice turns serious. "I can't stop thinking about you."

Why does he have to go and say all the wonderful things? He was a play-thing, a boy-toy. I was meant to never see him again.

Tell yourself what you want, Valentina. You gave him your number for a reason.

I can't stop thinking about him either. Memories of our day together have kept me sane the last twenty-four hours. But I can't tell him that.

"You are freaking out, aren't you?" he asks.

"No. I'm not freaking out." I pout as though he can see me, and he laughs again.

"Well, I need to get back to work. I just wanted to say, have a good day, and I'll be thinking about you."

"Thank you, Rory. You have a good day too."

"And?"

"And what?"

"And, you will be thinking about me too."

"Fine. I'll be thinking about you too."

I'm a bit panicked he might walk by my door, so I press the call button, and Sara's head pops in. I ask her to close my door for privacy, and she tells me she'll be right back with discharge paperwork.

The strangest feeling comes over me as I wait. I started out this journey homesick for the gym, for Chema, and for Pili. But now, my homesickness is more about time with Rory, and Mandy, and even the cousins Izel and Tlali. It feels strangely like Kansas City is home, not Mexico. I won't deny I miss Chema and my sister, but they don't beat in the same spot in my heart that home beats anymore.

Sara comes back to change the dressing over the two small laparoscopic incisions on my lower abdomen. I sign a stack of paperwork, get a prescription for pain medication I won't fill, and take a ridiculous cab ride the two blocks to my apartment.

I'm lying down and icing my belly when I get a text from Chema. My heart sinks. He knows nothing yet. The longer I've kept him at arms-length, the harder it has been for me to give him the excuse I had planned for him. I read all his texts in Spanish.

Chema: *Where are you?*

Me: *I'm sorry. I've been meaning to call you. I'm out of town.*

Chema: *Out of town?*

Me: *Yeah. I'm in the U.S.*

Chema: *What? You never cleared it with me. You haven't trained in a week!*

I don't answer him again because I'm a chicken shit, but minutes later, the phone rings, and it's him, and he's furious.

"What's going on?" he clips as soon as I answer the call.

"Hi, Chema. Miss you too."

"Don't be cute."

"I'm sorry. You don't deserve me disappearing on you."

"What? You're disappearing?"

"I wanted to tell you in person. I thought I'd get a break soon so I could say this face-to-face, but that didn't work out," I lie. My chest constricts at the betrayal I'm about to lay on him. "I got an agent."

"That's great, Tini! Why didn't you tell me? I knew you were starting to get attention. We even had a reporter here yesterday looking for you."

"You did?"

"Yeah," Chema says, all the anger gone from his voice. I imagine his hulkish frame that never quite seems to fit his warm smile.

"That's a first," I say, surprised.

"I know. I'll email you the details so you can tell your agent. If they want to do a feature at the gym while we train, that would be great for the gym too, Tini."

"Chema," I say and feel the tears in my throat. "There's more."

"What's wrong?" His voice is all concern now.

"My agent agency. They want me to train with someone else."

"You're dropping me?"

I take a deep breath. "I have no choice. It's the only way the agent would sign me. I had to agree to the new coach and new training plan."

Chema laughs bitterly on the other end, and the sound knocks the wind out of me. "After everything we've been through? After getting you this far? This is how you repay me?"

"I'm sorry, Chema. Please believe me, I never meant to hurt you. It just worked out this way."

"You know what the worst part is?"

All of it, I think, but keep silent.

"The worst part is I remember that gangly little kid with not a muscle on her body begging me and pestering me to train her."

"I remember," I smile when I think of our start. "It took me four months to persuade you."

"You never persuaded me, Tini. You're a force of nature. There isn't a goal you set you don't accomplish. You wanted me as your coach, and you showed up at my gym daily until you willed me into being your coach."

"I'm grateful for everything—"

"Which is why I don't buy this 'it just worked out this way' bullshit of yours. If you decided to drop me, that's fine, but I deserve the respect of being your mentor—of being your friend. Hell, Tini, you're my little sister. You owed it to me to tell me to my face. I'm your fucking family."

"Chema—" I croak out, but he is no longer on the phone with me.

I roll to my side and curl my knees to my chest. A shiver runs through me, and the fetal position provides warmth. I cradle the phone in my hand, hoping he'll call back. Hoping he'll let me apologize. Hoping he'll forgive me.

But there is no call, and I fall asleep like that.

CHAPTER 8

*B*eing sick sucks. The only good thing about it, and I really do mean the only good thing, is that I get to watch all the television I never got to when I was in training.

I'm halfway through the live-action version of *Beauty and the Beast* when my doorbell rings.

"Who is it?"

"It's me, girl." Mandy's loud voice fills my living room from the intercom, and I wince at the sound.

I buzz her in and unlock my door. I'm back on the couch when she enters my apartment.

"How's it going?" she asks.

"I've been better."

"I'm sure. Sorry I didn't visit while you were in the hospital—"

"It's okay, Mandy. I know you work there. I don't expect you to want to spend your time off there too."

"Wish that were it. I'm actually working overtime to get the pieces ready for the art show."

"That's right. How's that going?" I ask, and my face scrunches up with a short-lasting jolt of pain at the incision sites.

"Where are your pain meds?" Mandy asks.

"It's nothing," I say.

"Don't give me that. Where are they?" Mandy walks over to my kitchen and starts rummaging through my cabinets.

"I didn't fill the prescriptions," I admit.

"Valentina! Seriously? You're going to need them soon."

"I'll go to the hospital pharmacy at my next appointment. Happy?"

"Barely," she says and plops on the cushion next to me. "What are we watching?"

"*Beauty and the Beast.*"

"Oh, is this the one with Emma Watson as Belle? I love this version."

"Would you like me to start it over, Mandy?"

She grins. "Thanks for taking the hint."

We both relax, and I forget all about the pain as we watch the movie. Her presence lifts me somehow and props me up. I only hope I can be the same for her if she ever needs this kind of support.

My sister would be here now if I had told her and she was able to get away from her obligations. Who am I kidding? She could only be here if her husband were to give her permission, which is a big 'if.' I didn't want to put her in that difficult position. Having Mandy in that sisterly role almost made up for Pilar's absence. Almost.

The movie is nearly over when my phone dings on the seat next to me. I smile at the nickname I saved Rory under until I realize Mandy's gaze also followed the chime, probably thinking it was her own phone. Panic overtakes my smile.

"*Big Dick?*" her eyebrow raises suggestively. "Who's *Big Dick?*"

"Oh my god. Shut up," I say and grab the phone so she can't read his full text.

Mandy pauses the movie and turns to face me instead. "Come on, give up the goods."

"Fine. Just that one night stand I already told you about."

Mandy raises an eyebrow. "You exchanged phone numbers with a one night stand?"

"It was a mistake, okay? Chemo brain."

"Oh no, you don't. You gave him your number before you started treatment. Besides, it's too soon for chemo brain. Oh," she says, and her mouth forms into a smile.

"What?"

"You *like* him."

I avert my gaze.

She relents, finally, and starts playing the movie again. I read the text that came through.

Rory: *You end up being free?*

I sigh. It's Saturday, and he is claiming his date. If only I could go with him. It's not like I don't want to go, but I have no energy. I make up an excuse. I base it on truth, so it'll be harder to slip in my story. I was having enough of a hard time casting the web of lies with Chema and Pili as it was.

Me: *Yes. But I can't. I'm not feeling well.*

Rory: *What's wrong?*

Me: *Just a stomach bug. Raincheck? I wouldn't want to get you sick.*

I'm not sure how long I'll be able to spin that lie and keep Rory at bay, but I'm not ready to say goodbye to him yet.

"*Chica,* you should see the smile on your face," says Mandy.

I roll my eyes and grab a cushion, hugging it to my body. The credits roll, and Mandy and I both sigh after the Beast.

"You know," she says over the credits' music. "There's a massive plot hole in Beauty and the Beast."

"Oh yeah? What's that?"

"Belle should have totally tapped Gaston's fine ass."

"No, she shouldn't have!" I say, appalled at the travesty she just suggested.

"Oh, come on, tell me, if you had been in a little town like that with few options, you wouldn't have had a little fun with him?"

"He is really hot, isn't he?" I ask sheepishly.

Mandy nods. "And athletic, which I'm sure is your type." Mandy stands and stretches her arms over her head. "Between your text from Big Dick and watching Gaston grunt in that fight scene, I seriously want some. I'm going to go see what Chris is up to."

"Okay. Thanks for stopping by."

"Sure thing. Oh, tomorrow night, if you're feeling up to it—and only if you are feeling up to it—I'll pick you up for dinner. We have Sunday family dinners, and you can meet my parents."

"I'll let you know if it's a good day."

Mandy leaves, and I scroll through movie options to pick my next movie when a knock at the door distracts me. It's strange because I didn't buzz anyone up. I wonder if Mandy is back for some reason.

"Did you forget something—" I start to ask, opening the door, but freeze when I see him. For a long moment, I don't know what to do. My jaw drops.

Rory stands in front of me, handsome as I remembered him, with a grocery sack in each hand. "Can I come in?" he asks.

"Um, sure. Sorry." I move aside, and he steps through, making his way to the kitchen.

"No offense, but you look like crap," he says.

"You should have just said *offense*."

He chuckles, but the concern continues to crease his brows. "You lose a fight or something?"

I laugh. "Yeah. Something like that."

"Am I ever going to get to watch you fight?" he asks.

The question saddens me more than I would have thought. The truth is, I have no idea if I'll ever get back to the cage. "What's that?" I ask as I try to peer into the grocery bags he has placed on my counter. Changing the subject is safer. I avoid sitting at the barstool because barstools and Rory in the same room are a dangerous proposition, and I'm still weak from my first round of treatment.

"Well," he says. "You said you were sick, so I brought supplies. You know I'm a doctor, right?"

"Yeah, you mentioned."

He starts pulling out items and turns them on the counter so they face me. First in the lineup is a tall white container. "Chicken noodle soup," he says. I hope it's better than what they serve at the hospital, but I stay quiet. "Crackers." He pulls out a six-pack of ginger ale and puts that in the fridge.

"You really didn't have to do all this, Rory."

"I know." He shrugs. "I wanted to. And that's not all." He keeps pulling items from the bags, and I can't help but laugh when I see the rest of his purchases. There's a familiar blue container of Vick's Vapor Rub—or *vaporú* as we call it in Mexico—and a tall candle with the *Virgen de la Guadalupe* on it.

"You're unreal," I say through a laugh that sends a small shock of pain through my incisions. I play it off and keep talking. "How did you know?"

"You okay?" He asks with concern.

I scramble through my brain for a lie. "Yeah. Just a bit of a stom-achache."

He nods. "I searched online for Mexican home remedies, and these two items came up a lot. Sprite and lemon did too, but I thought it might be a bit much."

"Oh, *that* would be a bit much? How'd you think to do this?"

"Every culture has its own home remedies. It's kind of interesting to a doctor. Would you like some soup?"

I shake my head. "Not really hungry yet. Later?"

"Sure. You staying hydrated?"

"Okay, you know you're not actually my doctor, right?"

Rory's hands shoot up in surrender and then he places the soup container in the fridge too.

"Well, thanks for stopping by, and you know, checking in."

"You kicking me out?"

"No, I just—" I bite my lip and look away from him. "I can't imagine you'd want to hang out with me while I'm sick. And besides, it's kind of gross. I'm not ready for you to hear those sounds."

"If I may, I would like to counter those points," he says seriously as he counts fingers. "One, I'm a doctor. No sound to escape you should embarrass you. Two, yes, hanging out with you is exactly what I want. Three, if you are worried about getting me sick, don't. Work a year at a hospital, and you will have the immune system of a god. And four, I would cheer you up."

"Fine," I say, happier than I would have liked. "But no funny business. I'm just being lazy on the couch and watching TV."

"That's exactly what I would have prescribed," he says and kicks off his shoes before taking his spot on the couch. "Seriously, though. I'm sorry you aren't feeling well."

I sit next to him, and it must be too far for his liking because he wraps his arms around me and scoots me to his side so I can cuddle next to him. I bask in the warmth of his body, and he keeps one arm around me as we scroll through our options.

He makes me watch a sci-fi show about androids who raise children on another planet, and it isn't half bad. I make him watch the most recent female flyweight MMA championship. He's like a little kid, staring amazed at the screen. It's almost as if he can't believe women are so tough.

"I take it you don't like to watch sports?"

He shakes his head. "Normally no. I prefer to be active rather than sit and watch others be active, but that fight was pretty epic."

He picks another movie after that, but I fall asleep on him. When I wake up, I'm lying down on the sofa with my duvet over me, and Rory is in the kitchen heating up some of the soup. He brings it to the coffee table along with a small plate of crackers and a tall glass of water.

"I'd feel better if you ate something." He smiles at me, and it's all the encouragement I need.

"All right," I say. "I'll try."

The soup is eons better than the soup at the hospital, and I ask Rory where he got it so I can get some more.

"Oh no. I'm not giving you my secrets. You want this soup, you'll have to go through me."

I laugh and take another spoonful. I had been afraid to eat after my night at the hospital, but now that I was eating, my hunger opened up with a vengeance. Setting the spoon on the coffee table, I start drinking straight from the bowl like a savage.

Rory laughs next to me.

"Thank you," I say. "That was good."

He smiles. "You betcha."

After insisting with a look of warning that I am quite capable of cleaning up, I take the dishes to the sink, and soap suds drip from my hands when something in my stomach churns. I run to the toilet and barely make it in time.

The soup comes out nearly in the same state it went in, and it is revolting. I feel a hand on my back, and I push him away. "No," I manage to say. "I don't want you seeing me like this." I wave him away with my head hovering over the toilet bowl.

"Valentina, this doesn't bother me. Please, let me be here." He pulls my hair back so it's not dangling into the toilet bowl just in time for round two of the soup rejection.

I close the lid to the bowl and sit back as I wipe my mouth. "Real sexy, aren't I?" I say, attempting a joke, but Rory's face is all concern. "I really wish you hadn't seen that."

"Like I said, it doesn't bother me. Normally I would respect your wishes, but I know you don't have any family here."

"Can I have a moment to clean up a bit?"

Rory scratches his jaw through his beard, then nods. "Yeah, I'm just out here if you need anything, okay?"

"Thanks, doc."

After brushing my teeth and taking a shower, I find Rory scrolling through his phone. He looks up at me with a face-splitting smile that melts me.

"Better?"

"Yeah."

"What else do you want to watch?"

"I'm actually kind of sick of the TV for today."

"Okay. We can just chat."

"Sure . . ." I say reluctantly. "What about?"

"Anything. Let's see. Oh, I know. What's your favorite band?"

I smile, glad for the change in subject. "Easy. *Industrial November*. I always thought my walkout song would be either *Metal Red Day* or *Welded Dragons*."

"Those would be good fighting songs. I'm surprised, though. You listen to them in Mexico?"

"They're much bigger in Mexico City than they are here, I'll tell you that much."

"Well, yeah. Maybe not so much in the Midwest, but they have fans in the U.S. too."

"What about your favorite band?" I ask, content with the easy conversation topic that is also somehow really revealing.

"I have a lot. Let's see, well, lately I've been listening to a lot of *Kidneythieves*."

My eyes widen. "What?"

"You never heard of them?"

"That can't be a real band name," I say, horrified.

"Yep. That's their name—pretty good band too."

"I don't care how good they are; that's a horrible band name."

"It's not like we play it in the dialysis clinic," Rory deadpans, and we both roar with laughter.

"You laugh at really inappropriate things."

He shrugs. "Yeah. I have a pretty dark sense of humor sometimes. I guess I understand life is grim enough without us trying to make it dimmer. You know?"

"Would you laugh at anything?"

"Probably."

"What about death?"

"Yeah. I see myself laughing at death in the right circumstances."

"What about when I die?" I ask, not giving away I'm serious. "Will you laugh then?"

He looks at me, and a smile plays at the corners of his mouth. He does that a lot, giving away he is about to tell a joke like he needs to smile before sharing it. "That depends on how you die," he says, and we both laugh again.

I yawn, and Rory carries me to bed. He returns my duvet to the bed and tucks me in before placing a glass of water on my nightstand. "I'm still worried you'll get dehydrated. Please try to keep down some water, okay?" He kisses my forehead in the sweetest gesture any man has ever displayed for me, and I nod.

I drift off to sleep with a smile on my face.

andy's house is loud—so loud. Just like her. We sit at the table with her parents, Mr. and Mrs. Gomez, though they insisted I call them Enrique and Ana as soon as Mandy introduced us.

Mrs. Gomez—Ana—runs from the kitchen to the table as she piles *tortillas* onto the *tortilla* warmer in the center of the table.

"Mateo!" Ana screams at the top of her lungs, and a young man's voice bellows from down the hall in response.

"One second!"

"Sorry, Valentina," Ana says. "This kid drives me crazy sometimes." She offers me a sheepish smile, and I ask her to please not worry on my account.

"I'm so hungry I could eat a cow," says Enrique.

"Mom makes the best *albondiga* soup," Mandy says. "I thought a light broth might be good for you." She squeezes my forearm, and my heart swells that the menu was catered to me.

"Thank you," I say. "I haven't had any food that tastes like home in a while."

"Especially not at the hospital," Mandy adds.

I shiver at the memory.

"Mateo!" Ana yells again, her frustration growing on her face each time she has to yell her son's name. She tosses another pile of *tortillas* onto the heap and plops in her chair, a bit out of breath.

Ana is beautiful, and Mandy looks a lot like her. They have the same small frame with a lean muscular build, though Mandy's tanned skin is a shade darker, more like her dad's.

"Ama!" Mateo yells as he walks toward the dinner table. "I had to save my game."

"We have guests," Ana hisses.

Mateo and Ana continue to argue, and Enrique starts asking Amanda about work, ignoring the argument ensuing on the other side of the table. Each set of conversations has to raise an octave when the other conversation takes over the dining room's sound until they are all but screaming. I resist the urge to wince because it is also a little bit funny. I see now why Mandy is so loud.

The smack over his head silences Mateo once and for all, and he scowls.

"Hi, Mateo. I'm Valentina," I say to insert myself in the conversation.

"Hi," he says, looking down at his dinner.

"How old are you?"

"Thirteen," he seethes.

Mandy shakes her head at her little brother. "I'm going to have Valentina kick your ass," she says and smiles.

Mateo laughs. "She's a girl!" He snaps as if that disqualifies me from the job, and I press my lips together.

"She's an MMA fighter," Mandy says, crossing her arms.

Mateo's head snaps up with wide eyes like he can't believe what his sister just said. His gaze scans my arms, sizing me up, no doubt. "No way," he says, shaking his head. "You're too small."

"Yes, way," I say. "But I won't kick your ass. I promise."

He smiles at me, and for the rest of the dinner, he can hardly look in my direction.

"So," Ana says, "Mandy tells me you are getting treatment at Heartland Metro,"

"That's right—"

"Mami! I told you she doesn't want to talk about that," Mandy says.

"It's okay," I smile reassuringly at Ana. "I don't mind. Thank you for having me over for dinner. It's nice to eat with someone."

"All your family's in Mexico?"

I nod.

Ana's face twists like she is angry I'm alone.

"It's okay," I say. "They don't know about my treatment, or they would be here."

"I'm sure they would like to know—" Enrique says.

"Papi!" Mandy huffs, and I have to laugh. "Sorry," she says with an apologetic look of embarrassment.

"It's okay, Mandy. Your parents can ask me questions." I smile at them both. "Ana, the soup is delicious, by the way."

Ana smiles at me and digs into her own bowl.

Thankfully, Mandy manages to steer the conversation away from me. She hogs the attention, bringing everyone up to speed on her art show.

I listen halfheartedly as I watch this family that is so close my heart constricts. Why can't my family be like this? I would gladly give up the wealth of my upbringing if it meant we could have healthy relationships —if it meant we could be close.

So many 'if's' that would mean they would be here right now because I would have told them about my illness.

But I look at Enrique as he listens to his daughter talk about her art, and I know my father could never be like that. Enrique clearly has no idea what half the things she says mean, but he listens intently and offers encouraging words. Her mother, too, throws in a comment or two of support and several of pride. They don't understand Mandy's ambitions, but they support her anyway. Families can actually be like this? A longing for something I will never have creeps up and lodges in my throat.

Halfway through dinner, Mandy yells at her brother once again. "Give it back—or else!" she threatens.

"No," he sticks his tongue out at her. "You know the rules."

I blink as I stare at the fighting siblings. Enrique bites his lip as he tries to suppress his laughter, making his black mustache wiggle.

"House rules," he explains at seeing my confusion plain on my face.

"Hold on to your *tortilla*, especially when the stack is getting low," he points with his gaze at the *tortilla* warmer. I lift the lid to peek inside, and sure enough, there are none left.

Ana holds on to her spoon with one hand and clutches her own *tortilla* in the other. She takes a sip of water, but to do this, she lets go of the spoon, not the *tortilla*. She raises her glass toward me, showing that she is the victor of the game. I laugh.

Mandy must have kicked Mateo under the table because he drops both spoon and what's left of the *tortilla* on the table as he chokes on his last slurp of the broth. Enrique doesn't even skip a beat. He lunges forward and reaches for the *tortilla* that Mateo dropped on the table, snagging it just before Mandy's hand could get to it.

"Dad! That was mine!" Mandy is frustrated now, and Enrique gives me a little salute with the piece of *tortilla* left, and I lose it.

I laugh so hard and so long, they all stare at me. "I'm happy to get up and heat up more," I say through the laughter.

"That's not the point," Enrique explains. "By the time whoever heats up more, they will trickle back to the table rather slowly. There are only so many *tortillas* you can fit on the stovetop at a time. You wait long enough, your food gets cold."

I nod at the simple explanation, and I can't suppress the laughter again, but they join me this time.

"So finders keepers is the rule?"

Enrique nods.

The turn of keys at the front door turns all our attention, and we watch as Izel marches in. She drops her purse on the couch and rushes to the table.

She sits next to me and gives me a kiss on the cheek like we are old friends. "Hi, Vale," she says, and I smile at the nickname—a sure sign she considers me her friend.

I can't tell if the happiness of this moment has my mind in shambles, but a swell of emotion overtakes me. It is so natural to be inserted into Mandy's life. Izel looks at me like I'm not at all out of place in this family tableau, and I almost want to cry.

I want to cry because Mom and Dad will never be like this. Because we will never be at a family dinner unless it's an event Dad would force us to go to for publicity.

If anything, this night only cements what I already knew: I did the right thing by not telling them anything.

CHAPTER 10

The treatments are going as well as can be expected, and I am faithful to the new regimen. My routine is solid. Every weekday, I go into the hospital for chemotherapy, and three times a week, I go in for radiation in addition to the chemo. So far, I've seen no signs of Rory, and no one has commented on my disguise of sunglasses and a hat as I walk through the lobby.

My body is taking a hell of a beating, but Dr. Ramirez looks at me—and at my chart—with hope, so I push through the pain.

I lost five pounds in the first week, and some days are better than others with nausea. Days when the chemo is combined with the radiation are the worst, especially the next day. Mandy was right about absolutely everything. I'm hungry and can hardly keep anything down half the time. Drinking calories has been somewhat helpful, but the pounds are still shedding off my body.

I had radiation yesterday, and I haven't been able to keep anything down today. I'm due at the hospital in an hour, and I have a raging headache.

Rummaging through the cabinet, I grab for pain meds and stare at the vitamin bottle. Did I take my vitamins this morning like I was supposed to? I can't remember, and I panic.

Skipping vitamins one day isn't the end of the world, but so far, I've treated treatment with the same discipline I used to treat training. Missing supplements is not an option for me or for my routine.

The bottle rests next to the pain meds, and I grab them both. I stare between them, unsure why I grabbed them. My head pounds, and I remember the headache. I take two pain pills from the bottle and stare at the vitamin bottle again. What the hell is happening? My brain is misfiring, and I have no idea why. I shake my head, trying to clear it, and the movement makes the room spin.

The floor moves from under my feet, and I'm about to topple over, so I grab the edge of the counter. I try to lick my cracked lips, but my tongue is dry. Fuck. I'm dehydrated.

Holding on to the counter, I go to the sink and fill a glass. I try to chug it, but it only comes back up.

I pull my phone out to call a car. Looks like I'm heading to the hospital early today.

~

Nurse Sara replaces the IV fluids for the second time, and I look at her, a bit embarrassed.

"It's very common to get dehydrated when you can't keep anything down," she says soothingly.

"Yeah. I know. I'm glad I noticed before I passed out."

"You did good. You need anything else for now?"

"No. Thank you, Sara."

She walks out of my room, leaving me with my thoughts—another hospitalization. I get to stay overnight until I can keep down two full meals in a row. I'll need to make another large deposit to the hospital. Hospital stays in the U.S. are much more expensive than I thought they would be. I'm so glad I asked Pilar for more money than I thought I'd need to be on the safe side, though I have no idea how the hell I'm going to pay her back.

A new doctor I don't know walks into my room, followed closely by Dr. Ramirez.

"Valentina, how are you?" Dr. Ramirez asks.

"I've been better," I say dryly.

She nods. "This is Dr. Medina. He will be the new attending on your case."

Dr. Medina is tall and handsome, and I don't for one minute miss the twinkle in Dr. Ramirez's eye when she looks at him. I press my lips together because she can't hide her feelings at all, and it's adorable. Dr. Ramirez briefs Dr. Medina on my case like the residents do at morning rounds.

"Nice to meet you, Miss Almonte," Dr. Medina says. "I'm new to the clinical trial team, but we will see a lot of each other now that I am here."

Dr. Ramirez mentioned him earlier, when she was about to meet him. At the time, she thought he would be unattractive, but Dr. Medina is super hot for an older guy, and yet, I could see them together despite their age difference.

When he sits to read my chart and turns away, I mouth to Dr. Ramirez that he is hot, and I bang the air to get a reaction out of her. Her eyes widen with horror, and she pins me with a look begging me to stop. I press my lips together to seal the laugh inside of me.

"Thank you, doctor," I say to Dr. Medina as they excuse themselves. I can't wait to see how their relationship unfolds.

I'm bored out of my mind the rest of the day and drift off to sleep by eight p.m. The next thing I know, I'm awakened for rounds at 6 a.m. I hate hospital stays. It's been nice sleeping in for the first time in my adult life, but it never happens when I'm admitted overnight. It's as if they like to start rounds with me, so I'm the earliest every day.

The lights go on in my room, and the trail of footfalls follows. It's usually one attending and seven to ten residents and interns. I groan and pull my pillow over my face with annoyance.

Someone clears their throat, and I wave them to go on. A resident whose voice I don't recognize starts presenting my case. I hate hearing it. Every time they mention the details of my case, I feel like the stupidest woman on earth. Who skips their pap tests? Who ignores symptoms?

Me. I do all of those things, and my penance is my life. I only half-listen to the residents discussing my case. My philosophy on my involvement in my own treatment is likely as asinine as my prevention plan. I do what they say. All I ask is that they be aggressive with treatment and tell me where to be and what time.

"Miss Almonte, please," I recognize Dr. Medina's voice now as he tries to get my attention.

"What time is it?" I whine.

"Six in the morning."

I huff and take the pillow off my face placing it behind me. I stare among the residents, only half of whom I recognize.

"I hear you got a little dehydrated?" Dr. Medina asks as he glances through my medical chart.

"Yeah. I noticed it quickly, though, and came to the hospital right away," I say.

Dr. Medina faces the students, asking for their proposed plans for keeping food and water in my stomach. They have barely begun pitching treatment plans when the squeak of sneakers rushing into the room draws the attention of the small army of doctors. Someone is late.

And that someone is Rory.

He is staring down at his tablet and looking disheveled. His red hair is a mess, like he just woke up, and his white coat is nowhere near as crisp as the other doctors.

"Glad you could join us, Dr. Dennis," Dr. Medina says.

"Sorry, doctor. Won't happen again," Rory says as he squints at the room. He pats his pockets until he produces his glasses and brings them to his face.

Everything happens around me, but not to me. I'm looking into the hospital room scene from a faraway window like an out of body experience. My stomach burns, and I would grab for the bedpan if I didn't know there is absolutely nothing in my stomach that can come up right now.

Rory freezes when his eyes land on me. His hands clench around the tablet in his hands, and he looks down, undoubtedly looking at my chart, confirming the name that belongs to the patient. He looks up at my face, back at the tablet, and back to my face, freezing his hold on my eyes on the last glance. I swallow hard, wincing at the painful dryness in my throat. His hands fall to his sides in resignation. I'm not sure if it's the state of his crumpled doctor's coat, his slouched posture, or the weakness of his arms dangling at his sides, but Rory gives the impression of a crumpled napkin, discarded on a dirty old street.

The residents are mostly done with rounds by the time Rory arrives. I nod and say, "Sure, sure," not knowing at all what they have said. They trickle out of the room until only Rory remains.

His mouth parts like he is about to say something, then he shuts it again as he takes a step away from me. My eyes sting as I watch him withdraw. And it is so stupid because we barely know each other. It shouldn't matter. I don't care about him. He doesn't care about me. Not really. So why the hell has this heavy ball of lead settled low in my stomach?

"Rory, I—"

"I have to catch up to the group," he points with his thumb toward the door and leaves me alone.

THE LONG DAY drags after that. Pilar calls me around lunchtime.

"When can I come to see you?" she asks.

I know Felipe won't let her, so I bluff. "Whenever you want."

"I'm going to try to manage it. I think next month, I can get away for a week or so. I want to see your new place, the gym, everything."

"All right," I say, sure this will never happen.

"How are you liking it there?"

"It's great. I've made a few friends." Sticking with the positives will keep her at bay for a while.

"That's great, Tini! Tell me about them."

"Let's see, there's this girl, Mandy. She's an artist. And her two cousins, Izel and Tlali. Izel writes horror, and Tlali translates novels." I stick to describing them by their true trades instead of their day jobs. I'm afraid to even mention anything hospital-related to my sister.

"How Bohemian." Pilar sounds overjoyed. "And strange."

"Why strange?" I ask.

"All your friends here are gym rats. This is different."

"New leaf and all that," I say. "Trying new things. How about you, Pili? How are you doing? Really?"

"You know me. I'm always fine."

"Pilar, come on. I want to know the truth."

"I just miss you, is all."

"I miss you too. You should really think about making some new friends too."

She laughs, but it's bitter. "Do you think I could find some friends under the couch or in the kitchen?"

I wince. She is basically a prisoner in her fancy tower. "I'm sorry," I say. "That was insensitive."

"Don't worry about me. My problems aren't really problems."

"Just because you are wealthy and don't lack any physical comforts doesn't mean you can't have problems, Pilar."

She sighs into the phone. "I called to check on you, not to get the Spanish Inquisition."

I laugh. "Yeah. You're only okay with giving me the third degree."

"Speaking of which, did you speak to Chema?"

It's my turn to sigh. "Yeah."

"And?"

"He's pretty pissed at me."

"Were you expecting anything less?"

"No. I guess not. Do me a favor? Check on him if you can?"

"I'll try, but you know Felipe—"

"Yeah. I'm sorry. Forget I asked. I'll try to keep tabs on him with my gym rats, as you have so lovingly put it."

"I miss you," she says.

"Miss you too."

She promises she'll do her best to visit in a few weeks, but we both know better. Despite the lie, I'm glad for the call and the distraction from the boredom that is the dreaded hospital stay.

∾

I'M NOT surprised when Rory comes back. His white coat is gone, and I'm guessing he is off work late in the evening. The door to my room is open when he shows up, and he doesn't ask to come in. He sits on a chair opposite me and leans back, his legs apart, while he bounces one foot on the floor, making his leg shake.

The armrest props his elbow up as he grips a pen. He clicks the pen once, then twice, but doesn't say anything.

Being in the hospital gown without the armor of makeup or my knuckle-wraps, I shift in the bed uncomfortably. *Say something,* I think. *Anything. What are you thinking, Rory?*

The pen clicks again as his dark green eyes pierce through me. I open my mouth to break the hollow silence, but nothing comes out. I'm not sure how to explain this, or that I even want to. Rory swallows, and his Adam's apple bobs up and down. His eyes narrow as he waits patiently.

Another click of the pen.

The sound of it is so annoying, I want nothing more than to march up to him, snatch the pen, and throw it to the ground.

Click.

Mercifully, he finally speaks. "You didn't have a stomach bug," he says, and it's most definitely not a question. I shake my head. "What is it?" he asks.

"I'm sure you read my chart already."

"No," he snaps. "I wouldn't invade your privacy like that."

"But, I thought . . . earlier, you looked at my chart."

"I did. I looked to make sure it was you. I confirmed your name, then I stopped reading."

"Oh," is all I manage.

Rory stops tapping his foot on the floor, and the sound ceases. He also sets the pen on the hospital tray between us. "So? Are you going to tell me what it is? I mean, you're on the oncology floor, so I know it's cancer." His face betrays no emotion. I need to know if he's angry or if maybe he even feels cat-fished, for all I know.

"Does it matter?" I ask.

Rory scoffs. "Yes, it fucking matters," he sneers, finally betraying his stoic composure from earlier.

"There's a reason you were meant to be for only one night, Rory. This wasn't supposed to get complicated."

"We're a little past that, don't you think?"

"It's not too late. Feelings aren't involved yet. You can go on as you were before we met, and I'll go on with my treatment. No hard feelings," I offer, and do my best to smile in a way that might soothe him. Yet, the thought of him not being around aches in my chest.

"Is that right?" he asks, but it's clearly rhetorical. "You've decided, then? You have no feelings for me, and there's no possible way I have feelings for you?" His muscles are all tight knots, and I wince a bit because he is so wound up, I can almost anticipate him throwing something. But kind and gentle Rory wouldn't do something like that—I know that much.

"Rory, we hardly know each other. I won't begrudge you walking away if that's what you are worried about. I never wanted you to find out at all."

"That's what you think I'm worried about? That I would feel guilty about walking away now?"

"Well, yeah. Wouldn't you?"

His eyes soften, and he scratches his jaw, letting out a long breath. "Valentina, I care about you. You're right, we barely know each other, and it is too soon to talk about feelings. If circumstances were different, I would wait until we'd had more time together, but I meant what I said before. I want to get to know you and finding out you're sick doesn't change that."

"It does for me," I say, and now it's me who's angry.

"What does that mean?"

"You were never supposed to know. You were a fantasy—what I would have wanted if I wasn't sick—and I got to live it for one day. I was happy with that, but you had to keep pushing, didn't you?"

"Yeah, I did! Because I like you," he hisses. I blink because it's almost comical how he says the sweetest words with the roughest voice and so much anger. I want to laugh at how such a deep voice comes from the body of a man who has no business with that baritone.

"Rory," I plead. "Do you think I want you around for this? Especially when you know what I am without this illness?"

"Do you think you are any less remarkable because you're sick? Valentina, it only makes you that much fiercer. Don't you see? It's the fighter in you that I'm drawn to."

My vision blurs at the welling of my eyes. He says the most perfect thing he could possibly say to me, and I press my hand to my chest to soothe my aching heart.

Rory stands from his seat and lies down next to me on the hospital bed so he can embrace me. I curl up into his side like I did that night on the Kansas City grass and breathe him in. This time, it's the hospital's antiseptic scent instead of the earthy smells of the park that mingle with the smell of Rory, and it is no less remarkable because it is him. His embrace soothes like nothing in this world, and I fall apart in his arms. I break down for all the words I haven't said and all the people who don't know I'm sick. I sob into his t-shirt, and he lets me. He hugs me tight, encouraging me to let it all out.

The circles he rubs on my back bring me down from my cry, and I compose myself.

"Now, can you tell me what it is?"

"Cervical cancer," I say weakly.

Rory's chin rests on top of my head, and I'm so glad he can't see my face right now.

"Stage?"

I try to resist giving him any details, but in the end, I give in. I tell him every detail about my cancer and am relieved I don't have to explain what any of the terms mean because he already knows. His arms tighten around me like the words physically attack him.

After a long moment, I feel him shake around me. I look up, and he is holding back laughter. I wipe my eyes. "What?" I ask. "Are you laughing?"

"Nothing," he says, but this time he lets a little laugh escape.

"That's not nothing. Tell me!"

"I was just thinking . . ."

"Yeah?"

"It's a good thing you're dating an oncologist." Then he lets the roar of laughter out. I love that he can't help but laugh at his own jokes before he shares them out loud.

I smack his abs playfully. "That's not funny, Rory," I say, but I'm also laughing.

"Yeah, it is," he says and plants a sweet little kiss on my forehead.

"You really do laugh at anything," I say with a roll of my eyes.

"What else is there?"

CHAPTER 11

Four weeks of treatment down and only one to go, at least in this first round. Hopefully, it is also the only round if I achieve remission.

"I want to admit you," says Dr. Ramirez.

"No, I'm fine," I say. "I don't need any extra help."

"It's not about help. I don't like the amount of weight you've lost. It's getting harder and harder for you to keep anything down."

"How long will this hospital stay be?"

"That depends. I want to run some tests."

I wince at the prospect of a long exploratory admission. Between the apartment, treatment, and the dehydration admission, I'm getting dangerously close to needing to ask Pilar for more money. She'd give it right away, but it would make her suspicious. Her life is hard enough in her marriage; I can't add to her troubles.

After extensive testing, Dr. Ramirez walks into my room with Dr. Medina, both their faces grim.

I sit up and look between them expectantly. Dr. Ramirez stands a few feet behind Dr. Medina, and it is he who speaks first.

"Hello, Miss Almonte," Dr. Medina says.

"Valentina, or Vale, please," I say with a half-hearted smile as I wait for the bad news.

"That's right. I'm sorry. Valentina, I'm afraid the tests we ran today confirmed what Dr. Ramirez feared. The radiation is damaging your small intestine. That's what's been exacerbating your GI issues more than normal."

I suck in a breath and shut my eyes. No. This can't be happening. My body is shutting down, and I've lost all control of it. The blow is devastating. I have always controlled my body one hundred percent. But this? There is nothing I can do to make this better. I don't know how I manage to not cry—maybe because anger is vying for first place in my mind, but I keep it together in front of my two favorite doctors.

"Okay," I say as it sinks in. "So what do we do now?"

Dr. Ramirez sits in front of me and squeezes my forearm. "We have to do surgery to repair your intestine," she says.

I exhale. "So there is something we can do about it, then?" Can I dare hope I will get through this? Hope is dangerous, but I want it so bad. "Is this common?" I ask.

"It can be, for cervical cancer patients who receive extended radiation," Dr. Medina says.

"And the surgery?"

"I have scheduled it for tomorrow," Dr. Ramirez says.

What follows is Dr. Ramirez explaining the surgical procedure briefly and answering some of my questions. However, both she and Dr. Medina reassure me the surgeon will stop by before the procedure to answer anything more specific. Both my doctors are confident this is the only path forward, and I have to get over the fear of major surgery because I have no other choice.

"Can I go home today?" I ask.

"I'd rather you stay," she says.

"But do I have to?"

"I really think it's best," Dr. Medina interjects before Dr. Ramirez can respond.

～

I'M bored out of my mind and wonder if I packed a book or at least a magazine. I stand to grab my duffle bag and plop it onto my mattress so I can rummage through it. *Please tell me I at least packed my tablet*, I'm thinking, but I must have said it out loud because someone clears their throat inside my room. I spin around and smile when I see that Dr. Ramirez is back. "Dr. Ramirez!" My excitement dwindles when my eyes land on Rory standing behind her.

"Hello, Miss Almonte," says Rory. I cock my head to study him. He's never before called me that in our few interactions together at the hospital.

We never discussed it, but now I'm wondering if I could get him into trouble at work. Surely there are rules against dating patients. But we met before either of us knew . . . I doubt his superiors would see it that way. I decide to play along for now, and I'll be sure to ask him about it later.

"Valentina. Please," I correct and do my best to reassure him with my eyes that I won't give him away.

Most of what Dr. Ramirez says doesn't register. Something about consent forms that I've heard a million times, but I'm so nervous about giving him away, I'm afraid to speak.

"Well, missy, if you are that bored of my rambling, maybe I'll have the capable Dr. Dennis go over the paperwork with you. Do you mind, Dr. Dennis? I was paged."

"Sure," he says and takes the consent form from Dr. Ramirez.

The minute she leaves, I interrogate Rory. "Am I going to get you in trouble, Rory? Or fired?"

He shrugs. "Don't know. Don't care."

"Rory, please. I need to know."

"It's frowned upon. Let's put it that way. But I've never actually delivered any sort of care, nor have I broken any privacy laws trying to find out what's going on with you—not that I haven't been tempted. They will be able to tell I've never accessed your electronic record except for that first time before I knew it was you."

"What about the consent forms? Isn't you going over them with me part of care?"

"Yeah, I'll page another resident in a bit so they can go over them with you. Better safe than sorry."

"All right. And Rory? Thanks for not reading my medical chart. I appreciate you respecting my privacy."

He takes a seat and scratches his jaw—a move I've come to recognize as a sign of either concern or deep thought. "So," he starts. "You gonna tell me the truth this time, or will I have to pry it out of you again?"

"You have the consent forms, so you know it's surgery."

"No. I didn't read them."

I can't help but tell him everything Dr. Ramirez and Dr. Medina said to me about the procedure. Rory listens intently with a stoicism that I haven't seen in him yet. It's an entirely different side of him. I get the sense I'm looking at Dr. Dennis now, and not my Rory. There is no playfulness. His jaw ticks, almost as if he's angry.

After a long stretch of silence, I have to know what he is thinking. "What's wrong?" I ask.

"You."

"I'm wrong?"

"Yes. It isn't supposed to be this way. You're so young. So healthy. So . . . good. You aren't supposed to get cancer. Everything is all wrong."

"Rory—" I try to interject, but he won't let me.

"I wasn't supposed to find someone I—" His voice cracks, and he has to swallow several times before he can speak again. "Only for her to have to go through this—"

I close my eyes because I don't want to see Rory cry, and he seems to be on the brink. This is why I haven't told anyone about the cancer. I don't want this pity. I don't want it from him either.

"I'm sorry," he says, and his voice is firmer now. I dare to peek at him again, and all signs of incoming waterworks are gone. I relax and lean into my pillows. "It's just, I've seen this disease so much. I know what you're going through, more than probably even you do. I've never experienced cancer myself, but being on the other side of it, in this seat, I feel so fucking helpless, Valentina."

I let his words sink in and try to piece together what he is saying. I can't square this side of his personality with the man who, not too long ago, on hearing my diagnosis, laughed with me at his jokes about being an oncologist dating a cancer patient. His seriousness reaches a degree that leaves me uncomfortable.

I'm already in a somber mood after losing a big patch of hair this morning. Add to that happy-go-lucky Rory suddenly grim and I grow worried, really worried, that I am going to die from this. This is just too many bad omens for one day, not that I've ever believed in omens before.

"Look," I say. "Um. I've had a bad day. I appreciate you stopping by, saying hi, but I really want to be alone now."

"Yeah, um. I'll stop by after your surgery, okay?"

I nod, and he leans over me to place a short, sweet kiss on my lips. "Bye, Rory."

I'M in the worst mood when Sara walks into my room, pushing a cart. I can't stand her bubbly personality today. But she's been amazing to me, and I don't dare be rude to her. Dr. Ramirez walks in shortly after. As much as I love her, I'm starting to hate seeing her. She only ever comes to me with horrible news.

"Good morning," I say, but Dr. Ramirez only smiles. "What?" I ask, confused at why these women are in my room so chipper.

Dr. Ramirez places some items on the counter in front of my bed. A few seconds later, *Girls Like You* by Maroon 5 and Cardi B fills my room from what I can now see is a speaker on the counter. I sit up on my bed, confused at what's happening, and then prim and proper Dr. Carolina Ramirez starts dancing. *Dancing.* Dr. Ramirez—dancing. Her moves are a bit spazzy, but I can tell she is having fun.

When I turn to find Sara in my room to ask her what the hell Dr. R took, I realize Sara is also dancing. Several other nurses who have worked with me poke their heads in for just a moment to sing one line of the song's chorus. I throw my head back in laughter.

They are trying to cheer me up. They don't care if they look like fools doing it. Then Rory sticks his head in and sings the chorus directly at me. My face hurts from all the smiling, then I panic. Dr. Ramirez is looking at me with an eyebrow slightly raised.

The song ends and rolls straight into the next one as Sara uncovers her cart's contents: hair clippers. I nod at her with understanding and permission. She wraps me in a cape with raised edges to catch my hair, and Dr. Ramirez takes me by surprise and starts painting my toenails.

I appreciate what they are trying to do. They're treating me like any other girlfriend on any other day—not the sick person I am. There is no pity in their eyes as Sara leaves me bald. They keep singing until they run out of energy and turn their attention to boys.

If I could have had the guarantee my family would act like this around me, like I was still me, I would have told them.

I worry a bit as they keep talking about the men in their lives. First, because Dr. Ramirez implies that Sara's boyfriend isn't a good guy. Then I worry they are going to ask me about any romantic partners. I'm not sure I could lie to them after what they are doing for me.

Dr. Ramirez is so focused on painting my nails, she never notices Dr. Medina standing at the counter by the nurses' station, watching as she and Sara tried to cheer me up. I have a clear view of him through my open door. He smiles at me and brings a finger to his lips, asking for my silence. I gave a quick, discreet nod, and he stays there, his eyes glued to Dr. Ramirez as she works to cheer me up. It seems I'm not the only one with a secret doctor crush at this hospital. I smile at Dr. Ramirez. Not until they are nearly done and putting away all the supplies does Dr. Medina sneak away unnoticed.

Sara and Dr. Ramirez leave, and though my spirits are a bit lighter than they had been before they came, I'm left exhausted. Even talking as much as we did today took it out of me.

I rummage through my purse to pull out my pocket mirror. I'm not a vain person, and I have never paid any particular attention to my hair, but it was beautiful. I say 'was' because Sara just walked away with all of it in a trash bag.

I take a deep breath and remove the blue silk scarf Dr. Ramirez tied around my head. I steel my spine as I unfold the mirror in my hand and take a peek at my new reality.

To be honest, it's not bad. I mourn the loss of such beautiful, lush, thick hair, but the baldness gives me a certain edge. I almost look dangerous. Thinking of the future, I realize it might be a good look for the cage if I ever get back to it. The way a fighter looks can certainly affect an opponent's perception and potentially throw them off their game.

Yes. Bald is the best fighting look.

CHAPTER 12

"You ready?" Rory asks.

"For what?"

"We're going home today." He smiles warmly.

"We?"

"Yeah, well, I'm taking you home."

"I don't need any help, Rory." I sound about as annoyed as I feel.

The scarf Dr. Ramirez and Sara brought over to cover my head helps a bit, but I'm not ready for him to see me bald.

"No, you don't *need* help, but I would like to see you home. Make sure you're good."

"Rory," I let out a long breath.

"Please, Valentina. I worry about you being alone, and I'll feel better seeing you settled."

His brows are knitted together, and his longish hair is mussed. His boyish demeanor is long gone, replaced with sunken eyes like he hasn't slept in a while. He's been worried about me. Suddenly, my annoyance feels out of place. "Okay," I relent. "You can drive me home, get me settled. But that's it." This surgery was more invasive, and I'll have a larger scar than my other laparoscopic ones from before. I can anticipate more pain than before as well.

His smile is crooked, and barely a trace of his typically wide grin, but it's something. "Thank you," he says.

When we get to my apartment, Rory makes my bed and inspects my fridge. I know he is trying to determine if he needs to shop for me, and I hate that all I can be is angry.

We went from hot lovers to something else, though what that something is has not been defined yet. Is he my doctor and I his patient? Is he acting like a parent? Or worse still—am I his *charity case?* Long gone is the sexiness of our first day together. I almost wish I had stuck to my original idea and not given him my number to begin with.

I don't say any of this to Rory because ultimately, I understand he means well. He is caring and thoughtful and wants to take care of me. Now I'm mad at myself for being angry, and it's giving me a headache.

The medication bottle rests on the counter, and I grab for it.

Rory doesn't miss it. "Is the incision site hurting?" he asks.

"No. Just a bit of a headache," I say. After taking two pills, I go to my room, and Rory follows. He kicks off his shoes and lies next to me.

If he's going to insist on bugging me, then it is high time for him to give up some information himself. This couldn't continue to be as one-sided as it has been so far.

"It's time," I say.

"Time for what?"

"I was hoping you'd tell me on your own, but you haven't, so I'm forced to ask."

"Ah," he says. "You want to know about my scar?"

I nod. "You know more about me than I ever wanted you to know."

"That wasn't by design," he says.

"I know, but if you'd like to tell me, I really want to know why your chest was cracked open."

He turns on his side to look at me before he speaks. "I was born with a heart defect," he says. "I have what's called a pericardial patch on my heart."

"That's a pretty big scar if you got it when you were a baby," I say as I trace my finger over his chest where I picture the scar under his shirt.

"Good eye. When I turned eighteen, it had to be revised. I was growing, and so was my heart."

"You outgrew the patch?"

"Exactly."

"Open-heart surgery both times?" I ask.

Rory nods.

"Will it have to be revised again?"

"More than likely. Eventually, it will wear out."

My own heart skips a beat, and my mouth goes dry and not because of dehydration. Rory must see the worry plain on my face because he reaches to smooth out the crinkle between my eyebrows with his thumb.

"My cardiologist keeps a good eye on it. You don't have to worry," he says.

I purse my lips, and I can't tear my gaze from his chest.

"Is that why you became a doctor?" I ask.

"Mostly," he says.

"And?"

"And what?"

"You said mostly, so there's another reason."

He sighs.

"You're intimately acquainted with my medical chart, and with noises you shouldn't be familiar with this soon in the relationship. I think I deserve to know why you became a doctor," I say.

Rory grins, pleased with himself. I have no doubt it was me referring to us as being in a relationship that has him smiling. "Oh, grow up," I say, rolling my eyes.

His smile is gone when he speaks again. "I promise you'll know that part of me. Probably sooner than later, but do you think you can be a little bit patient?"

"It's not really my strong suit," I say dryly.

Rory scoffs. "Yeah. I've noticed."

"What's that supposed to mean?"

"You're a little bullheaded," he says.

"Occupational hazard."

Looking at Rory in my bed under the current circumstances makes my blood boil. The anger is quickly followed by guilt about being angry when nothing is his fault. Nothing is my fault. Nothing is our fault.

None of that is true. It's all my fault. If had only . . . so many things. If I had gotten my pap test when I was supposed to, or if I had gone to the doctor when the back pain started.

But I was built and trained to push through pain. It was nothing, I convinced myself, until it was too hard to ignore.

It's also my parent's fault because there is a vaccine for this cancer. If only they had agreed to get me the vaccine. Why won't parents give their children a cancer vaccine if it's available? My parents had only daughters. They should have known better. And even if they'd had only boys, they should have gotten the vaccine for them to protect their future girlfriends and wives. But who am I kidding? If we had been boys, we probably would have gotten the vaccine.

My family is estranged to begin with, but my resentment played a massive part in not telling my family what is happening to me.

Now, I'm lying in a bed with a wonderful man I wish I could keep, knowing I can't—a lover who gave me a taste of the life that still awaits. A lover I can't make love to.

"Hey," he whispers. "Where's that head at?" He smooths his fingers over my forehead again, and I blink my tears away.

"I'm sorry," I say.

"What do you have to be sorry for?"

"You're in my bed . . . and—I want to want you, but . . ."

"But you don't," he says.

I shake my head. "No. Sorry."

"Oh, Valentina. I know how this goes. Your sex drive will come back eventually. You have to be patient."

"Even if I had my sex drive," I explain, "I wouldn't want to. Not while I look like this." I avert his gaze, and Rory reaches to scoot me to him. His arm wraps around my waist, and he kisses my forehead.

"You silly woman. You're so beautiful, dontcha know. If you ask me, losing your hair and getting a little pale is only fair to other women." He chuckles. "They have a slightly more level playing field, but even then, you shine over all of them."

"You're just saying that."

Rory shakes his head. "Not even a little."

"It's hard for me to tell when you are joking, being sarcastic, or being serious."

"Always assume I'm serious and I'm joking. It's that pesky sarcasm you gotta look out for."

"Well, that narrows it down," I scoff.

"Can I ask you a favor?" Rory asks.

"Sure," I say.

"Mind if I take your apartment key and make a copy? I'd feel better that if you were to need anything, I could come in."

"That's sweet, but Rory, I'm feeling really weird about you taking care of me so much. We hardly know each other."

"I disagree. We know each other intimately."

I narrow my eyes, but he continues.

"I know, for example, that you prefer when I bestow attention on your left breast over your right. When I tease your left nipple, your back arches, and your toes curl. Nothing happens with the other one—"

"Oh, my, god, Rory!" I laugh—this man.

"I know you're embarrassed by your morning breath—don't think I didn't notice you sneaking to brush your teeth. I know you drink your coffee black but prefer it sweet. You've added increasing amounts of sugar each time we've had coffee together," he explains. "I know you have a lot of anger, and that's partly why you don't want your family to know you are here—"

"I—"

"I know that you're too stubborn and bullheaded to ask for help," his eyebrow arches high above the rim of his glasses when he says this. "And I know you don't feel beautiful bald, but I need you to know that you're more beautiful than ever—especially to me."

A sensation I can't identify lodges in my throat, and I have no words. What do you say to a beautiful man who says the most beautiful and comforting words? Nothing, that's what. You just hold on tight to that man.

RORY'S COMFORTING arms envelop me as I fall asleep, drawn in by the warmth radiating from his body. I don't know how long I've slept when movement in my living room wakes me.

The footfalls of more than one person alert me, and I hear voices. What the hell? Rory is not next to me anymore, so at least one of the voices has to be him.

I sit up and wince at the pain at the surgical incision. Looking at my phone, I realize I missed taking the last dose of my pain medication.

I readjust my headscarf that fell off while I slept. "Rory?" I say as I walk to my living room.

The apartment door is ajar, and Rory talks to another man who is bringing in a duffle bag. They both turn to face me as I walk over to them.

"Valentina, I'm sorry. Did we wake you?"

"It's okay. I had to take my meds anyway. What's going on?"

"Uh," Rory cups the back of his neck like he does anytime he is nervous. "This is my roommate, Neil. Neil, this is Valentina."

The tall, dark, and handsome man, who reminds me of Mandy's Chris, sets the duffel on the floor and extends his hand. His black eyes shine as he looks between Rory and me, and his grin spreads wide on his face. "Nice to meet you," he says, "Neil Campbell."

I wince at the movement as I shake his hand. "You too," I manage to say.

Neil's face turns to concern. "Are you in pain?" he asks.

I scoff. "Great. Let me guess. Another doctor?"

Neil chuckles and nods. "Yeah, but I'm in the surgery department."

Rory wastes no time in getting to my side. "Are you in pain?"

I nod. "I didn't wake up in time for pain meds."

Rory rushes to the cabinet, searching for them while Neil grabs my hand and leads me to the couch. "This all right?" he asks as he props a cushion behind my back.

"Yes. Thank you."

Rory offers a glass of water and two pills. I smile and take them. "Rory?"

"Yeah?"

"Why are there bags in my living room?"

"Okay, please don't get mad."

"Somehow, that statement alone makes me mad—"

"Well, that's everything from the car," Neil says. "I'm going to get going, man." He claps his hand on Rory's back and shakes his head as I watch him leave the apartment.

"Spit it out, Dennis," I say with little patience.

"You need help."

"I can hire a nurse."

"I can help while you get the nurse hired, and even then, the nurse won't be here twenty-four hours a day. You had major surgery. You shouldn't be alone, at least the first few days."

Looking between the bags and Rory, realization of what he has done sets in. My eyes widen with horror. No. He can't. I won't let him.

"So you moved in with me?"

"Well, um—" He at least has the grace to avert his eyes. "Just temporarily," he says.

"You didn't think you'd have to run that by me?"

"You have the extra room—"

It's barely a whisper as I manage to tame my anger. "Get out."

"Val—"

"Out, Rory! I don't want you here for this."

"Valentina, no."

He tries to stand his ground, but I know he sees the depth of my anger in my eyes. I stand and take a step toward him. He rears back only one step as he shakes his head.

"Out," I hiss and point to my door.

He doesn't budge, and I open the door. When he doesn't step out, I press my hands to his chest and shove him out. I am weak, but he follows the direction of my push voluntarily until I slam the door on his face.

Even that small amount of activity has me nearly panting, and I've never felt so weak. I rest my back on the wall next to the door, and the coolness of it is inviting.

A sob I didn't realize was building escapes me, and I can't stop it. My legs are noodles, and I slowly slide down toward the floor, my back gliding down the wall.

I'm a crumpled mess on the carpet of my rental apartment. My entire family and support system is a country away, and I've kicked out the only human I care for who knows about my cancer.

I never looked into hiring a nurse because I thought I could do without one for a while. I hadn't known then that I'd be having major surgery on top of everything else. Now was the time, though. I couldn't keep feeling sorry for myself.

This is that moment in the fight when every fighter is so tired and beaten up, you consider giving up. But then you remember that the other guy is feeling the same and considering giving up too, so you push just a little more until you rise.

I set my jaw and tighten my fists. Cancer is the other guy here, and I have to rise because soon, the other guy will be giving up. I move to place my legs under me so I can stand up, but the movement shifts my abdominal muscles, and a searing pain radiates from the incision site, forcing my legs to stretch out again. All the air leaves my lungs, and I pant until the pain ceases. I guess the medication hasn't kicked in.

The frustration deepens, and I fling my head to the wall. In my mind, I do this with force, but the effort is weak, so my head only gently taps at the wall.

Luckily, my phone is still in my pocket, saving me a trip crawling to it. I grab it, searching my contacts through my vision blurred by tears, and I call. It only rings once.

"I'm sorry," I say. "I can't do this alone. I need you. I need . . ." Saying the actual word is more challenging than I would have imagined. "I need help," I say, ignoring the pride that wouldn't let me say it until now. The weird thing is, saying the word out loud . . . is liberating.

The doorknob turns, and Rory is once again in my apartment. I smile weakly because I know he never left the other side of the door.

He crouches in front of me, and plants a kiss on my forehead. "Thank you," he says.

"For what?"

"Letting me help. I know that was hard."

"You do?"

"We're so much alike, you don't even know. I have a hard time asking for help too."

Rory places his hands under my armpits and lifts me like a doll. I wince at the sudden movement, and when we are both on our feet, he bends to place one arm under my knees, lifting me off the ground. I cradle my face in his neck and let him carry me back to bed.

"You've lost too much weight," he comments.

"*Et tu, Brutus?*"

Rory chuckles. "I'm guessing Dr. Ramirez already laid it on thick?"

I nod. "There wasn't much to begin with. You have to remember, my body was a fat-burning machine."

"In the morning, that's the first thing we will work on."

Once I'm settled, he inspects the room to make sure I have everything I need.

"Thank you, Rory. I'll hire a nurse tomorrow."

"You betcha, and no rush, really," he says with a wide smile.

"I don't want to keep taking your time like this."

"Valentina, you can have all my time, any way you want it."

I laugh. "Even in my sickbed?"

"*Especially* in your sickbed."

My heart sinks a little when I hear him settling in and taking all his things to my guest room instead of mine. It's for the best, though. I'm not sure what crazy thing my body will do next, and I probably don't want him right next to me all the time. He is respecting my privacy and trying to preserve what little dignity I have left.

CHAPTER 13

I hardly remember the next two days after Rory quasi-moves in with me. The pain from surgery has only gotten progressively worse, and I can do nothing but lay in bed.

Sleeping lets me forget about the pain, so I spend most of my time doing just that. I have a fleeting memory of Rory trying to wake me up. He had small, cool cubes of watermelon in his hands as he tried to feed me. The coolness of one pressed against my lips nearly tempted me, but ultimately, I pushed it away in favor of sleep.

The next vague memory is a blurry collage of the hospital lobby, Rory carrying me in, and a flurry of hospital images and sensations; the pinch of the needle going in, tubes of blood drawn, and the IV line set up.

When I wake, I'm not surprised to be at the hospital, knowing I would only be lucky if it had all been a dream, and luck is not on my side these days. It's morning, and my room is empty. How long have I been out? Is he back at work? I thought he took vacation time for a while to stay with me.

I lick my dry lips with a dry tongue and wince a little at the stiff skin peeling off my lower lip. They are so cracked it almost hurts. My throat is shut tight, and I'm thirstier than I ever have been. How long was I out?

The hospital remote rests conveniently by my side. I pick it up and press the call-nurse-button.

"Valentina, you're awake! That's great." A sunny Sara walks into my room and reads from some of the monitors next to me. "Welcome back," she says.

"How long have I been out?" I rasp.

"Oh, you must be thirsty. One sec." She comes back with a cup filled with water and adds a straw before handing it to me.

"Dr. Dennis brought you in last night. You don't remember anything? You were somewhat conscious when he checked you in."

I shake my head, trying to bring back memories, but nothing swims back. "What happened?" I ask.

"You spiked a fever. They think an infection from your incision. The docs put you on antibiotics, and you should be good as new soon. I'll have Dr. Ramirez come in and explain in more depth later today."

"Thanks."

"It was lucky Dr. Dennis was there." Sara places her hands on her hips and looks at me suggestively. "So you and Dr. Dennis . . . ?"

I glance away from her, then return my eyes to meet hers. "I don't want to get him in trouble," I say.

Sara smiles. "He's not your doctor, and he can't be involved in your treatment moving forward. It's not exactly against the rules, but—"

"But what?" I ask with wide eyes.

"It's frowned upon," she says.

I nod, understanding. "If it helps, I didn't know Rory was a doctor here when I first met him—"

"Listen, you owe me no explanations. I won't judge you," she pauses then adds, "for anything."

Sara says the word 'anything' pointedly like she has caught me with the hands in the dough, as Mom would say.

"Thanks . . ." I'm not sure I should ask her what she meant by that comment, so I trail off, hoping the silence will force her to fill the void.

"It's none of my business," she says finally, "but Rory left."

"Oh," I say.

"He was here all night."

"He stayed overnight?" I ask, and my heart swells.

"He did, until . . ." Sara trails off, and it's her who can't meet my eyes now.

"Until what, Sara? What aren't you telling me?"

"Until your husband showed up."

"Until my what?" I nearly yell. I shake my head. What the hell?

"Like I said, it's none of my business, but I do have to ask, Valentina, do you feel safe at home? Is that why you moved away from your family? Is your husband abusive?" Sara places a hand on my forearm and smiles warmly, inviting me to confess. Is this woman insane?

"There's a mistake, Sara, I don't have a hus—" I don't finish my sentence because a massive figure blocks the entire doorway to my room. I swallow hard.

Shit.

Chema stands with his arms crossed over his chest, looking at me with a face full of tension only reserved for when he is upset with me for slacking off during training.

Sara must confuse my look of panic with confirmation of her fears because she assumes a defensive stance between my bed and Chema. I twist in the bed so I can reach for her and gently pat her arm.

"No, it's okay," I say. "But he's not my husband."

Sara keeps pinning him down with a glare, and I'm in awe that Chema actually flinches. I've never seen him do that before.

"Did you lie to hospital staff to get patient information?" she asks defiantly.

"She *is* family," he says with an accent even thicker than mine.

Sara throws her hands in the air and finally turns to face me again. "Do I need to call security? Do you want him out of here?"

I shake my head but have a hard time finding my voice. "He's, um, he —is right. He's family. He can be here."

Sara's brows knit together, but she lets it go when I smile at her. "I'll leave you to it, then. Call if you need anything," she says before leaving my room and sending one last nasty glare Chema's way.

Chema walks forward, his nostrils flaring, and I can't help but recoil as I wrap my middle with the blankets. I wouldn't want to be his opponent in a fight.

I close my eyes for a second, then take a deep breath. He is going to yell. He looks so mad, so betrayed. I roll every lie I ever told him on a loop in my brain and know he has every right to be angry with me.

I've betrayed him.

But he doesn't yell.

Instead, he drags a chair to the spot next to my bed, and it's only when he sits that his shoulders collapse, and he buries his head in his hands. His shoulders start shaking, and I would think it's laughter, but the sob that escapes from deep in his chest leaves no room for interpretation.

"Hey, Chema, love, no," I say, switching to Spanish for him and place a hand on his shoulder. "I'm here. I'm okay."

His head snaps up, and his jaw sets with a fury I know all too well. "You are not okay," he hisses.

The tears streaming down his face deflate me. "You're right. But I'm working on it, okay? I am still here."

"What if you died and nobody knew, Valentina? What the fuck were you thinking?"

"I didn't, Chema, I'm right here," I say a bit louder, hoping the words get through to him.

He sits back, and it is only then, with his hands folded over his lap and the light flooding through the window illuminating his face, that I see his puffy, bloodshot eyes and red nose, like he has been crying for hours.

Or days.

"Chema, I'm sorry. I didn't want you to worry; that's why I didn't say anything."

"Worry? Valentina, you are going to send me to an early grave. I almost had a heart attack when I saw you."

"Lucky you were in a hospital, then," I say and grin. Chema glares at me with icy eyes, and I realize Rory's dark humor is starting to rub off on me, and it is not for everyone. Rory. Where is Rory?

"Chema?"

"Yeah?"

"Where's Rory?"

"You mean the *flacucho* who was here before I arrived?"

I nod.

"He left."

My eyes widen with horror. No. "Please don't tell me he thinks you really are my husband?"

Chema studies me until the smallest corner of his mouth extends into a hint of a smile. "Seriously, Valentina? A gringo? And a lanky one at that? I have more muscles in one *nalga* than he has in his entire body.

"Not true," I say. "He is deceivingly fit," I proclaim, and just like that, I'm in Chema's mind-game.

He grins. "You've seen these muscles?" he asks and raises an eyebrow.

I huff. "No. He's a runner. That's why I say that."

When my first text goes unanswered, and he sends me to voice mail on the first ring, I decide I have to go find Rory. I start shuffling blankets off me and trying to get to my feet when Chema pushes me back into bed with one finger to my shoulder.

"What do you think you're doing?" he asks.

"I have to find him, Chema. He thinks I'm married. I have to explain."

"Don't worry. He'll be back."

"How are you so sure?"

"He told me."

"*What?*"

"Yeah, he said he was getting a few things from your apartment, and he'd be back to drop off the key."

I sink back into the bed as my heart plummets low in my chest. "You shouldn't have told him—"

"Let's not start begrudging who should have told who what," Chema hisses.

Great, the two most important men in my life are mad at me at the same time. That thought jars me. When did I start thinking of Rory as equally as important to me as Chema? Chema, who is family at this point.

Rory is coming back, so I try to calm down in the meantime and shift the conversation away from him.

"How did you find out?" I ask, finally.

"Pilar called me."

"Pilar? How does *she* know?" A fresh wave of panic hits me. Do my parents know too?

"What did you think was going to happen, Valentina? Huh? You leave your family and your dreams for a half-baked plan to train away from home. Of course, she was going to get suspicious. If you signed on with an agent, why would you need the kind of money she gave you?"

The extensive web of lies I cast is starting to ensnare me. "Chema," I croak, unable to voice the question I am dreading. "Do my parents know?"

He nods. "They are on a flight as we speak."

I shut my eyes. No. The last people on earth I want to be seeing right now are my parents. "You had to tell them?"

"They had to know. But it wasn't up to me. Pilar made that call."

"Is she coming too?"

"No. Felipe, he . . ."

"Yeah, I know. Don't worry." The day she leaves that slime ball will be the happiest day of my life.

"I can't believe she told Mom and Dad," I say.

"Really? That's what you're worried about? God, Valentina, you can be so selfish sometimes." Chema shakes his head and stands to pace the small space in front of my bed. "We thought you were dying. Which, I guess you kind of are . . ." He trails off, and his bottom lip quivers.

"Chema, I didn't mean to . . ."

"I know." He sniffs. "You've always been too proud to ask for help, but I never thought you would take it to these extremes—"

"It's not about pride," I say in a small voice.

"Then what?"

"So many things. It's hard to explain."

"Try."

I want to tell him the truth. I never wanted this disease to define me. I didn't want to walk into a room and be the cancer girl. The sick girl. The dying girl. I've always been the strong one. The fighting one. The athlete. This is not who I am. I don't want to tell Chema I was afraid he would stop coaching me after—if there will even be an after. Or that I feared potential sponsors losing interest in my career. I didn't want them to see the failure of my body, because I wasn't a failure. But most of all, I want to tell him how angry I am. I don't say any of it. "I didn't want my parents to know. That's all." I say.

"Why not?" Chema wants answers, and he will not relent until I give them to him.

"Because I'm so angry at them, okay? I can't stand to look at them." That's not a lie, and I'm hoping a partial truth will appease him.

His eyes soften, and he retakes his seat next to me, cupping my hand not trapped by the IV line in his. "Did something happen before you were diagnosed?"

"You know it's always been strained between us. Dad had a lot of resentments toward me even before this happened. And I won't lie. I have a lot of resentment for him too. But Chema, that's not even it. There's a vaccine for this type of cancer. They refused it because they said it was for *sucias* only."

"And if you'd had it, you wouldn't have gotten cancer?"

"No. I wouldn't have."

"Then you have every right to be angry at them. Hell, I'm angry, but tell them that, Valentina. Don't shut the rest of your family out because you're mad at your parents."

Chema is right, of course. I'm bottling up so much anger for my parents, anger I've accumulated for so many years, anger that stretches far beyond their inability to give me a simple vaccine.

At first, the anger started when I was old enough to understand Dad's general disinterest in his own family. His business took up most of his time. His lovers took the rest, leaving nothing left for his wife and daughters.

For her part, Mom retreated into herself with the help of various little pills that a new doctor friend of hers prescribed. She slept or was awake but high—those were her two operational modes growing up. She became a hollowed-out, inactive participant in her own life, and I couldn't stand to watch her weakness. I was only fourteen when the dynamics of my family finally fit together in the jigsaw puzzle.

I swore I'd never be that weak and decided instead to be strong. I chose mixed martial arts in my quest to find my own strength, and I thought I had found it until my body told me otherwise.

"Chema, I know what happens next with my parents."

"What's that?"

"I will be an inconvenience for my father who has to be away from his *commitments*, and my mother will play the part of the perfect martyr whose daughter is sick. It's nauseating."

"Why don't you give them the benefit of the doubt?" He asks.

"Because I know better."

SLOWLY BUT SURELY, I get the full story out of Chema. Pilar became increasingly suspicious and decided to engage the services of a private investigation company. They found me out, easily tracked my mobile device, and took pictures.

Pilar hadn't thought to let me know, she simply wanted to know I was safe, but she knew I was sick when she saw the photos. I make Chema show me the images they've seen. He has them saved to his phone. The PI took pictures as I left the hospital. This was before I lost my hair. The image of the girl in the photo is unrecognizable even to me. She is me, but with no indication of muscles ever having existed, sunken eyes, and a greyish pallor.

The truth is, if at this moment Chema showed me a picture of Pilar looking like that, I would move heaven and earth to find her and make sure she was okay. I can't begrudge them for caring. Even if it means my parents were on their way.

How could I ever confront them? Neither of them will care about my anger and instead only be angry at me for hiding this. Not once, in my brief adult life, have I let them dictate what my life would look like —an ever-irritating sore on Dad's side, and this will only give them more ammunition to try to convince me they know what is best for me.

I take a deep breath. *Don't worry about them until you have to.* Instead, I focus my attention on my sister. I owe her an explanation. "Chema? Could you give me some privacy? I need to call Pilar." He nods and is about to go on a quest for decent coffee when Mandy rushes into my room in a whirl.

"Is it true?" she asks hurriedly. She brushes the hair off her face and eyes Chema up and down with a glint in her eye. "You're married? Way to keep a secret, woman," she scorns.

"He's not my husband," I say and glare at Chema. "He's my coach and more like family."

"Then why does the entire oncology floor think you're married?"

"I lied to be able to see her," he admits and hangs his head.

"Is that right," Amanda says, grinning at him and tossing her hair over one shoulder.

"Mandy! Stop it. You're with Chris." I can't believe this woman. She flirts with anything that moves.

"It's not serious, and we have never said we are exclusive," she says to me but looks at Chema the entire time. I roll my eyes.

"Well, I'm in a serious relationship. Afraid I'm—"

"Taken," I cut Chema off.

His eyebrows shoot up when he looks at me, but he extends a hand to shake Mandy's, and her face falls with disappointment for a beat before she takes it. "Chema. Nice to meet you."

"Yeah, you too," she says.

"Mandy, I need to call my sister. Chema was on his way to search for coffee. Give him the lay of the land?"

"Sure," she says and smiles encouragingly at me. I know she is happy I'm finally letting my family know.

THE VIDEO CALL rings only once, and Pilar glares at me through puffy, red eyes that match Chema's. She opens her mouth to speak, but I beat her to it.

"I'm sorry," I say.

"We've been so worried, Tini. You have no idea."

"I'm so sorry," I plead.

"I knew whatever you needed the money for was important, so I gave it to you even knowing you were lying out of your ass. But I never imagined it was life or death or I would have—"

"Would have what, Pilar? Come to see me? To help?"

She crosses her arms and looks away from the camera. We both know that's not an option, if her controlling husband has anything to say about it.

"I don't know," she says finally. "But I would have done something. You're my baby sister. You are a big part of the tiny light that exists in my life. I can't make it without you, Tini. Please don't ever pull shit like this again. You hear me?"

"I hear you. I promise I won't." And for the first time, I mean it. The heartbreak evident in my sister's eyes hurts more than any chemo and radiation side effects. She has been hurt enough in her life, and I can't be yet another person to let her down.

"I'm sorry. Mom and Dad are on their way," she says.

"I know you shield me from them as much as you can."

"You've noticed that?"

I nod. "Pilar, if I've learned anything from all this, it's that life is short. I hope I don't die from this, but even if I do, as brief as my life has been so far, I got to do what I loved. If you were in my shoes and you were facing death, could you say the same?"

"So that's what you're going to do. You're going to play the cancer card and hold it over everyone around you?"

"Only the ones I love," I say and smile.

Pilar doesn't engage the topic I tried to broach. Instead, I bring her up to speed on my treatment and we say our goodbyes and end the call, both of us sad but also a bit hopeful.

There's nothing left to do with the rest of my day but lay on my hospital bed and rehearse what I want to say to my parents. They need to know that while I share a big part of the blame for pushing off my regular checkups, they could have prevented it all. They need to know what a mistake they have made. And maybe, if I'm brave enough, I'll tell Dad precisely what I think of him. I was always too intimidated by him to do that. My young age and dependability prevented me from confronting him with his failures as a father, but now I am old enough to know better. My spine has strengthened, and this experience with cancer has matured me more than just physically. It would be now, or it would never be.

I'm saved from having the dread of time suffocating me by Rory finally showing up.

"Hey," he says but can't look at me.

"Rory!" I smile at him.

"Just came to drop off your key. I got all my stuff out of your apartment, and you don't have to see me ever again—"

"Rory, you don't have to—"

His voice deepens. "Yes, I do. I have to."

"Chema is my coach. Not my husband."

His head snaps up, and his eyes narrow, searching for the truth.

"He only said that so he could get my medical information."

"He can be arrested for that," Rory says.

"No. He won't. I'm okay with it. Frankly, I've put him through hell."

"So you two, you were—"

"No," I shake my head. "He is my coach and a good friend—that's it."

Rory doesn't seem fully appeased, but he takes a step forward, giving me hope.

Chema walks in then, clutching a mammoth cup of coffee that still looks puny in his hand and a bag with something that smells wonderful. "Brought you some breakfast," he says cheerily. "Hello." He smiles at Rory as he hands me the paper sack.

"Hello," Rory says but blinks as he tries to make sense of the situation.

I open the bag to find what I can only assume are burritos.

"Can you believe they put eggs in burritos?" Chema asks.

I shake my head and chuckle. My dear friend is about to have the same rude awakening with food I had when I first arrived. The truth is, I haven't eaten a burrito but a few times in my life. The last I remember was when my father had a trip to Chihuahua in Northern Mexico, where the burrito is king. It was one of those rare occasions when he brought his cumbersome family along. But those burritos had delicious grilled meat and beans with fresh avocado slices. Not eggs and cheese so greasy it leaks out of the flour tortilla rendering it soggy.

Still, I'm famished and take a healthy bite, which I have to admit, is not half bad. "I guess you two met while I was out of it?" I ask through the chewing.

Both men nod.

"I explained to Rory you're my coach," I say to Chema, "and not my husband."

Chema looks at Rory a bit sheepishly but still sizing him up with his glare. I'm proud when Rory stands tall, not at all intimidated by the meathead in the room.

"I'm sorry about that, buddy," says Chema. "I'm her coach. Actually, I'm—"

"Also a good friend," I say. Chema side-glances me.

"Oh." Rory cups the back of his neck.

"Sorry for the misunderstanding. As you can imagine, Valentina here had me and her family worried. I had to take drastic measures."

"Right, um, well, anyway, I assume you are staying with Valentina for a bit?" Rory asks.

Chema nods.

"Good. I'll be less worried," says Rory.

The proposed plan is appealing. The man I have the hots for doesn't have to see my physical decline, and one of my best friends can help me if I need it. I'm not sure when I became okay with the idea of help, but I did. It might have to do with the fact that not letting the people in my life who love me help me was in fact hurting them. I was hurting them, and I don't want to keep on hurting them.

"Chema? Are you staying for a while?"

"Until you're out of the woods," he says.

"And the gym?"

"It's taken care of. Don't worry."

"Well, um. I gave Valentina her spare key back. You can take that. I can show you to her apartment if you'd like," says Rory to Chema.

"Why don't we wait for me to be discharged, and we can go together?" I ask, suddenly nervous about leaving them together alone.

"They're keeping you overnight for observation, making sure you're responding well to the antibiotics, but you look much better, so I'm sure they'll discharge you in the morning," says Rory, who I know had to ask Sara for that information.

It's not ideal, but I have no further objections. At least not persuasive ones. I reassure Chema I'll be fine while he goes to freshen up and catch a nap before coming back.

"Rory?"

"Yeah?"

"I'll see you soon?" I ask because it is a question.

Rory's mouth upturns into a crooked smile, almost as if he were upset by the new arrangement. "Yeah, soon," he says.

Rory walks out of the room first, and Chema lingers for a bit.

"You aren't going to tell him I'm—"

"Don't you dare tell him," I warn my gentle giant, and he smiles knowingly at me. "Chema, thanks for coming. I'm glad you're here. Really."

"I'm always here for you, Tini," he says and walks out of my room after Rory. I can only imagine what they will talk about.

CHAPTER 14

"Oh my god," Mandy squeals. "You guys need to see him. He is so hot," she informs Tlali and Izel who are both huddled around my bed.

As soon as evening visiting hours started and everyone got off work, my room filled up. Chema is still at my apartment, but my new girlfriends keep me company. Sara even lingers after she checks on me to catch some of the girl-talk. When I first came to Kansas City, I never imagined I'd end up with a hospital room full of friends. I was prepared for lonesome and restless long stints in the hospital, but that has been the furthest from the truth.

"Is he coming back?" Izel asks and grabs a potato chip from a bag inside her purse.

"God, I hope so," Mandy says dreamily.

"Stop it," I warn. "You are taken. He's taken."

"You sound a little possessive there," she says and isn't even a little discreet when she glances at Rory, who is sitting in the corner of the room.

Rory's jaw ticks, and he stands up, probably not wishing to continue to let Mandy target him with her directness. "I'll leave you ladies to it, then. Valentina, I'll swing by tomorrow. I'm guessing you'll have your plate full tonight."

He tries to jab at the girls, who all giggle, but I already told him my parents would be showing up soon. "Yeah. See you later."

He steps past Mandy, and lands a peck on my cheek, then smiles at me. As he walks away, I don't miss Tlali looking between us as she presses her hand to her heart.

"He is so sweet," says Tlali.

"I couldn't believe Mandy when she told me you were dating a doctor here," says Izel.

"In my defense, I didn't know he was a doctor here when I met him at the bar."

"He looked a bit jealous," Mandy says with a mocking smile.

I smile back.

"I knew it. You are trying to make him jealous," Mandy accuses.

"No. I'm not *trying* to make him jealous," I say. "But I'll admit I'm not mad about it. He's kind of cute when he's angry, isn't he?"

"Guys, you're all missing the bigger picture here. Not that Dr. Dennis isn't super cute and everything, but Chema! We need to get back to Chema. Is his relationship serious?" Mandy asks. "Because I'd love to move to Mexico."

I roll my eyes.

"What does he look like?" Izel asks. "Like, compare him to a celebrity so we can have an idea."

Mandy's index finger taps her chin, and she chews the inside of her lip for a second. "I got it," she says. "He is ripped. And I mean *Ripped*. Think of the body of a young Arnold Schwarzenegger. His face, it's a cross between the manly features of Antonio Banderas, and the sculpted jaw of Henry Cavill." Mandy nods, pleased with herself.

I think about that description and picture, Chema. She kind of nailed it.

Sara laughs. "That's pretty accurate," she says, then excuses herself to check on other patients.

"Okay, *that* I have to see," Tlali says.

Mandy proceeds to fill us in with updates about Chris and her upcoming art show. I'm hoping I get to go. Izel and Tlali don't have much to report, though they continue to motivate each other with their artistic projects even after their long shifts at work. I'm glad they squeeze time to come chat with me here in there, as busy as they all are.

The conversation is upbeat, and I'm so grateful that my body's ailments are forgotten, if even for a moment. I don't see the sick Valentina reflected in these women's eyes. The hospital walls melt away from my periphery, and I can almost see myself having this conversation at a bar over dirty martinis. In my mind's eye, I'm healthy, pink at the cheeks, and my hair is still long. The distraction of this conversation is so welcome, I'm even glad Chema hasn't returned.

The happy mood doesn't last because late that afternoon before Chema has a chance to come back and be my reinforcement, I have two new visitors show up.

The last two people I wanted to see me sick.

My parents.

We are laughing and in the heat of our conversation when a booming voice fills the room, silencing us all.

"Valentina?" His voice is deep and cool, making my stomach drop.

We all turn to the door, and I freeze. My father walks in behind my mother.

"Hi," I say. All the levity that had been in the room evaporates, and Mandy, Tlali, and Izel all suddenly look at their purses, the floor, or their shoes. Anywhere except at my parents or me.

"Um, we'll get going," Izel says. "Come on, guys." She gestures for Tlali and Mandy to follow her. They both act like mutes, which is the first time Mandy has been at a loss for words. "Mr. and Mrs. Almonte, it's really nice to meet you." Izel is the only one with a functioning brain now, apparently. They all trickle out of the room, herded out by Izel, who closes the door.

I face my parents and attempt a smile, but I know it's awkward. My mom brings her hand to her mouth to hide her gasp. Her hair is mussed, something I've never seen before, and her designer outfit is rumpled. They came straight from the airport, then. Her eyes are swollen and red-rimmed. She grasps my Dad's arm for support like she can't stay upright if she lets go.

On the other hand, Dad breaks away from her hold and steps

forward toward the side of my bed. His gaze sweeps my body from feet to face, and he falls to his knees.

"Dad?" I'm momentarily concerned he has fallen, but he takes my hand in his.

"Honey. We were so worried."

I don't remember the last hug from my Dad, or the last gesture of kindness between us, so my hand in his is awkward—at least for me. For him, it looks like it's the most natural thing in the world.

His harsh, black eyebrows are drawn in with concern, and I notice the stubble starting to shade the lower part of his face for the first time. He never goes unshaven. Or out of his suit and tie, for that matter. He wears a polo shirt and jeans that don't look out of place here but would have him stick out like a sore thumb any other day back home.

He lets out a sob, and I don't know what to do. I look at mom for help, but as usual, she is useless. She takes a seat and clutches her chest like she can't breathe, as if she were the sick one and not me. I knew this would happen.

"Dad, it'll be okay."

He wipes a tear from the corner of his eye and kisses the top of my hand. I blink at him, unsure what to say. He stands then and grabs a chair to sit next to me.

"Valentina Almonte, how dare you keep this from your mother and me?" I can tell he is aiming for scorning, but his voice cracks, giving him away.

"I'm sorry. I would have told you if the treatment failed. I swear."

"And you would have robbed us of time together," he says.

"*Virgensita*," Mom says and looks to the ceiling. She makes a cross over her chest and starts muttering prayers toward the sky.

This is it. The dreaded moment. The moment of truth. I am sick, but I am still me, and my illness hasn't erased all the harm done to our relationship before now.

"You've never cared about time together before now, Dad." I don't mean to sound as harsh as I do, but I know that's how it's received because Dad winces. He knows it's the truth.

"I'm sorry, *Mija*. I've let work consume me, and I've overlooked so much. I'll make it up to you. I swear. Tell me what I can do to make it up."

"Why don't you start by taking Mom to your hotel so she can freshen up and let her have her feelings there. We can talk tomorrow when you're both rested and more calm."

We both look at Mom, who is rocking back and forth in her chair with a rosary dangling from her clasped hands, tears dripping from her chin.

Dad shakes his head. "No. We want to see your doctor. I want to know everything. All Pilar said is that you have c-c-cancer. That you've had it for God knows how long, and she didn't know how bad it was."

"Look, I'm getting treated now. I got myself in a very aggressive clinical trial. You can relax and know I'm being taken care of. As for the doctor, you'll want to talk to Dr. Ramirez or Dr. Medina. They're the team leading the trial and most familiar with my case, but Dad, it's late. They've gone home, and they'll be here in the morning."

Mom finally comes and crouches over me, placing a hand on each of my cheeks. I'm smothered, but I don't protest. "*Mijita*, when you get through this, I'm going to give you the spanking of a lifetime," she says. Her tears are dripping onto my face, but I don't wince. Now, in a span of twenty-four hours, Pilar, Chema, Dad, and now Mom all shed tears for me.

I wonder what it's like for them. Do they feel defeated, like this cancer will consume me? I'm still in fight mode, and I refuse to switch to flight until I know there is nothing else I can do. I'm not dead yet.

"Mom, stop. Please. I'm alive. Save your tears."

"Until you're dead? Is that what you're trying to say?"

She always exaggerates. "Yeah, Mom. But it won't be today or anytime soon."

She smiles weakly and dries up her tears. I know she's trying to keep them in, but she fails miserably.

"Okay," says Dad. "I'll take her to the hotel. We just had to see you. Make sure you're okay. You understand?"

"I do. And for what it's worth, I am sorry about how you found out. I wanted to tell you myself, if it came to it."

"You've always been so strong, Valentina. I never realized you would use that strength to pull something like this. But we'll talk more tomorrow. Okay?"

They both kiss me and walk away, though they glance back as they walk out the door. I take a deep breath. Okay. We can do this in small bites. We've ripped off the Band-Aid, and tomorrow we can do the rest.

~

RORY GETS to my room before my parents. He wears his scrubs and doctor's coat. Being hospital staff provides him the liberty to avoid visiting hours.

"How are you?" I ask and smile at him.

His face brightens when he sees my smile. "Good. How about you?"

"Feeling a bit stronger. But it won't last. I get chemo tomorrow, and that usually knocks me out for a few days."

"Think of it this way," he says. "You're almost halfway there."

He is right. I know this. The trial is a five-week treatment plan, and I'm entering week three. I hadn't let myself search for the light at the end of the tunnel, but there it is, reflected in Rory's bright green eyes.

Rory places a vase of yellow and pink tulips on the counter by the window.

"I love tulips," I say. "Thank you."

"Do you? Or are you just saying that?"

"Would I lie to you?"

"You *have* lied to me. And you seem to lie to a lot of people."

A kick to the jaw would have been less painful.

"I'm sorry," he says. "I'm new to being on the other side of this. Usually, I'm the doctor. Navigating everything else . . . that's harder," he says.

"I understand."

Rory takes a seat next to my bed and takes my hand, rubbing the top of it with his thumb in circles.

"I hate that you see me like this," I admit.

"Like what?"

"Sick. I look awful."

"Valentina, you have no idea how beautiful you are. I don't think you'll believe me, but I have to say it anyway. When I look at you, I don't see a sick person. I see *you*. And you are strong, and yes, beautiful. I don't care if you think I'm superficial."

My eyes mist over for the first time because Rory Dennis says the only words I want to hear. He hasn't let this disease alter his perception of me.

"Hey, don't cry," he coos.

"I'm not crying. You're crying." I shake my head to center myself and smile at him again.

I squeeze his hand, and he leans forward to land the sweetest and softest peck on my lips. It's not a passionate kiss like what we shared before, but the tenderness and rawness of it plunges us into a different level of intimacy. I place my hand on his cheek as our lips pull away, and he presses his forehead to mine. We're sharing this tender moment when a booming voice has us jumping and pulling away from each other.

"What is this?"

As he turns to face the door, Rory keeps my hand tight in his.

My father glares at him, his nostrils flaring, and his hands at his sides bunch into fists. His body shakes with fury, and my heart races.

"Dad, hi. Good morning."

He says nothing and takes a step toward us.

Rory lets go of my hand to stand and adjust his posture as he faces my father. "Mr. Almonte, it is a pleasure to meet you. Rory Dennis." He stretches out his hand, but my father doesn't take it, never breaking his glare from Rory's face.

"What is the meaning of this?" Dad asks.

"Dad, Rory is special to me. He helped take care of me when I was alone and has done nothing but help me and be kind to me."

Rory's rejected hand goes into his coat pocket, but he doesn't let my Dad intimidate him. "Valentina is very special to me too, sir."

Dad's mouth opens to speak, but he is interrupted when Dr. Ramirez walks into the room.

"Valentina, good morning," she says brightly. "Oh, hello. I'm Dr. Ramirez," she shakes my Dad's hand, but his glare stays frozen on Rory.

"Dr. Dennis, good morning," she says, smiling despite the questioning look on her face.

"Dr. Dennis?" Dad roars, and his chest rises faster with each breath.

"Yes, sir. I'm a physician here."

Dad turns to Dr. Ramirez, an accusation in his eyes. "Is it common for doctors here to kiss their patients?"

Dr. Ramirez's gaze scans the room from Dad's face, to Rory's, to mine, finally understanding what's going on. "Dr. Dennis isn't one of Valentina's doctors, Mr. Almonte. I can assure you, no lines have been crossed."

"Excuse me?" Dad huffs. "No lines have been crossed? My daughter is sick. He's clearly taking advantage—"

"Dad, no one's taking advantage. Please sit down so we can talk."

Dad shakes his head. "What kind of a sick bastard preys on cancer patients?"

"Dad! He didn't prey on me. He didn't even know I was sick when we met."

I can tell Dad's resolve wavers a bit, but he's also the person I inherited my stubbornness from, so I know he won't relent so easily. "I will sue," he hisses. "No one takes advantage of my daughter."

"No one took advantage of anyone, Dad. And you are not suing. If anything, you owe a wealth of gratitude to everyone in this hospital, including Rory. They have all made me very welcome knowing I was here alone."

"Mr. Almonte, I'm sure you have questions. I'll be back in an hour when everyone is calmer." Dr. Ramirez doesn't let Dad answer her before she is out of the room. I don't blame her for her quick departure, because the showdown taking place in my room is awkward as fuck. I don't even want to be in the room myself.

Dad takes a deep breath. "I need you to leave," he tells Rory.

"He's not leaving," I say and grab Rory's hand to make myself perfectly clear.

Rory never breaks eye-contact with Dad, and Dad's glare moves from him to me and back to him again.

"*Please,*" Dad says. "I have to speak with my daughter and her doctors." His voice is more placating now, and I'm more receptive to it. Rory looks at me, checking with me it's okay if he leaves. I nod.

My eyes widen with horror when Rory bends to kiss my lips one last time before heading out. When he stands, I look at Dad, who is fuming. Rory Dennis is a brave man to have made that move.

"Mr. Almonte, I'll be back later. I'm sure you'll want to chat with me too."

Dad looks stunned and frozen in place as Rory leaves the room. He starts pacing, pausing to glare at me every few steps, just as Chema had done. He seems a little better than he did last night when he first arrived. He has shaved, and his clothes are crisp once again, though more casual than what I'm used to seeing him wear. My mother is nowhere to be seen, and I'm not surprised. She's never handled family situations well. Avoidance being her modus operandi, I know she has knocked herself out cold with pills back at their hotel room. I don't have to ask Dad for confirmation.

We switch to Spanish for the rest of our conversation. "Dad, can you sit down? You're making me dizzy."

He stills and at last sits, taking the chair Rory vacated only moments ago.

"What on earth were you thinking?" he asks. "Were you even thinking? Men like that prey on weak—"

"Dad! Stop. You don't know him. He didn't prey on me."

"You're sick. Any man trying to, to . . ." He trails off, not able to finish his thought.

"Any man trying to be with a sick woman is trying to take advantage? I don't deserve to be loved if I'm sick?"

"That's not what I'm saying," he says and runs his hands through his hair, pulling on it with frustration.

"Then what, Dad? Please. Explain."

His head hangs for a moment before he looks back up at me. "I don't know, *Mija*. This is all too much of a shock. Seeing you yesterday like this, and then seeing that—" he points to the door in reference to the man who just left. "Love, huh?"

My eyes widen. "What?"

"You said he loves you."

Did I? "Um, well, I don't know if he does, I was just—"

"Do you love him?"

That takes me aback. I had used the word *love*, though I'm not sure why. "I don't know, Dad. I've only known him a few weeks. I don't think we can say we're in love yet, but he's special. And I owe him a lot."

"What do you mean?"

"He took care of me after surgery."

Dad shuts his eyes, his brows knitted together in pain. "You had surgery?" he asks as his gaze fixes on me once again.

I nod. "I'll let Dr. Ramirez fill you in on anything medical going on, but Rory, he took care of me and brought me to the hospital. If he hadn't been there—"

"Don't finish that sentence. I don't even want to know what could have happened."

I smile. "See? It's good he's been around."

Dad's shoulders finally droop with resignation. "I'll apologize to him later, though I don't like this. Not one little bit."

"Thanks, Dad."

When Dr. Ramirez comes back, I sign paperwork granting her permission to disclose my medical record to Dad. I ask them to leave the room so I can nap because I'm too tired to go through my entire medical history. Besides, I'd rather Dad ask Dr. Ramirez a million questions instead of me, and I'm glad she's more than willing to take one for the team.

When I'm awake again, he is in my room, smiling at me, but I can tell he's been crying from his puffed-up, red eyes, and I don't know how to feel about it.

He acts like the strain between us was all in my head, but I know it wasn't. Dad has never looked at me like this before, at least not in my adult life. It was always disdain and disappointment because I refused to marry the men he lined up for me.

He told me once that no man would want to marry a professional fighter—a woman who had more muscles than him. I told him that's exactly the kind of guy I would never end up with. When Pilar married, he finally stopped pushing me toward the destiny he'd drawn out for me since my birth. Since then, we've hardly spoken, and if we have, it has been mainly to argue.

Now, he is here pretending like that history never existed. Like I imagined it all. He is doting and loving like he had been once long ago when I was just a little girl. I bite my lip hard to hold back my emotions. I hate that it's taken me getting sick for him to care again. Why couldn't he show me his love before now, when it might very well be too late?

CHAPTER 15

The next day, Mom comes to visit with Dad. I'm feeling a bit stronger and glad they are here together because I have quite a lot to say.

But first, I let Mom nag and nag about keeping the secret from her.

"Are you done?" I ask after her tirade.

"I'm not even close to done, *señorita*—"

"Cecilia!" Dad snaps. "That's enough. This is hardly the time."

Mom's lips disappear into a thin line. Just once, I'd love to see her talk back to Dad. Today would not be that day.

"I'm angry too, you know," I say finally.

Mom glares at me. "*You're* angry? After you pulled this?"

"Mom, calm down. I'm trying to have a conversation with you. I'm angry about a lot, and for once, I wish you would just listen to me before you check out."

She looks away from me and shakes her head like I'm talking nonsense.

"Hear her out, Cecilia," Dad says, and I'm surprised he's on my side. Unfortunately for him, I'm angry at him too.

Mom takes a seat and crosses her arms. She taps her foot as she waits for me to speak.

I take a deep breath and decide to start with the easier one. "I'm upset you're never there for Pilar or me. You're like a ghost, Mom. We've never had your support, so I don't understand how you'd expect me to go to you for something like this when you always avoid hard situations."

"That is not an excuse—"

"Mom, Mom. Please. Just let me finish."

Mom glares at me but keeps her mouth shut. "Thank you," I say. "Neither of you has ever come to see me fight—"

"We didn't want to encourage—" Dad starts to say, but I cut him off.

"Dad, I know it's hard, but let's pretend for a moment this is the worst-case scenario, and I don't make it. Aren't you glad, as short as my life has been, that I got to do the one thing I loved most in the world?"

The silence hovers over all three of us like a dark cloud. Dad's eyes turn glassy, and he swallows hard.

"Wouldn't you wish, then, that you'd gotten to see my greatness? I know you don't think it was much compared to your business or Pilar's marriage, but Dad, I was good. So good. They don't call mixed martial arts 'arts' for no reason. I was an artist with my body. It's fighting, yes, but it's also a dance, and it's so beautiful. I was beautiful. And you never got to see it."

"You're not going to die, Valentina," he declares like he can somehow control it.

That's not what I wanted them to get from what I said, but I'm not surprised. They will never support my dreams unless they are dreams I share with them. I know now that if—when—I beat this thing, they will not change. It's time for me to move on from the hope that we will ever be close.

"I'm sorry you're angry," Mom says. "But I've done the best that I could."

"I know, Mom," I give her a sad smile because I believe her, and knowing that was her best is a bit disheartening.

Now for the harder one. The one they won't want to so much as hear me out on.

"That's not the only reason I'm angry."

Both my parents look at me intently, waiting for me to go on.

"This cancer is your fault—"

"Great. You're going to blame us for this—" Mom says, exasperated.

"Mom! Please, listen." I wait a moment, and when she doesn't speak again, I continue. "You could have prevented this if you had given me the HPV vaccine. I wouldn't be here right now if you had done that one little thing."

"I don't know about that sort of thing," Mom says dismissively.

"My doctor told you about it. I was there. You turned it down. Tell me I'm wrong."

"You have to understand. That vaccine is for young girls who are lost causes."

I shake my head, and I'm furious. "No, Mom. It's for everyone. Men and women. Everyone needs to get it when they're young—*everyone*."

"Everyone who does . . . *things*," she argues, not willing to put it into words.

"Say it, mom. Say what you mean."

She just shakes her head, and Dad's face is buried in his hands.

"You want to say it's only for whores," I snap.

"Watch your language, *niña*. These are not things we talk about." Mom stands and takes the small medallion on her gold necklace between her fingers so she can play with it as she paces.

"Mom, most women get HPV in their lives. It can take years to turn to cancer. Pilar could get this cancer too."

"No," Mom says. "Really, Valentina, I can't believe you would talk about this and with your father present. You have no shame. Besides, Pilar is married."

"Good. I'm glad Dad's here. He needs to hear this too. Pilar can get this cancer even if she's married, Mom. She could have gotten it before—"

"No!" Mom shakes her head. "She didn't get it before."

"She could get it from her husband, Mom! You could get it!"

Mom stops and blinks at me. She shakes her head. "I can't believe we are talking about this—especially in front of your father. Valentina Almonte, you were raised better than to talk about this."

I'll never get through to her, but at least Dad displays some form of shame. He hangs his head and pulls on his hair as he listens to me. At least I know he feels somewhat guilty.

"Mom, I haven't been a virgin for a long time. Why is that so hard to talk about?"

Mom turns to Dad, swinging her purse over her shoulder. "Benjamin, please take me to the hotel. This conversation is over." Then she turns to me. "If you want me to come back, missy, none of that talk. *No seas cochina.*"

At that moment, and with those words, I give up on my mother. "No, Mom. I don't want you to come back."

"Valentina!"

"I mean it. Dad, you are welcome back if you'd like, but don't bring her with you. Not unless she regrets not getting us that vaccine before it was too late." He nods, and I add, "I know you feel bad about this, Dad."

He clears his throat. "Um, I'll see you tomorrow, then." He kisses my forehead for the first time in I don't know how many years and looks back at me as he leaves the room.

THE NEXT MORNING, I'm happy to find Dad has respected my wishes and left Mom at the hotel, though I'm sure she didn't protest. After speaking with Dr. Ramirez yesterday, he looks less forlorn, though he admits he carries guilt for not being more involved in our health and leaving it up to Mom, who, let's face it, didn't do a good job. I tell him I forgive him because I really do.

"Why can't you forgive your mother too?" he asks.

"Because she doesn't believe she did anything wrong."

I'm relieved when Dad lets it go. I change the subject and tell him about all the people I have met besides Rory. He smiles when I describe how Mandy, Tlali, and Izel welcomed me and have kept my spirits up.

"This place suits you," Dad says.

I smile. "It does. Doesn't it?"

I tell him about Rory, though I only give him the PG version, and he laughs when I describe the confrontation between him and Chema.

"And he didn't flinch?" he asks about Rory.

"Not even a little."

Almost as if we had summoned him, Chema walks into my room. He hadn't come back after I texted him that my parents were here. For obvious reasons, Mom and Dad loathe Chema.

Which is why it takes me by complete surprise when Dad stands and hugs Chema. Towering over Dad, Chema looks over his head at me. His eyebrows float up in question, and I can only shrug. I mouth, *I have no idea.*

The men part, and I take the somewhat happy opportunity to give Dad my one request.

"Dad, Chema has agreed to stay and help me out while I finish the last few weeks of treatment."

"I don't know how I'll ever repay you," Dad says.

"I love Valentina like family," Chema reassures him. "I wouldn't take any type of payment."

"I'd like for you and Mom to go home—" I start to say.

"Out of the question." Dad shakes his head like he can't believe what I just asked him.

"Dad, please. Chema promises he'll call if things go south. But if not, and everything goes like I'm hoping it will, then what's the point of you and Mom being here, living in a hotel?" He's unsure, so I drive it home. "You know if she comes back, we'll just fight—and that's the last thing I need right now."

"*Mija,* I want to be with you."

"I know, but I promise I'll video call often, so it'll be just like you are here."

He reluctantly agrees after I swear I'll keep him in the loop, but I see his relief to be able to get Mom away from me—like this is the one thing he can do for me, so he will do it.

Dad hasn't done much for me in my life, but this small gesture means the world to me.

The olive branch extends from my hands, and he takes it in the first fatherly act of my adult life.

*A*fter my parents' departure, I stay in the hospital for two days during my next infusion. I spend the two days in bed without any energy. Luckily, it is Chema who sees me like this, and he keeps Rory at bay as much as possible, though the weasel sneaks in here and there.

On the third day, I have a burst of energy that Dr. Ramirez takes as an excuse to finally discharge me.

When we get to my apartment, I see Chema has made himself at home. He upgraded a bit of the decor so everything isn't so cream and beige. There are burnt orange cushions on the sectional sofa and several clear food organizers on the kitchen counter displaying oats, nuts, and shredded coconut. A few abandoned takeout containers sit on the coffee table, and Chema's many pairs of tennis shoes litter the carpeted floor. It's a mess, and it feels more like home than it ever has.

We settle on the couch, and I grab the remote.

"Wanna watch a movie?" I ask.

"No. Actually, my telenovela is on now. Mind if we watch it?"

Telenovelas don't appeal to me quite as much as they do to Chema, but I owe him too much to say no. "Sure. Which one is it?"

Chema takes the remote and fills me in excitedly. "It's called *Curvas*

Peligrosas. With Erica Moran. She's that new actress who's really popular right now."

"The curvy one who looks like she just stepped out of a fifties movie?'

"That one! It's so good."

We are watching the show, and I soon realize she is an anti-hero. She uses men as boy-toys, and they call her the man-eater because no man can tame her heart. I can see why Chema loves the show so much. It breaks away from every telenovela trope I've ever encountered. The actress is stunning, and she is also plus-sized. Not that there aren't gorgeous plus-sized actresses, but they usually play the best friend, not the main character.

I'm going over this character analysis in my head when I get a text from Rory.

~

RORY: *Please don't kill me.*

    Me: *What? Why?*

    Rory: *I swear it's not payback for making me meet your parents.*

    Me: *What did you do?*

    Rory: *My parents want to meet you.*

    Me: *Um, okay.*

I don't say I think it's too soon to meet the parents or that him meeting mine was a fluke thanks to my sister, but fair is fair, after all. I take a deep breath.

    Me: *Okay. Set it up.*

    Rory: *Already done. Open up.*

    Me: *What?!*

    Rory: *We're downstairs. I'm so sorry. They insisted.*

~

MY HEART RACES. "I'm going to kill him."

Chema's eyes don't tear away from the screen as he asks, "Who?"

I snatch the remote and shut off the television.

"Hey, what gives?" Chema's annoyed glare pins me.

"Pay attention. Rory's downstairs."

"So?"

"With his parents."

"Okay . . ."

"Chema!" I whine. "This place is a mess!"

"Oh." Realization lands on his face. "Oh. Shit. Sorry." He kicks it into gear and picks up shoes from the floor and trash from the coffee table as quickly as he can. Everything gets tossed in his room. I'm not able to help with much, but I go over to the intercom to buzz them up.

"I'm going to take a nap," Chema, the coward, tells me and shuts his bedroom door.

When I open the door, Rory stands in front of a couple a bit shorter than him, neither of whom is a redhead.

"Valentina, hi."

"Come in, please." I adjust my headscarf and straighten my sweatshirt.

"This is my Mom and Dad. This is Valentina," says Rory as we stand awkwardly by the door.

"Oh, she is darling, Rory. You didn't do her justice." Rory's mom takes me in for a hug that is so tight I have to suck in air. "Oh, I'm sorry, dear. Didn't mean to crush you."

"Hello, Mrs. Dennis. It's very nice to meet you."

"None of that nonsense. Call me Lisa. And this here is Tom."

"Lisa. Tom," I say and smile at them. "Please take a seat, make yourselves at home."

Lisa Dennis has dark brown hair and a light-olive skin tone. Her eyes are brown, and she is short and stocky. Nothing about her looks like Rory. Tom Dennis is only a few inches taller than his wife, and both his hair and eyes are a dark brown that is almost black. Neither of them has Rory's signature freckles.

"Your mom is right, son," says Tom. "She's a lot prettier than you said."

"Dad! I'm sorry, Valentina. Don't believe anything they say. They are both liars."

I laugh. I'm glad I'm up for company today.

"I'm sorry to spring up on you like this," says Lisa. "We wanted to surprise Rory with a visit, and he confessed he met someone special. He didn't want us to meet, but then the weasel told us you are sick and alone and, well, we had to come check on you. He's a sneaky one, dontchaknow." Lisa shoots daggers at Rory with her eyes, and I almost feel bad for him. Almost.

It's so strange to have his parents here and to have them so concerned about me—a complete stranger to them. I search Rory's eyes for a possible explanation. Rory just shrugs, not understanding the question I failed to ask telepathically. He must have said something to them that made me seem important enough for them to want to check in on me. But wasn't this move exactly like something Rory would do? He always shows up if he thinks I might need any help, whether he's been invited or not. Now his parents are doing the same. He gets it from them, and I'm starting to understand that this is simply how his family operates. It's intrusive . . . and loving.

Then I turn my focus to what his mom is saying. I remember Rory using that phrase before. Dontchaknow. The syllables running into each other like they are all one word. When he used the phrase, he had been talking about home. Now I know where he gets it.

I study Lisa with curiosity. I don't understand what made them visit with such urgency once they found out I was sick. They don't know me enough to care. *What did you say to them, Rory?*

"Oh dear," says Lisa. "We've really put our foot in it, haven't we? I only mean Rory's been through enough in his life. If someone he cares about is ill, we want to be here for Rory."

"And for you," Tom says, looking at me.

"I, um—I don't know what to say," I admit. I look between the three of them, trying to find some sort of resemblance between Rory and his parents, but there is none.

There is no similar curve to his nose like Tom's, and his wavy red hair couldn't be further from his mom's brown curls. I look like my mom—a lot, and still, I have a bit of Dad around the eyes.

"You haven't told her," Lisa says to Rory but keeps her gaze on me.

Rory shakes his head.

"Tell me what?"

"Well, we can get going if you two want to have a chat," Tom starts to say, but Rory cuts him off.

"No. It's fine. You can be here when I tell her."

"Tell me what?"

"I'm adopted," Rory says. "It's the rest of the scar story I promised I'd tell you one day."

"Oh," I say. "Wow. I mean, um. I don't know what to say."

"No need to say anything, dear," Lisa says. "We know he is our son, and so does he. There's no difference if I carried him or if I didn't. Rory Dennis is mine and Tom's."

Rory takes his mom's hand in his, making me smile.

"I'm confused," I say. "What does that have to do with the scar?"

"When my biological mother learned I had a heart defect and would need open-heart surgery as soon as I was born, she gave up her rights to me."

"The poor thing was very young, and a sick baby was more than she could handle." It's nice to see Lisa doesn't seem to carry any resentment toward Rory's biological mother.

"At the time, we had been praying for a miracle," Lisa continues. "When we got the news about him and that he had a heart condition, well that hurt as if he were ours. Because he was ours."

Tom listens to his wife tell the story with a small smile, letting her do all the talking.

"Is that why you wanted to be a doctor, because of your heart?" I ask Rory.

He nods, and I imagine a teenage Rory, feeling rejected by his biological mother and wanting to be a doctor so no other child would have to go through the same thing.

"Why oncology, then?"

"The plan was pediatric cardiology, but then I came to Heartland Metro and met Dr. Ramirez."

"Ah," I say, understanding. "She inspired you."

"Yeah. You could say that. I've had many passionate teachers before, but to her, fighting cancer is like a personal battle. She recruits physicians into oncology like she is drafting for war. She's a force to be reckoned with."

"No need to explain further," I say. "You never stood a chance."

Lisa and Tom both laugh like they already know everything Rory is saying and all about Dr. Ramirez. Does he talk to them about everything? I wonder what that's like. To have parents you can speak with and who listen—parents who support your dreams, even when they change. Rory may be adopted, but his parents are closer to him than my biological ones ever will be to me.

Lisa stands, inviting herself to my kitchen. She opens the fridge door, and meeting with scarce options, declares it won't do. In a blur, and before I can stop her, she goes into my room and comes out with a dirty clothes bin. "I'll take care of these for you, dear," she says.

I'm about to protest, but she glares at me with a look I don't dare confront.

"It's best if you just let it happen," Tom says and winks at me.

"Tom, would you drive me to the grocery store? I want to fill the fridge and—" Lisa starts to say.

"It's really not necessary. My friend Chema is staying with me. He's helping."

When I mention Chema, the corner of Rory's eyes tighten a bit.

"I don't see him anywhere," says Lisa.

"He's napping," I say.

"Good. While he naps, I'll get the laundry going and go get some things so I can make some soup."

"Mom's chicken noodle soup is magic," Rory says.

"Uh . . . Thanks. For everything," I say.

"You betcha, dear," says Lisa with a smile.

Lisa and Tom say a quick goodbye and leave my apartment, though Rory lingers for a little while.

"I'm sorry about all that," he says. "They mean well."

"Don't be. They are fantastic, Rory," I say.

Rory smiles and plants the customary peck on my lips before leaving. It feels familiar already, like we've known each other for years, and this is how we part ways.

I don't like it. Not one bit.

Rory was meant to be temporary. A tiny blip in my life, when everything was said and done. But somehow, he has already cared for me in my sickbed, met my parents, introduced me to his, and told me about his biological mother and his heart defect, which couldn't have been easy for him.

He thinks this thing between us is serious.

It can't be. Not unless I know I'm in the clear. If death weren't staring down at me, I know I'd let this happen, but everything is so much more complicated because of my stupid, stupid cancer.

Rory beamed when he introduced his parents to me. He was so proud for us to meet. He was not scared like I was when I was forced to introduce him to mine. My life is much too complicated to let this happen. His feelings for me are growing, and I can't break his heart.

I need to nip this in the bud.

CHAPTER 17

Rory pulls the wheelchair from the trunk and places it outside my door.

"Have I told you how beautiful you look tonight?" Rory asks.

I chuckle. "Yes. When you picked me up, remember?"

"Yeah. Right."

He is lying through his teeth, but I know he's just trying to make me feel good.

I dodged him after his parents went back to Minnesota, but we both committed to going on a date to Mandy's art show. I figure I can break it off with him after one last date.

If I'm honest, I want to see him one last time. One last time when we are both happy.

I feel okay today and insisted I wouldn't need the wheelchair, but Rory didn't want to push my luck with my energy levels. At the tail end of treatment, I only have one week to go, and then all that's left is to wait and see if it comes back. Finally leaving chemo and radiation behind me will be one of the best days of my life. I just hope I'm putting treatment behind me for the last time. I'm not sure I can put myself through this again.

I'm swimming in my wrap dress. I tied it as tightly as I could to make it seem more my size, though it's not fooling anyone. Rory looks dashing in dark slacks and a maroon button-up shirt that makes his beautiful green eyes pop. I'm going to miss him, but I try to focus on one last night together, enjoying his company for now.

Rory pushes my wheelchair into the nearly-empty gallery. The space has a modern vibe, and every wall is filled with colorful oversized landscapes and much smaller portraits.

Tlali and Izel huddle around Mandy, talking to a tall woman whom she introduces as the gallery manager and her art dealer, Debra.

"It's nice to meet you," I say.

"You too, enjoy the show. I have to check on a few things," Debra says and gets to work.

I turn to look at Mandy. "Are you nervous?" I ask.

Mandy nods. "A little. I've been working on this for so long. It's always a little nerve-racking putting work out there, hoping no one will trash something you've poured your heart into."

"It'll be great; you'll see." Tlali half-hugs Mandy and rubs her shoulder. "The paintings are great. You'll get rave reviews. I just know it."

"Thanks. I hope you're right," Mandy says, and nervous isn't a look that suits her.

Izel walks over to the hors d'oeuvre table and plops a tiny tart in her mouth, then grabs a glass of white wine. "You look good, Valentina," she says. "I'm glad you felt up to it."

"Me too. Thanks."

A few more people trickle in, and Mandy leaves us so she can greet them. Izel and Tlali both make their way to various paintings to admire, and I ask Rory to push me around so I can see them all.

One half of the room is hung only with portraits. I recognize depictions of Tlali, Izel, and Mandy's mom. The rest of the portraits are all women, though I don't recognize any more of them. Mandy's style is a bit abstract up close, but the further you step back, it's almost photorealistic. I'm no art expert, but despite my untrained eye, I can tell these are good.

I've seen modern art before. I don't understand most of it. A lot of it seems like things children would do, but somehow, Mandy has managed to merge classical-style painting with a modern twist. It's unlike anything I've seen before.

"She's really talented, isn't she?" I say to Rory.

"She sure is," he agrees. "One day, when I'm making a good salary, I'll commission a portrait of you from her."

Who knew that little package of loud would be this good an artist? I've always pictured artists as tortured souls suffering for their art. In my head, it was the Hollywood depiction of alcoholics and drug addicts starving for their art, only gaining recognition long after their death.

Mandy couldn't be further from what I envisioned an artist to be. Her life is chaotic, but she is fulfilled. She holds a regular job to support herself and has friends who support her.

"Take me over to the landscapes?"

Rory obliges, and we get in line behind a few people to start the procession in front of the significantly larger landscape paintings. The gallery is nearly full now, and I'm relieved for Mandy.

Her landscapes are crafted in a similar style to the portraits but on a grander scale. I can tell this is the playground where she experiments with light. The landscapes exude a feeling the portraits lack, and I know, just know, this is where her true talent lies.

We reach the end of the room to find a single painting larger than all the other landscapes. It's technically a landscape because I see land below, but clouds engulf the vast majority of the canvas, more like a skyscape.

I squeeze Rory's wrist, asking him to let me admire it a little bit longer. I haven't seen much art in my life, but I understand now why people seek it, travel for it, suffer for it. It moves something inside you. It makes you feel alive. It gives you a reason to live.

My eyes sting with tears as I take in the painting. I haven't seen enough. I haven't seen enough art. I've never seen clouds like these, sunrises like these—places like this. I've spent all my life in a big city surrounded by high-rises—a concrete jungle encasing me. While I love my city, there is so much more I haven't seen; not enough natural wonders, foreign countries, or art. I've never seen so much as a waterfall in real life.

I take a deep breath and swallow back my tears before they spill. Craning my neck to read the small card next to the canvas, I read: "Untitled, Not for Sale."

"That one is my favorite," Mandy says as she reaches Rory and me.

"Mine too," I agree, eyes still glued to the painting. I'm relieved the conversation distracts me from my fatalistic thoughts. "I was thinking about buying it, but it's the only one not for sale. Why?" I ask her.

We walk back to the food table as we keep chatting.

"I don't know," Mandy shrugs. "There are some paintings that you're just full of some sort of emotion while you work. You know? And then when you're done, it's like you can't believe you made that—that you have something like that inside you."

"No," I shake my head. "I have no idea what you are talking about, but I'll take your word for it."

"It would just be too hard to part with it, that's all. Though, I do think eventually I'll end up selling it."

Debra walks over to our spot and clutches Mandy's forearm. She speaks in small conspiratorial whispers, but Rory and I are close enough to hear too.

"You are not going to believe this, but we have someone wanting to buy the landscape that's not for sale."

"I do believe it," Mandy says. " It's my best work, but it's not for sale."

"He really wants it and is ready to prove it. He said to name your price."

"Who is it?" Mandy asks, scanning the gallery past Debra.

Debra points to a giant man almost as tall as Chema, though not quite as beefy. He is stunning, but in more of an Enrique Iglesias kind of way. My jaw drops, and I look over at Mandy, but her face is all scrunched up. "What's wrong?" I ask her.

Her jaw twitches, and I can tell she's grinding her teeth. "That's Dr. Bel."

"Wait, you know him?" Rory asks.

"Yeah. He's a surgeon at Heartland Metro."

"Why do you look like you are about to kick him in the shin?" Rory asks.

"He's a complete jerk. I've seen him every day for years, and he never remembers having seen me before if I say hello. Not that he'd say hello first. He basically fits every arrogant, god-complex, surgeon stereotype." Mandy's nostrils flare at the end of her rather picturesque description of Dr. Bel. "No way in hell I'm selling him my favorite painting."

"Hold on just one minute," Debra hisses. "Think about it. He asked for you to name your price for that landscape. You can make as much as you want here."

Mandy's resolve wavers, but in the end, she shakes her head. "No. I'd burn the painting before *he* could have it—"

"Mandy, hold on." I try to reason with her. "Why don't you set a ridiculous price no one in their right mind would agree to? That way, he'll probably say no and no harm done. And if he agrees, then you can make a small fortune at his expense."

"But he'll have the painting," Mandy says.

"But you'll have his money at a premium," I smile wickedly at her.

Most of the landscapes are priced at around fifteen-hundred dollars, depending on their size. I'm sure the gallery takes half of the sales price. She has the opportunity to make a killing on one painting alone.

Mandy bites her cheek as she thinks, then looks at Debra. "Fine. Valentina makes a great point. Tell him twenty thousand dollars—firm. I'm not going to haggle with him, Deb. I meant it."

"Are you kidding?" Deb hisses but plasters on a fake smile. "That's ridiculous. He'll never agree to that. You're not that established yet. One day maybe, but not—"

"I'm not trying to sell the painting, Deb. You agreed to this. We only included it because it's part of the narrative we were going for."

"Okay. Okay, but you're killing me here."

"Unless he agrees," Mandy smiles. "In which case, I just made you a shit ton of money."

Debra glares at Mandy, and I know she doesn't think Dr. Bel will buy it.

Rory, Mandy, and I all stare at Debra walking toward Dr. Bel. We can't hear anything they are saying from the other side of the room, but we see Dr. Bel nod. His head snaps up to look in our direction, and the three of us break our formation to pretend we were talking the entire time.

Debra walk-runs to us in the most comical way, a huge smile spread on her face. "He said yes!" she squeals.

Mandy's jaw drops. "What?"

"He said yes! He's buying it."

"We didn't set the price high enough?" Mandy asks, her brows creased.

"I honestly think he would have bought it no matter the price. He really wants it."

"See, that just makes me angrier. I just validated that he can get anything he wants," Mandy hisses. "And he gets to keep the one painting I didn't want to part with. It feels a lot like losing."

I nudge Mandy's arm. "Hey, you just made a shit ton of money. You can certainly be happy about that. And he paid a ridiculous amount for it. You have the upper hand here. Twenty thousand dollars, Mandy."

She smiles. "You're right. I can do a lot with that money."

Witnessing my friend's success shifts the mood of the evening, and I feel lighter now. I'm dreading the end of the night when Rory takes me home, but the rest of the time in the gallery is lighthearted. The gallery announces the sale of the untitled landscape and toasts Mandy with champagne. Within the hour of the announcement, the landscapes sell out, as well as a good portion of the portraits. Mandy's face must be in so much pain from all the grinning as she walks from patron to patron, explaining her artistic choices and thanking them for their support. I couldn't be prouder of her.

"Are you getting tired?" Rory asks, and I'm not too fond of the concern on his face.

"A little. Do you mind if we go home?"

"Don't ask me stupid questions, Valentina."

"I'm sorry. Yes. Please, take me home."

"Would you like to say goodbye to your friends?"

I shake my head. "Mandy's busy, and I don't want to distract from her happiness. Let's just go."

The drive to my apartment is short, and we don't say much. This is the moment of truth. I have to tell him. I sneak a text to Chema so he'll help me up to my apartment when we arrive. I don't want Rory to go into my building once I leave this car. I can't see him anymore. My pride can't take it, for one, and I can't part this world knowing I've broken his heart. I've let this go on far too long. I never considered myself a selfish person, but what I'm doing here with Rory—it takes the cake for selfishness.

CHAPTER 18

"We need to talk," I say as Rory parks. I glance over at my building, where Chema is sitting on the stoop. I signal for him to wait.

Rory takes off his seatbelt and faces me. The city's night lights render him more handsome than ever, and I know this will be harder than I thought. "Okay," he says with a wide smile.

"I want to thank you for being there for me and forcing me to accept help when I really needed it."

"Okay." Rory runs a hand through his hair, mussing it up in the sexiest bedhead way. "You've already thanked me for that. Valentina, I was happy to do it."

"You're amazing, and I really did need . . . someone, even if I wouldn't admit it."

"I know. What's really going on?" he asks.

I suck in a deep breath to strengthen my spine. "Now that Chema's here, and treatment's almost over, at least for a while, I'm set. You don't need to check in on me anymore."

"That's not what I'm doing here. I'm not checking up on you. I want to spend time with you—"

"Rory—"

"Don't you like spending time with me?"

"That isn't the point."

"That's exactly the point because that's all I'm doing."

His piercing gaze lingers on me, but I don't cower under those angry eyes. He knows what's coming. He has to.

"Rory, I don't want to keep spending time with you."

"Bullshit. You do, and I know you do."

I shake my head, though I know I'm trying to persuade myself as much as him. "I don't. Chema has agreed to stay through the end of my treatment. I'll also have Mandy and the girls around, so I won't be alone."

"You being alone is not what I'm worried about."

"You don't have to worry about anything. That's just it. I'm taken care of."

"Dammit, Valentina. I'm not trying to take care of you. I'm not your fucking nurse, and I'm not your fucking doctor. I'm just a man who has feelings for you, I—" he runs his hand through his hair more angrily now, then his eyes narrow. "Valentina, I'm in—"

"No. Don't say it. I can't handle it if you say it."

Rory's eyes remain narrow slits, but he stays quiet. I knew it almost the minute he started looking at me differently. It was a shift in his eyes when he would drift off, and I knew he was making plans for us—for our future together. He's taken steps, meeting my parents, bringing his parents to meet me—all of it to show me how deeply he cares about me. I should have stopped it sooner, but I couldn't.

I love him.

I love the man who didn't bat an eye to stay in bed with me and just sleep because I was too tired. The man who fed me watermelon cubes when I was nearly delirious with fever and hadn't eaten in days. The man who stood proud as he pushed me around in my wheelchair, never once giving off any indication that he was embarrassed by the sick woman with him during our date tonight.

But I can't tell him. He can't know I'm in love with him because I won't saddle him with a dying woman. My eyes prickle with tears, and for once, I don't draw them back in. I'm giving up perhaps the most perfect man in the world.

That small excursion to the art gallery, as brief as it was, took all the energy I had for the day. I'm a prisoner in my own body—the very body I once commanded with pride—and there isn't so much as the briefest hope of escape from this prison. I mourn for the loss of my health, the loss of what my body once was—what Rory got to enjoy so briefly so many weeks ago and that I will never be able to gift him again.

"Hey, hey, what's this?" Rory coos, all the hardness in his face gone. He adjusts in his seat to be as close to me as he can and wipes away the tear rolling down my cheek.

"I don't want to keep spending time with you. Before, you were just a meaningless one-night stand."

Rory shakes his head. "That's not true."

"And then I let you hang out because I didn't know anyone here, and I was bored. You were a distraction, Rory."

"You're lying."

"No. I am grateful, *I am*, to you for helping me when you did. I know that if you hadn't been there when the infection set in, I'd probably be dead. I'll always be grateful for that. But Chema's here now. I won't be alone, so you don't have to worry."

Rory's jaw sets, and he drops his hand from my face. He glances out the window past me and his nostrils flare. I know he sees Chema behind me. Then he focuses his gaze back on me.

"I know you don't want to hear it, but you have to. Valentina Almonte, I am so fucking in love with you."

My mouth dries up. I knew he wanted to start a serious relationship with me, and I know I love him, but I never imagined this outcome— that he already loved me back.

"Do you think maybe, your compassionate and caretaking nature as a doctor is bleeding over and clouding your feelings?"

"No. I love you, Valentina. Not sick Valentina. Not the athlete Valentina. None of that fucking matters. I love *you*. The person inside."

"Um, I'm sorry, I don't . . ."

"You don't what?"

"I don't know what to say."

"Just the truth. Do you have feelings for me? I know the answer, but you'll need to convince me otherwise if you're really breaking this between us off."

I clear my throat and sit up as straight as I can manage in the car. "I don't have feelings for you." I look him dead in the eye when I say it.

Rory chuckles, but it's bitter. "That's such bullshit."

"I'm sorry I let you think there was more here, but there isn't."

"Just stop, Valentina. We both know you are lying. Now I just want to know why? Is it because you feel bad for me, being with someone as sick as you, or is there another reason?" When he is done speaking, Rory glances past me again at Chema.

"What?"

"Do you have feelings for more than one person?"

I blink, trying to make sense of his words. "What are you talking about?"

"The way I see it, either you think you are self-sacrificing on my behalf and saving me for some reason, or you have feelings for someone else also. I say 'also' because I very damn well know you have feelings for me too."

"Stop telling me what I feel. I don't have feelings for you, Rory. Not like that. I'm grateful like I said, and I'll happily consider you a good friend and a good memory from my time in KC, but stop putting words in my mouth."

"Then answer the question. Is there someone else you care about?"

I turn and look at Chema, who stands and puts his hands in his pockets. His eyebrows are drawn together with concern and a questioning look in his eyes. I signal at him again to wait. I see now what Rory sees. He thinks I'm in love with Chema. This is my out. I swallow hard. I know if I take this step, if I dare utter this awful lie, I'll be putting the nail on the coffin of Rory's brief chapter in my life.

But for Rory, I do it. Because I love him, I can't tell him the truth. "You're right," I say finally. "I have feelings for someone else."

"Chema . . ." He says with a voice that cracks.

I turn to Rory again, and his eyes are glassy. I find no anger in his features, only hurt. I did that. I hurt him. But this hurt is less than the pain I would have caused by my death or by saddling him to a sick woman who would do nothing but take and take.

"Yes," I lie. "Chema. He will take good care of me, so you don't have to worry."

Rory takes in a deep breath and lets it out slowly. "Well, that changes things."

"I know. I'm sorry. I should have said sooner."

"No, it's fine. I'm glad we had the time we did," he says. "Does he love you?"

I don't lie because Chema does love me, even if I know it's not the same type of love Rory is asking about. "Yes. He loves me. And I love him."

Rory's eyes draw shut, and he drifts his head to the headrest. When his eyes open again, he smiles weakly.

"Does he love you more than I do?"

"That would be impossible to know, wouldn't it?"

"No, it wouldn't—" Rory takes me by surprise, holding my head in place so he can kiss me. His lips are tender at first, pressed against mine gently, until his tongue coaxes my lips open. He conquers my mouth hungrily for a few seconds, and I push him away, even though it's the last thing I want to do.

"I'm sorry," says Rory. "I believe that you love him. But I don't believe you don't have feelings for me too. If you weren't sick, and it wouldn't put you through hell, I'd fight for you. I'd do everything to make you see that my love is greater. But I don't want to put you through yet another emotional wringer."

"Thank you for respecting my wishes."

"I will. For now. But Valentina, once you beat this thing, all bets are off."

My eyes widen with panic. "What?"

"Go ahead and be with him now. Let him be your emotional support and caretaker until you get better—because you will get better, whether you believe it or not—and when it's all said and done, I'll be here. I'll be loving you. No amount of time will change that."

I turn from him, not able to look him in the eye after all those lies. I open the car door and call Chema over. Chema is at my side in an instant, and he ducks to get me out of the car. I'm only on my feet for a moment before he takes me in his arms like a child. I rest my head on his chest, as tired as I've ever felt.

"You okay?" Chema asks.

I nod. "I will be."

Another car door opens and shuts. "Chema!" Rory calls when we are almost at the door. Chema turns, so we both face Rory.

"Take care of her for me, okay?"

Chema nods and squeezes me a bit in his arms. "Always have. Always will."

Rory nods and gets back in his car.

CHEMA SETS me down on the bed, and I curl around my pillow, letting the sob out. "What happened?" Chema asks.

"We broke it off," I admit, the words like hot daggers searing my throat.

"Why? It looked like things were going so well." The bed shifts as Chema sits next to me. I stay facing away from him because I don't want him to see me cry.

"He said he loves me."

"And that's why you broke it off?"

"No, I, I—"

"Do you love him?"

I nod and keep sobbing into my pillow. Even the energy required for a good cry exhausts me. Chema's beefy hand wraps around my shoulder, and I put my hand over his.

"Then tell him that."

"No," I cry. "He can't know I love him."

"Why?"

"Look at me, Chema."

"I'm looking."

"How could you possibly think a man like that could be with someone like this?" I hiss out the question.

Chema shifts me on the bed so I'll face him and knows I can't fight it off. "Someone like what, Valentina? Someone strong and brave, smart and loving? Why wouldn't anyone deserve someone like that?"

I snort. "I'm not any of those things. I'm shriveling up and dying. Don't you all get that?"

"You are not dying."

I smile. "I used to say that when I first started treatment. I was so hopeful and thought I would live, and I'd say 'I'm not dead yet' a lot. I haven't thought it in weeks now—"

"Valentina, treatment is almost over. Just one week to go. Of course it was going to take its toll on you, but hear me when I say, 'you are not dying,' and I'm not going to sit here and listen to you tell me how you are going to die. I won't do it—"

I raise my chin so I can stare at my friend in awe. His voice crackles, but his face is furious. Fuck. I'm hurting him too. There is not a single loved one I've managed to spare from the circus that is cancer.

It takes all the strength I can muster, but I bring my hand to his cheek. "I'm sorry," I say.

"Don't do it again," he orders.

"Are you coaching me through the final week of treatment? Is that what this is?"

Chema wipes the tears pooling in the corners of his eyes and smiles. "Yeah. Guess I am. Now, rest."

He shuts the lights off before leaving my room. I hug my pillow once again. I want his optimism, an optimism I shared when I first started, but my body is so far gone, I can't imagine ever being what I once was. I was so naive to think I could hide this from everyone, that I could go back to fighting like nothing had ever happened. What a child.

My body will be altered for life, internally and externally. I will bear the scars as proof of this battle whether I die in weeks, months, years, or decades—I'll always carry the reminders.

I lie in bed and have a breakdown unlike any I've experienced so far. I'm surprised at how far I've made it, from what Mandy had told me. I let the tears flow as I mourn for the life I'll never get back even if I do live. I mourn the loss of the body I was once so damn proud of. I grieve for the loss of my physical strength.

The crying leads me into the early hours of the morning, and I can't stop the breakdown because I also mourn for the only person I could ever imagine being the love of my life.

My heart is bruised.

Contusions in every ventricle sending waves of pain with each heartbeat because Rory's gone. And no amount of ice baths, salves, or massages will ease the hurt.

I mourn for the loss of my love with Rory Dennis.

CHAPTER 19

SIX MONTHS LATER

WINTER

"I have an opening at three tomorrow. Does that work?" The hospital scheduler asks.

"Yeah, I'll be there."

I hang up the call, and my blood runs cold. Is it back?

It couldn't be, though, could it? I feel great. My energy is back, food tastes good again, and I've even put on some weight. My hair is growing in, including my eyebrows, and I thought, really thought, this was behind me.

Then I got the call to go back in for results from the tests I took last week. This is the news I've been waiting for so I can finally go home. Instead, I know they'll be telling me the cancer is back. Then they'll be suggesting another round of treatment—but I can't. I won't do it again. I would rather die than go through that again.

They asked me to come in. I know what that means. Bad news. If it was good news, Dr. Ramirez would have told me over the phone. But they asked me in instead, so it's bad news.

I squeeze the armrest on the sofa to ground myself to the time and place. My apartment looks much the same and also different. It's much neater now that Chema's gone. He left after three months of concluding treatment. He refused to leave until I proved I could go up the flight of stairs in my apartment without getting winded. When I finally managed it, he fought me on it, but I didn't want to keep disrupting his life, not when I was finally starting to feel fine.

He made me swear I'd call him to come back if there were any setbacks. Should I call him now? No. First, I need to hear it. I won't believe it until Dr. Ramirez says the words out loud.

～

I WAIT in exam room five, and the minutes feel like hours as I wait for Dr. Ramirez. Her face twists in concern when she sees me.

"What's wrong?" Dr. Ramirez asks. "Are you not feeling well?"

"You tell me," I say.

"Nothing's wrong, Vale, but you look like you saw a ghost."

I share my suspicions with her.

"Oh, Vale, honey—"

"It's back, isn't it?"

"No!" she nearly yells. "Valentina, I wanted to give you the good news in person. That's all. Please stop reading about treatment or procedures online. It's not the first time it's gotten you in trouble." Dr. Ramirez arches an eyebrow, almost making me cower.

"Good news?" I ask with all the hope I'll allow myself.

"Yes, Valentina. Good news." Dr. Ramirez grabs my shoulders and squeezes for a moment. A smile spreads the width of her face. "Six months remission. It's a great milestone."

"Really?" I have to confirm because it feels like a dream. I don't even know when I started crying, but I feel the tears rolling down my face.

"Really," she says. "I thought we should celebrate. I'm not working right now. Let's go across the street to the bar. Champagne. My treat."

～

I'M RELIEVED to see Sofia working the bar when we get there. In the last six months, I have come to the bar quite a bit—at first with Chema, who started to feel cooped up all the time in the apartment. Since he left, I've spent quite a bit of time with Mandy and the girls at *La Oficina*, though I didn't quite partake in any of the drinking myself.

Over that time, I've got to know Sofia pretty well. I haven't grow quite as close to her as I have to Mandy or Izel or Tlali, but she sure is one of the friends I have been lucky enough to make during the most horrific time of my life, and I am grateful for her. I'm glad she's here to celebrate this moment.

"What we celebrating?" Sofia asks when Dr. Ramirez orders champagne. Dr. Ramirez just looks at me, and I know she is waiting for me to answer. She can't divulge my health information unless I give her the green light.

"Six months in remission," I say proudly. This is as much Dr. Ramirez's victory as mine. From what I hear, the clinical trial is promising, despite being in its early phases.

"Wow. Congrats!" Sofia says, a face-splitting grin taking over her features.

When she comes back with two flutes filled to the brim with champagne, she sets them on the table. "On the house," she says. "All cancer ass-whipping is rewarded at *La Oficina*."

Sofia leaves us to our drinking, and Dr. Ramirez and I are grinning like idiots at our table.

Then, Dr. Ramirez's gaze shifts above and behind me.

"Dr. Dennis," she greets, and I freeze at the sound of his name. Does he know it's me sitting here?

"Please, Dr. Ramirez, call me Rory outside of work."

"Okay, then please call me Carolina."

Rory shifts to stand at the side of the table so he can see both our faces, and I panic. I remember I didn't wear a scarf today and wonder if my pixie hair is pointing in all different directions. I try to tame it with my hand discreetly, but I don't know if it's helping. Why did this joint have to be all classy and not have any mirrors?

"What are we celebrating?" Rory asks.

"You want to tell him?" Dr. Ramirez asks.

I look at Rory for the first time. I haven't seen those green eyes in six months, and I don't know how I keep it together. He's as handsome as ever. I have always regretted that we didn't take any photos during our brief time together to remember him by. Though honestly, I wouldn't have wanted to be in them at the time. But it would have been nice to have recorded our time at the park for posterity.

"I, um—" I clear my throat. "Remission. Six months," I say and sink a little in my chair, though I keep my plastered smile, hoping it looks natural.

"That's great!" Rory all but shrieks.

The pang of guilt forces my eyes to the ground. I should have messaged him at some point to tell him I was better. I force myself to look him in the eye again, and his smile never dissipates.

Our eyes are locked when Dr. Ramirez interjects in the exchange. "Rory, why don't you sit with us?" she asks.

Rory looks at me, waiting for me to echo the invitation. Part of me doesn't want to open this door again, but I know it's the part that will lose because I've missed him, and I need to know how he's been all this time, so I nod.

Dr. Ramirez gets another champagne flute for Rory, and the three of us clink glasses.

"To kicking the shit out of cancer," says Dr. Ramirez.

"To kicking the shit out of cancer," Rory and I both echo.

It's hard to include Dr. Ramirez in the conversation because we both have a lot of catching up to do, but we don't want to be rude, so we steer clear of any heavy subjects for the time being.

"So, I saw your fight with the Russian—what's her name?" Rory asks.

"Galina," I say.

"Yeah, that's right. It looked like you won. I can't believe the judges gave her the fight."

I smile, remembering that fight. At the time, it had seemed like the most unfair thing I'd ever go through. I hadn't been diagnosed yet. Now, it seems so minor and unimportant. "You weren't the only one," I say.

Rory keeps babbling about the fight, and I look over at Dr. Ramirez with concern. She is looking at her phone with her face scrunched up, and those eyebrows of hers are drawn together into twin frowns.

"Is everything okay?" I ask her.

"I don't know," she says. "I, uh, have to go. Do you mind?"

"No, please. I hope everything's fine."

Dr. Ramirez kisses my cheek warmly in a gesture I know is crossing a line, but I also think she is telling me she is no longer my doctor because I no longer need her. This was always the plan—for me to return to Mexico and get follow-up care close to home. Watching her leave the bar, though, makes my chest constrict a bit. I'll miss her immensely.

"So, you look good," Rory says.

"Thanks. I'm starting to feel a little like my old self."

"That's great," he says.

"Though I finally resigned myself to the fact that I'll never be what I once was—"

"Don't say that—"

"No. No, it's not a 'pity me' thing. It's the truth. My new reality is finally sinking in. A lot of things are different."

"You're more beautiful than ever," Rory says and winks at me.

"Rory—" I take an exasperated breath.

"Sorry," he says and hangs his head, but I can tell he is smiling.

"I'm different now," I say.

"Yeah?"

"You know how it is. My body's different. There are things it can't do anymore, and don't get me started on chemo brain."

Rory's eyes soften. "Yeah. I know how it is," he admits. "But you're looking a lot better than the last time I saw you. That alone is reason to celebrate."

We clink glasses again and each take a drink.

I don't give him details, but one of the worst changes to my body is chemo brain. I forget little things, can't find the right word sometimes— only made worse by my bilingualism. I shake my head, thinking of what a snob I used to be when people would speak in Spanglish and how sometimes I'm forced to do that now when I can't find the word in one language but can in the other. My reaction time has slowed, and I'm hoping I can work on correcting that if I have a shot in hell at fighting again. Now that I know I'll live, I have to at least give it a shot. If I didn't, I wouldn't be me.

"Thank you," I say. "For everything. Really."

Instead of his regular 'you betcha' that he customarily uses instead of 'you're welcome,' he says, "Stop thanking me. It pisses me off." But he is smiling.

"This is the last time. I promise. Thank you for respecting my wishes back then. I couldn't bear to have you around while I was going through that."

"I know. It killed me to stay away. But I know." Rory's hand reaches across the table to take mine. His thumb grazes over the top of my hand, and we smile at each other. God, I've missed him.

"I missed you," he says as if he is reading my mind.

I won't tell him I missed him back. I don't want to give him hope again. There is no point. I'm leaving for Mexico in a week or two—as soon as I can arrange everything—and then Rory Dennis will be nothing but a sweet memory from my time in KC, as I always knew he would be.

"You look good too," I say.

"Valentina Almonte, are you flirting with me?"

I draw my hand away from his and shake my head. "No. I'm just glad to see you looking so well."

Rory's smile falls for only one second before he regains it. "I'm sorry. I shouldn't have said that."

"It's okay. We're allowed to be happy to see each other."

"I'm glad you're happy to see me," he says.

I stand and put on my coat. Grabbing my purse, I toss it over my shoulder. Rory stands after I do, and I surprise us both by taking him into a hug. I take in his smell one last time. He doesn't know this is goodbye for good this time. "I have to go," I say. "Chema's waiting for me," I lie.

"Right. Say hi to him for me, will you? I think I owe him big time." Rory smiles weakly at me as I turn to walk away.

I leave him at the bar, holding my heart without his knowledge.

CHAPTER 20

FOUR MONTHS LATER

SPRING

The water rolls down my face as the shower fills with steam. I don't mind much that Chema never installed women's locker rooms. There are so few of us, and if the men didn't mind me here, then I had no complaints.

My parents never had to know.

I dress and try to try to rush past the front desk. My sister is expecting me for lunch, and I'm running late. I fail to sneak past Chema, though. He is at the front desk, wrapping up with a customer. He smiles as I try to dash past the desk.

"You did a great job today," he says.

Pausing to say goodbye, I face him. "Stop lying," I admonish.

"The best since you got back."

My smile is weak, and Chema picks up on my defeatist attitude.

"It's going to take a while, Valentina. We'll get you there."

"You know we won't, right? This is it. This is as good I'll ever be again."

"It's only been four months. Can you at least give it a little time before you throw in the towel?"

Nico comes up behind Chema and wraps his arms around Chema's waist. "What's this I hear about someone throwing in the towel?" He asks.

Chama pats him gently on the arms around his middle until Nico unravels his embrace and steps forward so we can both see him. He is wearing an athletic tank and shorts that complement Chema's outfit. They are so cute I feel like punching them in the face.

"Valentina's getting a little frustrated," Chema explains.

"Oh, honey," Nico says. "You don't remember when you first started, but I do. You were way worse than this."

I burst out laughing. Leave it to Nico to put things into perspective. I'll always be grateful to him. He was more than generous sharing his partner while Chema was in Kansas City taking care of me. Nico managed the gym while Chema was away. I hope I can one day have what they have—that kind of supportive partner with complete trust.

At least, I hope I'll have it again because I'm sure I got close to it once.

"Thanks, Nico," I say. "I don't know if that makes me feel worse or better."

"Any time, honey." He blows a kiss at me and kisses Chema for real before going off to teach a self-defense class.

Chema does his best to give me an empowering speech, and I try to hear it, but I think somewhere deep down, we are both aware I'm at the end of my professional fighting career. I know I'll always be in this business. Maybe I'll coach like Chema does or sponsor other fighters at some point, but *me* fighting, I know I'll have to let go of that notion real soon—if I haven't already.

"I'm going to see Pili," I say to Chema.

"Say hi for me. Tell her we miss her."

"I will. I have to swing by my place first, though, to pick up a present I ordered for her."

"A special occasion?" Chema asks.

"I don't need a special occasion to do something nice for her, especially after everything she has done—is doing—for me."

"You're late," are Pilar's first words when she opens the door. Her posture is impeccable, and her sensible, expensive outfit is well put together. Pilar is a mini version of our mother. I dealt with our Mom by avoiding her and leaving home as soon as I could, but Pilar tried, keeps trying, to earn her love by trying to mimic her. I don't think she realizes she's doing it, the mirroring effect, but it's such a big part of her personality, I doubt she'll ever be able to break it.

"I'm sorry," I say. "I was training." I follow her into the living room, where she has laid out artful canapés and an icy pitcher she pours from into our glasses.

"How's that going?"

"What?"

"Training, Valentina. Where's your head at? Seriously."

"Sorry, um—" I look around, trying to find a spot for the enormous gift I'm holding. "I brought this for you."

"What is it?"

"It's a gift, Pili."

She rolls her eyes and crosses her arms. "I know that, Tini. But what is it?"

"Well, open it and see."

Pilar can be such a smart-ass when she wants to be.

"I'll open it later. Set it down, and let's chat for a bit. Or do you have to go soon?"

The concern in her eyes melts away any of my criticisms of her. I'm the only human contact she's allowed other than her husband, parents, and many servants. "I can stay for a bit," I say and smile.

"Well, tell me about training."

I take a deep breath. "I'm improving, but it's slower than I'd hoped."

"It's only been four months. I'm sure it'll take time."

"Yeah. That's what everyone keeps telling me." I push a canapé around my plate with my fork.

"You're not hungry?"

"It's not that. I, um. I just think it might be time to give up. I'm a little disappointed I haven't accomplished much."

Pilar laughs, and I glare at her icily.

"I'm sorry," she says. "That is such bullshit."

I press my lips together, waiting for her to elaborate, though it's killing me not to pick a fight with her right now.

"Before you got sick, you won almost every fight. Your record was unreal. And we both know, if you hadn't gotten sick, the next step was the UFC. Don't kid yourself about that, Tini."

"But I did get sick."

"Yes. You did. And you beat it."

"It sounds a lot like you are saying I almost accomplished something, which isn't quite the same as accomplishing it, is it?"

Pilar raises an eyebrow in warning. "And you don't think beating the shit out of cancer constitutes accomplishing something?"

She looks a bit angry, but I can't bring myself to goad her further. I owe her too much. She was my first sponsor, when I first started fighting. She funded my training, bought my apartment, and paid a stipend so I could reach my dreams. Then I failed her when I couldn't make them happen, despite my best efforts. The cherry on the cake was asking her for a ridiculous amount of money for my treatment. Even then, she didn't bat an eye.

Didn't she care that I had nothing to show for it? I would if I were in her shoes. Wouldn't I? I had failed more than myself. I failed her and everything she has invested in me. Now I have no idea how I'm going to pay her back. I don't think I could even if I were to live several lifetimes.

"What is it?" she asks.

"What?"

"You went into your nothing box."

My 'nothing box' is what my sister calls it when I space off on her, which happens a lot since I got back.

"I'm sorry, Pilar. Your investment tanked."

"What on earth are you talking about?" Pilar asks.

"Yes, what investment?" We both turn to see Felipe now in the room.

Felipe Conde could be considered handsome by anyone who doesn't know him better. He is tall and muscular, and his face's chiseled quality wouldn't make the average woman gag—until they got to know him, that is.

My brother-in-law walks over to my sister, bends to kiss her on the cheek, and takes a seat next to her. He smiles knowingly at me, and I bite the inside of my lip so I don't sneer. Felipe crosses his legs and takes Pilar's hand in his possessively, as if it were another man and not her sister sitting in front of her. To put it plainly, Felipe Conde is a ridiculous man.

"What investment were you talking about?" he asks and looks between Pilar and me.

Pilar clears her throat nervously, and I shift in my seat. There has been exactly one thing Pilar ever allowed herself to defy her husband on. That was her sponsorship of my career. She tried to hide this simple fact from me, but Felipe hints and alludes to his dissatisfaction at her use of her own money to help me.

"Valentina is feeling guilty about me paying for her treatment. I was just about to tell her how ridiculous that is." Pilar pats Felipe's hand in a way that makes me think she is trying to placate him.

"Nonsense. You're family; of course we're happy to pay for your treatment."

He uses the word 'we' as if Pilar had used his money, or communal money, but all three of us know that money is, and always will be, Pilar's and Pilar's only. No one has ever openly admitted that simple fact, but I love that this is just one more thorn on Felipe's side. I love those thorns. Whenever I get a chance, I enjoy twisting them.

"Yes," I say. "Thank goodness Grandma Almonte had the foresight to secure Pilar's economic independence so she could do that. I'll always be grateful to her and Pilar." My words are pointed, and I try not to smile when Felipe's jaw tightens. His face twitches, barely, but I don't miss it. His presence dampening my time with my sister is almost worth it for this one moment.

"Yes, well. That's what we were talking about. Valentina thinks it's a wasted investment, and when you walked in, I was just about to tell her that her staying alive has been the best investment of my life."

My sister's sweet words change the mood in the room. I have to hand it to her. After years of marriage, she has mastered the art of diffusing tension. She talks about me beating cancer as if it was just another fight in the cage—as if it was something I accomplished, and I'd never thought about it like that before.

"I agree," Felipe says. "Best use of *our* money I can think of."

"Thank you," I say, if only to drop the standoff between us. I'll pick my battles with this idiot.

"What's that?" Felipe reaches for the present and flips it from side to side, likely looking for a card.

"A present for Pilar."

"A present?" he asks.

"Yes. You know, as a thank you for everything."

Felipe hands Pilar the gift and shifts further from her on the sofa so he can see the contents once revealed. Pilar shoots me a questioning look laced with panic, and I smile reassuringly that it's not something that could anger Felipe.

My smile is all it takes for Pilar to rip apart the wrapping paper like a savage. She has always loved presents and surprises, and this is both.

When she turns the canvas around, Pilar gasps. "Oh, Valentina. It's lovely."

"I'm glad you like it."

Pilar sets the painting down so she can stand. She comes over to my side of the room so she can sit next to me and take me into a hug. "I love it," she whispers in my ear.

"Yes, very lovely," Felipe says and stands. "Valentina, you look good. I'm glad you're feeling better. I do have to go to work, though."

"Thanks," I say.

"Working on a Saturday?" Pilar asks.

"Yes. I have a meeting," he hisses through his teeth, and my sister recoils a bit in her seat.

"Okay. Well, message me if you are coming for dinner so I can make sure it's ready for you."

Felipe delivers another kiss on Pilar's cheek, and I almost shiver.

We wait until we hear the door closing behind him before we continue our conversation. Pilar shakes her head at me but smiles.

"You could stand to be nicer to him," she says.

"He could stand to be nicer to me," I counter.

"I just wish you could get along better."

"I don't."

"Valentina!"

"I'm sorry," I say. "Let me just say this one last time. I know you don't believe it, but just because he doesn't physically abuse you doesn't mean he doesn't abuse you—"

"Not this again—"

"Please hear me out. Pilar, I love you, and if cancer has taught me anything, it's that you shouldn't waste your time on things and people you don't love."

"What makes you think I don't love him?"

"Please," I scoff. "I know you don't. He *is* abusive, Pilar. He has isolated you, made you lose all your friends, and even limits how much your own family can see you. He belittles you. It's subtle, but it's there. This is psychological warfare, and you need to start fighting back."

"Did you start watching telenovelas with Chema? Is that where this hysteria is coming from?"

Pilar knows all about Chema and Nicolas and the gym. Not because she is friends with them or interacts with them, or because she's ever come to the gym. She knows about them because her only connection to the outside world is me, and she doesn't realize she lives vicariously through me, but she does.

"Pilar—"

"I heard you. Okay? Thank you for your concern, but I'm a grown woman. I can take care of myself. Okay?"

I nod. "Okay."

This is a discussion we've had many times before. We fought the first time. Then I kept bringing it up, hoping slowly I could open her eyes. For now, I decide to change the subject.

"Where are you going to hang the painting?"

We both look around the walls of the grand room. For a cage, this mansion is rather lovely.

"I don't know," Pilar says and stands while holding the painting and admiring it. "Who did you say the artist is?"

"I didn't say. It's Mandy. You know, my friend I told you about. She helped me quite a bit when I was in Kansas City."

Pilar's gaze snaps from the painting to me. "Oh," she says

thoughtfully.

"Is that a problem?" I ask.

"No. It's great. I like landscapes. You know that."

"Pilar, come on."

"What?"

"Wait, are you jealous of Mandy?"

"What? No!" Pilar scoffs and sets the painting down again. "Why would I be jealous?"

"Gee, I don't know. She was there when you couldn't be. I confided in her instead of you. She visited when I was in the hospital—"

"Okay, okay. Maybe a little. I do wish I had been there, Tini. I swear."

"Then why weren't you? Mom and Dad visited. You could have gone with them."

Pilar's face hardens.

"Oh, that's right," I say. "Felipe wouldn't let you go see your sister while she was sick. Is this the man you want to defend?"

"Valentina!"

"What if I had died?"

"You didn't."

"What if I had, though? You wouldn't have seen me for the last time. All because you're a prisoner here. When are you going to see that?"

"I'm not a prisoner."

"No?"

"No."

"Shopping with a security detail does not exactly scream freedom, but whatever. I'm tired of having this conversation. Just think about that for one second. If I had died, how would you feel toward Felipe right now? Don't tell me. Just think on it."

A long moment of silence stretches between us, and Pilar takes a few bites from the tray in the center of the room.

"How are Chema and Nicolas?" She finally asks, changing the subject.

"Good. I think Chema has finally given in and let Nico start coordinating their outfits in the morning. It's like they are blending into the same person."

"Gross," Pilar says.

I roll my eyes, but am smiling. "Tell me about it. I'm the one who has to see it."

We both laugh, and our pattern repeats itself. We have the same fight, we don't resolve anything, and instead of acknowledging that, we change the topic to something we can both laugh about. It's not healthy, but nothing in our family ever is.

"Tell them hi for me," she says.

"I will."

I stay at Pilar's for three hours, and Felipe never comes back from his 'meeting,' though I'm doubtful that's where he went.

The similarities between Felipe Conde and my father are astounding. I have no doubt that's why Dad selected him as the winner from everyone who was courting Pilar at the time. I don't use the term 'courting' lightly. It's what my parents called it.

"I have to get going," I finally tell Pilar.

She finds a spot in one of the many guest rooms for Mandy's painting. I never imagined she would take the gift as she did. At least in the guest room, she won't have to look at it every day, reminding her she was not in Kansas City with me through one of the roughest times in my life.

Pilar knows everything—I've always told her everything.

Except about Rory.

I'm not sure why. I carefully left him out of any conversations we had about my time away and about my treatment. Dr. Ramirez, Dr. Medina, Mandy, and even Tlali and Izel featured prominently in all the stories I told her when I got back, but I was always careful to leave Rory out of those conversations.

I keep him all to myself.

Most nights, I close my eyes and envision him lying on the bed next to me. He's facing the other direction as I trace patterns over the freckle constellations scattered across the creamy skin of his back. The memory of him is so fresh in my mind, I can almost feel him under my fingertips when I think of him.

I spend my days back home suppressing my thoughts about Rory, hoping I can meet someone who'll help me forget.

Un clavo saca otro clavo.

CHAPTER 21

My hair is almost at my jawline and matted to the sides of my face with sweat, distracting me. I miss being able to pull it into braids. I breathe out with each blow I deliver. Chema positions the boxing pads in a jab-cross-jab combination that I follow easily. We repeat this several times, and I know he is starting off light.

He already made me run a mile before pad training, which is significantly less than he used to. By my pre-cancer standard, it's embarrassing, but this is the most my body has accomplished since concluding treatment.

After the fifth round with the same combination, he reaches for me, and I block with my shoulder, but I'm too slow, and he ends up hitting my shoulder with the pad.

"Agh!" I growl and step away from Chema. I shake my head to clear it.

"It's okay. We just got started. Come on."

I turn back to Chema and keep aiming for the pads. I successfully block with my right shoulder on his second try. We both smile.

"Chin down," he scolds.

"Sorry."

"Come on. Keep moving."

His commands are obeyed in this gym, so I start fluttering in a circle around him as he positions the pads in the air. He switches the combination; it's still a jab-cross-jab, but this time he wants a ratio of 3-2-3, and I can't pick up on it quick enough.

The never-ending haze, like walking through the cloud of my brain where my reaction time resides, envelops me. I know the combination Chema seeks, and once I had this muscle memory, but it's all gone now. I try again, messing up after the last cross before switching back to a jab. Fuck. Fuck. Fuck.

It's so incredibly frustrating. I step back and use my teeth to rip the Velcro on my gloves to yank them off.

Chema removes the pads from his hands and drops them on the mat. "Come on. Sit with me."

We sit cross-legged, facing each other on the mat.

"I'm sorry," I say out of breath.

"What for?"

"What do you mean what for? For fucking up!"

"You're not fucking up. Stop being so frustrated. Don't you see? This is the best you've done since we started training again."

"I know, but it's not fast enough."

"Think to the first day back at the gym. Did you think you'd ever be able to run a mile again? And here you are, in your gloves after running a mile. This is huge. You need to acknowledge that."

"I do. But I also acknowledge that I can't do a simple switch of combinations. My reaction time isn't there. Chema, we might be able to improve it a bit, but I don't think it will ever come back."

"We don't know that." He shakes his head, not wanting to believe it yet.

"I think I do. The glitches in my memory are minor, but they're there. It's like I can see the word I'm looking for, hovering just in front of me, but I can't grasp it. My synapses are short-circuiting. Eventually, my brain does what it needs to, but I can't fight like that. I can't ask my opponent, 'can you hold on just a sec, my brain is catching up?'"

"Don't give up. Not yet."

"I think it's time for my dreams to change. I can't keep mooching off Pilar forever."

"She'd be fine with that, you know?"

I smile. "Yeah. I know. I was only okay with it before because we had an end-goal in sight. I'd be sponsored soon and maybe even be able to pay her back. But I don't think that's the goal anymore, Chema. I don't think we can get me there."

"In time—"

I shake my head, and he doesn't finish his sentence. His bottom lip quivers, and I watch as his Adam's Apple bobs up and down.

"Are you sure?"

"Yeah. I'd like to keep training, I'll keep fighting, just for fun, but I'm done competing. It was beautiful while it lasted, but it's time to move on."

"What are you going to do?"

I shrug. "I don't know. Maybe I'll give you a run for your money and open up my own gym."

Chema laughs. "I'd love some competition, Tini," he says and musses my hair like I'm a child.

"Only Pilar is allowed to call me that."

"Uh-huh."

Something, or someone, catches Chema's attention from behind me, and he nods. I twist around to look where Chema's eyes are focused, and a stone so heavy drops in my stomach that I fail to stand up when I try.

Chema stands first and reaches out a hand to help me to my feet.

Too stunned to form words, I follow Chema wordlessly off the mat until we both reach the spot where Rory Dennis stands.

"Hey, buddy," Chema says and takes Rory into a hug.

I blink. 'Buddy?' What the hell is going on?

"Hi, Chema. Nice to see you."

"You too," says Chema. "Let's talk soon, but right now, I'm going to, um—I'm going somewhere else for absolutely no reason. Valentina, take my office if you want it."

I can only shake my head.

Rory's face lights up as he takes me in. "You look so good, Valentina."

"Um, thanks." I tuck my unruly hair behind my ear and start unwrapping my knuckle wraps with shaky hands. "What are you doing here, Rory?"

"Thought I'd check out the gym. Thinking about picking up boxing." He blinks at me when I stay quiet, staring at him.

Nothing's changed about him, while I look entirely different from the last time he saw me. Luckily, it's a change for the better.

"I'm joking," he says finally. "I'm here for you."

I peer around us to see if anyone is within earshot. Chema is on the other end of the gym with Nico, probably telling him everything about Rory. It's the off hours at the gym, my favorite time to train, so only a couple of other people are around.

"Here for me?" I ask.

"Yes. I can't stop thinking about you." Again I say nothing to that. "Do you think I could get a hug? I've missed you."

As if I have no control of my body, I step forward and wrap around him, resting my cheek on his chest right over where I know his scar is. Neither of us comments on my sweat dampening his shirt. His arms envelop around me and squeeze tightly while his cheek lands on top of my head. Being in his arms like this feels like finally being home. I thought I'd feel that way when I returned to my apartment, my friends, and family, but it hadn't. That feeling eluded me until right now, cocooned in Rory's arms.

"I'm so happy I don't have to be careful, worried about crushing you."

I pull away from him only long enough to look into his green eyes. "You're here."

"Yes. I'm here. I've missed you."

"I missed you too."

"Is it okay that I'm here? I know you wanted me to stay away, and I respected those wishes as long as I humanly could."

I shake my head. "No. I mean, I'm glad to see you, but I wish you hadn't come."

"That makes no sense."

"We live in different countries. I don't believe long-distance relation-ships can work."

"That's not what I'm proposing here."

"It's not?"

"No."

"Then what are you proposing?"

"This," he says and pulls away from my arms. He drops to one knee and looks up at me. He produces a small box from his pocket, and I take a step back, shaking my head.

"Valentina Almonte, I've had to face the possibility of losing you more times than my poor, scarred heart can take. I don't want to spend another second of my life without you. Will you marry me?"

I haven't yet processed his presence in this gym in Mexico—I certainly can't process the life-altering question he has asked me.

It suddenly dawns on me that he and Chema have been in contact with each other. How else would he know where to find me? Where I'd be and when? Chema. That's how.

"You've been talking to Chema?"

Rory's face falls, and he stands. "I'm sorry," he says, clasping the back of his neck. "I had to know you were okay. Please don't be mad at him. It was all me."

"How did you even get his number?"

"We did spend quite a bit of time together in waiting rooms."

I find Chema sitting at the front desk, grinning at me, but his grin disappears when he sees the daggers my eyes are shooting his way.

He stands and walks over to us. "Is everything okay?" Chema asks with a worried expression.

"You knew he was coming, and you didn't tell me?"

"I didn't know specifics, but I knew he would be coming to see you at some point."

"You two have been talking about me?"

The two guilty expressions look at each other, then they both hang their heads and stare at their shoes.

"I see," I say and take a step back, not sure what to make of all this.

Rory looks at Chema with a wide grin. "Full disclosure," Rory says to Chema, "I asked her to marry me."

"I saw that," says Chema with a grin of his own.

"I have to say, I thought you'd be angered by that," says Rory, looking confused.

"Why would I be angry?" Chema asks.

"I thought you—"

"Honey," Nico walks up to Chema. "I'm heading out early. I want to get groceries before heading home. I'll have a special dinner for you tonight." Nico winks at Chema and gives him a peck on the lips. "And who is this handsome fella?" he asks, reaching out to shake Rory's hand, scanning his body.

"Valentina's fiancé," Chema says.

"Valentina's what?" Nico's eyes widen with surprise.

"Well, she hasn't answered yet," Rory says, "but, um—you are . . ."

"Gay?" Chema asks. "Yeah. I'm gay."

"I thought you and Valentina—"

"Nope. Never," Chema assures Rory.

"Wait, he thought you and Valentina what?" Nico asks with a raised eyebrow.

Rory clears his throat and suddenly can't look at the two men standing next to us. "I'm sorry, I made assumptions—"

"Wait, you thought Chema and Valentina . . . No!" Nico squeals and lets out a roar of laughter. "Have you never met a gay man before?"

"Amor," Chema says, "we're ruining their engagement. Come on, let's go—"

I finally snap out of my stupor. "No," I say. "I'm glad you two have planned out my future without discussing it with me, but you have failed to recognize that I'm not property, and neither of you owns me."

The nerve.

I storm toward the locker room and don't hear the steps behind me from Rory following. I'm pulling my bag out of my locker when he finds me.

"I'm sorry. That's not how I intended things to go," he says softly.

"Really? You didn't intend to propose when I've been at the gym sweating my ass off? You didn't plan all this with Chema? Tell me, Rory, did he help you pick out a ring?"

"No, that's not what . . . um, I was going to ask you to dinner and propose then."

"Why did you do it here, then?"

"I saw you."

"So?"

"That's it. I saw you, and I couldn't stand it. I couldn't stand you being with anyone other than me for a second longer."

"Like property," I say.

"No. Not like property. I'm in love with you. That hasn't changed. And damn it, Valentina. I know you love me too. Be honest with yourself. Be honest with me. And don't get me started on how you let me think you and Chema—"

"Let's suppose for a moment you're right. It changes nothing. You live in Kansas City. I live in Mexico City."

"I'll move here, if that's what it takes."

I rear back and blink at him. "You would?"

"Yes. Nothing's more important to me than never again spending a minute apart from you."

"What about your residency?"

"I'll start over. Here."

I roll my eyes. "You don't speak Spanish."

"I'll learn."

"So let me get this straight. You're willing to drop your residency, move to a foreign country, get married, and practice medicine here? But to do all that, you'll learn Spanish first?"

Rory nods, and the corners of his mouth quirk up. He takes a step forward and cups my cheek in his hand. "I'm way ahead of the curve. I already know how to say *lagaña*."

I punch his middle playfully, and his abs are hard on impact. "I'm being serious," I say.

"I don't know, Valentina. If I can't, then I'll find something else I can do. None of that matters so long as you're healthy and by my side. We can work out everything else."

"You really mean it, don't you?"

"I do." He pulls out the box again. "Now, please. Will you *please* marry me, you stubborn woman?"

I grab the box and cradle it in my hand. It's open, and a simple round diamond glistens in the center, set in a minimalist gold band. My eyes mist over because I never imagined this outcome. I'd pictured every other outcome for my life, or my death, but not one where I lived *and* got to keep Rory.

"It was my mother's," Rory explains. "She gave it to me as soon as I told her what I was about to do."

"Oh, Rory. It's beautiful." I bring my hand to my mouth to hold my gasp.

The tears in my eyes blur my vision, so I have to bring the box closer to my face so I can keep looking at it.

"You haven't given me an answer," Rory says, his voice deepening with his frustration.

I want to scream, 'yes!' But I can't. There's too much at stake. Too much to consider. "Can I think about it?"

His face falls for a second, but he recovers quickly. "I guess I shouldn't have done this in a locker room, huh?"

"No, it's not that, it's just—we'd have to figure some things out before—"

His head snaps up as his mouth curves upward into a smile.

"I didn't say 'yes,'" I clarify. "Let's talk, and then we can decide if we are ready for this step. Okay?"

He answers by pulling me toward him and kissing me.

I missed kissing Rory. The sweetness with which he always starts and how it turns hungry so quickly without fail. Every single time.

Rory pushes me back against a locker and lifts me by my ass. I wrap both legs around his middle to stay up. I feel him hardening through his jeans, and my body awakens. It feels alive for the first time since before I started treatment. This part of me has been dormant for almost a year now, and only Rory has the key to free it.

His hand drops to the hem of my shirt, and I panic. Not only am I already self-conscious about being sweaty and smelly from my workout, but now I also have to worry about him seeing my scars. No one has seen those except my doctors.

Then there's the fact that anyone could walk in at any moment, plus the more important fact that I have no lube with me. I wince just thinking about Rory's size.

"Um—Rory. Please stop."

He listens and pants, his forehead pressed to mine. "Sorry." He says. "Got carried away."

I smile. "I know. Me too." I drop my legs to find the ground and give him one last quick kiss. "Want to see my place?"

Rory chuckles. "I'd love to see your place."

CHAPTER 22

We go to his hotel first to pick up his bags. I drive. I insist he shouldn't stay in a hotel but should stay with me instead. Rory is quick to grab his luggage from his room and check out. He is back in the car with me in no time, winded.

He smiles at me and kisses me on the lips like we have been apart for a long time instead of the fifteen minutes it took him to get back to my car. He keeps his hand on my thigh the entire time as I drive to my place.

Pilar's generosity has extended to getting me suitable living arrangements, but I've insisted on staying on the modest side, at least the 'modest side' by my family's standards.

We pull up to my apartment building, and I park in the lower-level garage.

"Well, this is it."

I help him with the smaller of his bags, and we make our way inside. I twirl the keys in my hand as we ride the elevator to the sixth floor. When we get inside my apartment, I glance around, hoping I haven't left anything terribly embarrassing lying about.

For the most part, I keep the place clear of clutter. I'm a fairly neat person, but it comes as second nature from the years of disciplined training more so than from an actual desire to keep a clean home.

"It's great," says Rory. "Mind if I look around? I want to see what kinds of things you like for when we move in together."

"*If* we move in together," I correct.

"Right. Assume I mean 'if' when I talk about plans, okay?" He asks.

"You could move in here," I say nonchalantly.

"Sure. Then you need to see my place for the kinds of things I like."

My apartment is small, with only one guest bedroom, and I follow Rory as he glances around every room. He enters my bedroom last, and I follow him there too.

Rory picks me up in his arms and carries me to the bed.

"I don't know if we'll live here or not, but just in case, I'm pretty sure I'm supposed to carry you in."

"I'm not a traditionalist, Rory."

"You sure?"

"Positive," I say and chuckle into his neck.

He sets me down gently on the bed so I can sit on the edge. He sits next to me and cradles my face in his hands. He kisses my forehead, but it's sweet, not sensual. He peppers kisses down my face until he reaches my neck. In that crevice between my jaw and my neck, the kisses turn hungry, and I feel his tongue tasting me. Rory lets out a groan from deep within his chest.

"Now, where did we leave off at the gym?" he asks. He reaches for the hem of my shirt, and I know he wants to take it off.

"Rory, wait. We have to talk."

"Uh-oh. I know the sound of that."

"No, it's just . . ." I trail off, unsure how to word this for him.

My brain flashes back to our first time together. We had stood in my apartment, and he'd seemed so scared and afraid that I would judge his body for the scar on his chest. It had broken me a little bit at the time that he had something on his body he had no control over that he had to explain before any sexual encounter.

In a mirror-opposite situation, I now have to explain my scars.

And the scars are just the tip of the iceberg we will have to climb together if we are ever to be intimate again.

"Rory—" I say, but my voice hitches. "I want to give you an out."

"An out?" he asks.

"Yes. An out. My body has changed significantly since we were together like this the last time."

"I'm aware," Rory says matter-of-factly. "I know how your body has changed."

"It's one thing to know it, though, isn't it? And another to experience it."

"There's nothing about your body I won't love."

"Don't say that. You don't know."

Rory brushes a loose strand of hair from my face. "Tell me what you need to feel comfortable—no—tell me what you need to feel as sexy as I see you."

This man is unreal. He can't be real. I clear my throat. "We can be intimate, but only if you promise that after, if you change your mind about proposing, you'll tell me."

"That's stupid, but from the look on your face, I think I better agree to this, if only to make you feel comfortable."

I nod. "You do."

"Okay. I promise if I change my mind, I will tell you, but I can tell you now there isn't a shot in hell—"

"Rory! Stop." I chuckle.

"Do you remember what you told me last year?" he asks.

"Can I get a hint?"

"Before I took my shirt off for the first time?"

I shake my head, unable to think about anything except Rory Dennis, naked and mine.

"You told me fighters find scars sexy as fuck."

"Oh," I gasp. I hadn't been expecting that. I'd forgotten those words from what seems like a lifetime ago.

"Is that what you're worried about? Because you don't need to be. You're a fighter, and if you're sincere when you tell me you find my scarred chest sexy, then you have to believe I'm sincere when I tell you that your scars of being a survivor are also sexy as fuck to me."

I nod. How could he know what I'm feeling without me saying it? He chips away at every insecurity I have. I was afraid he'd think my apartment is shitty compared to my apartment in KC, but he loves my home. I was worried he'd find my body lacking in its new form, but he is a doctor. He knows how much my body has changed, probably more than I do.

"That's part of it," I say finally.

"Look. I know you have tiny laparoscopic scars in the lower abdomen. I also know you had additional surgery and a larger scar in your torso. The small scars will match the dimples on your lower back that drive me wild, and the larger scar, well, that one will point me home. I'll love every inch of your body, even if it is covered in a hundred scars. I promise."

Bunching his shirt in my hands, I pull him in for a kiss because that little speech of his deserves to be rewarded. "Okay," I say. "If you trusted me to see your body, I'll trust you to see mine."

I hate that the confidence I once commanded is all gone, but somehow, the fact that it's Rory who is about to see me naked soothes me. I stand in front of him while he sits on the edge of my bed. I take a deep breath and pull my top over my head. The lights are on, and every cell in my body commands me to turn them off, but I refuse. I will trust Rory Dennis with my body because he once trusted me with his. I hadn't let him down then. I'm hoping he won't let me down now.

His hand floats upward to my breast, and he caresses me over my sports bra. His fingers wander and trail down my abdomen until they land on my scars. He traces the scars as he studies them, and I turn to the ceiling, not wanting to see his reaction. A rejection would hurt too much.

The heat of his mouth covers each scar, one by one, as he dusts kisses between them. His mouth leaves my body for only a second. "My little fighter," he whispers and continues to kiss and lick my body. I look down at him, kissing my abdomen. I stare at his red hair, and I run my fingers through it, encouraging him.

"Rory?"

"Yeah?"

"Make love to me," I plead.

His body stills. "I have plans for you, Valentina. I promise. But I'm not making love to you."

I step away from him and search for my discarded shirt. "What?" I knew it was too good to be true. I knew it was too much to ask. Why did

I ever think this could work? The hot woman he had sex with is long gone, and this is all that is left of her.

"No. Come here." He takes my hand and forces me to sit on his lap so he can look me dead in the eye. "I don't want to hurt you," he says.

He's worried about hurting me? I take a moment to consider that. "You won't hurt me."

He shakes his head, then smiles sexily. "I have many filthy ideas . . . Oh, Valentina, the things I will do to you . . . don't worry—"

"No, Rory. I—um—I mean, you can do those things too, but I want you to make love to me—"

"Valentina, I can't hurt you. I won't do it."

"Why do you think you'll hurt me?"

"You are all scarred inside from radiation. It's too soon."

I cock my head to the side to study him. He thinks I can't take his massive size. I grab onto his shoulders for support.

When I first concluded treatment, I told Dr. Ramirez my sexual life was a priority to me. She immediately got me started on dilator therapy to stretch me. The first and smallest dilator almost had me quit, but I pushed on. Months passed, and I kept with my therapy until I graduated to a larger dilator, then a larger one, until Dr. Ramirez suggested I graduate to a full-size vibrator.

Rory knows nothing of this. He was no longer a part of my life during that time post-treatment.

"You won't hurt me, Rory," I plead with him.

"We are not having penetrative sex, Valentina. I won't hurt you. I can't do that."

"Rory—"

"No. We can eventually get there. For now, there are plenty of things we can do to each other." He pulls me to him and whispers in my ear, "I promise I'll please you."

It's hard to pull away, but I do. "Will you just listen to me for one second."

Rory's lips disappear into a thin line, but he nods.

My face bursts into flames at having to discuss this at the worst of possible times, but it has to be done.

"I started dilator therapy as soon as treatment wrapped up."

Rory winces. "That sounds painful."

"It was at first. But that's what the therapy is for. I've kept up with it, Rory. I'm fairly certain I can take you."

He shakes his head. "I can't risk hurting you. Can you see my point of view here?"

"So long as we use plenty of lube, I'll be fine."

"No—"

"Rory, I want you. Do you want me?"

"I do, but—"

"Then can we at least try?"

He kisses me again, long and deep, leaving me breathless, and I forget what we are even arguing about for a moment.

"You're killing me, woman."

I grin at him.

"Fine," he says. "But only on one condition."

"Okay, what's the condition?"

"You promise you'll tell me if you're in pain. The minute it becomes too painful, we stop. That's the only way I'd be willing to try."

I suck in a breath. He is only trying to take care of me, even if this conversation spoils the moment's sensuality. I have to remind myself he is an expert and has seen it all. I try not to take it personally—this is not a rejection of my new body.

He loves me.

Everything he is doing—everything he is saying—is because he loves me.

The least I can do is reassure him.

"I promise I'll let you know if I'm in pain."

"Thank you," he says.

His hands snake around the back of my head until his fingers tangle in my hair. His mouth leaves mine only so he can lick and bite my neck playfully. The feel of his lips and tongue on my skin sends goosebumps of recognition down my body. His touch feels better than what I remembered.

We needed to have that conversation, but it didn't seem so bad once it was over. If anything, I think Rory and I now have a deeper understanding of the other's needs. It was embarrassing—I wanted to burrow my head into the dirt—but now there is nothing left to get in the way.

Rory's hands slide down my spine until he finds my bra strap and unclasps it. I spring free, and my muscles twitch with the reflex to cover my chest, but I don't. I have to let Rory in if I intend to say yes—because I really want to.

"Valentina," Rory whispers as he studies my body. I stand, and we keep undressing each other.

I'm shy in a way I've never been before. I know he senses my trepidation because he moves slowly, gently.

I lose my balance as he pulls me into him, and I land on his lap again, straddling him.

He runs a hand through my hair. "It's growing in great. I love it. You look beautiful."

My cheeks feel three-hundred degrees, and I bury my face in his neck.

"You mentioned lube?" He asks.

"Yeah, it's in the nightstand." I reach for the drawer and pull out the bottle and a condom, setting both items next to us.

I stand to help Rory out of his boxer-briefs, and I gulp when he springs free.

"We don't have to—" he says softly.

"No, it's fine. You promised me we could try."

He nods, but his brows are drawn inward, and his face is twisted with concern.

I take some lube in my hand and wrap it around his shaft, stroking him slowly. His face instantly relaxes, and his eyes draw shut. I can only hope I've broken through his concern.

"Valentina," he says my name in a raspy voice.

"Yes?"

"That feels so good."

"Does it?"

"Mmm-hmmm."

"Open your eyes, Rory."

He obeys and watches me take more lube. I return one hand to him, and his eyes widen when he sees me starting to pleasure myself with the other.

"Fuuck," he growls. "That is so hot, baby."

I take his mouth in mine so I can lead him to lie on his back and position my entrance over his hardness. I give it one last squeeze, and I swear it hardened even more in my grip.

"You promised," he pleads one last time.

"I promised. Let me drive; I know best how much I can handle."

Rory nods and lays perfectly still. So still, I almost laugh. This is not the time to tease him, though, so I keep it in.

He is a bit larger than my vibrator, but not by much. I would never admit I searched for a toy that resembled his anatomy, but I also couldn't deny the similar size.

I place my hands on his chest for support. Taking a deep breath, I brace myself and take the tip of him inside. I say a silent prayer this won't be painful because I want nothing more than Rory Dennis filling me to the hilt at this moment.

Dilator therapy isn't sexy. I hadn't felt sensual since the last time I was with Rory. But with just one look at him naked, my libido reared its head, and there is no way I want to tame it again.

I lower further until he is halfway in me, and so far, no pain. I take in another inch slowly, then another, and keep going until there is nothing left to take in. Rory bucks his hips upward once.

"Sorry, so sorry," he stammers. "I couldn't help it."

I shake my head. "It's okay. I'm fine."

"You are?" He looks up at me, so hopeful, I'm not sure I could tell him I was in pain even if I was. Lucky for me, there is no pain, and I don't have to lie.

I hadn't realized how tight I had clenched every muscle in my body. I relax and loosen myself. I clench experimentally around him, earning me a sexy growl from Rory.

"How does it feel?" he asks.

"Good," I say. "Really good." I circle my hips slowly, and Rory's hands drift up to grip my waist.

I grin down at him and lick my lips. I support myself with his chest as I ride him until I am spent, and our bodies are slicked with sweat. I know Rory strained himself, trying to keep still so I could have my way with him, and it took a toll on him too—his face and neck are pearled with sweat.

The room feels hotter, and my hair is nearly dripping with sweat. We are weak with exhaustion when Rory presses his thumb against my clit, and I shamelessly grind against it while he's inside me. I unravel around him as I come and collapse on his body. Rory pumps inside me twice more and steels with his own release. He rolls his head back, giving me a glorious look at his neck and the veins that bulge with his pleasure.

I pant to the rhythm of his chest rising.

"So, no pain," Rory says with a breathy voice.

I shake my head. "Only pleasure."

IN THE MORNING, I watch Rory as he sleeps in. It's been hours, and he has the sweetest little snore. I manage to get out of bed and back in again without him so much as stirring.

It's late morning when he finally wakes. "Hmmm," he moans.

"Good morning," I say.

He smiles. "Morning. How're you feeling?"

"Great."

"Great?" he asks.

"Yeah," I say.

"I need the truth, Valentina. Please."

"Very slightly sore. But no pain. I swear."

Rory smiles and draws circles on my shoulder with the pads of his fingers. "Good," he says.

He rolls up and over me so he's on top, and he kisses me. "Now," he says. "Almonte, what is it you need to think about to say yes?"

My face falls to the side, and Rory pushes it back by my chin, so I look at him. "If we get married, I'd like our marriage to be one of good communication. That starts now."

I blink. He is right. After last night, I don't think there's anything I couldn't talk to him about. I bite my lip. "Lots of things," I say.

"Okay." He kisses me gently, urging me to go on.

"I wanted to be with you last night so you could change your mind if you didn't like it."

Rory's eyebrow raises. "Did it look like I didn't like it?"

I giggle. "Right. Well, I guess that's a non-issue, then."

"Good. One down. What else?"

"I can't give you children," I admit.

That gives Rory pause, though I'm sure he had to know. He rolls off me and onto his side next to me, so we face each other. "Do you want children, Valentina?"

I shrug one shoulder. "That's not a future I ever envisioned, but when Dr. Ramirez asked about freezing eggs, I declined."

"Why?"

"It didn't seem important. There are so many children without parents—I guess I figured if I ever really wanted children, it wouldn't be important if they were biological. I'd rather give good parents to a kid with none."

Rory tucks a strand of hair behind my ear. "Valentina Almonte, you couldn't be more fucking perfect if you tried."

My eyes search his, and he smiles at me.

"Rory, don't lie to me. If children are important to you, this can't work—"

"They *are* important to me. And I intend to have them. With you. And they will be adopted, but they will be our children, same as if we made them the other way."

I laugh. "The other way?"

"You know what I mean."

He has already thought about this. Of course he has. Even if he didn't have access to my medical chart, he had to have known I'd more than likely fried my ovaries despite how hard we tried saving them. "You don't mind, then, if you can't have a child of your own blood?" I ask.

He shakes his head. "My children will be mine because they were meant to be. Just like you're meant to be their mom."

"Okay," I say.

"Okay?" Rory's eyes are wide.

"I'm not saying yes yet."

"What else do you want from me, woman?" We both laugh at his frustration.

"For one, I'd like a proper proposal. Preferably not in a locker room surrounded by the smell of feet."

"Noted. Won't happen again. Is that it, then? Are you saying yes?"

I shake my head. "I'd like to live together a little while first. Make sure we both want this and that we're committed to spending a lifetime together, because if I marry you, Rory Dennis, it'll be for life."

Rory smiles wide. "We can live together for a while first. I'm okay with a long engagement."

I turn to face away from him so he can spoon me because I don't want to see his face for what I'm about to tell him next.

"I have to confess something," I say.

"What's that?"

"While you were sleeping, I called my sister."

"Okay—"

"She wants to have you over for dinner. Meet you."

"That's not so bad. Why do you sound nervous all of a sudden?"

"She didn't say, but I'm pretty sure she intends to have my parents over."

"Oh."

CHAPTER 23

"I don't approve," says Dad. Rory is on the other side of the room, talking with Pilar. Dad's eyes are narrow as he looks at him and swirls the whiskey in his glass.

"I know," I smile and am surprised at how relaxed I am. I'm done caring. I no longer have to live my life for anyone other than myself.

"You know?" Dad asks.

"I know, Dad, but things are different now. Now it's about what I want. Not about what you or Mom want," I say matter-of-factly.

He'd never admit it, but I swear I saw the hint of a smile on the corner of Dad's mouth.

"Does he make you happy?" Dad asks

"He really does," I say.

Dad lands a peck on my cheek and walks back to his place next to Mom, but he seems happy in a way I'm not accustomed to seeing him.

Rory couldn't believe my sister's house. I hadn't seen it from an outsider's perspective in a long time. From his eyes, my world is new and filled with a wonder I have long taken for granted.

"Is she royalty or something?" Rory had asked as we'd walked up to the door.

Pilar's house is almost a palace. Her life lacks love from her partner, but in many ways, she has everything most women dream of—the perfect home and husband. My parents are happy and approve of her life, and I'm glad they have someone to approve of because I know it will never be me.

"He's great," Pilar whispers when she comes over to me. Rory is talking to Felipe about the home's architectural elements, even though I know Rory is faking it.

"I know," I say. "I'm happy."

"Are you?"

"What? Happy? Yeah, Pili. I'm happy in a way I never thought was possible. I only hope one day you can find that same level of happiness."

"What do you mean?"

"Do you really think Felipe is your happiness?"

Pilar's body stiffens, and I can decipher to the second the moment when her guard comes up. "This night is about you," she says. "Leave me out of it just this once. Please?"

I bite my lip. "I'm sorry," I say, and I am. This night is for Pilar to get to know Rory, and I have to keep reminding myself of that.

A maid announces dinner, and we all make our way to the dining room table.

Mom is a freaking painting. Beautiful, but a mere ornament on Dad's arm. Felipe and Dad monopolize the conversation, and I squeeze Rory's hand under the table. I whisper reassurances that him not feeding into their superficial bravado is perfectly fine.

"So, Rory, how much longer is your residency?" Felipe asks.

"Two more years" says Rory.

"That soon?" Felipe asks.

"Yeah. If all goes well—"

"And your plans after that?" Dad asks.

Rory clears his throat and swallows the bite of steak he is on. "Well, I'm not really sure. We have to decide where we want to live first—"

"Well," says Dad, "You'll be taking my daughter with you. I don't quite see how it would work for you to move here—"

I jump in. "Dad! Can we please not talk about this?"

Dad throws me a stern look of warning. "What? It's perfectly natural for your family to worry—"

"No, Dad. It's not. Things are different now. Everything's changed."

Dad shifts in his seat but has the decency not to comment further.

"Dad, I'm sorry," I say. "I just . . . I have to make my own choices."

"You always have," Dad says.

He looks at me but with no remorse. It's a fact. A simple fact. If he couldn't tame me before my outlook on life changed, he could never manage it now.

It's a relief when Dad changes the subject. He and Felipe turn their attention to business. Mom eats dinner, dainty and quiet for the most part.

Pilar can't stop smiling as she looks between Rory and me. We can't stop smiling ourselves.

Dad's passiveness the rest of the evening surprises everyone. Pilar and I half expected he would blow a gasket at my choice in a mate, but he doesn't. Dad had wanted me to marry an important businessman, lawyer, or politician from Mexico. Someone with influence. Someone who would add a certain type of value to the family that Dad craves. In the end, I think he sees how much I smile around Rory, how he holds me protectively by his side. There's also not a chance he has forgotten everything Rory did when I was in treatment even though he had absolutely no obligation to help.

Dad walks us to my car and takes Rory's hand to shake, but then holds it there. "I've told my daughter this, so I won't lie to you," Dad says. "I don't approve of this match. I am bitter that my daughter is leaving—"

"That hasn't been decided—" Rory tries to explain.

"As good as. And despite that, I see Valentina is in relatively good hands. I'm glad she'll have a doctor—someone who knows what to look out for . . ."

Dad trails off as he chokes on his words. I know what he is asking Rory. He wants him to watch out for recurrence of my cancer. To keep a watchful eye.

"I promise I'll take good care of her, sir."

Dad nods. "I'm sure you will," he says. "The alternative is a hell of a lot of trouble from me, son."

I bring my hand to my chest at hearing Dad call him 'son' even if it was a threat. Dad finally got the son he wanted in Felipe. He hand-picked him himself. But I know, deep down, Dad knows he doesn't make Pilar happy. And even though Rory is the furthest thing from what he wanted for me, he will be a better son-in-law than Felipe could ever hope to be.

~

My family, as expected, dragged out the dinner much longer than it needed to be. Pre-dinner drinks, five courses, port and cigars after dinner for the men who went off into Felipe's study, and endless, mind-numbing conversation. By the time we get home, Rory and I are exhausted. Rory barely brushed his teeth, and his head hit the pillow.

"That was better than I thought," I say.

"What dinner were *you* at?" Rory's voice is laced with sarcasm.

"I guess I should say, by my family's standard, it went better than I thought."

"They hate me."

"Not Pilar," I say with an encouraging smile.

"No, I guess not Pilar, but your Dad—I mean, I'm a doctor. He knows that, right? It's a noble profession, and no, I won't be a millionaire, but I will be financially stable. He talked to me like I was a, a, uh—"

"A what?" I ask.

"A chimney sweep," Rory says, satisfied with his analogy.

"A chimney sweep?" I laugh. "What is this? Oliver Twist?" I lay down next to Rory and take his hand in mine. "Poor little orphan boy is going to be a chimney sweep."

Rory's jaw drops, and he tries to break his hand away from mine. Then I realize what I said.

"Rory, no, I—that's not what—I just meant . . ."

"Yeah, go on, backpedal faster." Then he bursts out laughing.

"Come here, you." He grabs me and pulls me closer to him on the bed. "I'm not sensitive about being adopted. You should have seen your face, though."

I gently smack his shoulder. "That wasn't funny."

"I know. I'm sorry."

"Thank you for meeting my family."

"They're my family now, I suppose."

I haven't thought about it like this until Rory mentions it, but he is right. They are his family now too—poor thing.

"Even Felipe," I say.

"Yeah, that dude gives off a bad vibe."

"You are like a puppy," I say.

"What do you mean?"

"Dogs can sense evil without having to know a person."

"You're saying he is evil?"

"In his own way. I don't want to talk about sad things right now, though."

I CATCH Rory watching me sleep the next morning, as if we're taking turns with this ritual. He smiles at me, and I can't help but feel like I am exactly where I am supposed to be. His smile even feels like home.

"That's kind of creepy," I tease.

"You watch me sleep all the time."

"How do you know that?" I ask.

"I'm not always asleep."

I narrow my eyes at him, and he laughs.

"Can I ask you something?" He asks, his arm tightening around me.

"Yeah."

"Tell me about Chema and Nico."

I suck in a breath. "Are you upset I let you think we were together?"

"No. I know why you did it."

I squeeze his arm, thankful he's not mad about the second biggest lie I ever told him—the first being that I didn't love him back. But we don't dwell on those bitter moments anymore, so instead I tell him about Chema and Nico.

When I met Chema and Nico, they'd had the gym open for barely a year. Chema was coming down from the height of his fighting career after an injury, and has made his gym very successful since.

And because Rory will very soon be part of our inner circle, I need him and Chema to be friends. I need both of them in my life. So I also overshare on Chema's life; on how he and Nico were high school sweethearts in secret because their families didn't approve. They were both on their school's soccer team and were caught kissing by one of their teammates. The following day, three of their teammates cornered Nico alone and beat the shit out of him. Once he healed, Chema vowed he'd never let anyone hurt him again. They both took self-defense classes, and Chema fell in love with the sport. The fact that he could pummel anyone who dared look at Nico the wrong way was an added bonus of his profession.

When I'm done telling Rory the story of Nico and Chema, Rory's smiling at me. "Chema's really amazing isn't he?" he asks.

I nod. "Hopefully you'll learn to love him like I do."

"I already do. He took care of my precious girl when I couldn't be there."

"Precious girl?" I tease.

"Don't mock. You're precious to me, and Chema guarded you."

I smile, hopeful for the potential of our life together, and I lean in to kiss him. Shifting under the covers to get closer to him, I reach for the hem of his shirt, but he stills my hand. He shakes his head as he looks deep into my eyes.

"Why not?" I ask.

"You were sore yesterday—"

"I'm perfectly fine today."

"I'm sure you are, but can we please take it slow? I need to make sure you stay okay."

My instincts turn to anger, but I can't let it out because I know he only wants me healthy. It's coming from a good place, even as infantilizing as his desire to control my health is. We are both going to have to adjust.

"We can take it slow," I say finally. "Within reason. At some point, you have to trust me too."

"I know," Rory says. "We'll work on it. In the meantime, can loving each other be enough?"

CHAPTER 24

Rory has some sort of plan he isn't telling me about. Our flight was delayed, and everything Rory has done since we got to his apartment has been rushed. I'm tired from the long day of travel and can't imagine how he has all this energy.

"We're going out tonight, so get ready," he says.

I frown. "I'm too tired to go out."

"Please. It's important."

I cross my arms in front of me. "Rory Dennis, what do you have up your sleeve?"

"Please, can you just humor me? This once?"

I finally relent and hop in the shower before he does so I have time to dry my hair while he gets his turn. After drying off, and as Rory is in the shower, a lightbulb goes off in my head. I rummage through one of my suitcases.

As a parting gift, Pilar gave me a designer red camisole with matching robe. It's sexy in an elegant sort of way, and the feeling of the silk is divine. I put it on and wait for the shower to shut off. I give Rory a few minutes before walking into the bathroom with him. He is brushing his teeth and has a towel wrapped low on his hips. Water droplets roll down the rippled muscles of his abs, and I bite my lip at the beautiful sight. I lean on the doorframe and clear my throat. He turns to look at me, does a double-take stopping mid-brush, and when he eyes me up and down, rinses quickly.

"Valentina," he groans. "We're going out . . ." He says, but with less conviction now.

"You sure you want to go out? You wouldn't rather stay in bed our first night back?"

His eyes narrow as I approach him. I slide my index finger between him and the towel to unhook it, letting it slide down his body and pool at his feet. "Oops," I say, and he chuckles. "What's it going to be?" I ask, grabbing his hardening shaft and squeezing gently once, feeling as it stiffens further in my hand.

His green eyes darken under hooded lids. "It can wait," he says with a smirk, and I drop to my knees in front of him.

The silk clings to my skin with the steam from his shower, and the sensation forces my thighs to clench together. I pump him once more and bring him into my mouth. Rory has to lean back on the vanity as he loses balance, and I love what I can do to him. It's a power trip I haven't appreciated until him—like so many other things. I suck hard once, and he groans long and deep.

I suck and lick while I twist my grip around his shaft and then take him deep in my throat.

"Valentina, stop. I don't want to come in your mouth." I suck one last time before he draws away from my mouth. I stand and kiss him with an open mouth, our tongues dancing and playing.

Fucking Rory Dennis is so much fun.

He flips and lifts me until I'm sitting on the vanity, and he is between my legs. He feels the material of the chemise between his fingers. "This is nice," he says and nibbles my neck.

"You like it?"

"Mmm-hmmm. I insist you wear this to bed every night."

"You're very demanding, Doctor Dennis," I tease.

"I am," he agrees. "Lube?" he asks, and I hand him the small bottle I placed on the counter when I walked in. He pours it liberally onto his hand, warms it up, and my sex clenches at the sight of him sliding his hands up and down a now-shiny cock. Rory centers himself in front of me, and I wrap my legs around him.

He slides in slowly, slowly at first, until he bottoms out. I moan with pleasure, and he pulls out and slams deep and quick into me again. He kisses me, leading with his tongue, and comes back up for air as his thrusts quicken.

I forgot about the second mirror in the bathroom, and when I turn to the side briefly, an image of him thrusting into me as my legs quiver around him stops my gaze. It's so hot, seeing him—seeing *us*—like this. "Rory," I say. "Look." He turns in the direction of my gaze and stills deep inside me.

"Fuck, Valentina. You look so hot."

He fucks me harder, then, for the first time since we got back together. There is no hesitation, and I smile because I realize he couldn't stop himself from being a little rougher with me. We both look in the mirror now, watching how we fuck, and our eyes meet, catching the other doing the same. The corner of his mouth draws into a smirk.

My body shudders as I come, looking at Rory through the full-length mirror. He slides out, then slams in again, rolling my orgasm into two.

His hands wrap around me and grab onto my ass as he lifts me off the vanity and carries me to the bed, impaled on him. He lays me down gently and thrusts a few times before sliding out. I don't dwell in the absence of him too long before he flips me over, and grabbing onto my hip bones, pulls my ass up to face him. I smile, remembering his words from our first night together—this is his favorite part of my body. Rory Dennis is a booty-man, and he can't get enough of mine.

I look straight ahead to the empty wall, and before he is in me again, say, "We're getting a mirror right there—"

Rory slides in deep. "Agreed," he groans, and slams into me so roughly, my legs start to shake with my next orgasm. I'm afraid they'll give out soon, but Rory's growl breaks through the silence of the apartment, and he stills inside me.

I feel as he presses his forehead to my back and tries to catch his breath. Both his thumbs circle two spots on my lower back. "I love these dimples," he says, admiring my backside.

"They're all yours," I say.

We both collapse on the bed and stare at each other shyly. While it turned me on so much, somehow, looking at us through that mirror made me a bit bashful now that the deed is done.

I want to thank Rory for being rough and not treating me like a glass figurine, but I don't want to have another conversation like the one in Mexico, so instead, I trace the scar on his chest with my fingers. In turn, he traces my scars over my lower abdomen. We lie there, caressing each other's scarred and beautiful bodies without a word passing between us. His eyes search mine. "I love you," he says.

"I love you too."

CHAPTER 25

We are both sated but weak and tired, so it takes me by surprise when Rory starts getting dressed to go out. I don't understand his urgency to get to out the door until we arrive at our favorite bar, *La Oficina*.

The 'open' sign is off, and a flyer on the front door indicates the bar is closed for a special event, but the place is dark. Rory knocks, and Sofia opens up for us. As I step through, the lights come on, and a roar of "Welcome Home!" Blasts through me like heavy wind.

When my mind catches up to what just happened, I scan the room and see all the faces of everyone I met during my time in Kansas City. Dr. Ramirez, nurse Sara, Mandy, Tlali, and Izel all beam at me. They didn't forget me. I feel the tears coming on, and I try to sniffle them back in. All my friends are here—my new family.

Mandy nearly crashes onto me when she hugs me. "We missed you so much, girl. Wait until I catch you up with everything that's been going on." She loops her arm with mine, as she's done so many times before, and leads me to the bar to grab a glass of champagne.

When we get there, I realize Lisa and Tom, Rory's parents, are both here. I go over to them and give them both a hug.

"It's so good to see you, dear," says Lisa. "You're looking a lot better than the last time we saw you."

"Thank you. I'm feeling a lot better, and I'm in remission. Things are looking good."

"And you got some meat back on them bones," says Tom.

"Tom! Don't embarrass the girl—"

I laugh. "No. It's okay. You're absolutely right, Tom. I'm working on bulking up a bit again. Getting a little stronger."

"That's good," he says and winks at me. "The Dennis men like our women strong, with a little meat on the bone—"

"Tom!" Lisa scolds again.

"What? I didn't say anything wrong."

Luckily, Rory interjects before I laugh at his parents again. "I'm so sorry," Rory says. "Have they already gotten into trouble?"

"No, they're fine." I smile.

The surprise warms my heart. Rory had to have planned for this while he was in Mexico. I have no idea how he managed. I scan the room to see it's not only people I know. Neil, Rory's old roommate, who I remember from our one introduction, stands with a group of men at the other end of the bar. My mind flashes back to that moment at the bar when Rory told the group of men he was with he was bailing on them for someone else. I'm pretty sure it's that very table of men chatting it up with Neil.

It hits me, then, that Rory has invited all his friends and family, whether I know them or not. And this is a 'welcome home' surprise party? Something isn't quite adding up.

"Rory? What is this?" I ask.

Rory leads me to the bar and gestures for me to sit on one of the stools. With my back to the bar, I pin him with my eyes.

"What do you mean?" he asks.

"There are so many people here I don't know . . ." My thought trails off when Rory's mouth quirks into a playful smile.

He takes my hand in his and kisses it. He reaches behind me for something and then turns around to make his way to the center of the room. When he faces me again, I see a champagne glass in one hand and a spoon in the other. He clinks the spoon to the glass, and my heart rate quickens to the chime.

Oh god. What is he about to do? I want to run with the anticipation of his speech, but everyone is so silent and frozen to their spots, any movement from me will only draw attention. I curse Rory Dennis, and I curse barstools. There's something about a barstool and Dr. Dennis in the same room that always ends in disaster.

Then he speaks. "Thank you, everyone, for being here, and to those of you who helped me organize this, I am forever grateful. If you're in this room, you know the beautiful woman sitting at the bar." All eyes turn to me, and I sink in my seat a little. My face feels hot, and I want to run. But I can't. I'm going to kill him for this.

Rory goes on. "If you don't know Valentina Almonte personally, you know of her. You know of her because if you are here tonight, you're important to me, and if you're important to me, you know I can't shut up about her." Rory chuckles, and polite little laughs follow around the room. This isn't funny, Rory Dennis. I stew silently as he continues his speech.

"This year, I almost lost her. That experience only taught me to cherish her and have as much of her time as she'll allow me to have." Rory sets down the two items in his hands and holds my eyes. He fumbles a bit with his collar, then sticks his hand into his pants pocket, producing a familiar box.

Well-played, Rory. Well-played. The last time he tried to do this was in private. He won't give me a chance to say no; that's why he's doing this in front of everyone. If I hadn't already decided to marry him, this could be construed as manipulation.

Rory walks to where I'm sitting and gets down on one knee. I look down at the box in his hands, then back at him. His face is hopeful but strained, like he is holding his breath, and everyone around us quiets like they're holding their breath with him in solidarity.

I have my life back—a second chance. When I was diagnosed, all I wanted was to experience life, to see places, art, meet people, eat food I'd never dreamed of. Now I know that not only will I have the time to do all those things, but that Rory Dennis will be by my side for all of it. I know in my heart he is the man I will grow old with—now that I get to grow old.

"Valentina Almonte, will you do me the honor of being my wife?"

EPILOGUE

THIRTEEN YEARS LATER

The gym closes early on Sundays—by lunchtime, the place is dead. This is the one day a week I'll allow Nayeli and Miles to train in the cage. I can focus all my attention on them.

At ten-years-old, Nayeli towers over her eight-year-old brother. I try not to smile at how cute they are with their child-size gloves as they paw at each other like puppies with little strength. Miles struggles to put on his kid knuckle wraps, and Nayeli groans and protests, but in the end, she always helps him wrap so they can spar.

She won't let Miles win, though. I think not until he outgrows her will he have so much as a shot at winning, and even then, I don't see it happening.

Miles takes after Rory. He idolizes him and proclaimed years ago he was going to be a doctor just like him. He follows through, too, and spends most of his time hitting the books, ever since Rory told him that's what it takes.

For her part, Nayeli has no clue what she wants to do when she grows up, but she is physically gifted. I've never hinted at a career in sports—it needs to come from her—but nothing would make me prouder.

I watch my foster children play on the mat with equal parts hope and dread. Rory and I have petitioned to adopt them, and we are awaiting our court date. I'm sure everything will work out okay, but there's a little part of me gnawing at my insides with doubt, as if something could go wrong. It's silly, though. Miles and Nayeli's biological mom already lost custody. There's no reason for the judge to rule against the adoption.

They are my children. Before them, we had temporary foster placements, all children who were successfully reunited with their families, and I hope, doing well now. But the moment Nayeli and Miles came home two years ago, Rory and I looked at each other, and we both knew. I told him, "These are our children," and all he said was, "I know."

"Mom! Mom!" Miles yells. "I tapped out. Make her stop!"

"Nayeli, you know the rules. If your brother taps out, you have to stop."

Nayeli loses her chokehold's grip around her brother and raises her arms in surrender as she stands. "Sorry," she whines. "Mom, I really need to fight with someone my own age. The twerp is too weak."

"I am not weak!" Miles snaps.

"Are too."

"Am not! You're bigger. That's all. Mom! Tell her."

"Stop teasing your brother, Nayeli. If you behave, we can look into getting you someone else to train with," I say.

I stifle a laugh when Miles sucker-punches his sister when she's distracted. *Serves her right*, I think, but I don't take sides with them.

The front doorbell rings as it opens, and I walk over to help my next customer. "Play nice, you two," I call after the brawling siblings.

The first one to enter the gym is a little boy I know and love. "*Tía!*" my nephew yells and runs to me. I pick him up into my arms and embrace him as I carry him.

"What are you doing here, love?"

Pilar walks into the gym before he has a chance to answer me. "I'm so sorry, Tini," she says.

"For what?"

"For telling me where to find you," Dad's voice hits me like a ton of bricks as he enters my gym, the place he swore he'd never set foot in.

Mom and Dad didn't show up at my wedding. They sent a gift and claimed they were too busy with business and couldn't travel at the time. It was all horseshit, of course.

It was Tom, Rory's Dad, who walked me down the aisle that day. They've been a constant in our lives ever since. He and Lisa moved to Kansas City from Minnesota the minute they heard we would be fostering. They insisted they wanted to be a part of that with us. They are overjoyed at our adoption plans and already love Nayeli and Miles more than anything on this earth, dethroning even Rory from the number one spot. He is now third in their hearts—and okay with it.

My parents weren't quite so . . . graceful about it. When I told them over the phone, the roles reversed. Dad stayed quiet for the call, and Mom shouted. She couldn't believe I would adopt someone else's children. She yelled again at how stupid I was for not freezing my eggs so I could have a child of my blood. I hung up on them. I haven't spoken to them since.

"What are you doing here?" I ask Dad but then look at Pilar.

Pilar mouths, "I'm sorry," and I know she had little say in what happened.

"Can I talk to you, Valentina?" Dad asks.

"I don't see what we have to talk about," I say.

"Please. It's important."

It's then I notice the thick legal envelope in his hands. "Here." I hand Pilar her son, and she takes him over to the mat to play with Nayeli and Miles.

"We can go into my office," I say to Dad and lead him there. He takes a seat in front of me. I clasp my hands and lean back in my chair. "Well? What did you want to talk about?"

"This." He lets the envelope fall with a thud onto my desk. I take it.

"What is it?" I say as I empty the contents.

"Your dowry."

"My what?"

"I am legally obligated to give you your dowry."

I scan the paperwork, at least the first couple of pages, and the pieces of paper confirm what he is saying, but nothing explains why I'm getting it now. I've been married over a decade.

"Why now?"

"Believe me, if it were up to me, you wouldn't be getting it."

"Thanks? I guess . . ."

"You can thank your great-grandma for that."

I shake my head. "I don't understand."

"I never told you girls, for obvious reasons, that there were two pathways to getting the trust fund."

"Trust fund?"

"Yeah. We called it a dowry to ensure you and Pilar made acceptable matches, but marriage wasn't the only way to get the money. If my grandfather had his way, and I had my way, it would be the only way, but my grandmother felt differently. Most of the family money came from her side of the family, so she had significant control over its destiny."

"I don't understand," I repeat. None of this makes sense.

"She felt that a woman could start a good life either in marriage or in business. My grandfather insisted that with the marriage clause, the father had to approve. Grandma only conceded that the clause could be overturned if the recipient of the funds started a business. She felt a woman should have success in either married life or business life and that the funds would ensure that either way."

"Oh," I say, realization hitting me. I opened up my gym this year. Rory and I saved for nearly a decade to start this business. He wanted my dreams to come true as well, and we've skimped but have finally gotten here. His salary as a doctor helped loads, and I coached during that time. "My gym," I say finally.

"Yes. Your gym made you eligible for the funds."

"Dad, we don't need anything. We're doing fine."

"I know," he says. "But it's not about that. Your grandmother protected you and any daughters you have and their daughters. I can't do anything about it. Legally, she left that to you."

"I guess I can finally pay Pilar what's left of my debt to her," I say.

"She won't care about that."

"I know."

"Have your lawyers look over the documents. You'll want to give them account information so that the money can be wired. There's also preliminary paperwork for your children's trust funds."

"What?"

"You adopted them, right?"

"We are in the process."

"Well, they're your children once adopted. That makes them eligible for family trust funds."

"Let me guess. Grandma protected an adoption classification for this?"

"It wasn't grandpa," Dad says and smiles. "Listen, I'm sorry about how your Mom reacted. She doesn't understand what you're doing here. With all this . . ." he trails off and whirls his hand in the air, motioning to the space around us. "I don't think I fully do either, but I know it's a good thing. I can't promise I'll see them as my grandchildren, but I want to try."

"You do?"

Dad's shoulders relax, and I see the walls he's put up between us start to crumble. "I do. You think I could meet them?"

"They'd love that," I say. "But not today. I have to speak with Rory first. You understand?"

"I do. I'm here until Tuesday. I would love to meet them before I leave."

"I'm sure I can make that happen."

We stand, and for a moment, neither of us knows what to do. I clear my throat and offer him my hand.

Dad laughs and pushes it away. He takes me into his arms. "I know I don't understand you. But I do love you."

This is probably the first hug he's offered since I was sick, and the only 'I love you' I've ever gotten from him that I can remember. I sniffle into his shirt. "Love you too, Dad."

PILAR AND DAD are gone by the time Rory picks the kids and me up at the gym. Nayeli and Miles run up to him the second they see him.

"Dad! Dad!" Miles squeals. "I got Nayeli! Just the once. But it counts."

"Bet it does, buddy." He musses Miles's hair and hunches down to hug him.

"I was distracted," says Nayeli.

"Sure you were," Rory says, and Nayeli wraps her arms around his middle. "Anybody up for some ice cream? Maybe we can go to the park afterward?"

Both kids bounce with excitement, and both scream, "Yes!"

"Let me just lock up," I say. "Wait in the car."

WE GET OUR ICE CREAM, then head over to the park. Nayeli and Miles go straight for the playground, and Rory and I sit on a bench where I fill him in on everything that happened that day.

When I'm done, he says, "Wish I could've been there."

I'm still dazed as I try to process everything Dad said. "Me too. Well?" I ask. "Are you okay with Dad getting to know the kids?"

He shifts in his seat and faces me. "Maybe," he says. "Only if he's serious. I don't want to introduce anyone into their lives who doesn't plan on being there for the long haul."

"I don't think Mom will ever get on board, but I have to say, Dad looked sincere. I get the sense he has some regrets in life."

"Let me talk to him. We can go from there. But if he is serious, I have no problem with the kids knowing their other grandpa."

I squeeze Rory's hand. "Thank you," I say.

Rory scoots over to wrap an arm around me. He still uses the same aftershave from when we first met, and I take in the comforting smell of sandalwood and suede. My husband hasn't changed much over the years. He started working out more when I opened the gym to spend time with me, and he has bulked up a little. The hints of wrinkles barely begin to play around his beautiful green eyes, and he is not allowed to shave his beard. He is as handsome as he has ever been.

And he is a fantastic father. Because he is involved with our local foster care agency, he understands how slim adoption chances get the longer a child stays in the system—that's why he wants Nayeli and Miles. The older they get, the fewer chances they have to be adopted. They took to calling him Dad fairly quickly, not that it was a contest. It would have been a contest if they'd called me Mom first, but they didn't. Rory doesn't let me forget that.

Our kids didn't laugh when they first got to us. It broke our hearts. We watch them now when they play, and all the laughter they can't help but let out, and I know both our hearts are soaring.

For our part, Rory and I have a wonderful, healthy marriage. We could live our lives afraid of Rory's heart patch giving out or of my cancer coming back, but instead, each morning we wake up and choose to cherish each other and our time together like the privilege the gift of time is.

"So," Rory says, breaking my thoughts. "You're a millionaire? And so are the kids?"

I burst out laughing, and he joins me with his own laughter. "Yeah. Guess we are. And so are you, Dr. Dennis.

INCISION

HEARTLAND METRO HOSPITAL: A NOVELLA

INCISION

CHAPTER 1

I could be forcing the victims of a serial killer to run for their lives in my current slasher novel work in progress. But instead of my characters, I'm the one running—and not for a good reason, like to save my life, but rather for exercise. Ugh!

My sneakers paddle on the paved trail, sending a jolt of pain up my shins with each clumsy stride. It doesn't help that I'm wearing a workout top I bought a year and two dress sizes ago. The thin material rolls up my full hips and bunches at my smaller waist with the movement of my body. I gave up wrestling the hem down to my waist at the quarter mile mark. The result is an unintended crop top. And seriously, who runs in a crop top? To add insult to injury, I'm drenched in sweat, forcing the thin material to cling to my cleavage. And if *that* weren't enough, the top is white. The only saving grace is that jogging at this ungodly hour means fewer people to witness this debacle of a workout my roommate talked me into.

But Tlali, my cousin-slash-best-friend-slash-roommate, wasn't wrong when she hinted at how tight my jeans were getting around my hips and reminded me our forced modeling gig is only weeks away.

Why do I have to be such a people-pleaser? I need to work on saying 'no' more often. I cringe when I think back to how she talked me into working out.

"Izel," Tlali had whined when she got home after work and I had our favorite queso and chips at the table ready with a big pitcher of margaritas. "We can't eat like this. Mandy is going to have us nearly naked for her exhibit."

While our cousin Mandy hasn't exactly told us yet how much we'll be wearing when we pose for the day of the dead living sculpture we are modeling for, she's hinted, she's alluded, she's insinuated—it will be minimal. I don't care how much body paint she drenches me in—if she thinks I'm going to pose nude for strangers at the gallery—she has another think coming.

"But it's Friday," I'd pouted. "We always have margaritas on Fridays."

"After Mandy's exhibit, we can go back to margarita Fridays. Deal?"

I'd puffed air into my cheeks and then let it out. "I hate for this to go to waste," I'd said with a longing look at the food and margarita pitcher. "Guess I'll throw it out."

Tlali had basically lunged herself at the table to protect it. "Let's not get crazy," she said. "We'll start jogging Monday morning."

And why exactly wasn't my cousin running next to me on the trail at five this morning? She'd claimed to need her beauty sleep when I'd tried waking her. We work at the same hospital. She is a medical interpreter, and I work as a surgical technologist. We usually carpool to get to our seven a.m. shifts, so five in the morning was the best time for the run.

Mid-October in Kansas City is also too cold for her. But in truth, Tlali has the Ferrari of metabolisms and boasts perfect muscle tone on a slim figure with zero effort, while if I so much as look at chocolate, it goes straight to my hips.

I smile. Chocolate is so worth it.

While I'd never even dreamt of picking up running, Mandy coerced us into being part of an exhibit she is doing for a prominent art gallery. She calls it her Día de Muertos retrospective. And only because the three of us have been best friends since we were literally babies did

Mandy convince Tlali and me into being part of her living sculpture. We'll be posing as statues during opening night. She also enlisted one of our mutual friends, Valentina, who used to be a freaking professional athlete, and two other paid models. That's right. I will be nearly naked. With body paint. On a platform. Next to four other women with perfect bodies, two of whom are professional models.

Don't care. Chocolate is still worth it.

I will overlook the fact that I don't make it a full mile up the trail before I turn around and head back. I'm winded and have terrible shin splints. Not to mention my generous bust is strapped to my chest in the most uncomfortable sports bra in the world, which also happens to be the only thing making it possible for me to run without knocking myself out with my own boobs.

It's my first run. It'll get better.

I shut off my headlamp as the parking lot lights begin to flood onto the trail. Being on this trail before dawn feels like being in a dark forest. It's wonderfully spooky and has my creative juices flowing. I note details I know will make it into a scene for one of my horror novels, like how the shadows cast by the barren cottonwood trees slither toward the path like tendrils, even as the branches shake gently in the wind.

Joy Division's *Dead Souls* plays over my earbuds as I start my cool-down walk when something coils around my right ankle. I think it's a snake and let out a yell as I fall flat on my ass on the hard concrete. Whatever was around my ankle is now gone, and I yank my headphones out of my ears so I can hear any sounds as I frantically look for my headlamp and turn it back on.

When my eyes focus, I make out the silhouette of a person on the ground.

"Sorry," a man says.

I press my hand to my heart as my pulse races with fright.

"I didn't mean to scare you. Are you okay?" he asks.

That low, husky voice is one I recognize. I flash the light on the man's face, and he brings his hand up to block the beam as he uses the other to keep himself up in a sitting position. It's Dr. Logan Williams. The surgeon I've worked under for the last four months. What the hell is he doing on the ground?

CHAPTER 2

"Oh my god," I say. "Are you okay?"

"I had an accident on my bike and busted my ankle when I tried to stop."

I flash the light down his blood-speckled arm. I scan his body for injuries, but he seems fine except for the scrapes on his thick bicep. He's oriented, speaking, and holding himself up.

"Help me up?"

I cock my head to the side as I study him, trying to figure out if he's serious. Dr. Williams is about six one in height and I'd bet he weighs in at two-twenty—at least. No way my five-foot-five squishy-ass frame can help him to my car. "I don't think I can carry you by myself," I say.

"Only one of my ankles is twisted. I can put my weight on the other foot."

"Hold on," I say and jog the short distance to the parking lot.

A woman is stretching by her car, and I approach her with a smile. After she gets her headphones off, I tell her what's going on, and she agrees to help.

I think about how in a different place, this could be the start of a great serial killer movie—a couple who kills, luring victims to help in a dark, wooded area. Maybe that's the plot for my next novel?

But not in this part of Kansas City. This neighborhood is one of the safest.

She introduces herself as Stacy to Dr. Williams, and between the both of us, and after a lot of grunting, we have Dr. Williams on his foot, one arm around each of us. He hops his way to the parking lot with most of his weight on Stacy and me.

"My car's just right there," he says.

"Can you even drive? Your right ankle is busted."

"I can manage."

I roll my eyes. "How about I drive you to the hospital?" I ask as I point to my car so Stacy can help us in that direction. "You need to get that ankle x-rayed."

"You wouldn't mind?" Dr. Williams asks.

I have my change of clothes in the car, and I'd planned on showering at the hospital anyway. I shake my head. "No. I don't mind."

"Okay," he says and lets us help him into my car.

As he ducks to get in, I step back, not at all checking out his perfect, hard ass in bike shorts that are basically a second skin—or at least I'd never admit it to anyone.

"Thanks, Stacy," I say before getting in the driver's side of my little Hyundai SUV, and she waves before heading to the trail. When we're alone, I think about what he'd said. "Wait, did you say you were on your bike?"

Dr. Williams nods.

"Where's the bike?"

"Forget it," he says with a scowl. "Let's just go."

"Was it expensive?"

"It doesn't matter."

Before he has a chance to protest, I get out of my car and jog over to the spot where I'd found him. I get off the trail and carefully descend down the creek bank until I see the shimmer from a piece of hardware on the bike. I lift the bike, surprised at how light it is, and roll it back up the bank.

It takes me folding down the two back seats to get the bike to fit, but I manage to get it in despite Dr. William's many objections and interruptions, ordering me to leave it.

He's a stereotypical arrogant surgeon, but that bike looks expensive, and it isn't even that busted from the accident, just a bit scratched. No way I'd leave that bike behind.

Dr. Williams doesn't say much on the drive to Heartland Metro Hospital. Other than a few grunts and winces, silence fills the car. It's not awkward, though. In the four months I've worked with him, he's hardly said a full sentence to me, unless it was about a surgical case.

The only words he's really spoken to me have been in asking for the various instruments he requires for the heart surgeries we've worked on together. Until today when he asked me to help him up.

I don't play music during our ride because he has terrible taste in music. Like most surgeons, he plays music in the operating room, but he always shuts it off when he gets to the crux of the operation and doesn't resume it until he is back on safe ground. Even with that limited musical selection, I've come to realize Dr. Logan Williams has the worst taste in music of anyone in the entire hospital.

"So, how'd you end up down the creek bank?"

He doesn't turn in my direction, and I keep my eyes on the road.

"I'd rather not talk about it," he says dryly.

I press my lips together. If he weren't hurt—and technically my boss —I'd find this a little funny. About damn time his ego got a little bruised.

"I'm going to think about it all day if you don't tell me. I'm obsessive like that. Can I at least get a hint? I mean, I *am* driving you to the hospital . . ."

Dr. Williams huffs next to me and looks out the window as he speaks again. "I was trying to avoid hitting something."

My nose scrunches up. The trail is pretty clear of people so early in the morning, but he'd said *something*. "Something?" I ask. "Shall we play twenty questions until I guess what you were avoiding?"

He grunts. "I'm not in the mood."

"Then tell me—or we can go on like this forever—"

"Fine. It was a bunny, okay?" he snaps. "A little rabbit hopped out onto the trail, and I swerved to avoid hitting it."

I bite back my smile while he stews. His thick arms cross over a form-fitting athletic shirt that doesn't leave his pectoral muscles to the imagination. Somehow, I manage not to laugh at his scowl when I think of the arrogant, grumpy, hotshot surgeon flat on his ass to save a little bunny. It's actually kind of sweet. Who would have thought?

I pull up to the emergency loading bay, and a nurse approaches the car. I get out and ask him for a wheelchair after I brief him on the patient. The nurse helps Dr. Williams to the chair and thank goodness for that because I'd almost thrown out my back getting him off the ground at the trail.

Before the nurse gets a chance to do so, I kneel to lower the wheelchair's footrests, then take Dr. Williams's injured foot and place it gingerly over one of them. While I do this, I glance up at Dr. Williams to check for any grimaces indicating pain, but his eyes are fixed on . . . something. One corner of his mouth tugs upward, and I follow his gaze all the way to my boobs. My still-drenched, wet-t-shirt contest boobs in all the glory that is daylight. It takes everything in me not to grin like an idiot at having caught him gawking at my body. I don't call him out on it, though. Any other day, I'd say *hey buddy, eyes up here,* but today he's in pain, and endorphins can help with that. So instead, I linger two seconds too long until he peels his eyes from my chest and shakes his head.

"You don't have to come in with me," Dr. Williams says, his eyes fixed to the ground in front of him as I stand to follow when the nurse wheels him in.

"I don't mind. I want to make sure you're settled and okay."

His brows furrow together, but he stays quiet.

"Dr. Williams, what happened?" The ER doctor recognizes him, and he gets the royal treatment from then on, even as he refuses pain medication. I smile when he asks for a consult with Dr. Bel from the Orthopedics department, and I make a mental note to tell Mandy her husband is a sought-after ortho god.

"Well, you're all set," I say. I'm about to tell him I'll see him later, but since he is now a patient, I guess he won't be going to work today, so I stop myself. "I'll get going." I can always arrange to get his bike to him later.

Dr. Williams turns to me with confusion etched on his brows as if he's forgotten all about me, then he remembers. "Right," he says. "And, I'm sorry, um . . . but I don't think I got your name."

My head cocks to the side. What? "I'm sorry, I don't . . ." I trail off, realization hitting me like a freight train. He doesn't recognize me. I blink once, then twice. He has no idea who I am.

This entire time . . . he thought we were strangers.

Sure, he's always seen me in scrubs, with my hair in a surgical cap and a surgical mask on my face, my body swallowed in oversized scrubs, but we've been working together for four months.

Four months.

Shouldn't he know my voice by now? My eyes? Hell, shouldn't he know what my face looks like outside of the operating room?

To be fair, Dr. Williams is classically handsome and freaking hot. Those piercing blue eyes framed by thick black brows make many a nurse swoon around him. He would be hard to forget in or out of scrubs.

But while I'm not a major babe, I do all right. Sure, I'm curvy, but I've been told I have a great rack. And even if my face is a bit round, I'm kind of pretty. I wouldn't be quite so forgettable after four months of daily interaction.

Would I?

Dr. Williams's posture becomes rigid when I take too long to answer, my jaw slack as I think of what to say.

But I don't get the chance to correct his blunder because a nurse wheels him away to x-ray.

CHAPTER 3

As expected, Dr. Williams rescheduled his surgeries the day of the accident, but he showed up today for his regular schedule. He is curt and brief as always when he shows up at the O.R. He mentions nothing about the accident, so I don't either.

He never acknowledges me or gives any indication he now remembers me. He should be putting two and two together by now. I made excuses for him after I got home yesterday. He was in pain and embarrassed that he'd fallen off his bike—that's why he didn't recognize me outside of the O.R. uniform.

But then I reasoned he'd feel pretty silly when he showed up to work and realized it was me, his scrub tech of four months, who'd found him on the trail and driven him to the hospital.

But that realization never came, and I decided to keep his bike hostage as punishment. He could have it back when he pulled his head out of his ass.

When he asks the circulating nurse to wipe his forehead for the third time in the first hour of a three-hour surgery, I know something is off. We're repairing a heart valve in a fifty-five-year-old woman, a procedure he could do in his sleep, but his posture is . . . off somehow. He's standing; clearly, his ankle is only sprained. He has a brace on—I checked before starting on the surgical case—but he seemed fine initially. Still, he must be putting a lot of weight on it, and I figure he must be uncomfortable.

I am so distracted by his change in behavior, I don't realize when I snicker out loud as "Ice Ice Baby" starts playing on his playlist. Dr. Campbell, the first-year resident on the case, looks up at me, and I can tell he is smiling despite the surgical mask because it has spread to his eyes.

Dr. Williams clears his throat. "What's so funny?" he asks, not glancing up from the surgical field.

"Excuse me, Doctor. I didn't realize I laughed out loud."

"It's fine. Please share with the room what you were laughing at."

My eyes widen, and I look to the circulating nurse for help, but she only shrugs, offering none. Next, I turn to Dr. Campbell, who only gives me an encouraging nod.

It's my turn to clear my throat. "It's the music."

"You don't like my playlist?" he asks.

"Um . . ." Is it getting hot in the operating room? That would be impossible since the temperature is strictly controlled. It's definitely just me in the hot seat. "It's not really my style," I say finally.

"You've never complained about my music before," Dr. Williams says.

"No, Doctor. It's your O.R. I wouldn't."

He continues to work, explaining his next steps to Dr. Campbell until they get to a routine step.

"It's not just my O.R. It belongs to all of us. We should all enjoy the music."

I blink, unsure what to say. He's never expressed anything like this in the past. All surgeons pick their own music and make demands about when to start playing it or if they need it to stop so they can concentrate. None of the surgeons I've worked with have ever offered up music rights. For a man who has never said a word to me except for curt hellos before cutting open the person on the table in front of us, this simple statement surprises the hell out of me.

He asks the circulating nurse to track forward to the next song on the playlist.

"You don't have to do that—" I start to say, but he cuts me off.

"It's not a problem."

But then "My Heart Will Go On" by Celine Dion comes up, and it's everything I can do not to lose it. I hand Dr. Williams his next instrument, and my lips are pressed together, but Dr. Campbell must notice my shoulders shaking from the suppressed laughter, because he discreetly shakes his head at me.

The song goes on into the chorus, and I just can't. I let the laughter rip through me, and Dr. Campbell joins me. A heart surgeon performing an operation on a heart to "My Heart Will Go On"—priceless.

"What's so funny now?" Dr. Williams asks.

"Nothing, Doctor," I say, still chuckling.

"I'd like to know if I'm the butt of a joke in my own O.R. Answer honestly, please."

I think about that for a moment and hand him the next instrument I know he needs before he asks for it. "If I can speak honestly, without fear of repercussions . . ."

"Of course," he assures me.

"Well, um. Dr. Williams. No offense, but you have the absolute worst taste in music on the entire surgical floor."

Dr. Campbell laughs, and this time, the circulating nurse is laughing with us.

"I'm sorry," I say.

"No. No. It's good. I value honesty." Then after another moment he adds, "I take it no matter what plays next on my playlist, it will not be well-received?"

"I haven't yet heard anything worth listening to during any surgery I've worked with you." I think about the last four months and remember he doesn't know me even though I've been practically glued to his hip during that time, and the anger washes over me again.

"What would you recommend, then?" he asks.

"Your music is fine, Doctor."

"No, please. You sound like an expert on the subject. I'd like to know what you would enjoy during work hours."

"Oh, I don't know. Queen. The Who. Black Sabbath. Dragonforce. Though if you ask me, it's all about the original American punk before the British invasion."

"Punk?" he asks.

"Yeah. You know, Iggy, Television, Patti Smith?" Silence follows. "You have no idea who any of them are, do you?"

Dr. Williams shakes his head, so I continue, "Well, if you want something more contemporary, you can't go wrong with Tool, Evanescence, Kitty, Il Niño, or even Puscifer."

"Excuse me?" Dr. Williams snaps.

I laugh. "It's spelled P-U-S-C-I-F-E-R. Not what you're thinking."

"A bit of a music snob, Estrada? You only listen to rock?" Dr. Campbell asks.

"No, but it's my favorite, as well as Spanish rock, but you wouldn't know any of those bands. I listen to some electronic, like Infected Mushroom, too."

"Dr. Campbell," Dr. Williams says, "do you agree with the prescribed playlist?"

"I only know half the bands she listed," Dr. Campbell admits.

"I like Queen," the nurse interjects. "And Patti Smith."

Dr. Williams nods with approval at her. "What about you, Campbell? What do you like from her list?"

Dr. Campbell chuckles. "Puscifer's not bad. But I also like Patti Smith and Queen."

Then Dr. Williams surprises the hell out of Dr. Campbell and me when he asks the circulating nurse to find the suggested artists to play next on his phone. "Rev 22-20"—one of my favorites—plays first, and I smile. When the song wraps, I ask him, "So? What do you think?"

"Not bad. Thank you for the suggestions. Do you have a favorite band I should listen to?"

I smile wide. "Yes. Easy. Industrial November."

"Well, *them* I know," Dr. Williams says. "You'd have to be living under a rock to not know them."

You'd also have to live under a rock to not know your coworker of four months, but I don't say that. Instead, I stew as he plays Industrial November's entire first album, *Metal Red Day*, followed by Patti Smith's *Horses* album.

Three hours later, once the patient is closed after a successful surgery, Dr. Williams grabs his phone and exits the O.R., not once looking me in the face. Did he ever look me in the eyes? Hell, he hadn't even done it when I'd driven him to the hospital.

He will never know who I am because he'll never make the effort to see those around him as people worth his time.

～

"OH, NO," Tlali gasps when she sits in front of me at the cafeteria. "What happened?"

"Why do you think something happened?"

Tlali grabs the empty chocolate pudding cup from my tray as I take a spoonful of the second one. "You devour these when you have a bad day at work. You lose a patient?"

I set the pudding cup down. "No. I didn't lose a patient."

"Then what?"

I take a deep breath and tell her everything that happened, from the mishap during my run to the surgery we just wrapped up.

"No!" She draws her hand to her mouth.

"Yep. Four months, Tlali. *Four months* working together, and he doesn't even know my name."

"What an ass!" Tlali says with blind solidarity.

"You know what the worst part is?" I ask. "When I first worked for him, he started requesting me for all his surgeries. I'd been so proud back then. For a surgeon of his caliber to request me in his O.R., it felt . . ."

"Like you were special?" she asks.

"Yeah," I say sadly.

"We aren't indispensable, Izel. Not like surgeons are."

"I know. But it was nice, you know? To get a little recognition for all the hard work. Now I know he just wanted my robot hands and probably got used to my style and didn't want to change that up and have to retrain his next robot."

"Are you going to tell him it's you and give his bike back?" Tlali asks.

I shake my head. "No. That bike can rot in the garage for all I care."

"What will you do?"

"What can I do?"

"Ask the charge O.R. manager to change your schedule so you can work with another surgeon. You're friends with her, right?"

"Yeah, Gina's cool. Maybe I can get her to trade me with another scrub tech."

"There you go." Tlali opens the third pudding cup she stole from me. She doesn't need to worry about gaining weight before the living statue exhibit like I do. She could eat one hundred pudding cups and not gain a pound.

What a sucky day.

~

When I get home that night, I add a new character into the next chapter of my novel. The character's name is Hogan. He is tall, muscular, and has blue eyes. I snicker as I write his slow, painful death scene at the hands of my stealthy serial killer.

~

Gina has a box of chocolates coming her way because before my next shift, she's already moved schedules around. I don't have to see that jerk ever again. Hallelujah. My first case of the day is with a different surgeon, and everything goes mostly smoothly. I'm not used to her style, but I'm sure I'll be able to anticipate her movements better within a couple of weeks.

We wrap up the two-hour surgery, and I head to the front desk intending to thank Gina, but the look on her face stops me in my tracks. Her eyes widen when she sees me, then she shakes her head in defeat.

"What's wrong?" I ask her.

"I'm so sorry, Izel," Gina says. "I changed your schedule with another scrub tech for the week, but after his morning surgery, Dr. Williams came out requesting you back."

"No, Gina," I whine, though I know she tried.

I also know how much shit O.R. managers get from the surgeons. I wince, imagining Dr. Williams shouting at Gina because of me. I should get her those chocolates anyway.

"Is it something I should know about? Or that Human Resources should know about?" Gina asks, her brows pinched together with concern.

I hang my head. "No. Call it personality differences—"

Gina lets out a laugh. "Yeah, we all have those with the surgeons around here. You think another surgeon will be any different?"

"Fine, maybe I'd like to see a little more diversity in the cases I work. Why am I the designated cardiothoracic scrub tech? Why can't you throw me an ortho case or a general case once in a while?"

She passes me a funny look and rests her hand on her hip. "I thought you knew."

"Knew what?"

"Since his first week here, Dr. Williams has requested the same surgical staff for each of his surgeries."

"What?"

Gina nods.

I remember his first week on the job. Everyone in the cardio department had kissed his ass, trying to lure the world-class prodigy surgeon to Heartland Metro. I was a little nervous of fucking up when we were trying to make a good impression on him. But I didn't, and all the surgeries we worked on together that first week were successes.

How stupid had I been to believe all this time he'd been requesting *me* specifically? I am not special. It was the entire *surgical staff* he wanted a repeat of every day, not me.

And while a doctor making such a request wouldn't be common, I see how the hospital would bend over backward to get him to stay.

I take a deep breath. "All right. When do I get back on his service?"

"Your next case starts in an hour."

"In an hour?" I nearly shout.

"Yep. I had nothing to do with it. Get some lunch. I already had someone put together your case cart so you can go straight in after your break."

Small mercies. I sigh. "Thanks, Gina, you know, for trying."

～

THE NEXT SURGERY IS A DISASTER. Long gone is the conversation from the previous day about music. Dr. Campbell joins us again, and he sends me empathetic glances of solidarity when he can sneak them in.

I'm furious that Dr. Williams had the gall to request me again without even knowing my damn name. And still not a single thank you for getting him to the hospital after his bike wreck.

Nothing.

The anger spills over and starts to affect my work. Twice, Dr. Williams has to clear his throat to force my hands to give him an instrument he needs. I know a place or two where he could shove those instruments.

I've spoiled him. He doesn't need to ask for what he needs before I hand it to him. All surgeons ask for what they need. What makes him so special? The ass.

After the third clearing of his throat to grab my attention, he turns briefly to glare at me. I shrug and move my hands to keep working.

Once again, he says nothing before he leaves the O.R. when we are done. I stomp over to the front desk where Gina is standing in front of the board with the surgical case schedule. She's concentrating on something, so she doesn't notice me at first.

I take a deep breath because I'm about to do something I swore I'd never do. Not since my first year as a scrub tech when I used to take any and all shifts they'd give me until I had gained experience and established a reputation.

"Gina," I say.

She starts and turns to me. "How'd it go?"

"Not good."

"Wanna talk about it, sugar?"

"No. But I need to ask a favor—"

"I told you, I can't go against—"

"Give me the night shift."

"What?"

"Just for a month. I need a break from him. I'll take on-call the entire month if that's what it takes."

Gina's brow floats upward. "We won't have a shortage of techs who will want to trade; you don't need to pick up a month of call."

"Whatever it takes, Gina. Please."

I TEXT TLALI, who tells me she's on the third floor. I duck into the elevator to go vent to her when Dr. Ramirez gets in the elevator with me.

"Hi, Izel," she says cheerily at me, and I clench my jaw tight.

"See?" I snap. "It's not so hard!"

Dr. Ramirez turns slowly and blinks at me. "Uh . . ."

"Sorry," I say. "You hardly know me. We barely cross paths at work, and you know my name."

Dr. Ramirez laughs. "You're Mandy's cousin, and she was the best research assistant I ever had before she went and quit on me. Of course I know you," she finishes with a smile. "Everything okay?"

I shake my head.

"Is it about Dr. Williams?"

"That obvious?"

She nods. "If I may," she starts cautiously, "surgeons can be tough. But cut him some slack. They need to be arrogant to do what they do. As for you, just remember that you making your surgeon as efficient as possible is saving a life as much as he is—if not more. The lives you save are worth the bad days."

She's right, of course. His arrogance doesn't overpower the joy I have for my job. I take a deep breath. Dr. Ramirez is one of the smartest people in the entire hospital—and one of the most well-liked. I study her for a moment.

"You don't happen to need a scrub tech, do you?" I ask her.

She laughs. "If I were a surgeon, I'd take you in a heartbeat. But if you ever want to change fields, I'm always looking for good research assistants. In the meantime—here," she says and digs into her white coat pocket, producing a bite-sized Twix candy bar and placing it in my hand. "I hope your day gets better."

I would seriously consider working for that woman instead if it wouldn't mean a significant pay cut. I'm sought after, damn it! Logan Williams doesn't know how good he has it.

CHAPTER 4

uck my life. I'm called the very first night of my on-call night shift. I grab a disgusting energy drink because I haven't had enough time to adjust to the shift change. I'm all too glad it's nearly dawn when the call comes in.

I get to the hospital and prep the O.R. quickly. I am counting instruments and supplies when the on-call surgeon, Dr. Adams, walks in. I used to work with her quite a bit before Dr. Williams joined Heartland Metro but have barely seen her since.

"Izel." Dr. Adams beams at me when she sees me. "I've missed you." She starts scrubbing for surgery.

"I've missed you too," I say.

I'm glad the surgical case is a simple appendectomy that shouldn't take that long so I can go back to sleep, though it'll be morning by the time I get home. Not to mention, Dr. Adams is one of the few surgeons who has her feet firmly planted on the ground and actually learns her colleagues' names. Not that I'm comparing her to anyone in particular.

"Glad that hog Williams finally let someone else have you for a change," she says, and I laugh. If she only knew.

As I WALK over to the nurse's station, I skim the patient's chart to sign it and hand it to Gina, but Dr. Williams's booming voice gets louder as I get to the desk. He and Dr. Monica Lopez, the Chief of Cardiothoracic Surgery, are huddled around Gina next to the surgical board.

I get behind the desk, pretending I'm still charting as they argue.

"No. I want the same surgical tech on my service. Cancel today's surgery—" Dr. Williams yells.

"We're not rescheduling surgeries for staff preferences, Dr. Williams," Dr. Lopez says. Her voice is gentle but commanding. It's strange, seeing the short woman with cinnamon skin keeping her posture tall as this incredibly privileged, tall man yells down at her. But it shouldn't be strange because it's fucking fantastic. I almost want to high-five her.

She keeps her ground, her hands firm on her hips, a defiant look on her face.

"I'm not operating without my regular staff," he says more quietly but still huffing.

"Gina," Dr. Lopez says, "apart from the scrub tech, does Dr. Williams have everyone from his regular staff?"

"Yes, Doctor," Gina says.

"There you go, Dr. Williams," she says and smiles as if to say, *watch your tone, boy.*

Dr. Williams snatches his scrub cap from his head and starts rubbing his temples, his black waves falling in a mess over his forehead. "I need my regular scrub tech," he says with his eyes closed.

"What's your scrub tech's name?" Dr. Lopez asks.

Dr. Williams's eyes fly to her, a question in them. "Excuse me?"

"Their name, Williams. What is it?"

"I-I . . . uh," he stammers.

It's all I can do not to snicker. I want to kiss Dr. Lopez's feet for putting him in his place. Watching him squirm under her questioning glare tastes better than any queso dip in the world. I look up at Gina, the corners of her eyes tightening as they narrow at me. I discreetly shake my head, trying to convey telepathically that she shouldn't offer him help right now.

"Williams, I don't have all day," Dr. Lopez says.

He lets out a long breath. "I don't know."

"Here's a little lesson in leadership," she says. "People stay at a job for more than just a paycheck. They can get a paycheck anywhere else. They stay because they love their jobs, or they love the people they work with. In my experience, scrub techs love their jobs. Which leads me to believe it is the people they work with that would drive them away."

"You think she's avoiding me?"

"Well, at least you know she's a woman." Dr. Lopez scoffs. "Gina, how long has this tech worked with Dr. Williams?"

"Since Dr. Williams joined us," Gina says.

"What's that? Four months you've worked next to the same person without learning her name?"

All three of us are looking at Dr. Williams now, and he nervously scratches his jaw. "I'll learn her damn name. Just get her back!" he snaps and storms off.

Dr. Lopez and Gina give each other a look with a shake of their heads before Dr. Lopez leaves me to Gina's mercy.

Gina brings her hands to her hips, mimicking Dr. Lopez's body language, I realize, and pins me with her glare. It's all I can do not to cower into the chair I've settled in next to the computer.

I laugh nervously. "Thanks for not outing me."

"He didn't know it was you. You sat right here the entire time, and he didn't know it was you."

I shrug, and her eyes narrow to slits. "Is that why you wanted the change?"

"Mostly," I say truthfully, not wanting to get into the circumstances surrounding his accident. "Look, I don't want to cause any more trouble. Put me back on his service if you need to. Okay?"

CHAPTER 5

It's Friday night, and I'm not on call. So Tlali, Mandy, and I decide to have a bit of a girls' night and touch base on the sculpture and our roles, because el Día de Muertos is coming up right around the corner. Mandy has yet to tell us what exactly we will be doing.

As usual, Mandy is late to our favorite bar across the street from the hospital, and Tlali and I start on our first round of margaritas without her.

"How're you doing with the night shift?" Tlali asks.

I shrug. "I don't think I'll be able to keep it much longer. I'm just making things difficult for Gina," I say. "You? How's work been? I haven't even asked lately."

Tlali smiles. "Good. There's actually this—"

Mandy interrupts the conversation when she slumps in her seat. "I'm so sorry, guys. Lulu's driving me insane," she says about her son.

"You never have to apologize," I tell Mandy. "We know you're a mom. Is my nephew with Elio or your parents tonight?"

"Elio," she says with a dreamy smile as she thinks of her hunky hubby. I envy what they have. Mandy and Elio met at the hospital and are crazy about each other. Maybe that's why I'm still single. I measure everyone by Mandy and Elio's love story yardstick. *They didn't always like each other*, a little voice in my head whispers, though I'm not sure why.

"Anyway," Mandy says, "you two excited about the show?"

As Tlali says yes, I bring my margarita to my lips and start gulping it. I need the next one to be a double. Mandy's eyes narrow while she studies me.

"No, Izel. You can't flake out on me. Everything's arranged. I can't change things around now."

I raise my hands in surrender. "I didn't say anything," I whine.

"I know that look on your face. You want to back out," Mandy accuses me.

"I do want to back out, but I won't. When have I ever broken a promise?"

When our waitress stops by our table, I order queso dip with chips. I must look as nervous as I feel, because Tlali doesn't critique my order.

Mandy goes over the plan for the sculpture and our schedule for the day. I will go last, so I'll have less time to freak out once I'm in costume. She still hasn't told us exactly what we are wearing, though she has said it will be skimpy to show off the body paint she will be working on.

"You'll be great," Mandy says. "I promise you'll look beautiful. I wouldn't let you get on that platform looking anything less than spectacular. Do you trust me?" she asks.

I nod. "I need another one. You guys want a second round?"

"Get us a pitcher," Tlali says.

"Yeah," Mandy agrees. "Put it on my tab."

I head to the bar, and the pretty bartender gets my order right away despite how busy the bar is. "Thanks," I say while she starts putting together the pitcher.

Chewing on my bottom lip, I let my nerves take over. To be perfectly honest, I don't hate my body. I quite like it most days, even if I wish I were a little slimmer or didn't have those cellulite dimples on my thighs. But despite me being okay with all that, I don't enjoy displaying it in front of other people, let alone a room full of strangers.

Mandy better medicate me on the day of her exhibit if she intends to make this work.

"Hi," a man says. He's been sitting at the bar the entire time, and now faces me.

Logan Williams.

Fuck. Why can't I escape this man? The universe hates me.

I blink at him. "Hi," I say.

"Do I know you?"

My eyes narrow at him. "Nope, don't think so," I say and fix my gaze on the bartender. She has the pitcher on a small round tray and is rimming three glasses with salt. Why is she taking so long?

"Yeah. I think I know you," he says. I can tell from the corner of my eye he is leaning over to study my face. He gets so close to me, his beer-laced breath caresses my ear. It's hot, and the sensation raises goose-bumps down my arm.

"I'm Logan," he says, but I don't turn to face him again.

"That's nice." I smile tightly and take the tray the bartender hands me. I pivot on my heel and head back to the table.

"Oh my god, were you just talking to Dr. Williams?" Tlali asks when I'm back with them.

I nod. "He still doesn't know who I am," I say. "He just introduced himself to me."

Mandy pours her glass to the rim. "Wait, don't you work with Dr. Williams?"

"I do."

"Then I don't understand," Mandy says.

Tlali proceeds to tell Mandy the whole story, and I glance up at the bar to find Logan twisted around in his barstool so he can look at me. I look away immediately; it must be the alcohol that has my heart racing.

As Tlali rambles on about everything that's been going wrong in my life, I steal glances up at the bar, and he never stops looking at me. He leans back, his elbow propped on the bar-top, his jean-clad thighs wide in a man-spread. But his eyes are locked on me. What the hell is his problem? I have half a mind to march up there and tell him what's what, but Mandy grabs my attention when Tlali finishes talking.

"Please tell me you wrote him into one of your novels," Mandy says.

I nod. "His name is Hogan."

Mandy's head falls back with her signature obnoxiously loud laughter. It's contagious, and soon Tlali and I are laughing too.

"That is gold," Mandy says through the laughter.

Then Tlali lifts her glass, proposing a toast. Mandy and I raise our glasses to meet hers.

"To Hogan's painful death," Tlali says, and we all laugh.

Mandy and I both cheer, "To Hogan!"

CHAPTER 6

Two wonderful weeks—that's how much Logan-free time I have. I stay on the night shift for much of that time until Gina eases me back onto the day shift. Bless her heart, she actually gave me a couple of days to adjust back to the new schedule before returning me to Logan's service. Ugh. I have to see his face again tomorrow.

I'm prepping the O.R. for my last happy surgical case with Dr. Adams, and I am counting instruments and supplies when I hear foot-falls approach. I think it's the circulating nurse assigned to the case until I hear his voice, and my hands freeze mid-count.

"Izel," Logan says. "It is Izel, right?"

Crap. I lost count. My nostrils flair at the interruption. I spin on my heel slowly until we are facing each other. His eyes are locked on mine like they've never been before, and the breath trapped in my surgical mask heats up.

"Can I help you, Doctor?" I ask, confused as to why he is in the O.R. This isn't his case.

"Am I saying your name right?"

I shake my head. "No. It's not with a soft 'Z.' Pretend there's a 'T' before the 'Z,'" I say.

He tries it again, mouthing the syllables slowly, and I nod, giving him the approval he seeks. "That's right," I say.

Now he suddenly cares what my name is and how to pronounce it? After months working together? He shouldn't be doing this with me so close to a scalpel. Men are stabbed for less every day. At least in my novels.

Logan crosses his arms over his chest as he seems to mull over what he needs to say. Good lord, is he uncomfortable? Okay, this is a bit amusing, and I'm glad he can't see my smirk.

"I'm sorry, Doctor, but I have to finish prepping before my surgeon shows up. If there isn't anything—"

"Your surgeon?" he asks, his eyes narrowing.

I nod.

"I thought I was your surgeon," he says.

"You know what I mean—the surgeon on the case. I like to be ready on time," I say stupidly.

"Yes. I know . . . look, I was told you requested off my service." He pauses, waiting for acknowledgment on my part, but I'm not going to confirm what is glaringly obvious. "I thought we worked well together. Didn't we?"

"It wasn't bad," I say, because it really wasn't, not up until his accident and everything that followed. "Except for the music," I add. "That was bad."

"Is that why you left? My taste in music? Because you're more than welcome to pick the music from here on out. I actually listened to everyone you suggested and really enjoyed it all."

I blink at him. He listened to all my suggestions? Somehow, I find that hard to believe, given his tastes. "That's not why I requested off your service; as much as you tortured your O.R. with that noise, I had other reasons."

"Any you'd care to share?"

"Not really," I quip.

He sighs. "I can't fix something if I don't know what it is. I'm not a mind reader," he says.

"Fix?"

"Yes, Izel. I want to fix whatever I did wrong. Or apologize if I said something . . ."

There he went again. Saying my name. That's twice now since I've known him that he's said my name. "There's really no need. Gina already put me back on your service starting tomorrow. I thought you knew."

He nods. "I did, but I'd rather you come back because you want to and not because you're being forced to. If you're back, I'd like things to go back to the way they were before. You are a great scrub tech. The best I've ever had."

I chew my bottom lip as I think and let him squirm in the silence for a couple of beats. "It's hard to be honest, being your subordinate and all."

"Please. Speak freely. Anything you say in this O.R. today will be between us only."

"Okay. I'd rather not go back to the way things were. That's what I was trying to get away from. Like, think of Dr. Adams—"

"The general surgeon?"

"Yes. She walks into her O.R., says hello to every staff member, including environmental service when she wraps up, and," I narrow my eyes, "she knows all our names."

He has the decency to hang his head for a second before snapping his head back up. "I know I'm an arrogant asshole—"

"I'll say," I blurt out before I can stop myself. But fuck it. He gave me carte blanche to say how I feel, so I'm going to take it.

I almost wish we weren't in the O.R. so I could see his full features when I say that, because the way his eyes crinkle at the corners, I think he might actually be smiling under his mask.

"Would you give me a chance to do better? To be better?"

I consider his request for a moment. I don't believe for a minute he's willing to let me work for another surgeon, but I want to believe him.

I'm still a little hurt that he can't piece everything together. He has yet to match me, his scrub tech, with the girl who saved his ass on the bike trail or the girl he wouldn't stop staring at in the bar the other night. In his distracted brain, those three girls are different people.

But he did say I'm the best surgical tech he's ever had. That polishes a sense of pride deep in my ribcage. And for a surgeon like him to reduce himself to begging like this . . . let's just say I'm standing a little bit taller when I give him my answer.

"One more chance," I say, then take a liberty I never thought I would when I add, "but don't screw it up again, Logan."

WHEN LOGAN SHOWS up for our first surgery together since his apology, I force a chuckle to die in my chest when he stops to ask the environmental worker who's finishing cleaning up in the O.R. his name. He's trying, at least.

"Hello, Izel," he says, locking eyes on mine.

"Dr. Williams," I say and tip my chin.

"Not Logan today?" he teases.

"Wouldn't be professional now that my hall pass is over."

"I'll see you in there."

The circulating nurse on staff gives me a funny look when Logan asks me questions as he opens up the patient to start the operation. I just shrug at her.

"How long have you been a scrub tech?" is his first question.

"I started a year before you came to Heartland."

"That's it? Your hands seem more experienced."

"Thank you," I say.

"Is this what you always wanted to do?"

I shake my head, though he never glances up from the surgical field, so he can't see. "No. I'm not sure I'll do this forever, either."

"Oh?" His voice hardens, and I know he's wondering if I'm trying to quit being a surgical technologist all together.

"I have some . . . creative pursuits."

"Please elaborate," he says, and I shift my weight from one leg to the other. What is this? Twenty questions?

If he is trying to make up for years of not getting to know me in one day, he has another think coming. I glance at the resident and intern on the case huddled around the patient, but their eyes are glued to the now-exposed heart.

"I write," I quip.

"Really?"

"Yes."

"Are all your answers going to be that short?"

Apart from T'lali and Mandy, no one at work knows about my novels or that I have been trying to get a literary agent for the past year. I'm not sure I'm ready to reveal so many details.

Fear of failure has everything to do with my apprehension. What if I never get an agent? What if I never get published? I wince, thinking of all the dreaded questions in the years to come. How's the writing going, Izel? When can I buy your book?

"I don't want to be a distraction—"

"This bit's easy. We can talk for a while still. I'll tell you if I need quiet to concentrate, though you already know when that will be."

It's true. I'm always the one to ask the circulating nurse to cut the music when he needs it. His body signals his need for concentration. His hands stop moving, hovering over the surgical field, his head dipping the tiniest centimeter. But really, it's that moment when his chest rises with a deep breath as he makes his next call that lets me know he's about to make a risky decision.

"Okay," I say. "What do you want to know?"

"What do you write?"

If there is a time to speak my dreams into the universe, it is now. "Horror," I say.

"Really?" he asks, and even the two other surgeons look up at me for a second with surprise.

"Why do you sound surprised?"

"Pegged you for chick lit or children's books," Logan says.

I scoff loudly because I know he can't see my deep eye-roll.

"What?" he asks defensively.

"I'm a scrub tech. I'm just as hard-core as you. Not that there's anything wrong with chick-lit or children's books. I read both," I rant.

"I didn't mean any offense."

We say nothing for a long while, pausing for some questions from the intern and resident, but like he is on a personal mission to get to know me, he returns to his interrogation.

"So, you're going to be like the next Stephen King?"

"No. I want to be the next Lauren Beukes."

"Who's that?" Logan asks.

"I know you can't see me right now, but I'm rolling my eyes."

Logan lets a chuckle rumble up from deep in his chest. The sound is husky and surprising. It's also alien, and I don't know what to make of this new humor he seems to be hell-bent on injecting into his O.R.

"Stephen King is great, don't get me wrong, but Lauren Beukes is the best living horror author."

"I'll check her out," he says. "Given your music lesson a few weeks back, I get the feeling I'll like your taste in books. And maybe one day I'll get to buy a book by Izel Estrada from the bookstore."

The way he said it wasn't how I expected it to land. There was no expectation, no pressure. One day. He understands it's still a dream I'm working toward.

"If you do check her out, start with *Broken Monsters*, then *The Shining Girls*."

"Are you an only child—"

"Dr. Williams, what are you doing?" I ask.

He clears his throat. "I thought it was obvious. I'm trying to get to know my staff better."

"This feels more like an interrogation."

"What do you mean?"

"If you are trying to get to know your staff, you should open the conversation to more than just me. And if you are okay with a little friendly advice, part of getting to know someone is offering something about yourself too. Why don't you let us get to know you, too?"

"Maybe during our next surgery. We can take turns."

CHAPTER 7

"Nope," I say. "Not gonna happen. Nope. Not enough tacos in the world to make me do this."

Tlali and Valentina stand three feet apart from Mandy and me. They are both in costume, and the body paint line work is done on both of them, though they haven't started to fill in the color yet. Mandy's two assistants are painting the two professional models. They will paint Tlali and Valentina next, and I'm stuck with Mandy doing my entire body paint from start to finish.

"Here." Tlali hands me a glass of champagne. I tip my head back as I chug until it's gone.

"Please, Izel," Mandy says. "I have a vision!"

I blink at her, looking between her, the small fabric triangles she claims are my costume, and the sketches on the table in front of me.

The sketches are beautiful, and I have to hand it to her; she got my pear body shape perfectly. But it's one thing to see it on a sketch and a completely different thing to bare so much skin for an hour in front of strangers.

In her sketch of paper-Izel, the day of the dead Catrina makeup on one half of my face is spectacular. Half of my face and upper body is covered in black paint, with a meticulously drawn white skeleton over it. The side of my body not painted on with the skeleton is completely bare. Well, almost. Half my face has beautiful heavy makeup with a smokey eye and crimson lipstick that fades into skull's teeth on the opposite side of my face.

Then the paint dips down my neck, covers my arm, and crosses over my waistline to cover the opposite leg in the skeleton pattern. The other leg remains bare, long, and sexy, leading to a crimson stiletto slingback on the unpainted foot. The result is elegant, if a little bit creepy, but also intricate.

The problem is that the loincloth, because that's what it is, will only be secured over one side of my hip. I have yet to figure out how it's meant to stay in place or how it will cover my cheese-dip and margarita-loving rear. And don't get me started on the skin-toned backless, plunging bra. Does Mandy intend to glue these things onto me?

I committed to this. And I knew when Mandy refused to give specifics that today would be disastrous for my ego. I let out a deep breath.

"I'm going to need another one of those." I gesture to the empty champagne glass.

"Good," Mandy says, "but then I'm cutting you off. I need you to keep your balance and be perfectly still during the exhibit."

"How long are we supposed to be up there?"

"One hour as guests start arriving, then you have a thirty-minute break. We'll do any touch-ups needed during the break, then you go back for about half an hour while I say a few words and the photographer captures you in detail."

I chew my bottom lip.

"You're going to look fantastic," Valentina says.

I roll my eyes. Easy for her to say, with her perfectly honed muscles.

"I mean it," she says as if she can read my mind. "I'd kill for curves like yours and for a stomach as smooth as yours."

My instinct is to scoff because I definitely have a slight pooch with matching love-handles, but I'm glad I stop myself in time as my eyes roam over her middle and the battle scars from her fight with a disease that kills so many on display to the world tonight.

As if I suddenly have a key to Mandy's brain, I understand what she is trying to do. She doesn't want only cookie-cutter models as part of her living statue. She wants different types of women with varying types of bodies. Valentina's deeply tanned Mexican skin and Tlali's darker brown inherited from her Afro-Mexican father and Mexican mother will contrast perfectly against my pasty ass. My body is curvy and a bit fluffy; the soft edges will play against the hardness of Valentina's toned muscles, my smooth skin a foil to her scarred survivor's body.

"Listen to me," Mandy says after I stay quiet too long. She grabs my chin between her thumb and index finger to hold my gaze on her face. "You are Titian's *Venus of Urbino*, Botticelli's *Venus*. Alexandros's *Aphrodite*, Rubens's *Woman before the Mirror*. The greatest artists of all time painted and sculpted your body. And I want that body in my artwork tonight. If you really don't want to do this, I won't force you. But you're as beautiful as the other four women who will be up there with you."

"Hear, hear," one of the models calls out, and the other three co-conspirators answer in the same fashion. At the outpouring of encouragement, I get a déjà vu feeling of drunken experiences in ladies' bathrooms.

When Mandy lets go of my face, I lock eyes with Valentina, and for the first time since I've seen the sketches, I start to think about what my fellow statuettes are feeling. The models have done this a million times and are cool as cucumbers. I'm sure they are here for added professionalism. But I see insecurity in Valentina's eyes. She shrugs one shoulder and gives me a half-hearted smile. Tlali, for her part, stares at the ceiling, puffing up her chest, trying to make herself taller.

I'm not alone in my fears or insecurities tonight.

If they can do it, damn it, so can I.

"Okay," I say. "Let's get this over with."

As she works, I start to realize my paint is the most intricate. I glance down a few times to watch Mandy work, but she chastises me, not wanting me to see the work in progress until I can admire the finished product before the mirror.

She spends her time yapping, in true Mandy fashion, about the significance of Día de Muertos and how she did this exhibit to learn more about a part of her culture she knew little about. "Did you see any of my artwork on your way in?" Mandy asks, doing her best to distract me while she works.

"I'm sorry, Mandy. I'm being a shitty cousin, aren't I? This is your day."

"No, darling." She smiles up at me. "It's your day to shine."

"I only glanced at portraits quickly. I promise I'll come by later this week to admire them properly. But from what I saw, they were fantastic, Mandy. Really."

Mandy smiles and keeps painting my body. My face, chest, and arm are done when she goes into a rant about the Día de Muertos. She paints my waist, crossing over to the opposite hip before starting that leg as I listen to her. I only half know the history she's spewing, thanks to my Mom's ranting when I was a teenager. But I rejected everything about our culture when I rebelled, so not much stuck. I regret it now, but still, it's fascinating to learn about it now.

According to Mandy, it's a bit odd that we think of the holiday as a European celebration from our Spanish conquerors, because it all started with the Aztecs, though I suppose you could say the celebrations fused together. Mandy's portraits of Mexican women in Catrina makeup embody all that history in each canvas. I couldn't be prouder of her.

I have to hand it to her; she actually keeps my mind off what I'm about to do. Everything she talks about is so interesting, and I had little idea of most of it.

It takes Mandy nearly two hours to finish painting my face and body. I glance at myself in the mirror and gasp. My hair is up in braids now, and half of my round face is hollowed out into the painting of half a skull. The eye on the opposite side of my face has smokey eye makeup surrounded by a crimson flower spanning from above my eyebrow to my cheekbone, a delicate ruby-colored jewel on each flower petal.

The paint that covers my body conceals much of my flesh, giving the impression that I'm not entirely as naked as I feel. She painted half the bra on the side with the skeleton with black paint.

But I am not completely covered in paint, and the swell of my left breast visibly bulges above the bra. And absolutely nothing conceals the unpainted half of my stomach or love handle.

Still, her finished product is stunning. I'm stunning. Mandy crosses her arms over her chest and raises an eyebrow as if to say, *see?*

I nod at her because I do see. I see myself through her eyes, and hot damn, I look hot. With newfound confidence, I follow as she herds me and the other models toward the main gallery and places us perfectly on a three-foot platform just wide enough for the five of us.

"Oh, I almost forgot," Mandy says. She hops on the platform next to me and clasps a crimson lace choker around my neck.

I roll my eyes. "Right. Cuz I'd feel naked without *that*."

We each have ofrendas we must hold in our hands as part of the tableau. The first model holds a candle, and she lays horizontally at our feet. The second model has a bottle of tequila in her hand as she sits on a chair. Tlali stands to one side of me holding a small basket of pan de muerto, and Valentina holds a plate of tamales to my other side. Finally, Mandy hands me a glass of wine.

"It's not wine," Mandy says when I smile down at it.

"What?" I ask.

"Didn't want you going rogue. It's pomegranate juice."

"Thanks for the vote of confidence," I say and roll my eyes.

AFTER THE THIRD set of people walks up and gawks at us, leaning in to really admire the detail of Mandy's handiwork, my nerves start to settle. If my glass held wine, I wouldn't need to drink it to relax anyway.

In fact, as people sing Mandy's praises in front of us as if we are actual statues and comment on how beautiful we all look, I find it harder and harder to not smile.

"Keep your cool," Tlali whispers to me. Logan has just walked into the gallery with a date.

Easier said than done. The 'wine' ripples in the glass from my shaky hands. I don't move from my position on the sculpture, though. I'm a professional, damn it. I can do this.

As I track him with my eyes, I make note of the charcoal suit he's wearing and how it makes his blue eyes pop even more—as if that were possible. Underneath, a crisp white shirt and black tie. On his arm, a stunning woman, who I'm fairly certain is an anchor for the local news. In her perfect little black dress and stiletto heels, she seems nearly six feet tall—the ideal height for Logan Williams.

To my relief, they start with the massive portraits, which gives me time to collect my nerves before Logan and his date saunter over to us. The bell saves me before they reach us. We head out to the dressing room for our break and touch-ups.

I'm rattled and pace when we're alone.

"Are you okay?" Mandy asks. "I saw him."

"Yeah—no—a little shook, I guess. Wasn't expecting to see him here."

"Does she have to go back out there?" Tlali asks Mandy on my behalf, and they both look to me for answers.

"What?" I ask.

Mandy locks eyes with me. "Can you handle it? Having him here? I know he's your boss. I'd understand if you don't want him to see you like this. If you want to sit the next part out . . ." She trails off, not wanting to finish that sentence, and I see pain plain in her expression. The next part is the most crucial. If I'm not there for the photographer, Mandy will not have a full record of her art piece. "I can handle it," I say.

"Really?" Tlali asks, surprised.

"Really," I say, trying to reassure myself more than Mandy.

We get back on the platform, and everyone claps as we take our previous positions. The gallery manager announces that patrons will have ten minutes to admire the sculpture before they will need to clear the radius around the platform to make room for the photographer.

Several lines of people queue up around us, wanting a closer look before we dismantle. Right in front of me, three people back, stand Logan and his date.

My heart starts to race, and I clench the stem of the wineglass in my hand like a rock so that I don't shake it. The person in front of me leaves, and the next comes up, bringing them closer and closer to me.

Lord, give me strength.

When they finally get to me, they both eye me up and down. Logan's eyes flicker in . . . recognition? No. That's not it. I tear my gaze from him and look at the wall behind his head. They are just like any of the other people who got an up-close look at my body tonight. This is no differ-ent. I try—and fail—to soothe the nerves wreaking havoc in my chest.

I make the mistake of taking a deep breath, causing the swell of my breasts to rise in their tiny little bra. I take a quick peek down at my chest to make sure I'm still covered, though Mandy swore she'd keep an eye out and save my dignity if anything important was revealed. Finding the bra where it's supposed to be, I fix my gaze back at the wall.

"She is gorgeous," Logan's date says.

"Is she?" he asks and sips his white wine.

The woman throws her head back with laughter. "You don't have to do that," she says.

"Do what?" Logan asks.

"Pretend you don't have eyes when you're with me. You're human, and it's perfectly fine to admire that this woman has the best pair of tits I've ever seen—"

I don't flinch at the words, and somehow, they make me a bit taller. What is it with women fawning over me today? And why can't I always see myself through their eyes?

"Oh, I'm so sorry," she starts to say, looking up at my face. "Wow. That was weird. I forgot for a second that you're real and not an actual statue. Sorry, honey," she says up at me, but I stay frozen. Mandy will be so proud of me. I allow myself a half-smile at her before returning my face to stone.

They turn away to give the next person in line a chance to step up to the sculpture, and they think they are out of earshot when they continue their conversation.

They aren't.

"Admit it. That woman is gorgeous," she says, adamant as she teases Logan.

"If you say so."

"Anyone would say so," she says.

"Not my type. Too . . . curvy. I mean, look at her. She's too soft to pass for a statue."

"Too soft? You're joking! Those curves . . . my god, man, you are blind!"

I don't get a chance to hear the rest of their conversation as they move farther away. The juice in my glass is full-on sloshing with my anger, and I count to ten because I need to talk myself down from doing what I really want to do.

Too soft?

Too curvy? I LOVE my curves!

Maybe he is too damned hard and fit! Did he ever think of that?

Oh, the next time I hand Logan Williams a scalpel, it will be pointy end first!

"Cool, it," Tlali whispers.

"You hear that?" I ask, doing my best to not move my lips as I speak.

"Some," she says.

Mandy is at the other end of the gallery chatting with patrons and doesn't notice a damned thing. An eye on me my ass.

Too soft?! I try to remember everything Mandy had said to me earlier tonight about being Venus, Aphrodite, and the inspiration for all the artists she listed. I run her little speech over and over in my head, intending to distract myself, but then Logan's date says something funny, and their combined laughter booms in the gallery.

That does it.

"Excuse me," I quip at the man standing before me, and he blinks in surprise.

"What?" he asks.

"I need to step down, please."

The gentleman offers me a hand to help me down, and I smile at him, taking it while kicking off the single shoe and tossing it off the stage.

I march up to the still-laughing couple noiselessly as my bare feet stomp toward them. Logan's back is to me, and his date doesn't see me approaching on the other side of him.

When I'm right behind him, I step high on my tippy toes, and before anyone can stop me, reach as high as I can to let the pomegranate juice flow freely from the back of his head, down his neck, and trail all the way down his back.

"What the fuck!" he roars and spins around to face his attacker. When it registers that it's me, he takes a step back.

Several trails of red drip from his forehead, and the red stains on his white shirt are my trophies giving me all the courage I need. I take a step forward and jab a finger at his stained, hard chest.

"Too soft, am I?"

"No, I—"

"I am speaking," I hiss, and he blinks at me, his lips in a thin line while he wipes his brow with his hand, so I go on. "Don't interrupt me. Let me tell you something. It's an art event, so let's call it an education. I am Titian's *Venus of Urbino*. The same Venus birthed in Botticelli's painting. I am Rubens's *Woman Before the Mirror*. My body is Alexandros's Aphrodite, goddess of beauty, passion, and pleasure, unearthed from the depths of ancient Greece. But what do these great artists know about beauty? Clearly not more than you, sir. I will tell you one thing," I hiss through clenched teeth, "only a real man would know what to do with these curves."

His eyes widen, framed by crimson droplets speckled on his skin. His date, now at his side, drops her mouth into a small 'o,' then shoots me an apologetic look.

With a last burst of pride, I gather my breasts to secure the bra in place lest it fall off while I stomp back to the dressing room.

CHAPTER 8

I'm pacing, nearly naked, but unable to bring myself to put on a robe and ruin Mandy's work before the pictures when she hurries in the room with me.

"Oh my god, are you okay?"

I glare at her. I'm in this mess because of her. "No!" I snap. "The nerve—"

"That was amazing, Izel," Mandy says, and I stare at her.

"Amazing?" She nods and I start yelling. "I'm glad the most embarrassing moment of my life is amusing to you."

Mandy grabs a chair and sits, crossing her legs and flashing her bright, cherry-red platform heels.

"I'm sorry," I say, calmer now. "I ruined your piece, and now I'm shouting at you."

"Please don't be sorry. Remember my first real exhibit and all the drama back then?"

How could I forget? She'd loathed Elio before they'd fallen in love, and he'd been the cause of utter chaos on her first opening night.

"People love sensationalism. I sold every piece that night. And after your little stunt, I bet you every piece will sell tonight, too, or my name isn't Mandy Belmonte."

Small mercies, I think. At least I haven't ruined the night she's spent a year working toward.

"The art world loves this kind of thing. Don't worry," she says, the hint of a smile tugging at the corners of her lips.

To their credit, Valentina, Tlali, and the two models hadn't so much as flinched as I'd doused Logan Williams with blood-red juice. They are still out there in position. "I'm going to head out before the girls come back in here. I can't handle their pity right now," I say.

"Trust me, Izel. The only person being pitied tonight is Dr. Williams."

I snort.

"Do you want me to help you wipe the paint off before you head home?" Mandy asks.

I shake my head. "No. Go back out there. I'm sure you're missed. I'll shower when I get home and scrub it off."

THE STREET IS NEARLY empty as I head out to my car, and I start when I notice Logan loitering outside the entrance. I don't look at him and instead, walk right past him, wrapping my peacoat tighter around me.

"Excuse me," he says, and his dress shoes tap the pavement as he follows me. "Miss, I'm sorry. I, uh, I'd like to apologize . . ."

The words die in his mouth when I stop in my tracks and whip around to face him. I cross my arms over my body, comforted by the anonymity afforded by the face paint still obscuring my face. I angle away from him, hoping to hide as much of the non-painted side of my face as possible. "What exactly are you sorry for?" I ask, an eyebrow raised in warning. *Don't fuck with me tonight, Logan Williams. I've had enough of you.*

"I didn't mean to offend you—"

"But you did offend me," I say.

"I know. And I'm sorry." When I don't say anything, he speaks again. "Shit, sorry. I'm no good at this. Look, the woman I was with, my date, she put me in a no-win situation by asking me what I thought of your looks. If I'd agreed with her, she would have gotten mad at me, and if I didn't, well, the worst that would happen would be that we agree to disagree."

"But that's not the worst that happened," I say with an evil smile on my lips.

Logan chuckles. "No. I got a juice shower. And you ruined a very expensive shirt, let me tell you."

"You'd better not be asking me to pay for your dry cleaning," I say.

"No. Just looking for repentance."

"Consider it granted," I say and turn away from him, dashing toward my car.

"Can I at least get your name?" he calls after me without following.

"You should call the night a win while you are ahead," I yell back and get in my car to drive home.

CHAPTER 9

Given the face paint, I can't really be too mad that he didn't recognize me the night of the exhibit. He apologized, and I can take the higher road and not stab him like I've been itching to.

Besides, today, we have another attending in the O.R. with us. Dr. Foster is one of Logan's closest friends at the hospital, from what I can tell. I'd be outnumbered if they decided to gang up on me if I engaged in a tête à tête with Logan.

But because they are friendly, Dr. Foster asks about Logan's weekend.

And I strike gold.

"Had the worst first date of my life," Logan says in response.

"Really? I'm surprised to hear you're dating," Dr. Foster says, but Logan only grunts his annoyance. Dr. Foster continues with, "Well, spit it out. We've got plenty of time."

Logan is the leading surgeon on the case, but at the moment, Dr. Foster is taking care of the next several steps, allowing Logan to shift his weight. I smile because he's uncomfortable. As he should be.

"It was a first date."

"Anyone I know?"

"No. We went to an art exhibit, and there was an . . . incident."

"What happened?"

"My date, she asked me about this model posing in a performance piece. The model was nearly naked and covered in body paint."

"*Where* exactly is this gallery?" Dr. Foster asks with interest.

"Focus, Foster. The sculpture was live only on opening night."

"Pity."

As Dr. Foster keeps working, Logan proceeds to tell him everything that happened.

Dr. Foster can only laugh. "You were going to get the wrath of one woman or the other. I probably would have done the same thing," he says.

"Thank you," Logan says with triumph.

I chuckle, and it's just loud enough for them to notice.

"What was that, Estrada?" Logan asks.

I clear my throat. "I don't agree."

"You don't?"

"No, Doctor."

"Actually, I could use a woman's perspective on this. What should I have done? Let my date know I was physically attracted to the model we were both staring at, or try to reassure her as I did and feign disinterest? There's no winning here, Estrada."

I shake my head. Men can be so dim. No wonder I've been single for nearly a year. I'm standing next to two world-class surgeons, and they are no smarter than my high school boyfriend was when it comes to women. How do they give out medical licenses like this?

In the end, I decide to be honest. "You're making your choice based on the wrong assumptions," I say with firmness in my voice as I hand Logan his next instrument, now that he'll be jumping in with Dr. Foster.

"What assumptions are those?" Logan asks.

"That the woman was testing you. What if she was simply admiring the art piece? If you liked the art, all you had to do was say so, and you wouldn't have gotten a drink over your head."

Dr. Foster snickers under his surgical mask, making me smile.

"I don't think so," Logan insists. "That *was* a test. How do I tell a first date, 'yeah, that woman is hot?'"

I gulp at his admission. Had he said *hot*? I replay his words from before, and for a moment, I must have forgotten that the 'model' he's been talking about is me. He'd said he was physically attracted . . . *to me.* And I'd completely missed it the first time.

Because there's no way. Right? For this Adonis with his chiseled body and stupid-perfect face to be physically attracted to me. It seems like something that's against the laws of the universe. "You thought the model was h-hot?" I stammer.

"Yes! She was spectacular. I couldn't tell my date I was attracted to another woman. She would have tossed *her* drink in my face before the model had her chance to."

Doing my best to ignore the pitter-patter of my heart, I try to sound confident when I speak again. "Look, I'm sure your date was beautiful in her own right. For all you know, she was confident enough to ask you if another woman was attractive for the sake of learning about your tastes. Everything you're saying sounds like you're assuming she's insecure about herself, and I have to tell you, I don't think she is, if she apologized to the model for ogling her."

"Maybe," Logan says, more resigned now.

"And what happened to the model?" Dr. Foster asks, looking up from the surgical field.

Logan lets out a long breath. "I tried apologizing, and she somewhat accepted, but she wouldn't give me so much as her name, so I didn't dare ask for her number—"

"You were going to ask for her number?" Dr. Foster and I say at the same time.

"Well, yeah. I wanted to see her again, but she really didn't seem interested."

"Can you blame her?" Dr. Foster asks. "After you called her fat?"

"No. I suppose not. And I didn't call her fat. I, uh, just said she was curvy."

"Was she?" asks Dr. Foster.

Logan shakes his head. "Yes. She was curvy, but . . . in a sensual way. I was lying to my date to save face, but I really thought we were out of earshot. I tried calling the gallery to get her information, but they won't release it."

If I weren't the professional that I am, I would have dropped the instrument I held in my hand to the ground.

HE'D TRIED to find out who I am. What the actual fuck? He's never showed any interest in me. I had caught him staring at my rack the morning I'd rescued him after his bike accident, but I catch most men doing that, so I hadn't thought much of it at the time. And besides, he hadn't tried getting my number then.

What was it about that damned statue? Could it really be as simple as I was nearly naked? Or was Mandy's painting simply that good? I suspect the anonymity of the mask might also have had something to do with this bizarre reaction from my boss.

I'm shoving a massive spoonful of mashed potatoes in my mouth, my surgical cap still on my head, when Logan finds me in the cafeteria.

"Estrada. Hey. Can I join you?"

"Mmmhmmm," is all I manage to say between the glob of potatoes bulging my cheek.

Perfect-fucking-Logan has a thermos in his hands. I swallow my bite and ask, "Is that your lunch?"

He smiles. "Yep. Protein shake."

I laugh and point at the chicken tenders on my plate. "This is my protein."

Logan blinks down at my plate. "Those actually look good. Can I bum one?"

"Have at it."

I'm sharing my lunch with Logan Williams.

And he thinks I'm hot.

And he was physically attracted to me—or a version of me.

This is the Twilight Zone. It has to be. Or Friday the thirteenth . . . or *something* that sent the planet into a tizzy. I shove a big nervous bite of my chicken tenders in my mouth.

"Listen," he says after he devours his own chicken tender. "I wanted to check in with you."

"About?" I ask with muffled words through my nervous chewing.

"Our conversation this morning. Did it make you uncomfortable?"

I blink at him, not sure I understand where this is coming from. "Um, about your date and stuff?"

He nods.

"No. Why would it?"

Logan shrugs. "I don't know. Foster likes locker room talk, and I guess I don't want you to think I objectify women."

"Do you?" I ask. "Objectify women?"

"No," he hurries to say. "At least, I never intend to."

"Then you have nothing to worry about."

"Good. Things have been great since you got back on my service. I'd hate to lose that over some stupid discussion about one of the most embarrassing moments of my life."

"You were embarrassed?"

He nods, and I add, "I'm sure she was too."

"My date?"

I shake my head. "No. The model."

CHAPTER 10

I agonize for a week over whether or not to help him connect all the dots. In the end, I decided waiting for him to figure it out himself would leave me waiting forever. Sometimes men need a nudge.

Friday afternoon, after our last surgery for the week, seems like the best time. The surgery, which only lasts two hours, feels like a year as I anticipate his reaction. I'd practiced what I was going to say to him in front of the mirror last night.

Like the biggest dork who ever lived.

I should've told him when he'd told me about the art exhibit. I'd let too much time pass, and now the conversation wouldn't be anything other than awkward, just like me.

"Dr. Williams. I have a technique question for you. Do you mind staying behind when we close?"

"Sure," he says, but he side-eyes me as if he is wondering why I couldn't just ask him now.

When the O.R. empties, Logan joins me in the scrub room.

"I take it this isn't about technique?" Logan says. "Is everything okay?"

My breaths quicken. As I take off my surgical mask, I start chewing on the inside of my cheek and shake my head. "No. It's not about technique."

"What is it?" Logan takes a step closer to me, and I instinctively step back. He towers over me in his baby-blue scrubs, looking as handsome and authoritative as ever. If he weren't my boss, or so damned attractive, speaking up wouldn't be so difficult.

"Um, that Day of the Dead exhibit. Did you ever find out who the model was?"

A wrinkle forms between his brows. "No . . . why?"

I shrug. "Was just curious."

"Estrada, it's been a long day. I want to get home. Spit it out."

"I wanted to know if you tried seeing her again."

"No. The gallery contacted the artist with a request to pass along my number to the model, but the artist declined."

I am going to END Amanda Belmonte for not telling me this. "I didn't have you pegged as someone who would give up so easily."

"I'm not," he says. "But I am someone who respects when a woman shoots me down, and this particular woman doesn't want to be found. At least not by me. Not that I can blame her . . ."

"What if she does?" I peer up at him, forcing my eyes on him. I shouldn't feel this intimidated, so out of place. He has already admitted he found me attractive. That he tried looking for me.

Me.

What did he see in me? I've had a few boyfriends—and many hookups—in my life, and many of them were handsome, but none like . . . him. None *that* blindingly beautiful. The kind of beauty that almost hurts to look at because the longing is too painful. And yet, he wanted to find me.

I take a deep breath, take off my scrub cap, undo my hairpin, and let my hair fall around my shoulders.

"What's going on, Estrada?" he asks, confused by my shady-as-fuck behavior.

"Would you like your bike back?"

"My bi . . ." His eyes narrow. "Wait. You! It was you!"

I flinch at the accusation but straighten my height. I nod. "Yeah. I have your bike. It's in my garage. Whenever you want to get it, you're welcome to stop by." There I went, feeling dumb as hell. This is not how it went when I'd practiced it. Not even a little. My speech in front of the mirror had been so . . . eloquent. This is not.

"You helped me on the trail that day?"

"I did."

"I've been looking for you."

"I've been at arm's length."

Logan hangs his head. "I'm so sorry, Estrada. I was so embarrassed and in pain, I didn't even put two and two together—"

"Apparently, you can't put four and four together, either," I say with a roll of my eyes that is so reflexive, I don't even bother playing it off.

Logan's chest rumbles with a chuckle. "What's that supposed to mean?"

"Nothing. I, uh, just wanted you to know. I've been holding it hostage this entire time."

"Why didn't you say anything before?"

"Because, you jerk, you never said thank you, and I'd been working with you for *four* months, and you didn't know what my face looked like, or what my voice sounded like, or what my name was—"

"Okay, okay. I get it." He exhales deeply. "I'm sorry, Estrada. Believe me, I know my head's up my ass most of the time. You're not telling me anything I don't already know. But I don't mean it. I'm just . . . aloof."

The laugh that escapes me is so loud, he joins me.

"What's so funny?" he asks.

"You. You're a surgeon. And aloof. Please never tell your patients that."

"I guess I owe you an apology," he says.

"Oh, was that supposed to be it?"

He chuckles again, and I could get used to that sound. "No," he says. "Izel Estrada, would you please accept my apology for being an ass?"

The way he says it is so sincere, so . . . raw despite the humor he seems to try to inject into his apology. It seems like he's saying so much more than the words that have actually left his mouth.

And I must be under some sort of hot guy spell because, without permission from my brain, my body steps closer to him until I bunch up the fabric of his scrub top in my hand and pull him down to me.

Our lips mold as if they were sculpted to fit together like jigsaw puzzle pieces. My senses electrify, and only the smell of his smokey cedarwood aftershave overpowers me. The only sound is my blood pulsing in my ears, the only twin sensations in my body, one on my lips, the other around my waist where he's wrapped his arm around it, pulling me closer to him.

He pulls away briefly, then pecks my lips once again, smiling against my mouth. "Estrada," he says in a low, breathy voice.

My feet return to the ground from the high, and I release his top so I can step away. As my heart slows down, my eyes widen with the horror of what I've just done.

I step away from him, and all I can say is, "I'm so sorry, I don't know what that was, what I—"

"Estrada," he whispers, grabbing my wrist to pull me into his arms again.

This time, it's him who dips his head to find my lips, parting my mouth with his tongue, and I have zero desire to resist. I melt into his arms. His tongue finds mine, gently, slowly, like he's enjoying every corner of my mouth. I groan, and some sort of super-human strength enters my body to pull away because, fuck, we're at work.

"Logan, stop," I say, though they're the last possible words I want to speak at that moment.

His forehead drops to mine, the scrub cap on his head cool against my skin, helping me ground myself to time and place.

How did we lose ourselves like this? If someone had seen . . . I don't even know what would have happened, but if anyone were to get fired as a consequence, it would be me a million times over the world-class surgeon.

"We can't do this here," I say.

His arm unravels from around my middle, and he steps away. He looks at our surroundings, coming to the same conclusion. "Right." He shakes his head, coming down from our high. His mouth opens to say something, but he stops himself, shutting it again.

"I have to go," I say as I dash out of the scrub room before anyone sees us alone. "Have a great weekend!" I yell behind me.

I'M TOO DISTRACTED to join Mandy and Tlali for Friday night drinks, but I'm also too distracted to write. It's still early, so I lay in bed replaying that kiss in my brain. He'd kissed me back. He'd pulled me into his arms. It wasn't all in my head.

I bring my hand to my lips, closing my eyes so that a flash of our kiss slices through my mind. That was the best kiss of my life. My eyes fly open when a ding sounds from my phone, and I open the text from an unknown number.

Unknown: *I can't stop thinking about your lips.*

Me: *Logan?*

He probably got my number from HR.

Unknown: *Who else have you kissed lately?!*

I snort-laugh and type my response.

Me: *I don't kiss and tell.*

Logan: *Estrada! You are heartless.*

Me: *Good thing I know a good heart surgeon.*

Logan: *Very funny.*

Logan: *When can I get my bike back?*

Me: *I'm home tonight.*

Logan: *Address?*

I get cold feet, realizing I have no idea how long Tlali will be out, and I'd hate for her to run into him. He's been public enemy number one at our house since the exhibit, and I have yet to explain everything to her. I can just see her chasing after him with a baseball bat—Logan running down our driveway to the safety of his car.

Me: *Actually, my roommate's due home anytime now, and I don't want her in my business just yet. Can I bring the bike to you?*

He responds with his address, and I maneuver the bike into my car before heading over to Dr. Logan Williams's house.

His garage door rolls up as I pull into his driveway.

He walks out barefoot, wearing a ribbed white tank, and grey, name-brand sweatpants. I bite back a knowing smile. This man knows *exactly* what he's doing with that getup.

But so do I with mine. I've shown up in my best hip-hugging jeans and my bubble-gum pink, second-skin sweater that dips a perfect shadow between the valley of my breasts.

I get out of the car, even though he needs no assistance getting the bike out.

"Thanks, Estrada."

"Sure." I stick my hands in my jeans pockets and avert my eyes. "I'll see you later then," I say, grabbing for the door handle.

I'm almost in the car when he calls after me. "Wait. Can I offer you a drink? Coffee? Or dinner? Maybe we could chat for a while?"

I glance between him and his house, a bit nervous now. But what do I have to be nervous about? He's made it more than clear he wants me.

I grab my car keys and shut the door to the car. "Sure," I say, following him in.

We don't get that drink. Or dinner—unless we go with an unconventional definition of 'dinner.' I don't get the chance to admire his beautiful, modern home when we get inside before he has me on my back on the couch in his living room. Logan's length presses painfully against my hipbone through my jeans and his sweats. He grinds against me, my hips welcoming the friction, matching his rhythm.

"Izel," he groans, and the sound of my first name from his lips is everything. "I want to fuck you."

I smirk up at him. "Fuck me, then." The challenge is there in my eyes, just like his acceptance of the challenge flickering in his irises.

"Fuck," he hisses. "How did I not see you?"

"You were blind," I say and nip his bottom lip.

He rises to his feet and offers a hand to help me up. When I'm standing again, I take off my pants, letting him watch as I undress. I will send Mandy a thank you card and some chocolates, because somehow, my experience for her living statue prepared me to not flinch in front of this freaking Dionysus as I undress.

Logan gasps when he takes me in. I know what he sees. Because I mostly exist in an unattractive uniform of scrubs, and since I don't have to invest in work clothes, instead, I invest in top-tier lingerie. My matching set today consists of a deep crimson, eyelash-lace balconette bra and matching mesh G-string. I squeeze my arms together to push my breasts out, offering him a better view.

His gaze roams over my chest, and his eyes snap up to my face. Then his eyes narrow again like they did when he recognized me from the trail.

"It was you," he whispers.

I nod.

"You are the . . . what did you say? Venus and Aphrodite?"

I nod again, taking a step toward him until my hand floats up to his hard chest. His quickened breaths expand against my palm.

"How'd you figure it out?" I ask.

His gaze dips low again, and he brings his hand up to hover over my breast. His beautiful blue eyes then lock on mine, a questioning look in them, and I nod my approval. His index finger lands on the small beauty mark like a target over the swell of my left breast.

"This," he says hoarsely. "I remember it vividly."

"You do?"

Logan nods, his eyes hooded. "I've thought about this beauty mark every night since I saw it."

Nothing in my face gave him a clue, but one look at my boobs, and suddenly Logan's memory is freaking fantastic. I can either be offended or take the win. And hell, if he's been thinking about my body, I can't find it in myself to take offense.

"You recognize me by my boobs?"

"Only the one that had no paint on it," he says and chuckles. His finger circles the beauty mark several times, forcing my chest to heave with quickened breaths. I stretch my arms behind my back to unclasp the bra and let it fall next to my feet. Logan trails his hand down from the beauty mark toward my puckered nipple, catching it between his thumb and forefinger.

My back arches at the sensation of his hands on my naked skin, pushing my pelvis toward him. Logan groans and snakes his free hand around my waist, pulling me toward him.

His mouth finds mine, and I have to rise onto my tippy toes to deepen the kiss. My hands bunch up his shirt as our tongues explore each other.

I pull away long enough to say, "How is it I'm standing here in only my G-string, and you're still fully dressed?"

"An oversight I intend to correct immediately," he says and leads me to sit on the comfy armchair.

The sun from the floor-to-ceiling windows in the living room illuminates Logan as he chucks his shirt to the wind. He lowers his sweats until he stands before me in nothing but his white boxer-briefs.

My lips dry up, and I lick them instinctively at the sight of him because Logan Williams doesn't have a six-pack.

He has an eight-pack. And seriously, what the fuck? When does he have time to work out that much?

I don't know how long I'm frozen as I look at his body before his chuckle brings my attention back to his face.

"See something you like?" he asks.

I swallow hard and nod. I sit up toward the edge of the chair, and he takes a step toward me. My eyes roam those insanely toned cyclist's thighs, and I almost want to take a bite out of one.

Once he's within a foot's distance from me, I see the mushroom tip of him poking through his waistband. I peer up at him through my thick eyelashes, watching his jaw tighten when I hook both my thumbs in his waistband and draw down his boxer-briefs.

My eyes widen when he springs free. My core clenches at the sight of his massive shaft, but really, what was I expecting when everything about Logan Williams is so . . . big? And to be brutally honest, I'm not sure I can take him. I've never been with anyone quite this size.

His hand falls to the top of my head, caressing it gently and drawing my attention back to his face. "Don't worry, Izel," he says. "I'll make sure you're ready."

"Wha . . ."

He smiles the most seductive crooked smile and drops to his knees in front of me. Logan's hands gently push me by the shoulders until I lean back into the over-sized chair.

As exposed as I feel, I'm too far gone with a carnal need for him; I don't even think to feel self-conscious, so I widen my thighs as far as I can stretch them.

"Fuck, Izel," he gurgles out. "That's it, baby. Open up for me." As he says this, his massive hands wrap around my thighs, massaging them a bit before moving his right hand up to the apex of my thighs.

Logan's thumb presses over my engorged clitoris through the flimsy mesh fabric. The pressure is light, and he circles it deliciously, forcing my eyes to close with pleasure.

"You're so wet already, baby," he says.

I feel him pull the fabric to the side, and he returns his thumb where it belongs. "Holy hell," he groans, "you are fucking perfect." He fixes his eyes on my pussy as he works it with his hand. "It's so . . . slick—perfect."

Despite everything we've said and done, I can't help the heat that climbs up my neck and settles on my cheeks. And thank the heavens I didn't skip my last waxing appointment.

He bends over to make out with me while he plays with my center. My eyes fly open when he sinks one finger inside me, swirling and thrusting in and out of me until I squirm in the chair.

"Logan!" I pant. The sensations are too much—he's too much, too hot, too good at what he's doing with his hand.

"Yes?" the bastard teases.

"That . . ." I bite my lip. "That feels so good."

He draws a second finger inside, and all coherent thought leaves my body. Izel Estrada ceases to exist, leaving a more primal being to take over her body.

I grind my hips against his hand, working in tandem with his rhythm. "That's it, baby," he says. "I need you to come. I need you to open up these pretty little swollen lips and make room for me."

His dirty tongue sends me reeling, and I can almost feel the orgasm building. Before I know it, he leans back on his legs and finds my clit with his tongue while his fingers are still inside me.

I look down at him—at the sight of his head between my legs, and good god, I can't believe this is my life.

Logan Williams is on his knees.

Between my legs.

His tongue swirls in a rhythm over my clit, and I can't take the sensations any longer. My center clenches further and further around his fingers, pulling a growl out of Logan's chest until I let go and fall over the edge with my release.

My legs start to quiver, and only when my center's pulsing slows down does he stop licking me. He comes up for air, his lips glistening with my arousal, smirking because he knows precisely how he affects me.

He stands and lifts me off the chair to flip us, so he's now the one sitting, and I'm on top, straddling his lap. I didn't even notice him grabbing a condom, but he has one between his fingers now, and he tears it with his teeth, not once breaking eye contact with me.

That gaze of his, so intent on my features, sends a wave of goosebumps through my body, and I shiver. Once he's sheathed himself, Logan grabs my waist and lifts me up and over his erection. "I need you," he whispers in my ear, then drops his mouth until he drags his teeth over my neck.

I let his tip part my sex, and I take a deep, nervous breath.

"Shh, it's okay," Logan coos. "Take your time."

I nod and grab onto his shoulders for support, lowering myself further and further down his cock. It feels fucking fantastic, and I'm relieved there isn't an ounce of the pain I anticipated.

His fingers tighten around my hips as I reach the root of him, steeling himself to give me time to adjust to him. "You okay?" he asks.

"More than okay," I breathe out. I clench around him, adjusting further, and he bucks his hips.

"Izel, fuck, you feel so good."

We both lose it, then. It becomes a race for him to get deeper in me. His hands grip onto my hips painfully, but I don't care about the pain because he feels so good inside of me. He lifts me off him, then slams me back down with force. I take over the movement, my thighs lifting me off him and down again in long strokes.

"Izel, stop!" he growls. "Stop. I'm going to come!"

I lean back to look at him, his neck straining, veins bulging to the surface as he tries to hold himself back, and it's me doing this to him—me making him lose himself.

It's *me* forcing the most controlling man in the world to abandon all control.

I don't stop.

I lean forward until my breasts hover over his face, and he doesn't disappoint—he takes my nipple between his teeth and sucks on it gently.

I pick up the pace, riding harder, and say, "Come, Logan. I want you to come in my tight, slick cunt."

My breast drops from his mouth, and he growls. My dirty talk does something to both of us, because we become frantic as we both chase our orgasms. Mine hits first, and I spasm around him, milking him when he comes. "Fuuuck," he hisses and tightens his grip on my hips to still me when he's too far gone.

My forehead drops to his, my breathing coming in hard as I try to calm my heart rate.

"I'm sorry," he says.

"What on earth for?" I ask.

"I didn't want to come so fast."

I chuckle, and he frowns. "I'm sorry," I say. "I came, Logan. Hard. Twice. I don't care how long it took."

He smiles.

"Still. I want you to know . . . it's been a while. I'll be able to please you a lot longer next time."

Next time. My heart somersaults when he says 'next time,' and I can't hide my face-splitting grin because he wants more of me.

"Don't tell me once is all you have for tonight?" I smirk down at him with a challenge. His arms tighten around my waist in response, and he plants a gentle peck over the beauty mark on my breast.

He stands, taking me with him, and my legs wrap around him tightly as I yelp with the surprise. He walks down a hallway, I assume to his bedroom, and he squeezes my ass in his beefy palm. "We're just getting started, Estrada," he says and tosses me onto his bed.

I don't cover myself up despite the sun flooding through Logan's bedroom window. We're on our sides, staring at each other, a bit shy, for some reason. Our legs are tangled; Logan grabs my hand to interlace his fingers in mine.

"That was . . ." I start to say but am unsure of the words I'm willing to actually share.

"Yeah," Logan smiles. "It truly was."

I snicker and bury my head in my pillow for a second before peering back up at him.

"What?" he asks.

"I kind of attacked you at work," I say.

Logan chuckles. "I'm so glad you did."

I cup the side of his face in my hand, and he responds by closing his eyes. I still can't believe I had this handsome man. "Anyone ever tell you you're obnoxiously handsome?" I ask.

He shakes his head. "Never. And you Estrada, you're obnoxiously hot."

The Izel of only a few weeks ago would have scoffed at hearing those words from those lips, but the thing is, I actually believe him. My mind races back to only minutes ago. The way he touched me, exploring, in awe—and the way he looked at me, with dark eyes emblazoned with hunger . . . when he says he finds me hot, Logan Williams fucking means it.

I turned him on just as much as he did me, if not more. Having him hard and throbbing inside me, pumping into me, nibbling my lower lip, will be a memory I cherish always.

"What're you thinking about?" he asks.

"Nothing," I say timidly.

"You're lying. You're blushing." He dusts my cheekbone with one finger, tracing the length of it until he reaches my ear and caresses the shell of it.

"You ever get those flashbacks? You know, when you have unforgettable sex, and then out of nowhere, you get this little flicker of it?"

"Is that what just happened?"

I bite my lower lip and nod. "Yeah." I bite my lip again, unsure about asking him what I really want to. Before I can change my mind, I blurt it out. "How come you were such an ass to me before?"

Logan lets out a long breath next to me. "It wasn't my intention. I"—he clears his throat—"I've always been too focused on work . . . I don't really take time for . . ."

"People?" I offer.

"Yeah. I'm sorry if I was an ass. Does it make a difference if I didn't intend to be?"

"A very, very tiny difference." I squint at him between my thumb and forefinger, and he laughs.

I get the sense there's a deeper story behind why he's so detached from everyone, but I don't want to ruin this perfect moment by bringing up any bad memories for him.

As if sensing my wandering thoughts, Logan leans forward to kiss me gently, and he smiles against my lips while wrapping his leg around my waist. I grunt under the weight of it, earning me a chuckle.

"We've done this a bit backward. Haven't we?" he says.

"What do you mean?"

"I'd like to take you on a date."

I raise an eyebrow at him, trying and failing to hide my satisfaction at his request. "You want to date?"

"Yes. I do," he says with a smirk that melts me into the mattress.

Trying not to sound too eager, I say, "Yeah. I'd like that," even though my insides are screaming, *Yes, please, I'd like that very much! Is now too soon?*

"Good." Logan nods like it was some business meeting, then locks eyes with me. "Oh and, Estrada, one thing you should know about me before you agree to date me—I don't share what's mine."

HERE'S what Logan meant when he said dating: he whisked me away to a cabin for a weekend where we could disconnect from the world and basically fuck until I could barely walk straight.

It was fantastic.

We didn't do much besides going out for dinners and burning the calories with glorious naked time in bed. We continued to work together over the next couple of weeks and did our best to act professional, so no one at work got wind of our new relationship, though who were we kidding? We had absolutely no one fooled. Gina even approached me to say that she doesn't really care so long as it doesn't affect our work.

We've also spent nearly every night together since that first day when I revealed my 'secret identities,' as he now calls them. To hear him tell it, you'd think I was some mastermind sleuth to escape his radar like I did. I don't roll my eyes at him anymore—at least not to his face.

But when we're alone, he lights up when he talks about surgery. It seems a relief he can talk about cases with me because I was right there experiencing all of it with him. Then we discuss the plot or characterization for my horror novel, and he always begs for me to let him read chapters, but I'm not there yet. Maybe one day.

Now we're on our way to Mandy's for a dinner she's hosting. We pull up to the mansion—because that's what the estate is—and it still trips me up that this is where my cousin lives.

Logan opens the car door for me and grabs the bottle of wine he brought as a hostess gift from the back seat. Yeah. That's the kind of thoughtful Logan is.

"I still can't believe your cousin is married to Elio," Logan says as we walk up the stone pathway to the front door.

"Why?"

"Small world is all," he says with a crooked smile.

I hadn't realized how close Logan is with Adelio Belmonte. Freaking Elio never mentioned that they play basketball together with a few other surgeons from the hospital.

"This house is nice," Logan says.

I look up at the house's stone façade. It looks more like a castle than a private residence. "You didn't know?" I ask him.

"Know what?"

I cock my head. The kind of money Elio has is way beyond his surgeon salary. But Elio is one of the humblest guys I know. I'm not sure he wants everyone at the hospital in his business, so I'll let him tell Logan what he wants. If he wants.

Luckily, Elio opens the door before I can answer.

"Izel!" He beams down at me and pulls me in for a hug.

Elio, or 'the mountain,' as Mandy likes to call him, is an inch taller than Logan, so I feel like I'm standing between two trees. To see them next to each other, it's almost like looking at brothers. Though Elio's light olive complexion is the tiniest bit lighter than Logan's barely sun-kissed one, they have a similar athletic build. Elio looks up to Logan, then back at me, and throws me a teasing smile earning him an eye-roll from me.

"Hey, man," Elio says to Logan, and they step into a bro-hug complete with a gentle fist tap to the other's back.

Mandy peeks around her mountain and squeals. "You came!" She smothers me in a typical Mandy tight-as-a-cobra hug that I return. "And you brought Dr. Williams," she says, eying him in such an obviously suggestive way that I want to bury my head in the sand.

"Please, call me Logan," he says and offers her the bottle of wine.

"Oh, thank you!" Mandy says. "Izel, if you get yourself a man with good taste in wine, you don't let him go. Come in, come in. Tlali's inside."

❧

"The food was fantastic," I tell Mandy as I rub my belly. "You're a great cook," I tease with payback for what she said about Logan and the wine.

Elio snorts, and Mandy whips her cloth napkin at his arm.

"I'm sorry," Elio says and leans in to gently hold his wife's chin. "You're a fantastic cook."

Mandy roars with laughter. "Elio Belmonte, you're a terrible liar!"

Elio turns to me. "We hired a caterer for tonight, Izel."

I raise my wine glass in cheers. "Thank heavens," I say.

"Hey! That's enough ganging up on me," Mandy protests.

Tlali jumps in. "Out of the three of us, I'm the cook."

Logan withers a bit under Tlali's glare because she still hasn't forgiven him for what he said about me at the gallery and has been scowling at him all through dinner.

Elio looks between Logan and Tlali, realizing something's off. "What's going on here?" Elio asks, pointing between the two.

I sigh. "Tlali is still upset about the art exhibit."

Elio looks at Mandy with a questioning look. "You said the exhibit went great."

Tlali lets out an exaggerated snort, and I wince.

"Will someone please tell me what I'm missing?" Elio says.

"You didn't tell him?" I ask Mandy, and she shakes her head.

"I wanted all of you to be comfortable, so I asked Elio to sit out on opening night and stay home with Lulu," Mandy says, referring to their son.

I look over at Logan, whose jaw is set despite the slight red at the tips of his ears. "I wasn't very nice to Izel," he confesses. "I've apologized. It was a misunderstanding. That's all."

"What happened?" Nosy Elio asks again.

Tlali's chair groans under her as she drags it away from the table so she can stand, then pulls out her cell phone from her back pocket. "I'll show you what happened," she says, narrowing her eyes at Logan.

My eyes widen. "Excuse me?"

"You stormed out," Tlali says, "and you were too mad to notice the half dozen cellphones that were pulled out during your little outburst."

"Outburst?" Elio asks, still whining for information.

My hand flies up to my mouth. "No," I gasp. "Please tell me it's not—"

"You're damned right it's online." Tlali pushes a few buttons and slides the phone over the table toward Elio, who catches it, before retaking her seat. She leans back, crossing her arms with satisfaction etched around her mouth.

Elio roars with laughter at my little speech, wincing when the splash of the pomegranate juice connects with Logan's head.

"Look," Logan says, facing Tlali's direction. "I know Izel tells you everything, so you already know, but I didn't mean any of the things I said. I was in a tough spot, and I handled it poorly. Izel has accepted my apology and is willing to give me a second chance. I also know you're her best friend. I'd love for you to give me a second shot, too." He smiles weakly at her.

Tlali's crossed arms unravel, and her face softens. "Fine," she says after mulling it over for a few beats. "But so help me, god, Logan Williams, I don't care that you're some hotshot surgeon. You hurt her, I will kill you exactly how Izel wrote your death in her book—"

"Oh, I took that out," I say.

"What? Why?" Tlali whines.

"Don't worry. I can always put it back if he fucks up again." I smirk up at Logan, and he shakes his head, but there's amusement in his eyes.

"You never did tell me. How did you kill me off?" Logan asks.

I take a sip of my wine and offer him my sweetest, most innocent smile and say, "I skinned you alive."

Elio throws his head back with laughter and replays the video on the phone a third time. I cringe at the sound of my own voice and shut my eyes tight, trying to shake away the memory.

When the video gets to the part where I claim the title of the goddess of beauty, passion, and pleasure, Logan squeezes my thigh under the table. My eyes fly open, and I look up at him. He dips his head low so he can whisper in my ear, his breath hot against my skin. "You are all those things, Estrada. And so much fucking more."

The End

ALSO BY OFELIA MARTINEZ

The Industrial November on Tour Series

Sofia & Bren's Story: Hiding in the Smoke

Lola & Karl's Story: Running from the Blaze

Erica & Friedrich's Story: Scorching to the Touch

The Heartland Metro Hospital Series

Carolina & Hector's Story: Remission

Valentina & Rory's Story: Contusion

Izel & Logan's Story: Incision (Novella)

Camila & Leonardo's Story: Palpitation (Novella as part of the *Heroes with Heat and Heart Vol.2* anthology)

Sara & Ramiro's Story: Sensation

Mandy & Elio's Story: Adhesion

Anthologies

Camila & Leonardo's Story: Heroes with Heat and Heart Vol 2

Collections

Diagnosis Amor Vol. 1: A Heartland Metro Hospital Collection

ABOUT THE AUTHOR

Ofelia Martinez writes romance with Latinas on top. Originally from the Texas border, Ofelia now resides in Missouri with her partner and their dog, Pixel.

She loves good books, tequila, and chocolate. She proudly shares a birthday with Usagi Tsukino. When not writing, you can find Ofelia making visual art.

Visit OfeliaMartinez.com to learn more.

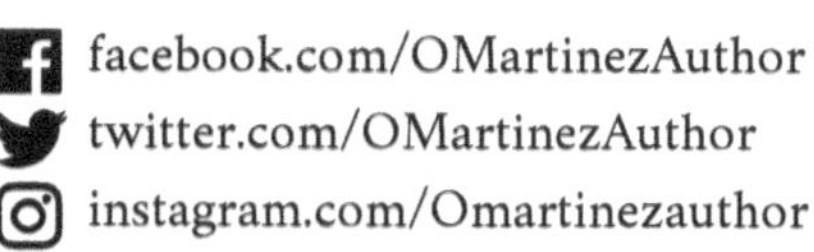